INTO THE VOID

Also by Joshua A. Johnston

THE CHRONICLES OF SARCO:
Edge of Oblivion | BOOK ONE

INTO THE VOID

THE CHRONICLES OF SARCO

BOOK TWO

JOSHUA A. JOHNSTON

an imprint of
GILEAD PUBLISHING

Published by Enclave Publishing, an imprint of Gilead Publishing,
Grand Rapids, Michigan
www.enclavepublishing.com

an imprint of
GILEAD PUBLISHING

ISBN: 978-1-68370-078-4 (print)
ISBN: 978-1-68370-079-1 (eBook)

Into the Void
Copyright © 2018 by Joshua A. Johnston.

Edited by Reagen Reed
Cover design by Kirk DouPonce
Interior design/typesetting by Beth Shagene

Printed in the United States of America

For Megan

THE FIVE RACES
OF THE CONFEDERACY

The Aecrons. Brilliant, arrogant, and secretive, the Aecrons are the scientific and technological backbone of the Confederacy. Hailing from a planet of domed cities, their blue-skinned, black-eyed bodies are small and fragile.

The Riticans. A society that emphasizes peaceful coexistence where possible and violent retaliation when threatened, the Riticans excel in strategic decisions. They are large methane-breathers capable of enduring harsh environments.

The Hazionites. A race of matriarchal tree-dwellers, this once-expansionistic society survived a near genocide by the Riticans and now fills diverse roles within the Confederacy. To varying degrees, they can smell the feelings of those around them.

The Humans. Average by both mental and physical standards, Humans have little knowledge of their homeworld's history prior to the current Index era, which began thirteen centuries ago. They excel as diplomats and leaders, and the Confederacy's capital is situated in their home system.

The Exos. Asexual and individualistic, the Exos have no government, little culture, and a mindset oriented around task completion. They are adept with mechanics and engineering and have bodies tough enough to endure the vacuum of space.

THE CONFEDERAL NAVY

Navy Command, Nevea, Titan

Admiral Wr Ghiri—*Hazionite female, Head of Navy Intelligence*

Admiral Nhile-tonna-amel-fro-tigh-Garvak (Nhile Garvak)—*Ritican male, Head of Navy Special Operations*

Navy Cruiser *Hattan*

Captain Jared Carter—*Human male, ship's captain and fleet commander*

Commander Tir Bvaso—*Hazionite female, first officer*

Senior Lieutenant Vetta-parso-bonna-truph-Quidd (Vetta Quidd)—*Ritican female, senior security officer*

Senior Lieutenant Garo-konna-ichen-Ball (Garo Ball)—*Ritican male, weapons officer*

Lieutenant Omarami (Rami) Del—*Human female, communications officer*

Lieutenant Orel Dayail—*Aecron male, communications officer*

Lieutenant Aioua Horae—*Aecron female, sciences officer*

Lieutenant Kilvin Wrsaw—*Hazionite male, navigator*

Deck Officer Darel Weye—*Aecron male, assistant medical officer*

Deck Officer Triphox—*Exo, engineer*

Hattan Battle Group

Senior Commander Redelia Aroo—*Aecron female, senior interceptor commander*

Senior Lieutenant Eil Morichar—*Hazionite female, interceptor commander*

Senior Lieutenant Amun-also-xixit-orrcsa-Plau (Amun Plau)—*Ritican male, interceptor commander*

Senior Lieutenant Venzz Kitt—*Human male, interceptor commander*

Lieutenant Brigg Drews—*Human male, interceptor commander*

PROLOGUE

A sword, a sword is sharpened, and also furbished:
It is sharpened to make a sore slaughter;
It is furbished that it may glitter . . .
And he hath given it to be furbished, that it may be handled:
This sword is sharpened, and it is furbished,
To give it into the hand of the slayer . . .
I have set the point of the sword against all their gates,
That their heart may faint, and their ruins be multiplied.

    –Excerpt from a Human religious text, origin unknown

The short, golden, stubby grass crunched uncomfortably under Nho's feet as he picked his way up the path that wound through the Bvaso Mountains. As it was so many years before, the path was strewn with rocks that could twist an ankle or stub a toe if one wasn't paying attention. The sun overhead beat down with that same merciless power that only worsened under the humidity. And the wind was light, carrying a strange organic scent that triggered endless memories in Nho's mind. The sense of familiarity here was almost overpowering.

As he reached the crest of the hill, Nho could see the giant lake off to his left and the mountain pass to his right. With a smile tainted by the deep sorrow in his heart, he made his way over to the lake. Setting Sarco's staff down beside him, he splashed water on his face and cupped a small quantity to drink. The water had a sharp mineral taste.

Strange, he thought. *I once hated drinking this water. Now I find I've missed it.*

He stood and made his way to the pass, which curled around for a short distance before running into a cave entrance. As the cave came into view, he could see people. Tens of them, dressed in plain garments, many of them standing just outside the mouth of the cave. Two of the Humans spotted him, momentarily forgetting their place and shouting his name.

Others outside the cave door looked his way, their astonished expressions quickly giving way to a small stampede of sentients running directly at him. He barely had time to brace himself before several bodies collided with his, hugging him fiercely. They buried themselves in his arms and tears streaked onto his clothes from their weeping eyes.

"It is so very good to see you all," he said softly, leaving unsaid the tragedy that had brought him there.

"It is good to see you, too, Mentor Nho," whispered one of them, the man called Yarden.

Nho had many questions surrounding Tsi's death, but now was not the time to ask them. He knew that Saidor Wheit, the influential Hazionite politician, had taken exception to Tsi's influence over her daughter, Haus Wheit. Saidor had exploited the chaos surrounding the Malum crisis to order Tsi arrested and imprisoned. Just days before Malum was defeated, Tsi was beheaded. He also knew that an official inquiry was underway, though it was unlikely Saidor would face any consequences.

Nho wondered what, exactly, had transpired on the night of Tsi's arrest, although the answers to that, too, would have to wait. One potential clue emerged as he looked more closely at the open area immediately outside the cave. The great stone, which for years had been used to seal up the cave at night, was cracked in two, presumably by weapons fire. *They must have attacked in the dark, then,* reasoned Nho. That the local police would come here at night, when the most treacherous predators were afoot, only further convinced Nho of Saidor Wheit's madness.

Trailed by his friends and followers, Nho stepped quietly up to the threshold of the cave and peered inside. A number of Hazionites were seated in the center of the main room, the men in the back with the women in front of them. In the far end of the main room, beyond the women, was a large black coffin that contained the remains of his good friend. They were fortunate to have even that.

Nho stepped farther into the cave. He could now make out some of the faces. Many were familiar, including that of Haus Wheit, the now-estranged daughter of Saidor Wheit. The female Hazionites were unaware of his presence; Haus and the other females were in the quiet, catatonic state they lapsed into during the Hazionite death ritual. He marveled at this: it was unusual for Hazionites to experience the death ritual over a non-Hazionite. It spoke to how close Tsi had been to his disciples, and how deeply his loss hurt.

He made his way over to the males and sat next to them, a few of them acknowledging him silently as they tended to the females. Although he could not sense emotion as the Hazionites did, he knew full well that there was much despair here. He felt it himself. Tsi's followers were adrift, shaken by Tsi's senseless death. They would no doubt be questioning Sarco, in spite of the great stories of how Nho, through the power of the One, had defeated Malum.

Nho's course was clear. He would remain here for some time, building them up until they could once again walk on their own.

1

Titan

Earth Index 1305.350

"And so it is my belief," rasped the old historian, leaning forward as he spoke, "that there is no conclusive evidence that Malum, the Aecrons, or the Sarconians were responsible for the loss of historical knowledge that predates the Human Dark Age. The evidence instead points to internal factors on Earth, perhaps of an environmental or political nature."

The old man raised a crooked finger in the air. "However, I do believe that the presence of Sarconian artifacts on Earth before the current Index age indicates that the Aecron government may yet possess knowledge on the lost past of Human history."

Several of the Aecron scholars in the audience shifted visibly in indignation.

"I therefore call upon the Aecron government to make available to us on Earth their archives of pre-Index visits to Earth, so that we might reclaim our lost heritage. The time for obfuscation is over!"

The Human members of the audience, who made up the majority of the several hundred in attendance, broke into loud applause which was quickly accompanied by another Human cultural expression—a standing ovation. The few Hazionites and Riticans in attendance were somewhat more subdued, and polite, in their applause. The Aecrons, numbering around fifty or so, sat coldly in their seats.

Above, next to the exit, Senior Commander Jared Carter stood quietly, observing the entire spectacle. Standing next to him was Coto Ute, a one-time study peer and a current historian with the Confederal Archives.

"Well, Jared," Coto said in his deep voice, "what do you think?"

Jared shrugged. "He certainly created a sensation, but we both know nothing will come of it. This is an old and tired debate. The Aecron government still denies that it ever visited pre-Dark Age Earth."

"Do you believe them?"

Jared gave Coto a friendly pat on the shoulder. "If I knew the answer to that, I'd be standing up there instead of him. As it is, he'll get some attention on the feeds, but little more."

"Perhaps you should take up his cause," said Coto, laughing. "The last time I noticed, he wasn't the hero of Malum."

Jared groaned. "Don't even start. Listen, I have to get going. I have an appointment over at Navy Command."

"Finally getting back into a ship, then?"

"Let's hope so. I didn't leave academics just to wind up back in an office."

Jared took his leave from Coto and strolled out the exit, headed for Nevea's central walkways. He had just taken his first step through the door when a voice from his left called out, "Senior Commander Carter!"

Jared turned to see a young Human walking up to him. Jared stopped and extended his hand. "Delegate Carson."

Troye Carson took Jared's hand and shook it warmly in the traditional Human style. "Commander, I'm glad I caught you."

"I'm afraid I'm in a hurry," Jared said. "I have a meeting with Command in less than an hour."

"I'll walk with you, then." As they started walking, Troye leaned in conspiratorially. "What does the admiralty want with the hero of Malum?"

Jared stifled another groan. *Not again.* "They haven't told me," he said, "and Nho Ames is the hero. I just gave him a little help when he fell down."

"You're too modest, Commander Carter," Troye said, flashing a broad smile. "Nho himself said that he would have never succeeded without your help. Whatever Command has for you, I'm sure it will befit your accomplishments." He straightened a little. "I just returned from a visit to my constituency back home, and I wanted to reiterate just how proud they are of what you did at Aeroel."

Jared resisted the urge to ask the man what he wanted. Troye Carson could be insufferable, but he also represented Jared's home nation, Earth's Western Territories, in the Confederal Congress. Jared was no fan of the political game, but he'd learned enough from his father to know that a politician who was both one's representative and a member of the group that supervised one's employment was a relationship best kept amicable.

"Thank you," Jared said, hoping that would be the end of the conversation.

It wasn't. "What would you say to coming to work for me?"

Jared kept looking ahead as he walked, but he couldn't stop himself from flinching in surprise. "I'm committed to the Navy right now."

"It would not be hard for me to secure a release from your Navy contract, especially if it involved Confederal business."

Now Jared looked at him. "What sort of Confederal business?"

Again the broad smile. "I wish I could tell you specifics, but I can't. I can say this: it would involve the best of your talents."

"I'm listening." Jared wasn't, but he knew the only way out of this conversation was through it.

They were passing into a busier part of the Confederal Capital. Jared had to change direction to avoid colliding with a contingent of Aecrons chattering amongst themselves. Troye adjusted his path to match Jared and continued. "Let me indulge in some guesswork. In an hour you fear you will get assigned to desk duty. That's probably the last thing you'd like to be doing. You'd rather be in command of a ship, out there doing the work you love. But you also have the background of the historian, and returning to that role in the search for those Sarconian parchments was invigorating. You'd love to do it again. Take up my offer, and I not only promise something worthwhile, but something that will compensate you well beyond your current Navy pay."

"If you know me that well, you also know I'm a deliberate thinker. I can't make any commitments right now."

"Of course," Troye said, parting ways, "but if Garvak's assignment doesn't work out as planned, come see me. The offer will still be there."

Jared nodded and kept walking. As he did, though, he asked himself, *Did I specifically tell him I was meeting with Garvak?* He couldn't remember.

• • •

An hour later, Jared emerged from his shuttle into the largely empty corridors of Complex 14, home to Navy Special Operations. It had been less than a year since he'd last set foot here, back at the outset of an assignment to recover a set of obscure ancient parchment pieces. That assignment had set in motion a series of events that had transformed his life, events that had culminated in a dramatic victory inside the planet-ship known as Malum.

Had it really been less than a year since this all began? It seemed much longer.

In many ways, he felt as if he'd left his sanity back on that giant fleet-destroying sphere orbiting Aeroel. His ordered understanding of the universe had been rattled by the simple miracle of Nho Ames, an eccentric Human devotee to an obscure Aecron religion. Trapped inside Malum with millions of others, Nho had challenged and defeated Malum's warden, a large cloud-being. Nho's only weapon? An ancient wooden staff reputed to have come from Sarco, an Aecron who claimed to be incarnated from the Creator of the Universe.

While Nho's role in the ordeal was irrefutable—hundreds had

witnessed it—the Confederacy's intelligentsia had grasped for other explanations. The Aecron Science Institute was cynical at best about Nho's explanation that it was the supernatural power of the Incarnate. Instead, the Institute officially concluded that Malum had failed as a result of an "aberrant cataclysmic failure."

In layman's terms, they believed Malum's defeat to be the result of a massive internal accident.

"Do you know what the odds of *that* are?" scoffed Nho when he'd read the report.

"1,134,578,963,542 to 1," sciences officer Darel Weye had said with a straight face. No one knew if he was serious or not.

Nho was the hero, but Jared had also earned substantial (and in some ways unwelcome) glory for his role. He was the envy of his friends and enemies alike, but he found the parade of commendations, interviews, and speaking engagements overwhelming. He never sought fame for himself and simply wanted to return to a normal life of Navy work.

Maybe today will be that day, he thought as he turned down a southwest corridor along Complex 14. There, ahead of him, was the familiar sight of Admiral Nhile-tonna-amel-fro-tigh-Garvak's office. He passed through the doorway, taking in what he had seen once before: a large space with a decidedly brown and crimson theme, and a trace scent of Ritican atmosphere. Admiral Nhile Garvak's massive, hairless, rust-colored frame occupied a seat behind a desk at the far end of the office.

"Senior Commander Carter," said Garvak, looking up.

Jared gave a Navy salute. Garvak stood, returned the salute, and gestured for Jared to sit in a chair nearby. "I trust that this meeting finds you well," said the admiral.

"Yes, sir, but restless," Jared said candidly as he sat.

"I can certainly understand your feelings. Were it not for Titan's scenic beauty, I doubt I could manage this life."

Jared shuddered. Only a Ritican could appreciate the frozen wasteland that was Titan.

"But let this experience be a lesson to you," Garvak continued, "for the day will inevitably come when necessity may force you behind one of these." He tapped the desk with his fist. "Think on your options before that day comes, so that when it does, you may find work you truly enjoy."

"I will remember that, sir."

Garvak set down his portable. "So, let us talk of your situation. As you know, there is something of a shortage of ships in the fleet. You are fortunate to have a job at all. Congress nearly disbanded half of the Navy."

"So I've heard. I'm obviously thankful they chose not to."

"So am I. Discharging good, motivated officers is a waste, though we are still scrambling to assemble new ships. That effort will take longer than the Navy would rather admit to the public, which means most of our best remain grounded. For you, though, I have different news. You have been given a new assignment."

"Glad to hear it, sir. What do you have in mind?"

The admiral leaned forward, resting his massive hands under what passed on a Ritican as a chin. "I should first warn you that some of what I am about to tell you is highly classified information. Some of it is, in fact, so sensitive that it is known only to a few select officers at the highest chain of command, as well as a few very trusted members of Congress. President Wheit is not among them. This information is not to be shared except with very specifically authorized officers named by me. You know the potential consequences if you fail to comply."

"Understood, sir," Jared said, although in reality he wasn't sure he understood at all. Information so sensitive even the Confederal President didn't know? Where was the Admiral going with all of this?

Garvak sat back in his chair. "Commander, some of us at Command are concerned about Malum."

"Malum?"

"Specifically, we are concerned about whomever or whatever created it, since we do not know where this *bkslah* came from or if there are any more. The Confederacy is still in disarray, and I am worried that if more forces arrive, we will not be able to stop them."

"You have reason to suspect another imminent threat." It was a not a question.

"Possibly. Ten months ago, when Malum was first approaching Aeroel, two Confederal ships nearby detected a particle stream emanating from the planet-ship. We think it was a transmission. We have not been able to decode it, but we have managed to pinpoint its trajectory. The destination was well outside of known space, beyond the Great Void. Rumors of this particular fact have leaked into Congress, and they have asked for a buildup of defensive elements along that stretch of the Far Outerlands. A few of us have determined that this course is far too passive given the circumstances.

"That is where you come in. Senior Commander Carter, I am assigning to you a deep-space exploration mission. Your job is to locate the recipient of Malum's transmission and assess its threat to the Confederacy. You will be journeying farther than anyone in the Confederacy has traveled before."

Jared reeled in shock. A deep-space exploration mission, beyond the bounds of the Confederacy? He couldn't recall the last time the Confederacy had launched such a mission, if ever. It was uncertain, risk-laden, even terrifying. It was also the sort of assignment every Human child on Earth grew up dreaming about.

"As you know," Garvak said, "a deep-space assignment requires much more than a simple interceptor could bear. To that end, I have been authorized to grant you command of the most suitable vessel we currently have for such an exercise."

The admiral reached over and manipulated a display, causing an annotated projection of a Navy ship to appear in the air above his desk. It was a cruiser-level vessel, a blocky hull built around a massive cylinder. The cylinder terminated at the front of the ship with a large round orifice, which was closed.

Jared recognized the ship before Garvak could say its name.

"Effective immediately," the admiral said, "I am placing you in command of the *Hattan*."

It took a moment for the statement to register with Jared. The *Hattan* was an experimental Navy cruiser that had been deployed—disastrously—against Malum. Jared had seen the ship on two occasions: once during its departure from Titan at the outset of the Malum crisis, and a second time after it had been left empty and adrift by Malum following the battle over Obaiyo Colony. The ship's former captain, Traves Walbirg, was currently awaiting trial on a variety of charges stemming from the Obaiyo debacle.

Jared said the only words he could think of at that moment. "The *Hattan*, sir?"

"You heard me correctly. Is there a problem?"

Jared balked. He could think of a lot of problems. "May I speak candidly, sir?"

He almost immediately regretted the statement. The last time he had used those specific words with Garvak was in the midst of a heated debate with the admiral not long before the Battle of Aeroel. He had incurred Garvak's full wrath that day, and he had little desire to do it again.

If Garvak remembered Jared's use of that question, he did not show it. "Go ahead, Commander."

"Admiral," Jared said, carefully choosing his words, "it's been years since I've been on a ship of that size, and I know there are other, more decorated commanders out there. While I'm more than willing to take up the command—why choose me?"

Garvak's face, partially hidden behind a rebreather, looked almost like it was smiling. "An honest question, Commander. Perhaps too honest. I will also be honest: you were not Command's first choice. However, you were the first choice of the one sentient in the Confederacy who fought and defeated Malum."

"Nho Ames."

Garvak nodded. "As you are aware, Nho returned to the Sarconian enclave on Hazion Prime several months ago, not long after your group was extracted from Malum. We have been in contact with him since then. He has agreed to join this mission, but has made it explicitly clear he will only do so if you are in command."

Jared wasn't sure whether to be flattered or insulted. Garvak went on, "Moreover, you assisted him that day, so you, too, are viewed as someone who can also contend with Malum. For better or worse, fate has tied the two of you together."

Garvak shifted in his seat, placed his massive arms on his desk, and continued. "You will also be assigned a small escort fleet. Under Navy regulations, fleet commanders rank at the level of captain or higher. Accordingly, I have been authorized to promote you to the full rank of captain. This is a permanent designation, not a field promotion."

Captain. Jared was stunned. He was still getting used to his promotion to senior commander. Captain of the Navy cruiser *Hattan*, and fleet commander of the *Hattan* exploratory fleet, or battle fleet, or whatever the Navy would choose to call it. He managed a brief nod. "It's an honor, sir, if a daunting one."

"Be honored, Captain Carter," the admiral agreed, "but it is more daunting than you may realize. Even given the *Hattan*'s resources, this is a dangerous mission, filled with grave uncertainties. There is a reason why no Confederate vessels have ever ventured outside of the galactic region."

On this Jared stated what nearly all historians agreed on. "Politics. The Confederacy is more concerned with maintaining economic stability inside its own borders than expanding outward."

Garvak said, "That is the publicly circulated reason."

Jared hadn't expected that. He felt a sudden sensation of being off-balance, as if Garvak was about to upend a part of his world and there was no stopping it. "I don't follow you, sir."

Garvak projected a series of floating graphs above his desk. "The true reason dates back two centuries. As you are aware, the Aecrons were in the midst of an era of exploration when the Invasion of 1124 took place."

Jared knew well the stories of the Invasion of 1124. Long before the advent of the Confederacy—before Humans had developed fold drive technology—a mysterious race had tried to overrun the galactic region. The Aecrons had repelled that assault, albeit at great cost.

Garvak was still talking. "Before that time, the Aecrons were, by our best standards, an arrogant, condescending culture who felt at ease to explore, and manipulate, whomever and whatever they wanted."

"Some would say that little has changed."

"So it would appear, at least on the surface. Certainly their awareness of their superior intellectual abilities persists. But there is a fundamental difference. Following the Invasion of 1124, Aeroel's policies—their actions—shifted dramatically. The abductions and other acts of interference on your world and on Hazion Prime ceased permanently, as did their deep-space exploration projects. Even to this day, their most distant colonies have fully cooperated, as has the rest of the Confederacy. Have you ever wondered why that is?"

"I assumed it was because of lingering fear over inadvertently bringing about another invasion. Or perhaps it was to consolidate resources against possible future invasions. At least, that's what the history readings say."

"That might have held true for a generation," said Garvak, "but any permanent change is inconsistent with our knowledge of Aecron psychology. In time, their people, and their government, would again be lured to explore the unknown and manipulate what they saw as lesser beings, regardless of past concerns."

Jared was getting tired of being rebutted, but something about Garvak's words gnawed at his curiosity. "So what happened? What changed?"

"The answer to your question came approximately fifteen years ago, when a Human embassy on Aeroel—operated by Earth's Western Territories—inadvertently found themselves in the posses-sion of a collection of journals from over a century and a half ago."

"You said the embassy found them fifteen years ago? My father was the lead diplomat for the Western Territories on Aeroel around that time."

Garvak's voice was impassive. "Rowun Carter was involved."

Jared stared at the ground, trying to make sense of this revelation. "I thought it was just another routine political post. He never mentioned anything important happening there."

"He had very good reason not to. What the embassy found was a secret so deep and so dangerous that it risked his life and the lives of everyone else stationed there. According to the intelligence I have seen, Aecron agents tried and failed to recapture the journals by force, and Rowun was recalled from Aeroel not long after the incident."

Jared stared down at his hands in disbelief. He and his father were distant; Jared had lived with his mother after the dissolution of his parents' marriage, and between that and his father's life-consuming political career, Jared and Rowun rarely met or even spoke. Still, the arc of his father's pursuits was public enough that he always assumed he knew some things. Rowun's world looked like one of straightforward political ambitions; Jared never fathomed that his father would ever place himself in serious danger.

Garvak said, "The journals were written by an Aecron scientist involved in a secret government operation on Aeroel. Apparently the Aecron government of that era was very concerned about repeating the mistakes which they felt led to the Invasion of 1124. To that end, they developed a program, one so clandestine that no one today even knows its name. The program, we believe, was designed to psychologically condition all living and future Aecrons to never seek either further exploration or the manipulation of lesser cultures."

Jared stared at him blankly. "My apologies, Admiral. Could you repeat that, please?"

Garvak exhaled loudly into his rebreather. "The Aecron government psychologically programmed the Aecrons to never explore beyond their current exploratory borders or manipulate any species within them."

It sounded even more ridiculous the second time. "And that includes their descendants?"

"To the best of our knowledge, all living Aecrons are affected. The journals are elusive in their language, but they make general reference to the program on several occasions, specifically speaking to the idea that the Aecrons will never again trespass the borders of explored space."

Jared hesitated. "Sir, you know how that sounds. The writer could have been delusional, or deliberately lying."

"I had those same doubts when I first heard of it. It was only after viewing the totality of the evidence that I became convinced, including to what lengths the Aecrons went to recapture the journals from the Human embassy."

Jared decided to put off asking about the evidence for a moment. He said, "How did the Aecrons accomplish this . . . this *change*?"

"We do not know. No one does. The ruling government at the time made sure that the program was not only completely effective, but they also took great pains to eliminate any clues that might lead others to discover its methods. There are no physiological markers. No technological signs. Whatever it was, it was a flawless procedure. Were it not for the writings the Human embassy found, we would not know such a program ever existed, although there are certain . . . *peculiarities* . . . that sentients in high positions have been trying to make sense of for some time now. The journals brought clarity to those events."

"That is—I'm not sure how to—" Jared cut off saying what he really thought—that this was sounding more and more like one of the absurd conspiratorial rantings that surfaced in the dark corners of the civilian feeds.

"I realize this is difficult to accept," said Garvak, "but we have seen it manifested repeatedly over the course of recent history. One of the earliest recorded examples comes from over seven decades ago, when Human and Hazionite expansion was brought to a halt by the outbreak of the Corridor Wars. While the most common explanation for the outbreak of the Wars was Hazionite greed, that is only part of the story. There are clear indications that Aecron expatriates may have had a hand in encouraging the Hazionites to expand into Ritican territory rather than elsewhere."

Jared shrugged. "Those expatriates may have had other motives. They may have been trying to distract the Hazionites from attacking the Aecrons."

"Nevertheless, consider the outcome. After the Wars, during the negotiating of the Titan Accords, the Aecrons succeeded in including a moratorium on expansion in order to prevent future conflicts. This included privately financed expeditions."

"That may just be a formality. Exploration is prohibitively expensive absent government support. There would be very few private organizations with the desire or resources to take on such endeavors."

Garvak lifted a portable off his desk and searched through it for a moment. "While that is true, there have been a few private attempts, and they are instructive, because in those rare ventures, disaster has inevitably followed." He began reading. "Thirty-six years ago, a Human exploration project was canceled when its chief financiers were pressured to do so by the Aecron government. Twenty-two years ago, an interspecies research vessel under an overzealous Human commander ventured outside of the region. The Aecrons on board mutinied and piloted the vessel back into Confederal space, claiming the commander had lost his mind. Eleven years ago, a Ritican vessel heading into the Void was attacked and destroyed by an Aecron patrol ship, which claimed it had mistaken it for a pirate vessel. Later that year a privately owned Hazionite vessel heading toward the galactic core was destroyed when its ordnance mysteriously detonated. An Aecron had overseen the stocking of the armory. Seven years ago a Human vessel that ventured into the Great Void was destroyed, apparently by an Aecron sciences officer on board who went mad. I could list a multitude of other strikingly similar examples."

"Those are unusual stories. I've never heard any of them before."

"And you have never heard of any successful private expeditions, either."

"No, sir. I guess I haven't." *Could this be true?*

"There are still other examples—more subtle ones. Have you been following the debates in the Confederal Congress regarding the response to Malum? Specifically, the Ritican initiative for a military counterstrike against Malum's creators?"

"Yes. The initiative failed on a floor vote. It was"—Jared searched his memory—"defeated, having been vigorously opposed by the Aecron delegation. They insisted the Confederacy lacked proper intelligence."

"Yet another example. By themselves, none of them look incriminating. Taken as a whole, a clear pattern develops." Garvak shut off the display. "Even so, this information is still kept classified, and for a multitude of reasons. I trust you can discern what they are."

"With respect, sir, I can't. Why not expose it to the public?"

Garvak stared at him. "That should be obvious. The Aecrons wield tremendous political and technological influence in the Confederacy, and revealing this would have far-reaching repercussions. It could even be a pretext for war, which is the last thing we need right now. As it is, only a select few in the highest levels of the sentient governments know of this."

"Are other races affected?"

"There is no evidence that they are. For whatever reason, the Aecron government chose not to apply their conditioning to other sentients. Since we do not know how they did it in the first place, it would be useless to speculate on why they did not use it on others."

"Perhaps there are experts in the Aecron Sciences Institute that could help with that."

"They do not care."

Jared's eyes narrowed. "Do not care?"

"Some in the Institute know, and they do not care. It is quite likely that their very apathy toward the issue was part of the conditioning process. The Aecron government wanted to ensure that none of their own would ever desire to undo what had been done, even if they did discover what had happened. As a result, this conditioned apathy is an intrinsic part of who they are. To them it is no more a malignant condition than your ability to breathe oxygen."

Something didn't quite fit in Jared's mind. "But you also said the Aecrons reacted violently when the Western Territories embassy acquired the journals."

"We believe that the conditioning impels the Aecrons to make certain none of their allies try to do that which they are conditioned not to do. Plainly put, they will actively subvert any outside attempt to understand the conditioning or press into the unexplored regions of space."

Jared had been struggling so hard just to comprehend what he was hearing that he hadn't given any thought to why Garvak was telling him this. Now that thought emerged, and it was an unsettling one. "The Aecrons would not react well to the Navy sending a ship out of the Confederacy, and—wait." Jared paled.

Garvak said, "You are being assigned to an exploration mission outside of the Confederacy, across the Great Void. Not only would the Aecron government move to stop you, should they learn of your assignment, but any Aecrons on your ship might also try to stop it. If history is any indication, they might well try to destroy your ship, even at the cost of their own lives."

Jared stood and paced around the room. After a short time he stopped and, staring at Garvak, said, "Are you suggesting I carry a crew without Aecrons?"

"We both know that would be severely difficult, if not impossible. There are no other sentients with the capacity to fully operate the scientific instrumentation the Navy uses. Venturing into unknown space with only basic sensory capabilities would put your fleet at a serious disadvantage."

"That puts me in a very difficult situation."

"I fully agree. Unfortunately, as you can see, our options are limited, but one thing is clear: we cannot afford sit around and wait for a large-scale invasion of more Malum planets, nor do we have the time to develop instrumentation technology and associated officers to circumvent the Aecron problem. We must know what the source of this threat is, and Aecron crew members are pivotal to the success of that mission."

Garvak set down his portable and continued. "My team, however, has a plan. First, only a few select members of your crew will be told of the specifics of your real mission, at least at the outset. Your official assignment will be a simple test flight to assess and optimize the *Hattan*'s systems. Stationed aboard your ship will be a unit of non-Aecron medical officers whose primary expertise is Aecron physiology. The unit will coordinate with a trusted team of security officers and, before you leave Confederal space, will implement a protocol to detain your Aecron officers. Once so detained, you will inform the Aecrons of your mission and the unit will monitor their reactions. They will then research proper medical and psychological countermeasures. Our hope is that they can develop a cure."

"What if they fail?"

"Your mission has many risks, including that one. We do have contingencies in place should the *Hattan* be unable to proceed."

Jared considered that. "Such as Human ships with Human-only crews."

"I cannot be specific," said Garvak, "except to say that we have contingencies, although they, too, have their own pitfalls. Regardless, we believe the *Hattan* to be a far superior option to our other contingencies, enough to justify this attempt."

Garvak again picked up his portable and began manipulating it. "Now, let us speak to your crew. We have assembled some of the best officers from across the Navy, including some that you know, to serve under you. This manifest includes both the *Hattan* and the five interceptors that will serve as escorts and reconnaissance for your battle group."

Jared walked over to the desk, took the portable, and looked over the list. Many of the names were unfamiliar, but a good number of them were not. There were several officers retained from the original *Hattan* crew, including its first officer, Tir Bvaso. Also on the list were crew members from the battle carrier *Sydney*, which fell to Malum at the confrontation over Ahtog 3.

But the names that most caught his eye were the five he knew best: Vetta-parso-bonna-truph-Quidd, Kilvin Wrsaw, Omarami Del, Darel Weye, and Triphox. The crew of the former Navy interceptor *Retaelus*. The crew that had served with him for years—and fought with him in the Battle of Aeroel—were once again at his side.

Garvak stood up. "If you will excuse me, Captain, I have other matters to attend to. You will receive more mission details once you have reported to your new ship. For now, I will dismiss you to Complex 18. There you will meet with Admiral Dal Wrsaw, who served on the *Hattan* project. She will brief you on the ship's systems. Admiral Wrsaw is one of the few within Command aware of your true mission, although I would advise you to exercise caution when speaking to her outside her office. There are powerful forces that would stop at nothing to make sure this mission does not happen if they were to learn of it."

Jared nodded, then came to attention, saluted, and was dismissed.

As he left, a tempest of feelings filled his mind. The elation of being assigned a ship—the *Hattan*, no less—was dampened by the reality that he was not Command's first choice. Were it not for Nho, Jared would not even be a consideration. And why should he be? He was a former interceptor commander. He'd served on a large ship before, but was he really ready to lead one?

But even that was insignificant compared to what Garvak called the Aecron problem. The more Jared considered that it could be true, the more the whole scenario frightened him. He was being sent into deep space in a large, unfamiliar ship where a sizeable minority of his crew might somehow seek to sabotage his mission or possibly even destroy the ship entirely. It seemed an unworkable arrangement.

2

To the Outerlands
Earth Index 1306.106

"What is *this*—?"

Jared started to tack an expletive onto the end of his remark, then caught himself. Two years ago, he would have done less catching and more cursing.

"This," the senior deck officer explained cautiously, "is our support fleet."

Jared stared across the *Hattan*'s primary cargo bay. All he saw were towering stacks of boxes. "Our *what*?"

The young, short Hazionite flinched, her words coming out in a stammer. "Command said that they do not have . . . time to build a . . . sup—support fleet for us, so they said we were pect—expected . . . to do it ourselves."

Senior Commander Redelia Aroo—an Aecron and the lead interceptor commander assigned to Jared's battle group—was standing next to the captain. "And how many ships are supposed to be here, exactly?" she asked, gesturing vaguely in front of her.

"Five, Commander."

Jared wandered a few steps forward. The boxes ran nearly to the ceiling of the vast room. "I don't suppose Command was kind enough to send assembly instructions, were they?"

"Well, yes, sir, in fact, I have right here—"

Jared put up a hand. "Stop, stop, Nenkin. How long will it take the teams to assemble them?"

"I—I don't know, sir. We'll have to examine the parts to make sure they meet integrity specifications, cross-correlate the manif—"

Jared cut her off. "Just get it done. Before the next Index year, please."

"Yes—yes, sir."

Jared turned and started to head out, but Redelia was standing silently in his way, giving him a knowing stare with her large, opaque eyes. In his head he could almost hear her saying, *You were pretty hard on her.*

Jared stared her down for a moment, then, with a resigned look, turned back around and called out, "Nenkin!"

Nenkin Fiwdl's head jerked up from her portable. Her tiny Hazionite eyes flickered anxiously. "Sir?"

"I know"—he tried to soften his tone—"I know this was not of your doing. And I realize I'm asking a lot of you. This assignment is asking a lot of all of us. Do the best you can with these ships. If you need any additional resources, contact Commander Bvaso. Understood?"

"Yes, sir."

Jared moved away, Redelia next to him. "Thank you," she said.

"No, thank you. You were right."

"Not always, but today, yes."

Such was the way his friendship with Redelia operated, a friendship forged through their time together inside Malum. He had been a council member for Hope Colony, an impromptu government created by many of the nearby Malum survivors to keep order and elevate spirits while they waited to be rescued. She had arrived later, part of the migrations seeking to join the Colony. Jared had other officers he called friends, but most of them still treated Jared with a degree of deference due his rank. Redelia did not. While they had both been commanders during the Malum crisis, Jared's promotion to captain had not altered her disposition toward him.

Their relationship was not romantic; for a variety of reasons, such things almost never developed between the different species. Instead, his connection with Redelia was more like family. Bright, gracious, and considerate, she was the antithesis of what Jared had found Aecrons to be and certainly not what he expected in a Navy officer of her stature. She could be firm, but her crew found her refreshingly kind as well, one of the reasons she had earned the right to lead Navy ships.

For all that bond meant, the inescapable reality was that she was also Aecron. She was no ordinary Aecron—he knew she was a quiet follower of Sarco—but the specter of the Aecron conditioning hovered over her just as it did every other of her race on the ship. Knowing she might turn on him made it hard for him to sort out how to interact with her. Redelia, with her ever-likable personality, made it even more difficult.

Redelia said, "I have a meeting later today to interview prospective interceptor commanders. I will let you know how it proceeds. Also, I received something today you might find interesting. It is a large database, apparently academic, sent by way of an encrypted data packet transmission."

Jared looked at her with mild interest. "From who?"

"It did not say, but there is a note attached to it. I have passed it along to your workstation and would like to ask you about it later when you have time."

As Jared turned to leave, he said, "I'll take a look at it after my shift is over."

• • •

Several hours later, Jared walked out the door of the bridge, weary from yet another torturous day. His tenure as captain of the *Hattan* was now some three months old, and from the start had been a succession of steep difficulties. The first month in particular had been a nightmare. The ship had so many faulty parts, technical problems, and unresolved design quirks that Jared wondered how it had ever fought Malum in the first place.

"I do not know that *fought* would be the word I would use," first officer Tir Bvaso had once explained to him. "Nearly all of our weapons systems failed when we arrived in the battle space above Obaiyo. We did not manage even a single shot."

Not much had changed. Following the *Hattan*'s defeat at the hands of Malum, the monstrous planet had stripped out most of the Navy cruiser's internal components. The replacement parts since installed had proven just as unreliable as those originally installed. In some extreme cases, the Exos on board had resorted to reverse engineering and designing their own parts instead of using the ones sent from the Navy shipyards.

Jared constantly reminded himself that beneath all the setbacks was a ship of extraordinary potential. The Navy's most recent technological advances were apparent in nearly every station and location, from its peerless siege cannon to its experimental collider torpedoes, down to the specialized medical equipment in the infirmary and even some of the recreational equipment. The Navy envisioned the *Hattan* as something special, even if that vision had not yet been realized.

That job fell to this crew. At Jared's orders, the crew had undertaken an exhaustive—and exhausting—inspection of the ship during the test flight. Over one thousand officers—even Nho helped—went tric by tric over the ship, tightening loose armor plating, replacing faulty conduits, rebalancing energy outputs, and refining collider reactions. It was painful, tedious work.

Much to Jared's surprise, the crew did not take well to the task. In the first month alone there had been at least twenty reported skirmishes, and rumors of several more that were not reported. More often than not, the ship's psychologists found frustration to be the root cause. Tir Bvaso, one of the very few people who knew the *Hattan*'s true mission, had tried to explain why during one of their private conversations.

"Try to see it from their perspective," she'd said. "This crew was selected for this mission specifically because they are well-suited to a deep-space assignment. Even the Aecrons, with this conditioning of theirs, seem restless. The crew wants to do something *important*, desperately, but right now they are doing the work of a technical crew, not a Navy crew. They believe the Navy is just trying to keep them occupied in the face of the ship shortage, and they hate it. I can smell their anger and frustration nearly everywhere I go."

"One would think they would be happy to be in space again," said Jared.

"They are not. They want something more."

Jared knew she was right, and it didn't take emotion sense to see it. It was one of the many hard lessons he had learned as the captain of this ship.

Over time, things slowly improved. At the outset, many on board were strangers to one another, pieced together from other ships, which had exacerbated the internal discord. As they suffered together, they also grew more familiar with one another and began evolving into something more cohesive. Jared and Tir encouraged that development by implementing organized competition, which in turn helped diminish the frustrations that had led to the earlier conflicts.

And with progress came those little moments of victory. The entire crew went wild with excitement the day the *Hattan* went out to fire the siege cannon for the first time. The massive weapon, which ran the length of the ship, blew a large asteroid the size of a small moon into a billion pieces. It was the first successful field test of the weapon in the ship's existence, and a proud moment for all who had toiled to bring it to working order.

For others, there was the quiet satisfaction as more mundane benchmarks were met. The lab teams looked on with accomplishment as their equipment finally began working the way it should. Communications took up a low-key celebration when the experimental long-range communications array came online. Then there was the moment in engineering when the fold drive operated at peak efficiency for the first time, sending a resonant hum across the decks that brought smiles (or the racial equivalent) to the entire crew—even the Exos.

Vetta and Tir also boosted morale considerably when they

quietly spread the brazenly false rumor that the ship was headed for a massive border campaign against pirates.

Jared smiled a little at that memory. At least not everything on this tour had been bad.

He rounded the corner and headed into his personal quarters, taking off his shoes and dropping into a chair to decompress. He was about to reach for something to eat when he noticed a flashing light on his workstation. Reaching over, he turned it on and saw the database Redelia had mentioned to him earlier that morning. He decided to take a look.

• • •

Tir Bvaso sat down and began to write:

To Kebrun, my husband-mate,

I hope that this message finds you well. By the time you receive this, we will be well into our test flight of the Hattan, *bound for a series of tests in the outer regions of Confederal space. It has been strange to be on this ship again; it is at once the same but it is also different. The bridge looks as it did before, and there is still nothing quite like sitting in the command station and seeing the many other stations in its orbit, like planets around a star. It is ever the grand setting; my mother would say it befits a cruiser of such high ambitions.*

But the people have changed. So many new faces, including the one at the top: Captain Walbirg is gone, and Captain Carter is here in his place. I of course do not regret Walbirg's current situation—the fool brought it upon himself—but I have been slow to warm up to Carter's leadership style. While I came to know him well inside Malum, and I certainly marveled at how he intervened with the Human cleric Nho during his fateful hour, I was not sure how a commander of such a small interceptor could effectively command such a large ship as this one.

Naturally there is more to it than that: you know me too well for me to be able to conceal this from you. I hoped that command of the Hattan *would be mine. Instead I remain the only first officer this ship has ever had.*

While I am not happy, I must admit to you (and perhaps no one else) that Jared Carter has earned my respect. I did not believe that his small-ship leadership would work here, but the crew has embraced him as a leader, more than many other, more experienced capital ship captains I know. He inspires more than just obedience: he inspires loyalty. Even Aioua is impressed, and her former ship commander, the late Cersius Pelleon Monabee, was one of the greatest admirals in Confederal history.

As you have so selflessly supported me, so have I tried to support Captain Carter, providing support as he learns the subtleties of this ship. It will come as no great shock to you that Carter is a better diplomat than I, but I have my own skills to offer. Carter has expressed appreciation for my "tyranny," when the situation has demanded it.

For the most part, the rest of the new crew has acquitted themselves well. As difficult as the work has been, they have worked hard, and each day they become less like a thousand separate trees and more like a canopy. And there have been many surprises. One of the most unexpected has been a young Wrsaw, the navigator from Captain Carter's interceptor crew. I was suspicious of him; although you might feel differently, I did not feel the bridge of such a ship as this to be the place for one of our males. In this, too, I was wrong. He possesses a ferocious ethic and has adapted far more quickly to the station of a large cruiser than I would have thought possible.

Another one of Captain Carter's former crew members has also caught my attention. She is a Ritican, now a security officer. She reminds me of your mother—

Tir's link chirped. "Jared to Tir."

She leaned back from her workstation. "Yes, Captain?"

"Could you join me in my quarters for a moment? I have something interesting to show you."

• • •

Redelia Aroo:

This is information the Aeroel government does not want you to have. I hope and pray that it might assist you. Please be judicious in how you share it.

In Sarco's name,
A friend.

"Does Redelia know who sent it?" Tir asked, sitting across from Jared and Vetta.

"I don't think so. There are any number of Sarconian sympathizers who might want us to have it, including some working for Aeroel or in the Aecron Sciences Institute." Jared did not add that Redelia's father, a legal counsel and secret Sarconian devotee, was known to represent his fellow Sarconians. It might be related, but Redelia had told him that information in confidence, especially as her unit father's faith was a secret.

Tir eyed the database description. "It appears quite large. What is it?"

Jared brought up three images. "It's three separate databases collated into a single encrypted transmission. The first is a repository of findings from the research teams sent into Malum by the Aecron Sciences Institute, conducted after the rescue work was completed. The second and third portions are lexicons. The first lexicon is the smaller and more incomplete of the two, but it's potentially invaluable. It is preliminary research into Malum's language. According to its annotations, it is based on Malum's particle transmissions as well as stores of information uncovered inside Malum."

"Interesting," said Tir. "And the second lexicon?"

"That's the real shock. It's the language of the Invaders of 1124."

Tir sat straight up. "The Aecrons have the *Invader* language?"

"A substantial amount of it, at least. According to the annotations, the Aecrons were able to harvest quite a bit from derelict Invader ships and Invader transmissions intercepted during the war two centuries ago."

"They have been secretly studying that language all this time?" Tir looked beside herself with shock. "The linguistic community would be in an uproar if they learned of this."

Vetta spoke in a dark voice. "This is timely information. Too timely. I do not like it."

"I don't either," Jared admitted. "The Malum data by itself wouldn't be alarming; it could simply be the work of someone out to subvert the Aecron leadership's handling of the planet-ship. But including all of it—the Malum data and the Invader language—is another matter. It is hard to conceive of a reason one would pass that information along, unless they believed we might somehow need it."

"And the last thing we want is for someone to know that we need this information."

Tir rested her long hand digits on the sides of her chair, her pinprick eyes deep in thought. "Has our mission been compromised? And, if so, how?"

"I don't know," said Jared. "Besides the three of us, Nho is the only one on board who knows about our actual mission. He insists he has not spoken to anyone of it, but he is also a civilian. He may have made remarks to his friends on Hazion Prime that unintentionally signaled where we are headed, and it somehow found its way to Sarconians at the Institute."

"It is also easy to envision how the knowledge may have leaked out at Navy Command," Vetta noted. "Trying to effect a mission of this scope without drawing the suspicions of the many Aecrons in higher positions would be very difficult, perhaps impossible. If the conditioning is indeed real, just one Aecron admiral or intelligence officer learning of our assignment would be problematic."

Tir lifted her portable and gestured to it. "Or an Aecron supply officer who reacted suspiciously to our requisition list."

"We could probably spend hours debating this subject," said Jared, "but the immediate question before us now is what to do next. We are not scheduled to attempt our departure of the frontier for another two months. How ready are we to get under way now?"

Tir gave the Hazionite version of a frown. "Not as ready as I would like. The ship could still benefit from more extensive testing, and we have not even had time to fully assemble a single interceptor."

"So I saw. This is a decision we will have to bear on our own." He tapped the table absently, thinking. "Our orders call for strict communications silence with Command. Garvak is very concerned the Aecrons might intercept any contact we might make with him regarding our true orders. I don't know that we can even readily get this packet's information to them, at least not until we are out of the Confederacy."

"Even with our current shortcomings," said Vetta, "I believe our best course is to depart for the Void as soon as possible."

Tir said, "I reluctantly have to agree."

Jared stood. "Then it's settled. Vetta, start making preparations for the Aecron detainment."

"I will, sir." Vetta paused. "What will you tell Commander Aroo?"

That was a question Jared was trying not to think about it. Redelia had sent him the packet hoping to solicit his feedback on what he thought of it. Now that he'd seen it, he wasn't sure what to tell her.

"I'll think of something," he said.

3

The lab went dark. In the center of the room, an asymmetrical black object floated in the air. At once the object began to hum audibly, translucent waves radiating out and away from it. The waves crashed against invisible barriers in the air.

A few steps beyond the barriers, a Ritican security officer leveled a pulse rifle at the black object and fired. The translucent pulse passed through the invisible barrier, cut through the waves, and struck the object, rattling it.

The lights came back on. Standing on the other side of the room, Jared nodded approvingly. "That looks promising."

"It is a start," said Aioua, standing next to him. "The force waves still diminish the potency of the pulse, but it is now hitting the target. The first time we attempted this experiment, the pulse did not even clear the defense fields."

"As impressive as the pulse is, I'm more impressed that the defense fields aren't destabilizing."

"We are farther along in addressing that problem. Although the Malum piece we have here puts out only a fraction of the power the planet itself does, our scaled trials suggest some promising adaptations at the ship level. The physics are too complex to try to explain, but suffice it to say, we believe we can resonate our fields in such a way that the waves will wash over the fields rather than push the fields in on themselves."

Jared gave her a searching look. "You never did explain how you acquired the piece."

Aioua's features were unreadable. "No, sir, we did not."

So it wasn't legal, Jared reasoned. Both the Aecrons and the Confederacy had made it very clear during the rescue process that anyone caught smuggling anything off of Malum would be dealt with most harshly. Whoever had acquired this piece—whether it was Aioua during their captivity or someone else then or later—had taken a grave risk in doing so. The less he asked about it, the better.

The room burst into a momentary roar, the floor quaking beneath their feet. Aioua lost her footing and careened into Jared, who caught her before she hit the floor. Even as he steadied both of them, he was shouting into his link. "Bridge, report!"

"There was an explosion in engineering," came the voice of the Hazionite duty officer from the bridge. "Our fold destabilized, and we were forced to make an emergency stop. The Exos are trying to assess what happened."

"Was anyone hurt?"

A pause. Then, "No injuries. They report the damage was confined to a small area."

"Tell them I'm on my way down," said Jared, running out of the lab.

• • •

"Below," clicked the Exo, "is a fold drive tertiary coupling. It is a standard part, found on all Navy and Human military ships of this size."

Jared peered over the railing in engineering and looked down at the large object. Wisps of smoke still drifted away from it, causing a couple of Human workers to cough as they walked by.

"And you said it cracked, correct?" said Jared, looking back at his engineer.

"It cracked," repeated the Exo.

"Was it a faulty part?"

"It is not clear."

A Human engineering assistant walked up. "I checked the database, sir. This part has a nearly flawless service history. A failure of this type as a result of usage is almost unheard of."

"It is improbable," the Exo admitted.

Tir Bvaso came up behind Jared, addressing the Exo. "Is it possible that this was an act of . . . tampering?"

The Exo tilted its head, processing the question. After a moment it said, "Uncertain."

"Have someone from sciences come down here and analyze it," Jared said. "I want to know exactly what happened. Velocitox, how soon can you have it repaired?"

"It cannot be repaired. Microfractures are developing at the point of damage."

Jared blew out an impatient shot of air. "Then how long until it can be replaced?"

"We do not have a replacement part."

"What?" His mouth fell open. "Why not?"

"The Vorsbun shipment did not have the part."

Now he remembered. During a layover near one of the Ritican colony worlds, the *Hattan* received a shipment of spare parts in advance of their field tests along the frontier. Half of the parts that engineering had ordered did not arrive with the shipment. Apparently, replacement fold drive tertiary couplings were among the missing.

• • •

A few hours later, Jared met privately in the bridge's conference room with Vetta and Tir. "So what happened?"

"The investigation was inconclusive," said Vetta. "The crack seems consistent with a fault line at the molecular level, but no one in sciences can recall seeing one like that before. The Exos assigned to that section in engineering are also at a loss."

"Could it be sabotage?"

"There is no evidence of external stimuli."

"Who was on the investigative team?" asked Tir.

"Several Aecron scientists," said Vetta, "but also other sentients as well. The conclusions they reached were unanimous."

Jared looked back and forth at the two officers with a questioning gaze.

"I do not like it, sir," said Tir.

Vetta grunted, "Nor do I."

Jared pulled up a star map in the air above the table. "The more immediate problem is how we are going to repair the ship. We're stranded in deep space without that part, and I'm concerned about what will happen when we contact the Navy for help."

"Given the current state of affairs in the Confederacy, it could take a month or more for a ship to deliver a replacement coupling. Command would also most certainly order us back to drydock for an inspection and further investigation, which could effectively put an end to our assignment."

"There is another option," said Tir, manipulating the star map. "Kilvin located a Ritican manufactory less than a day's fold from our current position. They service the drydocks of several Ritican frontier colonies, as well as the militia border patrols."

Vetta pointed to a star system. "And other clients."

Jared leaned in to look, his eyes narrowing. He knew that star system well, and Vetta knew it even better. A star gone nova, a scorched planet serving as a haven for pirates and other undesirables. Dio.

Jared brought his eyes to meet Vetta's. "Are you sure?"

"Yes. My father made that run many times."

Tir looked at both of them. "I sense there are things you both know that I do not."

Jared gently waved her off. "I'll explain another time. Let's talk about this manufactory. I assume they specialize in Ritican parts. Can they service a Navy ship?"

"According to our database, they do manufacture a limited number of non-Ritican parts. The coupling we use is a common part on both Human and Navy ships. We will not know for sure until we arrive, but I would be surprised if they do not."

A small risk, but they didn't have much choice. "You said the colony is a day away by fold. How will we get there?"

Tir brought up a graphic of the damaged part. "Engineering says they can reinforce the microfractures long enough to make a few jumps."

Jared took a step back. "Then instruct the Exos to begin work. It's not ideal, but anything is preferable to languishing at a Navy base for the rest of the year." Then, to Vetta: "Assign a security detail to keep a quiet eye on engineering. I'd rather not have any more . . . *accidents*."

4

RAMAS-EDUJ
EARTH INDEX 1306.124

Located on an inhospitable mass of rock, the Ramas-Eduj Manufactory was home to society's outcasts, sentients trying to survive in a galaxy that did not want them. The operation was managed by a Ritican cartel, and as such maintained strictly enforced rules of discipline. Those who caused trouble were exiled from the complex to the surface, where death would soon follow.

While the *Hattan* reached the planet without incident, the sudden arrival of the cruiser attracted considerable local attention. The manufactory primarily serviced Ritican ships, and a Navy presence was neither expected nor welcome. Defusing this problem fell on the shoulders of Lieutenant Orel Dayail.

Orel was not an officer Jared knew well, but he was happy to have him, especially now. A former communications officer on board the battle carrier *Sidney*, Orel was an Aecron who, in contrast to most Aecrons, carried an unusual touch for diplomacy. He was cognitively impaired by Aecron intellectual standards, which meant little, since he was still brilliant compared to most non-Aecrons. He also got along very well with his peers, although Jared had observed that he was so friendly that it almost seemed like he was trying to sell something. Being the unit child of an Aecron ambassador probably had something to do with it.

JOSHUA A. JOHNSTON

Orel didn't disappoint. Once he explained that they had a business proposition for the Riticans, the manufactory generously offered their services—for the right price, of course. Orel hammered out appropriate compensation with the management, who in turn granted the *Hattan* permission to send a shuttle and secure the necessary equipment.

Jared felt a senior officer should command the expedition and oversee the transaction, but in that area there were some complications. Tir Bvaso was Hazionite, and lingering animosity toward her race might impede her ability to deal with the Riticans running the colony. Vetta Quidd was an obvious choice, but she was immersed in critical preparations for the Aecron detainment.

Things being as they were, Jared opted to lead the mission himself. He brought Kilvin Wrsaw along to pilot the shuttle. Kilvin had spent much of the interim period between the Malum crisis and the *Hattan* assignment hauling cargo shuttles to and from the Navy shipyards, and was better at it than most of the cruiser's actual shuttle specialists. Kilvin did have the disadvantage of being Hazionite, but Jared figured that as long as Kilvin stayed on board the shuttle, his presence would probably not be an issue.

Nho also asked to go along, citing only vague intuitions as his reasons. Jared agreed.

• • •

Jared moved into the seat next to Kilvin at the front of the Navy shuttle *Disgnin*. They were a little less than eight minutes removed from the *Hattan*. The other occupants of the shuttle—an Exo engineer, Nho, and three Ritican security officers—waited silently in the seats farther back.

Jared watched with quiet interest as Kilvin deftly kept the shuttle on a steady course in the planet's light gravity. This shuttle, like most attached to the *Hattan*, was considerably larger than the two-person models he used when he was an interceptor commander. And today it was even larger than normal, owing to the bulky cargo pod attached to it.

Jared finally broke the silence. "I remember the last time we were in a Navy shuttle together."

Kilvin's expression turned sad. "Hazion Prime, when you came to find me after my mother's funeral." He paused. "That day continues to give me no shortage of trouble."

"Then you are still receiving messages from your aunt?"

"Several times a month. She continues to demand that I return to the homeworld."

"She didn't like you volunteering to work for the shipyards?"

"Most definitely not."

"You told me before that she was considering legal action to force you to come home."

"My association with Nho and yourself inside Malum made that politically difficult. Instead she has taken to other tactics, including applying pressure through other relatives. I have received multiple contacts from my father, imploring me to resign from the Navy. I know him well enough to know that his words are not of his own choosing, but it does not matter. I cannot return to Hazion Prime, and Hrez will not sanction any marriage I might try to enter into."

Jared shrugged. "I thought the whole point was that you didn't want to marry."

Much to Jared's surprise, Kilvin hesitated a little. "I have met . . . a few possible mate-candidates on the *Hattan.*"

Jared's initial surprise was now full-fledged shock. He didn't necessarily regard Kilvin as one who would remain unmarried for a lifetime—Jared didn't even assume that about himself—but he had taken for granted the idea that Kilvin's only route to marriage was through his aunt's directives. Apparently that was not the case.

"What?" Jared asked. "Who?"

Kilvin's voice grew quiet. "I would rather not say, sir. I assure you that there are no supervisory conflicts."

Jared took a moment to process this. "I thought Hazionite marriages were arranged."

"Most, but not all. Some of our colony planets permit unarranged pairings."

"So your aunt's injunction is moot, then?"

Kilvin gestured to the negative and his voice grew frustrated. "Even in an unarranged union, it is only valid if the two mate-candidates do not have any Hazionite injunctions. I currently do, so I would not be able to lawfully settle on any Hazionite world. It is a complication for any potential wife-mate, although some members of the crew are less concerned about that complication than others." He brightened a little. "In fact, some of them are in similar situations, or in minor tribes that do not care what the larger tribes do."

A bemused grin crossed Jared's face. "I never thought I'd see the day when Kilvin Wrsaw would be talking about wife-mates. Next you'll be telling me that Rami Del is in a serious relationship."

Kilvin looked caught off-guard. Jared's eyes grew wide. "No. It can't be."

The navigator lowered his voice again. "It is not exactly what you think, but she has changed. Apparently Nho has had an influence on her. She is different now. More serious about . . . certain things. Less like . . . the way she was when we were on the *Retaelus*."

Jared's jaw dropped. Rami, like Jared, had struggled through the absence of a father, but where Jared was notoriously cautious about romance, Rami was notoriously casual. Her lifestyle of frequent, transient partners was an open secret among the crew of the *Retaelus*; because it did not appear to impede her professional duties, Jared never brought it up with her. He'd long ago accepted that it was an immutable part of who she was.

Except now it wasn't. *Apparently Nho has had an influence on her*, Kilvin had said.

Jared looked over his shoulder. If Nho overheard them, the old man gave no indication. He turned back. "Are you saying she *is* seeking out more serious relationships?"

Kilvin didn't respond right away; Jared assumed the navigator was weighing whether to answer the question. "Ever since Malum," he said at last, "Rami has . . . avoided romance. She says she has decided to step back and think about those things more carefully."

They had all been changed to different degrees by the Malum

experience, but this one left Jared dumbstruck. Kilvin said no more on the subject, and Jared didn't press it. They passed the remainder of the trip in silence.

• • •

Twenty minutes later, Kilvin navigated the *Disgnin* into the hangar bay of the Ritican manufactory, and the bay doors closed behind it. After the shuttle landed and the bay was pressurized, Jared, Nho, the Exo engineer, and two Ritican security officers disembarked. Kilvin and a single Ritican security officer remained behind.

For safety reasons, there was no oxygen or methane in the complex's atmosphere. As a result, Jared and Nho wore environmental suits, while the Ritican security officers wore rebreathers. In accordance with the conditions of the negotiations, none of the Navy officers were armed.

They were greeted by a contingent of Ritican factory workers who looked the part. Marked with scars and what Jared took to be some sort of body art, the Riticans of the manufactory looked more unpleasant than even the most aggressive of those who served in the Navy.

"Welcome to our humble operation, Captain," roared the manager, a Ritican with an absolutely massive frame who stepped forward from among the waiting crowd. "My name is, of course, beyond your range of hearing. You may call me Tack."

Jared extended his fist in a traditional Ritican greeting. "It is good to meet you in person, Tack. I am Captain Jared Carter of the Navy cruiser *Hattan*."

Tack gave the Ritican version of a laugh, which sounded to Jared rather like a large dog in the throes of death. "We do not engage in formalities or flattery here, Captain. Equipment is our formality and currency is our flattery. But your taste of civilization is nevertheless appreciated. Come, let us get your couplings."

Tack turned and headed down one of the large corridors, flanked by his entourage. Jared and his team followed. The Exo engineer, at the rear, pulled the utility pod, which floated effortlessly above their Aecron-designed suspension buffers.

The manufactory was an open floor plan with three levels of construction equipment on both sides. The complex, roofed by a sheet of rock, was set below the planet's surface. Everything around them was a cacophony of light and sound. Construction projects were under way everywhere, and the flash of ardor torches combined with the grinding sounds of assembly. Jared wondered how such a remote construction facility could be so busy, even servicing illicit clients. *This doesn't just look like a manufactory for parts. If I didn't know any better, I'd think they were assembling entire ships. But why?*

Jared's thoughts were broken by a voice coming from just off to his left. Despite Tack's larger stride, the Ritican walked slowly to match his pace with Jared and began talking. It soon became clear that the Ritican enjoyed talking a great deal.

"We do not get many non-Ritican vessels out here," remarked the manager. "Your ship's arrival is one of the most interesting things to happen here in months."

Jared said nothing.

"By the way, you never did tell me what your crew was doing out this far."

"Research mission."

"Is that so?" remarked Tack loudly. "That's an awfully impressive warship you have up there to be doing science projects with."

"It has superb scientific facilities."

"Of course it does. And just what are you researching, Captain? Or, better yet, let me guess. It is classified."

"Naturally."

"Well," bellowed Tack, "who am I to stand between a warship and its classified scientific research? It is unfortunate your important work has been interrupted by flawed Navy technology."

"You'll be well compensated for helping us fix that," said Jared, "much better than what those Dio raiders are giving you."

Tack gave him an indignant look. "We do not do business with pirates here, Captain. I can assure you of that. And, of course, even if we did, it would be classified."

Tack's entourage laughed. It sounded like a pack of injured wolves.

They reached a junction point and Tack stopped. "If you will give me a moment, I will see if the parts are ready." The large Ritican turned and, with some of his followers accompanying him, headed down a side tunnel.

Nho's voice floated out of Jared's link—a private channel the Riticans could not hear. "Did you see that mark on his arm?"

Jared cut his external communication and replied, "I saw it. I don't know what it is."

"I met others with that mark on Alsis," Nho said.

One of Jared's Ritican security officers, Senior Lieutenant Thorno Garn, said, "The mark means he is a veteran of the Corridor Wars and has killed Hazionites in battle."

"The ones I knew who had that mark did not hesitate to kill again. This Tack is more dangerous than he seems."

Thorno said, "I would agree."

Jared suddenly wished he had a pulse pistol or maybe a gibeon rifle. Here they were, deep in a distant Ritican manufactory surrounded by workers who were skilled in the art of killing. He would be happier once this transaction was over and they could leave.

Tack walked back up the tunnel. "This way, Captain."

Jared put up a hand. "If you'll give me a moment, I need to check in with my ship."

"Of course, Captain. Take your time."

Jared keyed his link. "Jared Carter to *Hattan*."

There was no response. Jared tried again. And again.

After the fourth time, Tack finally let out a long-winded Ritican laugh. "Captain, did I forget to mention? The planet's surface wreaks havoc with communication. There is only one way to talk to anyone from this colony, and that's through our contact room. Do I need to take you there, or should I worry that your warship may panic and come after you?"

"No, don't worry," Jared replied calmly. "Our science teams will no doubt determine the composition of the ore and reach the same conclusion. I'd give us at least a good half hour before my Hazionite first officer gets impatient and destroys your colony."

"How about that!" observed Tack, breaking again into the horrible laughter. "A Navy Captain with a sense of humor. I think I like you, Human, even if you do associate with Hazionites. Just for that, I won't kill that young Hazionite pilot of yours back on your shuttle. And I'll even get you your parts. Come with me."

• • •

Darel Weye carefully applied a stabilizer to Sesin Bvaso's arm. The young Hazionite had been sparring with another Hazionite in the gym and had been thrown from her feet, landing and tearing her arm's muscle core. Darel never understood the Hazionite affinity for physical violence, but it was not his job to understand, only to repair. And he had done a lot of repair work during his tour of duty on this ship.

It had been a difficult transition, moving from a general sciences officer on a Navy interceptor to working as a full-time medical officer on a cruiser. He missed his life on the *Retaelus*, where he had carved out a familiar professional routine working in his small lab and treating a small crew. Here on the *Hattan*, everything was larger and more specialized. As a medical specialist—a profession his family had pressed him into against his wishes—it was a foregone conclusion that he would be assigned to the infirmary once he moved to a large ship. Sarco, writing thousands of years ago, had written that it was best to accept one's profession with grace. Darel wondered if Sarco would have felt the same way working in an infirmary treating injury-seeking Hazionites.

Darel directed his patient to stand. "You will need to keep this on for about five days. And remember to turn on the regeneration wrap before you go to sleep each night. If you forget, you will have to wear the stabilizer for another week. Understood?"

"Yes, Doctor," she replied.

Darel took from her tone that she was not happy about the arrangement, but few of his patients were. He looked over his shoulder. "Oael, could you bring me . . . Oael? Deck Officer Oael, where are you?"

No response. Darel instructed Sesin to remain seated for a moment, and walked to the outer infirmary area. There was no sign of his Aecron medical assistant. In fact, there was no sign of any of the current shift's staff. He looked out in the hallway, but to no avail.

Darel looked back in on the Hazionite. "Did you see any of the staff leave?" he asked.

"No, Doctor."

"Strange. Infirmary to Deck Officer Oael."

No response over his link. Darel repeated the call. Still nothing. He paged the other members of the current infirmary staff. No response.

The situation was unsettling. He took a short breath and said, "Infirmary to Bridge, Sciences Station."

A disembodied voice on the other end spoke. "Aioua here. What is it, Darel?"

"It appears that my staff has departed the infirmary, and I do not know where they have gone."

"Departed?"

Darel gave what passed among Aecrons as an impatient snort. "Yes. They are not here."

"Did you page them?" asked Aioua. She sounded amused.

He was not. "Of course," he snapped.

"Give me their names, and I will find them."

Darel did so, then waited.

When Aioua Horae spoke again, her voice was more serious. "All of your missing officers are on deck ten, rearward section."

That made no sense. The infirmary, like the bridge, was on deck four. The only thing in that section of deck ten was the armory.

• • •

55

Senior Commander Redelia Aroo had the problem of being a commander without a ship. The construction of the first interceptor was coming along well and was only a few weeks away from its test flights. As the senior interceptor commander assigned to the *Hattan* battle group, that ship would be hers.

In the meantime, she was without a command to call her own. That was difficult. She had supervised much of the interceptor's construction, but she was no engineer and could only stand and watch for so long. Jared, for his part, had placed her in the *Hattan*'s bridge command rotation, which helped keep her skills sharp and also exposed her to the stark challenges of running a large capital ship.

But there was still too much free time and Redelia was not always sure how to spend it. Today, she had rather spontaneously decided to work on her small arms combat training. It was time well spent; interceptor crews were more likely than most Navy personnel to wind up leading boarding parties or other combat excursions outside of a ship. The *Hattan*'s presence in the battle group, with its accompanying legions of specialized security officers, made such exigencies less likely, but interceptor commanders never knew when their ships might have an emergency to deal with. If nothing else, it kept Redelia busy.

Now finished, Redelia strolled back to the window next to the armory, carrying an Aecron handpulse. The watch officer, a Human female, said nothing as she took the weapon, signed it in, and handed it off to another officer who placed it back with the main stock.

Redelia turned away, retracing her steps down the hallway. Already her mind had drifted to the next item on her agenda for the day, a meeting with one of the prospective weapons officers for her new interceptor crew.

As she reached an intersection, she stopped.

Up ahead was a group of Navy officers, perhaps ten or twelve. All were Aecrons. They were all walking purposefully down the hallway, presumably toward the armory. Almost immediately, though, a sense of alarm rippled through her mind. The look in the officers' eyes was wrong. It was anger, or something beyond it. Rage. She had not seen the look often, but she knew it when she saw it.

She noticed movement out of the corner of her eye. Glancing to her left and right, she saw still more Aecron officers approaching at a brisk walk. Their eyes were the same.

She suddenly felt nervous, even fearful. Suppressing those feelings, Redelia summoned the authority of command in her voice. "What are you all doing down here?"

No response. They pressed forward, now no more than a few trics away.

"Answer me. Now."

From inside her mind came a still, small voice.

Run.

Pushing aside her confusion, she pivoted around and retreated back in the direction of the armory.

Her return to the watch officer's station drew a puzzled look. "Is there a problem, Commander?"

"Yes," Redelia said quickly. "Take up a defensive position outside the armory."

"Sir?"

"That is an order. Draw your weapon and prepare to fire at my command."

"But, sir—"

Redelia nearly shouted, "Do it *now*."

As the Human weapons officer stood and fumbled for a weapon, Redelia was already on her link. "Redelia Aroo to Bridge, Command Station. Commander Bvaso, I need to speak with you right now."

• • •

"Commander Bvaso, can I speak to you for a moment?"

Tir, seated at the bridge's command station, looked up from a report she was reading. She said to Aioua, "What is it?"

"I am not sure what is going on, but I am reading about fifty officers headed toward the armory. Mostly medical and sciences officers. I just spoke with medical officer Darel Weye, who reported that the entire infirmary staff left their post without explanation."

Tir stood up and took a step toward Aioua. "Aecrons?"

"Yes, all of them."

Tir's link chirped. "Redelia Aroo to Bridge, Command Station. Commander Bvaso, I need to speak with you right now."

"It will have to wait. We have a potential problem up here."

Redelia's voice was insistent. "Commander, there is a large group of Aecron officers converging on the armory down here on deck ten. Something is wrong with them, and they are not responding to my orders. I have ordered the watch officers to take up a defensive position."

Tir's core muscles tightened in apprehension. She had dutifully followed Jared's orders regarding the Aecron detainment, although she wasn't completely convinced the conditioning was real. At that moment, though, it was hard to ascribe the situation to anything else.

And Redelia is an Aecron. Does that mean this is a ruse? No, she told herself. Redelia was a good officer and one of the most honest and reliable people Tir knew. For the moment, she had to trust that this communication—and that of Darel Weye—was true.

"Redelia," said Tir, "do not let any of them reach the armory. Try to minimize potential fatalities, but use force if necessary. Keeping them out of that armory is your top priority. I am sending reinforcements to assist you."

Tir reset her link. "Tir to Vetta. We need a security detail down to the armory immediately. Implement the Detainment Protocol."

Tir looked around the bridge. Several Aecrons were situated at various stations. Most of them were standing straight, staring at her with odd looks in their eyes. Tir felt a wash of emotion as their scents reached her. They were angry. Enraged.

The Hazionite first officer took a few steps back and reached down to the command chair, where a pulse pistol was concealed inside a compartment. She withdrew the pistol.

A wave of bodies crashed into her, sending her sprawling on

the floor and the pistol flying out of her hands. Aecron officers swarmed over her, biting and clawing. Through the pile she could see other Aecron officers attacking nearby non-Aecrons or trying to damage their consoles.

Tir saw the pistol. She reached for it, but it was knocked away again, landing a couple trics distant. She watched in horror as Aioua Horae stepped out from around the sciences station, picked up the pistol, and pointed it directly at her.

• • •

Vetta Quidd had implemented the Detainment Protocol even before she received the order from Tir. Vetta was down in the cargo bay when a call came from guards watching over the torpedo bay on deck twelve, forward section. A large number of unauthorized Aecron officers had converged on the bay, overrun the guards, and were now trying to force their way into the racks of explosive ordnance. The detonation of just one torpedo would trigger a chain reaction that would obliterate the entire ship. While the torpedo bay was stoutly sealed, there were Aecrons on the ship who were skilled enough to override the door if given enough time.

Rounding up a few nearby officers, Vetta rushed up to deck twelve, where she quickly found herself engulfed by a horde of the rabid, blue-skinned Navy officers. While the others with her, most of them unarmed, launched into a desperate brawl, Vetta fired her pulse pistol into the Aecron crowd, sending numbers of them flying off in various directions. Up ahead, she could see several of them working surgically to break open the torpedo bay door. She had no illusions about how close they might be to succeeding.

• • •

Aioua fired the pulse pistol.

The shot blew several Aecrons off of Tir, sending them crashing onto the far floor. Aioua quickly stepped forward and fired again, the pulse bolt striking two more Aecrons. Tir whipped her arm against one Aecron and planted a fist in the last one.

JOSHUA A. JOHNSTON

Aioua reached over and helped her up. Tir took her hand, making note her smell: fear, but no anger. Aioua seemed to be unaffected, at least for now. Nearby, bridge officers were trying to restrain other angry Aecrons, the opaque-eyed officers screaming wildly in protest.

Tir smelled a spike of anger nearby. She looked around for the source of the scent. Communications.

Orel Dayail hoisted a conduit access plate over his head and brought it crashing down on the communications panel, sending sparks flying everywhere. He did it a second time and then a third before Aioua gathered her senses and pulled the trigger, sending him crumpling to the floor.

Tir turned to Aioua. "Hand me the pistol," she ordered.

Aioua complied without protest. An Aecron officer slipped away from a Human and charged at Tir. Tir leveled the pistol and fired, knocking the officer to the floor.

She glanced back at Aioua. "Get back to your station and find out where the Aecron numbers are concentrated. We need to make sure they don't destroy the ship."

• • •

Jared Carter and the rest of the Navy team arrived at the central hub of operations for this portion of the manufactory. Archaic rail lines served as the roadway for moving ore and equipment throughout the vast building.

Human operators drove two separate, noisy railcars into the room where Jared and the others were standing. Each railcar was carrying a large metal circular object: a Ritican fold drive tertiary coupling. The *Hattan* only needed one, but Jared and Tir had concluded that a spare to replace one that never arrived was prudent.

Jared's Exo engineer surveyed the couplings carefully, running a sensor over them to verify that they were what the *Hattan* required. Satisfied, he addressed Jared. "These are suitable."

Before Jared could speak, Tack clamped a fist the size of an Earth watermelon on his shoulder, nearly causing his knees to buckle. "Good!" said Tack. "My workers will help you load the parts into your pod."

Tack shouted and gestured to a group of men—mostly Riticans and Humans—who began affixing the couplings with levitators. As they went about their work, Jared could hear Nho murmuring something to himself.

"It's not possible," the old cleric whispered, his eyes transfixed on something.

"What?" said Jared. "Is something wrong?"

"It's not possible."

"What are you talking about?"

Nho kept his voice low. "It's Rete."

It took a few moments for the name to register. Rete. Nho's old friend. Rete had been on Bate Mur when its sun went supernova. While on a refugee colony, Rete's traveling companion, Suda, had turned on Rete, selling him into slavery. On his last assignment, Jared had tracked Rete's whereabouts as far as the pirate haven of Dio, but the trail had gone cold there.

Jared scarcely expected to hear that name here and now. He glanced in the direction Nho was looking, at a man loading ore into one of the manufactory processors along a wall. "That one in the middle?"

"Yes. It's his eyes. It's has to be him."

"Are you certain?"

Nho reflexively squeezed his staff. "Yes. I'm certain."

Jared regarded the man closely. He was, like the others in his area, laboring hard. Something about the man's body language stood out, though. He was behaving differently than the others.

He looked nervous.

Nho stepped forward, walking toward the man, calling out, "Rete? Rete?"

No answer, but Jared saw the man cast a sidelong glance over in their direction.

"Rete?" Nho asked again, drifting closer. "It's Nho Ames."

The man did his best to ignore Nho, continuing to do his work.

Tack did not. The Ritican was halfway up another tunnel when he heard Nho's voice and doubled back, calling out, "What is going on here?"

By this time, Nho was within a few trics of the man he called Rete, still calling out. The man continued to focus on moving the ore, though it was apparent to Jared that the man was looking at Nho out of the corner of his eye.

"Rete Sorte! It's me, Nho."

Nho started to take another step forward, but he suddenly found the massive Ritican manager blocking his path. "Listen, *Human*," Tack said, towering over him, "I would appreciate it if you would allow my men to do their work."

Nho was silent for a moment. Then, without a word, he took a step back and rejoined the rest of the Navy officers.

"Keep your men in line, Captain," the manager snarled. "I would hate for them to do anything to jeopardize our business arrangement."

Jared nodded but said nothing.

• • •

Tir stood nervously next to the sciences station as Aioua continued to track the rogue Aecron groups running loose across the ship. The security teams swarmed toward them, implementing the Aecron Detainment Protocol that Jared, Tir, and Vetta had drawn up earlier in the year. At that time, only a few select members of the *Hattan* security force knew about the plans. Now the entire security team—and the rest of the crew—were trying to effect the orders in the midst of a chaotic and dangerous situation.

On Aioua's display, a group of red dots, representing a large Aecron contingent near the commons, stopped moving. A group of green security dots moved in. "Team Seven reports that the commons is secure," Aioua said.

Tir took little joy in the statement. The ship was still crawling in red. "Current count on the Aecrons," Tir said.

Aioua looked over her numbers. "Fifteen dead or dying in

various parts of the ship. Security estimates that ninety have been incapacitated. Most of that number are currently in the brig or the secondary cargo bays."

That left perhaps seventy still unaccounted for. Far too many, Tir thought. "And the rest of the crew?"

"Total injuries close to one hundred, some more serious than others. No deaths."

Among the injured were, mysteriously, nearly every member of the specialist team that Admiral Garvak had assigned and briefed to study and treat the Aecron conditioning. Three of them had been attacked, alone, in their personal quarters. Most of the others had been assaulted by roaming mobs of Aecrons. The only one left unharmed was a lone Human xenophysiologist who was so badly shaken by a brush with death in the corridors that he had difficulty even using his equipment properly.

Tir scanned the map further. "What is the status of deck ten?"

"The group that arrived there two minutes ago has been incapacitated. Commander Aroo reports no new threats."

Tir allowed herself a measure of relief. Redelia Aroo's fierce, organized defense of the armory on deck ten was a major reason why things weren't worse than they were.

Redelia was one of twelve Aecrons that appeared to be unaffected by the conditioning, and thus were excluded by Tir from the detainment. All twelve had acted in ways that were not only nonthreatening, but heroic. Tir did not have the time to consider why those twelve differed from their peers, but a dim part of her hoped that insight into the differences might help them find a cure.

She glanced at Aioua, her sciences officer and friend—another excluded from the detainment on the basis of her actions, including the pulse shot that had saved Tir's life. Aioua did not look back, engrossed in her work.

Tir's link chirped. "Darel Weye to Tir Bvaso."

"Yes, Deck Officer."

"Commander, could you *please* tell the security team to stop trying to keep me from doing my job?"

Tir suppressed a profanity. Every new wave of injured crew members coming into the infirmary brought a new group of suspicious security officers trying to detain the lone Aecron medical officer still able to function. She said, "Who is it?"

"Qora Vocks."

To the Ground Curser with these Riticans, she mused angrily. She started to contact Senior Deck Officer Vocks when she heard a voice in the background of Darel's link.

"He does not smell like the other ones," the voice said. "And we need him."

Tir recognized the voice as Hazionite, and sure enough Darel said, "It is under control now, sir."

"Tell that Hazionite officer to stay with you," Tir snapped. "My orders."

"Gladly, Commander."

Tir ran a digit over the small shock of hair atop her head. If this crew didn't sabotage themselves, just maybe they'd be able to stop the Aecrons from sabotaging the ship. She said to Darel, "Please tell me you have made some headway on understanding what is causing this."

Without any formal decision, Darel Weye had assumed charge of the investigation. With the specialist team out of action and the other Aecron doctors out of their minds, Tir had no one else to turn to.

"I am confounded," Darel said. "The Aecrons on board—except for a few of us—are obviously out of their minds, but I cannot find a physiological cause. I will run more tests as soon as I have stabilized the injury situation down here . . . provided no one else tries to drag me off to the brig."

The connection closed, and Tir placed a hand on the sciences station to steady herself. It was an overwhelming situation, and she could smell her own frustrations in addition to those around her. Mentally, she knew that the crew had performed admirably given the unexpected onset of the mutiny, but the situation nevertheless remained precarious.

• • •

After the utility pod was reattached to the *Disgnin*, Jared completed the currency transfer and headed for the shuttle's airlock, where Nho and one of the Ritican security officers waited. The rest of Jared's team was already on board. Through his link, he heard Kilvin advising everyone that the extra weight was going to make their exit a little awkward. As Kilvin finished speaking, Jared keyed the controls to close the airlock door. The door slid silently closed—but not before a body dove through and landed face-down on the floor.

For a frozen moment, the body lay there on the floor of the airlock. Then a helmeted face looked up, directly at Jared.

Nho, his voice muffled by his environmental suit, shouted, "Rete!"

"Captain," the man said, pulling himself to his knees and wiping his faceplate, "I am Rete Sorte, a slave on this planet. I would like to formally request your protection."

Jared regarded him warily. "Can you verify who you are?"

The man looked to Nho, who said, "It's him, Jared. I'm certain of it."

"That's not enough, not for what he's asking." He stared hard at the man. "How did you meet Nho?"

The man got to his feet. "We were friends on Hazion Prime many years ago," he said, brushing off his suit. "I left with a Human named Suda for Bate Mur, but Suda sold me into slavery. I passed through several planets before ending up here."

Outside, they could hear angry voices screaming in protest, growing louder as they got closer. The shuttle shook.

"Captain, someone just fired on us with an ardor weapon," Kilvin said through Jared's link. "There are other armed workers also moving into position."

Nho turned to Jared with an imploring look. "Please, help him, Captain."

Jared frowned. This was a complicated situation of the highest order. Slavery was illegal, both under Ritican law and Confederal accord. In that regard, the *Hattan* had every legal right to offer the man protection pending an investigation. But a Ritican frontier world, particularly one with ties to the Dio Market, likely cared little for Confederal jurisprudence, despite Tack's pretense of respect. He would care somewhat more about Ritican law, but the Ritican government was far away right now and would be reluctant to involve itself with such a distant and valuable manufactory, especially if it serviced Ritican border patrols.

The Ritican manager might hesitate knowing that the *Hattan* was in orbit above, but Riticans were not always rational when they felt invaded. Jared had little doubt Tack felt violated now that one of his purchased slaves had been taken from him. Even if Confederal or Ritican law eventually confirmed Rete's story and punished Tack's colony, it would matter little if the occupants of the shuttle were dead, which they might shortly be.

By now the airlock had cycled and was open to the interior of the shuttle. Jared stepped through and saw that the shuttle's communications display was lit up, with Tack's face dominating it. Jared did not need to be a Ritican to know the manager was livid.

Jared moved over to the display and keyed the audio. Almost immediately the manager's voice came blasting into the shuttle's interior.

"Captain, you have one of my men."

Jared's glare was cold with anger. "Your men fired on my shuttle."

"And they will do so again if you do not return my worker."

"He is requesting protection. He claims he is a slave and is being held here against his will."

"I am not concerned with what he says. He is one of my men, and I expect him returned."

Jared made no attempt to conceal his indignation. "He is entitled to an investigation under both Ritican and Confederal law. We are returning him to our ship pending the outcome of that investigation."

"You will do no such thing."

"Is that a threat?"

"It is a statement of fact, Captain. Your ship needs those parts, and unless I open those hangar doors, you will not leave here with them."

Jared muted the display. "Kilvin, can we contact the *Hattan* from here?"

"I already tried. Nothing is getting through the rock or that door."

Jared turned to one of his Ritican officers, Thorno Garn. "What do you think will happen if we open that door and I try to reason with Tack?"

"I would not count on reason. Our lives are in danger each moment we sit here."

"That's what I thought." Jared glanced out the shuttle's forward observation window, where more of Tack's workers were lining up with weapons. "Kilvin, take us up. Also, keep trying to contact the *Hattan*. Let them know we may be in danger."

"What about the hangar doors?"

That was a problem. The shuttle had defense fields but was unarmed. Jared looked to Thorno, who responded by gesturing to the two other Ritican security officers—one female, one male—sitting next to him. The three stood up and made their way swiftly to the back of the *Disgnin*, where they opened up the shuttle's storage locker.

The locker was modestly stocked. In addition to standard survival equipment and a store of rations, there were also weapons: two ordnance-launching gibeon rifles, two pulse rifles, and four pulse pistols. Two sets of self-fitting Navy-issue combat armor, complete with visors, hung next to the weapons.

The three Ritican officers took the two gibeon rifles and one of the pulse rifles; Jared walked up behind them and took the other pulse rifle. As they did, Kilvin activated the *Disgnin*'s thrusters and elevated the small ship vertically into the air. Dull thuds from enemy fire could be heard impacting against the shuttle's defense fields.

Thorno walked up behind Kilvin. "Turn us so the airlock is facing the hangar door. Lower the defense fields when I give the signal."

As Kilvin rotated the small ship around, Jared and the Riticans crowded into the airlock and closed it to the interior. Once in position, Thorno opened the exterior door.

The Ritican security officer looked through the sight of his gibeon rifle. "I spot a seam along the hangar door. Match my target. Navigator, lower the fields now."

The four officers—Jared and the three Riticans—fired rapidly into the hangar door. The pulses landed first, splashing against and denting the thick metal. The gibeon ordnance arrived shortly thereafter, exploding into balls of light. Smoke drifted from the spot, and through the haze, Jared could see fissures developing where the hits had landed.

A blaze of ardor whipped by the shuttle. Down below, several miners were firing up at the *Disgnin*, trying to bring it down.

"I'll take care of the ground attack," said Jared. "Keep on that door."

The three Ritican Navy officers pummeled the door with their rifles as Jared swept his weapon down on the attackers below. One of Jared's shots struck a worker dead-on, blowing her into a stack of metal crates. The others attempted to return fire while retreating behind cover, their shots landing wide of the mark.

Thorno and the other Navy officers continued their assault on the door, the gibeon explosions in particular now beginning to create serious fractures in the door. Jared maintained steady fire on the miners, who for all their perceived toughness were obviously not used to being shot at, much less by military-grade weapons.

Almost unexpectedly, the hangar door blew open. The explosive decompression pulled at Jared like a rope. He grabbed a handrail with one hand while holding his rifle with the other, barely keeping a foothold on the airlock floor. Nearby, the Ritican Navy officers fired a few more shots from the gibeons to add some size to the now-gaping hole in the hangar door, then quickly withdrew into the shuttle and closed the outer airlock door.

Kilvin oriented the vessel toward the hole, reinitialized the shuttle's defense fields, and pushed the small vessel through the exit. Jared scarcely had time to sit in his seat before the *Disgnin* rose up and out of the Ramas-Eduj Manufactory.

• • •

Tir Bvaso rubbed her shoulder gingerly. She was in need of medical attention but did not have the time right now, not while the ship was still in its current state. She hobbled over to the engineering coordination station, where a Human female was trying to manage the various repair teams scattered about the ship.

"What is our status?" Tir's voice came out more tired than she'd intended. The bridge climate was a mixture of tension and fatigue.

"None of the damage is serious, but it is widespread," replied the officer. "External communication is down, repairs estimated at two hours. Internal communication is unreliable, although at present it is functional. Engineering does not yet have a repair estimate."

"Propulsion?"

"We are stable in orbit, but right now we're limited to basic maneuvers."

At least we won't crash into the planet. "What about weapons?"

"Everything is down. Forward torpedoes are down, pending an inspection, and a group of Aecrons managed to sabotage the rearward tubes before they were apprehended. Several other groups were able to damage various turret systems. Both the pulse and ardor turret systems are out."

Tir rubbed her shoulder again, trying to massage some of the pain away. It didn't work. "How long will repairs take?"

"There is no immediate estimate on the torpedoes; they will not know for sure until their examination is complete. Engineering believes they can have the turrets operational in approximately one hour."

"It would seem the Aecrons were specific in their targets."

The Human officer sighed. "It would appear so, Commander. Most of their targets were locations that could conceivably be used to damage or destroy the ship. The exception was communications, which may have been disabled to prevent us from calling for help."

"How many Aecrons do we still have out there?"

Aioua, the lone Aecron currently on the bridge, looked up from her display. "Only four are still at large, and security knows where they are. None are in critical areas."

A new shower of data flowed from sciences. Aioua spoke again. "Also, I have just received a reading on the *Disgnin*. The shuttle is on its way out, but there seems to be a problem."

Tir wondered silently how this day could get any worse. "What sort of problem?"

"It is hard to tell from the rock interference, but the shuttle appears to be holding to a low altitude in its departure from the manufactory."

"Could it be the weight from the couplings?"

"I do not think so. That shuttle has more than enough power to escape the planet's atmosphere, even with twice the weight it is carrying, and I do not see any signs of damage to the propulsion system."

"Commander, there is one possible reason." It was the Ritican weapons officer, Garo Ball, who had just taken over the weapons station for an injured Human. "They may be attempting to avoid an attacker."

• • •

"I have the *Hattan* on sensors," reported Kilvin. "They are just coming around in orbit on the far side of the planet. So far they have not responded to our communications."

Jared didn't like the sound of that. "Is it because of the rock?"

"I do not believe so. We have a clear line of sight to the ship."

"Is there perhaps damage to the shuttle?"

Kilvin pulled up the shuttle diagnostics. "Everything reports operational."

"Then what's the problem?"

Nho, who was sitting next to Rete, leaned forward. "Something is wrong on board the *Hattan*. I can't explain it, but something is wrong."

"Captain," said Kilvin, "the shuttle sensors report two Ritican gunboats leaving the manufactory. They are pursuing us."

• • •

"Ritican gunboats?" Tir had just taken her seat at the command station.

"Two of them," said Aioua, "armed with ardor cannons and civilian-grade missiles. They appear to be pursuing the *Disgnin*."

The question, of course, was why. With communications down, there was no way to find out, but Tir knew there were many things that could go wrong between a Navy crew and a group of semiautonomous Ritican miners.

Tir pulled up a tactical map on her chair display. "How long until they overtake the shuttle?"

"Given current speeds, twenty minutes."

"How long until the shuttle reaches us?"

"At least thirty minutes."

No weapons, no ability to maneuver, and a shuttle carrying the captain and a critical shipment of parts twenty minutes away from possible destruction.

Tir looked over at Garo Ball. "Do we have any means of attack at our disposal?"

"No, Commander. The Aecrons were thorough in their work."

"I need options, Garo. Perhaps we could manually launch a torpedo out of the cargo bay, or override one of our turrets to fire by sight. Anything."

"What about the interceptor they are building down in the cargo bay?" asked Aioua. "Is it ready?"

Tir stopped to think about that for a moment. She was not

directly supervising its construction, so she did not know its current state. Working her display, she pulled up the reports on the in-progress interceptor.

After she finished reading, the Hazionite first officer keyed her link. "Tir to Redelia."

A voice spoke in her ear. "Redelia here, Commander."

"What is your status?"

"The armory is secure and security has nearly cleared the area. I was about to head up to the infirmary to assist Darel Weye. Do you need something?"

"What is the status of the interceptor in the cargo bay?"

"Sir?"

"Is the interceptor ready for space flight?"

Redelia hesitated. "I—what is this about?"

"Our team returning from the surface appears to be under pursuit and possible attack by two civilian gunboats. We cannot help them, as the *Hattan*'s weapons are offline."

There was a moment of silence on the other end. When Redelia finally spoke, she said, "Commander, send an interceptor crew down to the cargo bay. I will meet them there."

· · ·

Flanked by a security escort, Redelia ran to the cargo bay where the interceptor waited, her mind developing the beginnings of a plan. Five others met her in the cargo bay: a Human female navigator, a Human male weapons officer, a Hazionite female communications officer, an Exo engineer . . . and an Aecron male sciences officer named Udos Beyole.

For Redelia, the sight of the Aecron sciences officer triggered several thoughts at once, which converged into a web of understanding that turned an inexplicable day of events into something cohesive and understandable. She did not know Udos Beyole well, but she knew he was a practicing Sarconian. More recently, so was Aioua Horae. She also suspected Darel Weye was, although he was reluctant to admit it.

She was a Sarconian herself. When Redelia was first assigned to be the lead interceptor commander in the *Hattan* battle group, Jared told her that the honor of naming the first interceptor would be hers. After hours of contemplation, she settled on the name *Belico*. Belicos were large, omnivorous sea serpents who ravaged the oceans of Aeroel, eating living creatures and occasionally even Aecron-made vessels and structures. Aecrons stationed on the *Hattan* were liable to assume that her choice was a nod to those massive water animals, and in part they would be right. But Redelia also intended it to be a subtle nod to her faith; Belico was the name of the man who founded the now-uninhabited Sarconian world of Teirel over 2500 years before.

According to the reports she received over her link, there were approximately twelve Aecrons who were unaffected by whatever had turned the others against the *Hattan*. She had not researched the question exhaustively, but she was aware of about ten to twelve Aecrons on the ship who were followers of Sarco. Somehow, followers of Sarco were not affected by whatever had happened on the ship—"the conditioning," as Vetta called it over her link.

She momentarily banished the train of thought. She had a more immediate issue—that of saving the two people on the *Hattan* she was closest to, both of whom were on that shuttle.

"Everyone on board the *Belico*," she ordered. "We have no time to waste."

Minus the Exo engineer, Redelia and her crew swarmed onto the bridge and took their stations. The *Belico* was a mess, reflecting its in-progress state of construction. Dust and parts were strewn everywhere, and various conduit plates hung open or were missing entirely. The bridge was somewhat farther along than many of the other areas on the ship, but it, too, had plenty of incomplete areas and potential hazards.

The good news, as far as Redelia was concerned, was that although the *Belico* did not look it, it was far along with respect to its completion. Many rudimentary systems had been installed, including life support, a fusing core for basic power, and—perhaps most critically to the current situation—an ardor engine for sub-light travel. The fold drive, among other things, was still missing, but interstellar travel was immaterial at this point.

Redelia wiped dust off her display as it lit up. "How long until we're at full power?"

Vidra Najik, the Human navigator, perused her station. "From a low-output state, just a few seconds."

The main viewscreen popped on, revealing the cargo bay. Nearby, various officers scampered out of the *Belico*'s way. In short order a buffer field would enclose the *Belico*, and it would be sent out into the vacuum of space.

The cargo crew cleared out, and the ripple of the buffer field filled the viewscreen.

"Full power," Vidra announced. "Buffer field initialized."

"Take us out."

The bridge rumbled and shook as the interceptor's ardor thrusters roared to life. The *Belico* rose off the floor of the cargo bay, turned, and sailed out into open space. "We're clear, Commander."

"Udos, do you have a bearing on the shuttle?"

Chains of data poured through the sciences station. "Sending the location to navigation now."

"Vidra, plot an intercept course, half-burn."

The Exo, working down in engineering, clicked, "Ship diagnostics are not yet complete."

Redelia leaned forward slightly in her seat. "We do not have the luxury of running tests. The captain and those couplings are about to be blown out of the sky. Navigator, try out the thrusters to make sure they are fully responsive, then initiate the course."

"Yes, Commander." Redelia had skimmed Vidra Najik's personnel file; she was a seasoned interceptor navigator and would probably notice any thruster irregularities before most others in her position would.

On the viewscreen, the planet slowly grew in size as the ship accelerated. Redelia rotated to face weapons. "What do we have to work with?"

"Not much. The forward and torpedo tubes are both installed and probably operational, but the cargo workers couldn't get to the *Hattan*'s torpedo stock because of the . . ." His voice trailed off.

"The mutiny. There is no need for pretense, Lieutenant. I was shooting at tens of them less than an hour ago." Her voice hardened. "I am not one of them."

"No, of course not, Commander. My apologies."

Redelia was ready to move on. "What about the rest of the weapons?"

The weapons officer looked over the ship's weapons suite. "The pulse cannons are installed, but they are not showing any power readings."

She cocked her head and spoke into her link. "Decatrix, what is the status of the pulse cannons?"

"The conduits are not yet connected to the fusing core."

"Can you effect a temporary connection?"

"No."

Exos rarely minced words. Redelia looked back at weapons. "And the ardor turret?"

The weapons officer's demeanor brightened somewhat. "It reads operational."

"Defense fields?"

The weapons officer tested them. A ripple crackled across the screen. "They're not optimized, but they appear to be responding."

An operational rearward ardor turret and some semblance of defense fields. It would have to do. Redelia asked, "Communications?"

"Working. I have readied a secure channel to the *Disgnin* on your command."

• • •

Kilvin kept the *Disgnin* low and close to the ground, skirting the rocky mounds and craters that marked the landscape of the barren, empty world. His hope was to make it difficult for the manufactory's ships to track his shuttle and attack it, particularly if they had any sort of long-range missiles. So far the tactic appeared to be working, as they had not been struck yet. The shuttle did possess defense fields, but they were not designed to handle the sort of fire-power that a gunboat could produce. The fields were further compromised by the additional bulk of the pod the *Disgnin* was towing.

Jared remained seated next to Kilvin, his eye on the communications display. The *Hattan* had remained ominously unresponsive to the *Disgnin*'s calls for help, which reinforced Nho's sense that something was wrong on board Jared's ship. The Ramas-Eduj Manufactory had not been so silent; Tack had bombarded the shuttle with angry threats over the last several minutes. Jared had, on the advice of his Ritican officers, declined to respond.

A new face appeared on the display, on a secure Navy channel. "Navy interceptor *Belico* to *Disgnin*. Captain Carter, are you there?"

Jared let out a deep breath. "This is Captain Carter. Redelia, it is good to see you."

"We are on our way to assist you, sir. What happened?"

Where to begin? thought Jared. Then, out loud: "We negotiated the coupling transaction successfully, but one of the miners requested political protection. His name is Rete; he's an old friend of Nho and claims he was sold as a slave to the colony. The manager took exception to our interference and threatened to kill us unless we turned him over. We're now being chased by two of the colony's gunboats."

Redelia briefly looked away from the display. "At our current combined speeds we should reach you in seven minutes."

That would be cutting it close. Kilvin estimated the gunboats would be close enough to fire, even with the restrictions of ground cover, in less than eight minutes. And there was still the matter of clearing the ground and getting up to the *Hattan*.

"What then?"

"We will take up a defensive position behind you. We are limited with respect to our weapons, but we do have operable defense fields and an ardor turret."

Left unsaid was something Jared already knew—the interceptor was theoretically operable but untested. "What about the *Hattan*?" he asked. "We have been unable to contact them."

Redelia's face contorted to what passed in Aecrons as sadness. "There was a mutiny. Nearly all of the Aecrons on board went insane and tried to destroy the ship. The crisis is contained, but many of the ship's systems are disabled, including weapons, most propulsion systems, and communications. I gather from Vetta's institution of a detainment protocol that you knew this was a possibility."

Jared's lips tightened. He wondered how much that fact might have hurt her. He faced her squarely on the display and nodded. "Yes, but not this soon. You said *nearly* all the Aecrons were affected." He gave her searching look. "I'm assuming you were not."

"Yes. There were twelve of us in total, including an Aecron sciences officer on board the *Belico* with me now."

"Do you have any idea why?"

"I believe that all of the unaffected are Sarconians."

Nho, who was sitting behind Jared, leaned forward. "Do you think that is the reason?"

Redelia said, "I do not know. It is only an observation. Darel Weye, who is also unaffected, has been overseeing the testing of the affected Aecrons and cannot find any physiological causes."

Jared's eyes widened. "Darel? Why is he in charge? What happened to the . . ." He paused as he tried to figure out how finish the sentence.

She answered without hesitation. "I know about the specialist team, sir. Vetta briefed me. The mutineers targeted them. All of them are alive, although none are in any position to do the work."

Jared caught sight of the sensory data at Kilvin's station. The two gunboats were closing in more quickly. "We can discuss it more if we make it off this planet alive," he said. "For now, I would like to have your navigator talk with mine. We are just a few minutes from coming under fire, and we have a defense to coordinate."

• • •

Under normal circumstances, a Navy interceptor would be more than a match for two civilian gunboats. Although an interceptor and a gunboat were roughly the same size, Navy technology far surpassed that of most nonmilitary ships. A year earlier, Jared's former interceptor, the *Retaelus*, had engaged two Ritican pirate frigates in the space above the water world of Alsis and had more than held its own. And frigates were significantly more powerful vessels than gunboats.

With the *Belico* in its current condition—untested and barely flight worthy—the odds in this case were considerably more even. The navigator, Vidra Najik, struggled mightily to preserve stability using thrusters that suffered intermittent outages. The Exo engineer worked furiously to maintain various systems that all seemed intent on failing simultaneously. The defense fields flickered, the life support wavered, and at times it appeared the very seams of the ship might come apart.

Even irrespective of the ship's technical problems, Redelia knew her options in this engagement were limited. Ritican psychology when it came to combat was as lethal as any species: the methane-breathers were relentless and calculating even in the midst of fierce rage. Humans—and, to a lesser extent, the infamous piracy-waging Minor Race known as the Ussonians—could be baited by taunts and threats, but such techniques had no effect on the Ritican psyche. Riticans were equally impervious to placations or bribes, and Tack had already rejected any diplomatic solution.

Regardless of what Redelia might say to Tack, the two attackers would chase the shuttle until one side or the other was destroyed. The gunboats would fire on the interceptor if it stood in the way, but any notion of Redelia drawing the gunboats away so the shuttle could escape was unlikely.

The *Belico* bore down on the *Disgnin* from above, the interceptor traveling in nearly the opposite direction of the shuttle. Redelia watched as the *Disgnin* and its large utility pod nimbly weaved in and out of the various rock hills and outcroppings of the airless planet. True to Kilvin's reputation, it was brilliant piloting of an unwieldy vehicle. The gunboats had not been able to line up even one shot.

The gunboats were also skimming the ground, opting to close the distance as fast as possible rather than gain altitude and try to gain a line of sight from afar. It was also likely they were keeping low amid concern of exposing themselves to possible attacks from the Navy forces above. Had the *Hattan* been fully operational or the *Belico* fully armed, those fears would have carried much merit.

Redelia's plan was to bring the *Belico* down to the shuttle, then orient the interceptor so it was stationed between the *Disgnin* and the Riticans. The shuttle would then accelerate up toward the *Hattan* while Redelia's crew provided a rear guard. It would be a long ten minutes.

The gunboats had other plans. As the interceptor approached, the two attackers shifted their attention away from the shuttle, their wide, flat noses coming to bear on the *Belico*. Almost in unison, the two Ritican ships opened fire with everything in their arsenal. Gunboats, particularly civilian ones, were armed with no more than ten nonmilitary grade missiles and a single rotary ardor cannon, but the sight of twenty missiles and a salvo of ardor floes suddenly flooding the space ahead of them was no small spectacle.

Clever, Redelia thought, *especially given our weakened condition.* It seemed the Riticans' plan was to unload a swift and brutal volley on the interceptor in hopes of quickly knocking it out of the fight. Should the full force of the attack hit the target, the *Belico* would be disabled or destroyed and the gunboats would still have several minutes to use their ardor cannons to penetrate the shuttle's meager defense fields.

Unfortunately for the Riticans, their pre-emptive attack, while tactically sound in theory, was poorly executed. The two gunboats fired their missiles and floes while they were still some distance from the interceptor. To the untrained eye, the eleven-second interval between the launching of the missiles and their estimated impact on the *Belico* would appear quite brief, and that would be true . . . if the Navy ship were a larger capital vessel. Interceptors were much more agile, however, and could effect any number of evasive maneuvers.

In a fraction of a second, Redelia considered why the gunboats had erred. Most of the manufactory workers were probably lifetime laborers with no actual combat experience. Some of them, like Tack, were veterans, but that did not mean they had experience in space combat or in combat involving ships like interceptors. Even if they had relevant military experience, it was doubtful any of them had found themselves in battle in some time, much less against an actual military ship.

As quickly as those thoughts raced through Redelia's acute Aecron mind, they gave way to a plan of action. With little wasted time or speech, Redelia sent her orders directly to the navigator's display. Vidra executed them flawlessly, forcing the small ship sharply down toward the rugged terrain. The Ritican ardor floes, lacking any form of guidance, passed harmlessly overhead, leaving the twenty missiles in pursuit.

Etched along the hills of the planet's surface were a series of strange outcroppings, rock formations that seemed out of place on a planet with no atmosphere. Vidra expertly sliced between the ground and the outcroppings, while several of the missiles, possessing only rudimentary civilian guidance systems, missed the gap and careened directly into the rock ceiling. The explosion sent rocks down on several other missiles, detonating them as well.

For Tack's men, it was a disaster. Only four missiles out of twenty escaped to continue tracking the *Belico*, and they were easy targets at the hands of the interceptor's rear ardor turret. The gunboats had expended their entire complement of missiles and a full round of ardor and did not have a single hit to show for it.

On board the *Belico*, there was no celebration. Nimbly, the navigator whipped the interceptor around, laying a course to chase down the shuttle, which had raced by in the other direction during the *Belico*'s evasive maneuver. The gunboats had also turned their attention back to the shuttle, and while they had no missiles left to fire, they were close enough to begin landing hits with their ardor cannons.

Most of the ardor attacks by the Riticans slapped uselessly into a crater hill or off into empty space, although a few now started to find a mark on the lumbering shuttle. The *Disgnin*'s fields crackled, but so far showed only minor evidence of strain. That would change as the two Ritican ships drew closer and had fewer obstructions.

Rocketing in between them was the *Belico*, which had leveraged its superior speed to interpose itself between the attackers and the shuttle.

"The engines are strained," the Exo engineer warned. "They could fail at any moment."

"Make sure they do not," snapped Redelia. Breaking off was not an option.

Ardor floes splashed against the *Belico*'s untested fields, sending ominous rumbles through the ship. The interceptor's rear turret replied with spits of its own ardor, splashing against one of the gunboats. The Ritican vessel's defense fields shimmered but held.

• • •

The next several minutes were among the longest in the lives of Jared Carter and Redelia Aroo. The former sat tensely in the shuttle, which shook under the force of the withering rounds of Ritican ardor. The shuttle's fields strained and began to give way, allowing slivers of the superheated attacks to seep through and slap against the utility pod's reinforced plating.

The latter gripped the command chair of her interceptor as it continued to absorb a much greater proportion of the Ritican assault. The *Belico* had performed far better than anyone would have reasonably expected, but its defense had been anything but flawless. More than once, the interceptor had nearly dropped out of the sky before the Exo engineer was able to restart the unsteady ardor thrusters. Those moments left the shuttle briefly but dangerously exposed.

Equally unreliable were the *Belico*'s defense fields, which would occasionally flash off for no explainable reason. Most of these failures had happened in between volleys, but a couple had allowed the gunboats to hit the interceptor unimpeded, damaging a wing and part of the interceptor's underside.

On the other end, both Ritican gunboats had absorbed significant fire. One of them, in particular, had taken a vicious hit through its weakening fields and was now lagging behind its companion. The Riticans, undaunted, continued to fire as often as their ships would allow them.

Up ahead, growing in the distance, was the *Hattan*. The cruiser orbited the planet casually, showing no sign of the chaos within and seeming uninterested in the desperate situation approaching. The *Disgnin* was now close enough that Jared could make out the *Hattan*'s idling pulse turrets on one of the shuttle displays. *What I wouldn't give for a single round of fire*, he thought.

Almost on cue, several of the *Hattan*'s turrets stirred. Jared watched in stunned fascination as the weapons rotated into position and fired. A barrage of translucent fire shot out, slicing past the shuttle and the *Belico* before smashing into one of the gunboats. The small ship's defense field gave a feeble protest before collapsing spectacularly, allowing most of the barrage to smash directly upon the gunboat's hull. The Ritican ship exploded in the emptiness of space.

The second gunboat, in a fashion uncharacteristic of Riticans, apparently wanted no part of battling an enormous Navy cruiser. It turned around and set a course back to the surface.

• • •

The shuttle *Disgnin* touched down in the cargo bay and was greeted by a formidable security presence and several Exos. Vetta walked up to Jared as the captain disembarked. "It is good to see you are unharmed," she said, offering a Navy salute.

Jared returned the gesture. "It's good to see the Exos were able to get the weapons online."

"Only a few of them, but it was enough. Have you been apprised of our situation?"

Jared looked around the cargo bay. "I was told the Aecrons tried to destroy the ship."

"They were not far from succeeding, but the situation is now under control. Our medical staff is still trying to determine what is causing their behavior." She then looked behind Jared. "Who is that?"

Jared glanced over his shoulder. A few trics away, Nho and Rete were talking quietly. "That," Jared said, "is Rete, Nho's old friend from Hazion Prime."

Jared watched Vetta's face contort as she searched her memory, much as Jared had done when Nho first said Rete's name inside the manufactory. Finally she said, "The one we were looking for on Dio?"

"Yes."

"That is unexpected. I assumed him to be lost forever, if not dead."

"As did I. It turns out he was a slave in the manufactory. When he asked for help, the Riticans tried to destroy us. That's how we wound up fleeing for our lives."

Nho and Rete walked up to where Jared and Vetta were standing. Nho was holding onto Rete's arm with one hand. "Rete has said he does not feel well," Nho said. "Should we have him examined by a doctor?"

The captain exchanged looks with his Ritican security officer. "I will have someone escort them up to the infirmary," said Vetta, "although he may have to wait a while to see someone. Most of the medical staff was lost to the Aecron madness. Those who remain are stretched thin."

Jared watched as the Exos pushed the couplings out of the shuttle pod and across the cargo bay. He turned back to Vetta. "Are any of the afflicted Aecrons in the infirmary?"

"Darel is examining one of them right now."

"Then I'll go with Rete. I'd like to see one of them for myself."

Nho said, "I would also like to see this."

"I was going to ask you to," said Jared. "If . . . well, perhaps your insights might be helpful."

Vetta looked confused. "Sir?"

Jared shook his head as if to say, *I'm not ready yet.* "I'll talk about it later."

• • •

Jared, Rete, Nho, and their security escort arrived to find assistants still cleaning up the mess in the infirmary and various staffers coming in and out for supplies. Each of their faces indicated something beyond exhaustion. *If there is any evidence of the scope of the mutiny*, thought Jared, *it is here.*

On one side of the room, Darel Weye was running tests on a young Aecron, a precocious medical officer named Mollo Nairu. Nairu looked rabid, pulling violently on his restraints and issuing an intermittent scream that filled the entire room.

Jared walked up next to Darel. The doctor briefly looked his way but said nothing. Jared asked, "What have you learned?"

"Nothing, unfortunately. His state is unlike anything I have ever seen. Hyperviolent, if there is such a thing. His vitals are far beyond anything normally observed in an Aecron."

Jared leaned in slightly to examine Mollo, who responded by shouting in the captain's face. Jared took a step back. "He looks pretty bad."

"He is currently on a week's worth of sedatives. You should have seen him without them."

Jared arched his eyebrows. "Any theories on the cause?"

"I have run every conceivable test and found no physical or physiological cause. Whatever is doing this is a mystery to me."

"Could it be psychological?"

"The evidence might suggest some sort of mass hallucination, but among one hundred and fifty-three different Aecrons in separate decks? It simply is not possible. Some of them were in the middle of their sleep cycles. It was as if someone had manipulated a panel that activated something inside of them all at once."

Out of the corner of his eye, Jared saw Mollo Nairu run his hand along a blank edge of the table. His restraints retracted, and before Jared could say anything, the rabid Aecron was on his feet, racing for the exit.

Jared sidestepped to cut him off, and the two collided. Despite Jared's superior size and strength, he bounced backward from the Aecron and landed roughly on the ground, while Mollo reeled for just a fraction of a moment before once again taking off in a run. A Hazionite security officer nearby lunged for Mollo but missed.

Nho, standing at the door, had been conferring in private with Rete and did not initially notice the commotion nor the small blue form barreling toward the exit they were blocking. Rete was the first of the two to see the Aecron; he let out a short yelp and hopped back. Nho, reacting with less awareness, was caught-flat footed by the oncoming charge; he had no time to do anything except raise his staff in front of him in a defensive posture.

Mollo skidded to a halt in front of Nho, latching onto Sarco's staff with both hands as if to wrench it away to use as a weapon. But rather than completing the act, the Aecron simply froze in place. For a second there was just Nho and Mollo, each holding the staff. Then Mollo screamed. It was a long, piercing, prolonged scream, and it was right in Nho's face. Jared thought he could feel the floor rattling.

The staff started to glow. Nho's eyes at first went wide, then closed in apparent concentration. His lips moved, although Jared could not make out what he said. Mollo replied with a stream of angry protests in an Aecron dialect, then went abruptly silent, releasing the staff and slumping to a sitting position on the floor.

Darel and the security officers rushed over. Mollo looked up, searching the room as if he had never noticed it before. "Darel, what am I doing in here?"

Darel stood over his fellow medical officer, running a sensor over Mollo's body. "One moment, Lieutenant," he said. "Captain, his vitals are normal." He looked to the Hazionite security officer now standing next to him. "What do you smell?" he asked.

The officer's nose curled, and she looked at Darel in surprise. "His anger is gone. He smells confused, tired, but no longer angry. As far as I can tell, he is as a normal Aecron should be."

"Darel," pleaded Mollo, "what is she talking about?"

"I will explain in a moment," said Darel quickly. Then, looking at Nho, he said, "What did you do?"

"I . . . I invoked the power of Sarco," said Nho.

"How?" Darel demanded.

"I don't know." Nho gestured to Mollo. "You saw it. He charged me and I felt something, someone. It was telling me to have faith. I concentrated on placing my faith in Sarco. I felt something flow into the staff. It was like when I faced the warden inside Malum."

Darel considered this in silence. He said, "Can you do it again?"

"I believe so."

"In that case," said Jared, picking himself off the ground, "we may need that show of faith one hundred and fifty more times."

"One hundred and fifty-*two* more times," said Darel.

5

FAR OUTERLANDS
EARTH INDEX 1306.131

"Officers and crew of the *Hattan*, this is Captain Jared Carter speaking.

"Over the last few weeks, we have ventured toward the fringes of Ritican space. Officially our assignment has been to field test the capabilities of this ship along the frontier. There is, as some of you may have suspected, more to our mission than that, although necessity dictated that the exact nature of our orders be kept a secret until now.

"Last year, our civilization was almost brought to an end by Malum. No one knows this truth better than this crew. Each and every one of us holds in common the experience of captivity aboard that evil planet. Earlier this year, Navy leadership concluded that we needed to know where Malum came from and to determine what threat its makers may pose to the Confederacy.

"To that end, we have been assigned on a reconnaissance mission. Our task is to cross the Great Void and investigate the region of space Malum transmitted to before it was defeated. We are to collect what information we can and report back to the Confederacy. Navy Command selected this specific crew for this specific mission because all of us were evaluated as the Navy's best officers for a task of this nature.

"This mission is a dangerous one. Already we have witnessed firsthand some of those dangers. Just a few days ago, our fellow Aecron officers rose up against us and nearly put an end to our voyage. What you do not know—what few others know—is why. The answer, as we best understand it, is that long ago the Aeroel government somehow conditioned its people to resist leaving Confederal space, even to the point of madness. They did so to prevent a repeat of the events that led to the Invasion of 1124. We do not know how they accomplished this, but we do know that the mutiny we witnessed was the result of that conditioning. Our Aecron officers are victims; they did not ask for this conditioning, acting outside of their own reason. We believe they are now cured, apparently by the same power that stopped Malum. They are once again our allies in this cause.

"And we will need them. From here we will be voyaging farther than any known Confederal vessel ever has traveled. We will be facing the unknown regions of space, and quite possibly hostile forces. The *Hattan* is a powerful ship—the Confederacy's very best—but we will be but one ship and a few escorts against what may well be an empire. Success will be measured by our ability to endure and survive so that we may help protect those we care about back on our homeworlds.

"As your Captain, I ask for your best over these next several months. I ask for your courage against the unknown. I ask for your perseverance in the face of a long mission. Most importantly, I ask for your solidarity with and understanding toward your fellow officers. We cannot win against the forces of Dar if we are turned against one another.

"In each of your personal workstations will be what information we can share with you about the specifics of our mission. You are the Navy's finest, and I have the utmost confidence that we will do the rest of the Confederacy proud. Thank you."

• • •

Sarco, help me.

Nho Ames sat wearily in a chair in the far corner of the commons, the spacious social gathering space located along the forward section of the *Hattan*. Sitting across from him was a Hazionite male, a staff member in the xenoanthropology department. The Hazionite had spent the last twenty minutes talking about how difficult it was working with the Aecrons who had, not long ago, tried to kill him. With visible emotion, the xenoanthropologist recounted the pure anger he smelled as several Aecron colleagues had swarmed him in the lab, clawing at him and attacking him with lab tools.

Nho tried to be empathetic, but it was difficult. It was not that he did not care; it was that he had listened to countless such stories since the mutiny. Every day there seemed an inexhaustible supply of people seeking an ear, prayer, counsel. They were met by the ship's counseling department, as well as Nho's friend, Rete, but the crowds seeking help far outnumbered those available to speak with them. Nho always drew the most attention (including, of late, some of the other counselors) and he was emotionally and physically spent. It was only by the grace of Sarco that he had managed to maintain the calm and understanding demeanor these people so desperately needed.

Out of nowhere, Nho was suddenly struck with a deep dread. It radiated from the pit of his stomach, a sense of foreboding spreading throughout his body. It was as if total darkness had cast a shadow across him, sending him spiraling into an abyss from which he could never return. The world around him ceased to exist. The Hazionite male continued to talk, but Nho heard nothing.

Nho reached out from the depths of his soul, calling out to his Creator, seeking understanding. Was this a mental breakdown from unending hours giving himself to the despair of others? Had his sanity finally been broken?

No. It was not that. This dread, this . . . thing . . . it was not coming from within him. His soul was still vital, his mind still intact.

Great One, what is this thing? Why am I suddenly as the man toppling off a cliff?

What happened next was completely unexpected. In the recesses of his mind, a voice said:

I am the one who is casting the shadow.

That was not possible, Nho thought to himself. Sarco could not be the architect of such darkness. Yet Nho knew that He was. From without, Sarco had planted the seed of oblivion into Nho's heart, stabbing him with a blow that tore him from his present reality and sent him searching for answers.

Why? pleaded Nho. *What is your purpose?*

The shadow is a portent. Evil draws near.

Just like that, the feeling was gone. Nho was sitting in his chair, the Hazionite talking, the world as it had been.

Nho, however, was changed. He had emerged from the abyss with a certainty about one thing. What he must now do was as clear as anything he had ever done in his life.

"I'm sorry," he said, interrupting the Hazionite. "I cannot explain why, but I must do something right now."

Nho picked up Sarco's staff and hurried out of the commons, ignoring the many eyes wondering where he was going when they so badly needed him.

• • •

"What do you make of it?"

"You are right. That is odd."

"Should we tell the captain?"

"Yes. Absolutely. Captain? Can we speak with you?"

Jared looked up from his portable, rose from the command station, and walked over to Rami and Aioua, who were staring at Rami's display. On the main viewscreen, the spectrum tendrils of a fold filled the space before them. They were about four days out of the Ramas-Eduj Manufactory.

He placed a hand on Rami's station. "What is it?"

"I'm not sure." She glanced up, her lips compressed in puzzlement.

For a split instant, he thought of what Kilvin had said about her on the shuttle. The moment passed as she continued. "When I came on for my shift this morning, I noticed a long-range foldparticle transmission."

Jared crossed his arms. "That would seem impossible. I didn't think foldparticles could penetrate a ship fold."

"Normally they cannot," Aioua said, "as the transmissions exist in their own discreet folds. In this case, however, the transmission is not coming to us. It is being sent *from* us, through the *Hattan's* experimental long-range communications array."

"From us? Who is sending it?"

"I don't know," said Rami. "The transmission is encrypted. I haven't been able to decode the contents."

Jared didn't like the sound of that. His ship had been through enough unexpected problems already. "Can you pinpoint where the transmission is being sent to?"

"Not while we are in a fold," said Aioua. "It appears that whoever activated the transmission set it to broadcast continuously, presumably before we made a jump."

"Any idea how long it has been going on?"

"No. Engineering has reported ongoing problems with our communications stations. It is conceivable this has gone unnoticed for days."

Jared pondered that for a moment. "Is it still transmitting?"

"Yes," said Rami.

"Kilvin, how long until we emerge from our fold?"

"Just over a minute, sir."

"Aioua, once we emerge, see if you can triangulate a destination."

"Yes, sir."

Jared moved to return to his seat at the command station. He had taken a few steps when the bridge doors opened and a voice called out his name.

"Jared! Jared!"

It was Nho. The old man was breathing heavily, as if he'd been running hard. His knuckles were white as they clutched Sarco's staff. "Jared, I must speak with you right now. It's urgent."

"What's wrong?"

"The ship is in danger."

Jared regarded him suspiciously. "How? What is it?"

Nho drew a deep breath, slowing his respiration and focusing more steadily. "I don't know, but when I was in the commons, I was possessed of a sense that something terrible was about to happen. Something evil." He held up a hand as if to forestall Jared's next question. "I cannot explain it, but trust me when I say we are in imminent danger."

Jared looked at Aioua. The Aecron sciences officer looked at her display. "Nothing out of the ordinary, sir—except the foldparticle transmission, of course."

"Could the transmission somehow pose a danger to us?"

"I do not see how."

"Try to cut it off anyway. Navigation, how long?"

"Twenty-five seconds."

Jared looked out at the viewscreen, where the end of the fold was now in sight. Nho's intuition was not something to take lightly. He moved quickly to his chair. "Garo, what is the status of our defense fields?"

"Initialized at reduced power."

As Jared anticipated. That was a standard procedure to accommodate longer fold jumps. He said, "Bring them to full power."

Garo Ball did just what Jared expected the veteran Ritican weapons officer to do: no questions, no hesitation. "Yes, sir."

Before them, on the viewscreen, the fields crackled to life. Beyond, the terminus of the fold was closing rapidly. Suddenly, they were through, into normal space.

And into a galaxy of explosions.

• • •

Flashes of light from every direction. Chaos, as if the entire universe were crashing in from every angle simultaneously. Bodies thrown up and around, caught by passive restraints and held at their posts from the onslaught of death.

Defense fields crackling, bending, valiantly struggling against forces of destruction.

"Combat stations!" someone screamed. "Combat stations!" As if it even needed to be said.

Pulse turrets coming alive in retaliation, waves of flak spitting into the night. So many targets, so many small, fast-moving targets. Powerful targets, pouring bolts of impossible might upon the defense fields. Pulse turrets with their showers of reply.

One attacker destroyed.

More attacks from the many, the unknowns. Vicious attacks. The fields bowed inward, shimmered. The telltale sign of imminent failure.

Two more attackers destroyed.

"Reinforce the fields!" a voice shouted. "Do not let them fail!"

One attack breached the fields, struck the cruiser's armor. The armor cracked open, the blast cutting through to the bone. A near-miss; the hit struck nonvitals. Two more grazed the hull, leaving ugly wounds on the body of the great vessel.

More attackers cut down by the rain of pulse turrets.

The attacks softened, weakened. The attackers were still frenzied, but reduced in number. The cruiser's defense fields reinitialized, once again blunting the many points of attack. The turrets focused in on the remaining targets, cutting through their fields, disabling them, destroying them.

In a matter of moments, it was all over. A single Navy ship alone in the night, surrounded by debris.

• • •

Captain Carter leaned against his chair, his hair disheveled and his face covered in grime. The officers around him looked just as bad, some worse. The infirmary was inundated by requests from all over the ship, but had promised to send someone to the bridge as soon as possible.

Jared leveled a weary gaze at Tir. "Where do we stand?"

"The Exos report moderate to serious damage to multiple decks on the ship. There is some damage to the hull and varying degrees of damage to weapons, sciences, engineering, and life support. They are still gauging the full extent of the damage."

"Had the fields not been initialized," Garo said, "we would almost certainly have been destroyed."

"Casualties?"

"Medical teams are still assessing the situation," Rami said. She had a darkening bruise on her forehead where a falling conduit had grazed her. "Preliminary estimates indicate six possible deaths and over two hundred injuries, most of them minor."

"Aioua, what do we know about our attackers?"

The sciences officer brought up a schematic of the ships on the bridge's tridimensional display. "They were roughly the size of Navy torpedo bombers, but their power output was comparable to a gunboat or interceptor. A ship that small would not have lasted long with such a high output. They were designed to kill quickly, but possibly at the cost of their own lives."

"What were they doing with all that power?"

"It was channeled into the weapons they hit us with. They were armed with weapons I have never seen before. The attacks were focused pulse attacks, but instead of concussive packets, they were high output pulse streams."

Jared started. "Pulse *streams*? Is that even possible?"

Aioua gestured to the negative. "Under different circumstances, I would say no. The concussive feedback of a stream is so great, it tears the attacking ship apart, which is why both the Aecrons and the Navy use focused pulse packets. These fighters, however, were able circumvent that problem through their hyperbolic power output. Each of them poured massive amounts of energy into maintaining their hull integrity. It offset the feedback, at least for a time."

"Long enough destroy us, if not long after," said Garo.

"That appears to be their design," Aioua agreed. "And they nearly succeeded. Most ships, even large capital vessels, would never have survived an attack of that magnitude. We were fortunate."

Jared sat back down, resting his arms on his knees and venturing a glance at Nho, who was clearly shaken. "So, the big question is, who were they?"

Aioua spoke quietly. "Our initial analysis suggests they were Aecron, Captain. While their physical profile is different from standard Aecron ships, there are telltale markers that would be very difficult, if not impossible, to duplicate by other races."

"How certain are you?"

"I do not see how they could be anyone else."

Jared sat there in disbelief. Even Garvak's warnings about the conditioning didn't capture just how malevolent it was. "That fold-particle transmission, the one we found before we were attacked. Is that how they ambushed us?"

"It would explain what happened." She shifted the tridimensional display to show a star map. "We were unable to stop it before we exited the fold, but we were able to trace its destination. It was apparently directed at a point in Ritican space, but I am not sure the recipient was Ritican."

Jared took a closer look at the map. "The Riticans will not appreciate that. Are we still transmitting?"

"No. The array was damaged in the attack."

"Make sure that transmission is off for good before we finish repairing it." He walked back to his station "Tir, are we fit to make a jump?"

Tir had already been conferring with engineering. "It would not be ideal," she reported, "but we should be safe if the fold is short."

"That will have to be good enough. Navigation, make ready for a short emergency jump. I do not want to be here if more of those things arrive."

• • •

Some time later, Jared met with Rami, Garo, Aioua, and Tir in the conference room. Orel Dayail and Darel Weye also joined them.

Jared got right to the point. "So how did those fighters ambush us?"

Rami spoke. "It appears that someone on board the *Hattan* triggered a continuous transmission from our long-range communication array. It was sent to the Aecrons, who were able to use the transmission to determine our fold trajectories and orchestrate an ambush."

"As we feared. So who did it?"

"It had to be me." It was Orel Dayail. Everyone looked at him. No one spoke.

Orel looked downcast. "I am the only person with the expertise in both communications and sciences to accomplish it. I must have done it while under the influence of the conditioning back in orbit around Ramas-Eduj. It is possible I might have sabotaged the communications station to conceal my actions. It is only a hypothesis, though, because I have no memory of doing it. I simply know I have the ability, and could do it relatively quickly."

"The pieces fit together," said Garo. "Once the Aecrons on board suspected we were leaving Confederal space, Orel would have been conditioned to contact the Aecrons by the best means available, perhaps right as the mutiny began."

"And with the communications panel damaged, we would not know the array was transmitting," Rami said. "The Aecrons would have been able to track our movements and set an ambush."

"It is not the only example of sophistical subversion we saw during the mutiny," Darel added. "I am still trying to determine how Mollo released his restraints in the infirmary."

Jared looked at him. "Nho thinks the Aecrons on board are no longer under the influence of the conditioning. Do you agree?"

"I have seen no evidence of it since we left Ramas-Eduj. I cannot be certain, since I am not even certain what caused the conditioning in the first place. Based on my observations, however, the Aecron crew seems to be—to use your word, sir—cured."

"If they had wanted to destroy the ship," Garo added, "the ambush would have been the ideal opportunity."

Jared mulled that over. "Thank you," he said to them after a moment. "That's all for now. You're dismissed."

The group filed out, leaving Jared alone with his thoughts for a time.

6

The Unknown Regions
Earth Index 1306.142

"With respect," Redelia said, "it is too soon. If there is a chance the Aecrons might still be able to track us, we need to keep it offline, at least until we are farther into the Void."

Rami Del, standing between Redelia and Tir inside Tir's office, inhaled deeply through her nose. Redelia was a good officer and a decent sentient, but Rami did not enjoy being challenged on a subject she felt so strongly about—in this case, the *Hattan*'s experimental long-range communications array. *Stay calm*, Rami told herself, *but don't back down.*

"This isn't just about us," she insisted, her hands resting on Tir's desk. "It's about telling Command what happened to us. They still don't know, and that worries me. If Orel says the array is no longer compromised, I believe him. We need to let Garvak know what happened."

"I agree Garvak needs to know," Redelia said, "but I am not sure he would want us to take any unnecessary risks in telling him."

"It's not an unnecessary risk," Rami said. "Our department has been working on this for days. Engineering has certified the work."

"Who in engineering?"

"It was . . ." Rami paused. Realization struck her like a bolt. "Is this because of the Aecrons working on the team?"

"I trust in what Nho did," Redelia said evenly, her opaque gaze frank and patient. "But I think we need to be careful. I say this as an Aecron."

Tir said, "And what do you think, Lieutenant?"

Rami drew her lips into a thin line. "I think the technicians are genuinely remorseful for what happened and they're trying to make amends in the only way they know how." She gestured to Tir. "Surely our Hazionite xenopsychologists can smell it."

Tir did not respond to Rami directly. Instead she looked at both of them and said, "I will take both of your recommendations under advisement. You are dismissed. Rami, thank you for volunteering your off-duty time to come down here."

"Of course."

Rami departed, crossing the hallway and taking the lift down to the main artery of deck six. She took her time. It was a good morning, and she was content. It was not the sort of feeling that came from self-indulgence—the things that marked what she called in her mind her "old world"—but the feeling that came from being at peace with the larger universe.

Rationally, she ought not to feel this way. The *Hattan* was less than two weeks removed from a savage ambush that had nearly destroyed the ship, and less than three weeks removed from a terrifying mutiny that had nearly done the same. Ahead of her lay months of lonely travel across the emptiness of the Great Void, followed by whatever dangers awaited them on the other side. And in between was difficult work. She knew, for example, that this morning's debate would not be the last.

But, in a way she could not explain, her own sense of well-being was detached from all of this, as if she were outside herself looking in. Maybe, she thought, it was because of pride over how she had handled herself through the recent crises. Maybe it was because she was embarking on this mission with people she had come to call good friends, including her crew from the *Retaelus*.

That's part of it, she thought. *But not all. It's because of something much greater than me. This thing inside of me has changed.*

She smiled to herself and resisted the urge to skip down the hallway.

A familiar face emerged along the far corridor. Captain Carter. He seemed lost in thought, focused intently on a portable in front of him. Judging from his trajectory and her knowledge of his schedule, he was probably headed for the bridge. She was going in the opposite direction, toward the dining hall.

She thought about how difficult the last weeks had been for him, at the top, leading a big ship through situations few Navy captains, if any, had ever faced. And as a captain who had never before led a big ship. She knew it had to be hard, but she could *see* it, too, in the lines around his eyes and the tone of his voice.

He wasn't happy right now.

But I am. Maybe I can spare a little for him today.

Her stomach rumbled a little, but she ignored it, diverting off to the same hallway, speeding up just a little to catch up with him.

"Good afternoon, Captain."

Jared's gaze, which had been boring into the display he carried, popped up in surprise. Apparently he hadn't heard her approach. "Hello, Rami," he said. "How are you doing?"

"Well, sir. How are you?"

He blew out a breath. "Busy, but I'll manage. Where are you headed?"

"To lunch."

"I just came from there. I recommend you give the cook a wide berth today."

She laughed. "Warning taken." Her smile fell away, and she studied him openly, noting the few gray hairs at his temples, which hadn't been there just a year ago. "There was something I wanted to tell you, sir, if you have a moment."

Jared slowed his walk just a little, dropping his portable to his side and giving her his attention. His eyes were tired but congenial. "What's on your mind?"

She gathered her thoughts. Despite being a longtime communications officer and linguist, dispensing compliments was a relatively recent addition to her repertoire. "I just wanted to let you know how much I respect how you've handled things the last few weeks."

"Thank you." His tone was polite, but she could tell he was not totally convinced.

"I mean it, Captain," she pressed. "I've served with you for a long time, and I have to say I am genuinely impressed by how you have commanded the *Hattan*. I felt that way during the first months, but you have a lot to be proud of in these last weeks. I know the rest of the crew feel the same way. It's a big reason why morale is high despite what might be ahead."

Jared said, with a smirk, "Are you lobbying for a promotion?"

Had it come from anyone else, Rami's feelings might have been hurt, but she knew Jared well enough to know his brand of teasing. "Only if I get to command my own ship, sir."

He chuckled. She said, "In all seriousness, I just wanted you to know."

"Thank you," he said again. This time, she thought he seemed a little more convinced.

They reached the lift and he stepped in, turning and meeting her eyes squarely for the first time. "I appreciate it, Rami," he added. "Really. Have a good day. I'll see you at the communications briefing later this afternoon."

"See you then, Captain."

The lift closed. Rami smiled in satisfaction, then wheeled and headed the other direction.

A few minutes later, she set foot inside the *Hattan*'s dining area. It was a large, spacious facility with numerous round tables orbiting a series of food processors. Most of the crew, including many of the senior officers, came here to eat, and since sentient eating patterns varied widely, the room was almost always busy.

Off to one side was the kitchen, where the ship's cook served up food for those who, either by necessity or preference, opted for prepared dishes. The head cook, a cantankerous Ritican with gnarled, rust-colored skin and dark green eyes, was the one member of the crew not to be trifled with, lest he decide to fulfill his oft-repeated threat to serve nothing but Ritican cuisine for a full Ritican *orthwuk*.

Contemplating the effect on morale (let alone digestion) if the crew were forced to eat nothing but toxic Ritican food for thirty-eight Index days, Rami turned to her left, from whence a round of incessant clicking and snapping assailed her ears. Exos. She watched as most of the morning engineering department, fresh off of duty and evidently quite hungry, hovered next to the kitchen window as the Ritican cook furiously opened boxes of radioactive packets to distribute to the engineers.

What a different arrangement it was compared to what she'd experienced on the *Retaelus*. On a small interceptor, the single Exo engineer would take its meals alone in its work space. Because of the high amount of Exo and non-Exo traffic in the *Hattan*'s engineering section, such an arrangement was impractical, so the Exos were served in the dining area with the rest of the crew.

The Exos pressed in closer to the kitchen. Rami, who understood the Exo language, could hear the engineers chanting "food" over and over again. Although Exos were task-oriented and comparatively emotionless, they could be impatient when their necessary tasks were delayed.

The cook would have none of it. "Get back," he shouted, "or you will all be feeding out of the fusing core until the Festival of the *Glosurhot!*"

The captain wasn't lying about the cook's mood. The Exos went silent and backed away.

Nearby, a group of Ritican security guards, watching the exchange, broke into cringe-inducing laughter. The cook cast them an annoyed look, and the guards, too, went quiet.

The power of the stomach, Rami mused. Or, in the case of the Riticans, eight of them.

She went to gather something to eat from one of the Human food processors, then scanned the room for a familiar face. A few trics to her right, she noticed Rete Sorte, sitting alone. Rete, who was just a few years younger than the grandfatherly Nho, was quietly reading off of a portable even as he took a bite of some unidentifiable military ration.

Maybe, she thought, *I can spread a little more joy this morning.* That, and she'd been wanting to talk with Nho's friend—a Sarconian linguist, supposedly—for a while now.

Her approach went unnoticed until she was standing right in front of the table. "May I?" she asked.

Rete put his portable down and gestured to a nearby seat. "If you'd like," he said.

She sat down, placing her tray in front of her. "I don't think we've had a chance to meet. I'm Rami Del, a communications officer."

"Rete Sorte, although I'm guessing you know that."

"The civilian clothing tends to give it away, yes."

"What do you want?"

Rami flushed a bit. "What?"

"I assume you need counseling?"

"No, not at all. I just thought it would be good to meet you." She cocked her head inquisitively. "Why are you asking? Have people been asking you for counseling?"

Rete regarded her with a grim expression. "Nearly nonstop since I arrived here. I'm more tired now than I think I ever was as a slave. One day I'm processing ore for eighteen Index hours a day, the next I'm in a Navy cruiser filled with half-crazed Aecrons and traumatized officers on some suicide mission into deep space because of some giant alien planet I've never heard of."

Rami opened her mouth to speak but Rete kept going. "My old friend Nho, who used to antagonize almost every government official he ever met, is now some sort of Confederal legend, and the first person one thousand Navy officers come to after nearly killing each other . . . and I'm their second choice if Nho is occupied, which he always is. I have officers who barely know who I am baring their souls to me just because they've decided I must be Nho's best friend, and they *never go away*."

Rami was about to take a bite from her plate of noodles but

stopped. This was not turning out to be nearly as pleasant as her conversation five minutes ago. She said, slowly, "I had no idea it was so hard for you. I've been so busy with my work, I haven't even had time to think about seeking counseling."

"You might be the only one."

She rested her utensil next to her plate and folded her hands. "It sounds as if you could use someone to talk to."

Now it was his turn to flush. He sighed and rubbed his eyes. "I'm sorry."

"It's not a problem. You've been through a lot. Nho was devastated that we couldn't find you during our search for the parchments last year."

Rete sat up a little. "You were part of that search?"

"I was on Jared's interceptor crew. Has Nho talked much about that?"

Rete smiled, but it was a sad one. "No, nothing. We barely have time for any talk between us. I was told that there was some sort of expedition to gather the Sarconian parchments, and that those parchments were related to the war against that giant planet . . . Milum?"

"Malum."

"Yes, that."

Rami took a bite of food. "We were. On an expedition to find the parchments, that is. We found Nho in a prison on Alsis, the Corridor world, while looking for one of them. He said he'd been searching for you when he was imprisoned. We later located Suda and learned that he'd been responsible for Nho's arrest and your enslavement."

Rete's expression turned dark. "Suda."

She paused, trying to figure out how to respond to the sudden flash of emotion. She said, slowly, "I am sorry for what he did. If it is any consolation, Vetta Quidd spoke to him and said he was very remorseful."

"It is a small comfort to those of us whose lives he destroyed," Rete spat. When Rami did not respond, his expression softened a bit. "I'm sorry. Forgiveness has not come easy on this matter." He sighed. "Please, continue your story."

She nodded. "Vetta's conversation with Suda led us to Dio, where we found your parchment piece. We lost your trail there. We assumed you were dead."

Rete's expression suddenly changed to one of realization. "So if you were part of that crew, that means you also spent time with the Sarconian parchments. Is that right?"

Rami brightened. "That was something I hoped we'd able to talk about. Nho told me once that you knew the Sarconian language."

"More than the others," he said with a shrug, "although I'm not an expert. I couldn't figure out the parchment pieces."

She felt a stab of disappointment. "Really? I was told you knew but kept it a secret."

Rete shook his head. "Everyone *assumed* I knew because I'd studied the lexicons. They thought I was being intentionally elusive when I didn't answer their questions. The truth was that I was younger, more foolish, and less willing to admit that the lexicons I had access to translated into nonsense. Eventually I simply told them what another in the enclave advised me to say: that their full meaning would come forth in the One's own time, rather than my own." He tore off a bite of his ration. "Were you able to decipher them, then?"

"With some help, yes. Did Nho tell you where they took us?"

"Like I said, he and I haven't had much time to talk."

Rami was about to speak when Rete's link signaled him. He could hear a disembodied voice saying, "Rete, are you there?"

It was Nho. Rete answered. "Yes, Nho, what is it?"

"Could you join me in the commons? I need your assistance with something."

"Of course," said Rete, although his tone of voice suggested something otherwise.

After the link closed, Rete took a deep breath. "I have to go, but I would very much like to hear the rest of your story. Perhaps another time?"

"Perhaps another time," she agreed. "It's quite a story."

• • •

The *Hattan*'s senior officers' lounge was set on a different deck than the general dining area. According to Tir, Jared's predecessor, Captain Traves Walbirg, had taken every meal in the officer's lounge, holding court with his senior staff as if he were royalty. Walbirg had the additional virtues of being both unpopular and incompetent, having been responsible for the *Hattan*'s humiliating defeat at the hands of Malum.

Jared, conversely, tried to take his meals in the main dining area from time to time, as he had during lunch earlier in the day. He thought it good to fraternize with the larger crew population when he could. Sometimes it made for a more tiring meal than he wanted—crew members talked to him from start to finish—but other senior officers reported that it made him popular with his crew, and crew morale was extremely important in a deep-space mission like this one.

Nevertheless, while Jared ate in the senior officer's lounge less frequently than Walbirg, he did take the majority of his meals there. One main reason was simply that he needed a respite from the constant demands of captaincy, and the lounge represented a quiet place where he could gather his thoughts. A second reason was that it allowed him to confer in private with his senior staff without fear of nearby crew hearing sensitive information—or worse, hearing half a conversation and developing rumors based on incomplete information.

Tonight Jared was joined in the lounge by his Hazionite first officer, Tir Bvaso, and his Ritican security officer, Vetta Quidd. Eating frequency was quite variable among Humans, Hazionites, and Riticans, but the three of them tried to arrange times like this when possible. Sometimes Redelia Aroo would also join them, although she was at present the watch officer on the bridge.

Jared sat down to a simple Western Territories-style meal of meat, potatoes, and bread. Tir ate a typical Hazionite meal, all of it approximations of Hazion Prime plant life. Vetta's meal was hard, cold, and decidedly animal. Vetta had her rebreather off and sitting to the side on the table; Riticans could survive for a half-hour or so without them in an oxygen atmosphere.

Tir was the first to speak. "I am not sure that my mind has fully accepted that we have passed outside of the Confederacy."

Jared looked over at the viewscreen on the wall, which offered a spectacular view of the *Hattan*'s current fold. "I've heard that a lot this week. I've been thinking about what we can do to help the crew cope beyond what we've implemented already."

"I have spoken extensively with Nho and with the members of the counseling staff. A recurring point of personal difficulty among the crew is the prospect of lengthy separation from family and other close associations back home. This sentiment seems to persist across all the races, except, of course, for the Exos."

"Any ideas on how to deal with it?"

"I have spoken to several people, and I am working up a report on the subject."

Jared sipped a fruit drink. "I'd be grateful for any insight you might have. I have to admit, I'm at a bit of a disadvantage on this subject. I'm not very close to most of my family back on Earth, and most of my close friends are on this ship."

Tir lapsed into what looked like reflection, her pinprick eyes staring out across the room. "I will be out of contact with my husband-mate and offspring for at least a full Index year, and likely longer . . . presuming we return at all. I could not tell them where I was going, or for how long. I told my offspring I was defending the border from another Malum attack. My husband-mate knew I was lying but did not question me."

Jared wasn't sure what to say. "I'm sorry, Tir."

She looked at him. "Do not be. I accepted this position without objection, even knowing the hardships. But there are still hardships. While Garvak's circle was very deliberate in who was selected for this mission, not all are as accepting of it as I am. It is not a reflection on your leadership—the crew respects you—but everyone is here involuntarily, no matter how much they support being part of a mission this important. And many are leaving loved ones behind. I tell you what I have experienced so you will understand what others on board might be going through." She looked at Vetta. "I know you also miss your progeny."

Vetta grunted noncommittally.

Vetta's response alone wouldn't have been enough to arouse Jared's suspicions, but in concert with things he knew, it gave him reason to press the matter. "Vetta, I saw in your file that you did not return to Lutnum 9 after we were rescued from Malum."

Vetta looked at him but did not answer. Tir said to Vetta, "If this matter is private, I can excuse myself."

Vetta gestured to the negative. "No, that is not necessary. Captain, you are correct. I did not return to Lutnum 9. There was no reason for me to do so. During the Malum crisis, Monnux secured work with the Ritican Protectorate. He and the progeny have returned to Ritica."

Because of an incident that took place during her service in the Ritican militia, Vetta was no longer welcome on the Ritican homeworld; that was why she had moved to the more distant colony of Lutnum 9. Her union with Monnux had suffered because of the incident. Jared asked, "What does that mean for you?"

"There is no Ritican equivalent to Human marital dissolution, but on a practical level this places my union with Monnux at an end. As you are aware, it was nominal even before, but this relocation impacts much more than just my association with him. As long as he lives on Ritica, my involvement in the lives of our progeny—beyond long-distance correspondence—will now be all but impossible. Monnux knows this. Because of my history with the militia, few in my family or in the government will be sympathetic to my disadvantages."

"What he did was wrong," Jared said.

Tir added, "You have my deepest condolences. I agree with the captain. It is not right."

Vetta looked at her. "I, like you, fight for my family, but mine is a family I cannot return to. I cannot tell you whether this makes the distance easier or more difficult. It is not easy for me to say this in front of you, but I say it because there may also be others on board in similar situations, including other Riticans."

"I will be mindful of that," said Tir.

Apparently, Jared thought, there was a lot to learn today.

Jared knew Vetta well enough to know she probably was done talking about the subject. He moved on. "I saw that we've had a pair of security incidents over the last twelve hours."

Vetta lifted her portable and showed it to Jared. "This morning, a Hazionite deck officer down on the interceptor assembly team shouted at an Aecron engineer, a lieutenant, and later in the day a similar incident took place in the dining hall involving a deck officer Human male and a senior deck officer Aecron male. We issued reprimands to the offending officers."

"I also personally spoke to both officers," added Tir. "I would not expect further trouble from either of them."

"Good," Jared said. "I'll be much happier once we can stop dealing with problems among the crew and focus instead on the actual threat."

"Some lingering tension toward the Aecrons is probably unavoidable," said Vetta. "It will likely be an intermittent issue until we near enemy territory."

"Just as long as it does not cause problems."

"It is worth noting," said Tir, casting a sideways glance at Vetta, "that none of the past week's incidents have been incited by our Ritican officers."

"The Riticans have already shifted their focus to Malum," explained Vetta. "It is an instinctive reaction in campaigns like this. Rarely does the Ritican militia deal with internal discord on their ships the way some other sentients do."

Jared took another sip of his drink. "What about the Aecrons?"

"Other than being intimidated by other members of the crew, they have been no trouble."

Tir said, "I would say it goes well beyond that. Every supervisor I have spoken to reports that the Aecrons are different since the mutiny. They have been working exceptionally hard, almost too hard in some cases. It is clear they feel the need to prove they are valuable members of the crew. I have also been told, repeatedly, the condescension that Aecrons historically exhibit has vanished. They have almost universally been described as humble."

"Humble?" Jared almost choked on his drink.

"Consider it yet another miracle on this voyage," said Vetta.

"There seem to be no shortages of those," Jared coughed.

Tir placed her arms, with their elongated digits, on the table. "There are still a lot of unanswered questions about what caused the mutiny. Many on board, including the Aecrons themselves, remain confused and, in some cases, frightened. It does not help that the medical staff has not been able to determine a cause."

"Given the cure, I would think that to be obvious," said Vetta.

Tir cast a sharp look at the Ritican. "I did not take you for one of them." Jared detected a distinct edge in Tir's use of the last word.

"I did not say that I was," replied Vetta calmly, "but all three of us saw what happened that day in Malum. All three of us saw what happened the day the mutiny ended. Nho possesses a power."

"It remains difficult to believe that it was the work of a deity."

"Nho believes it is," said Jared, "and he's the one who's responsible for all this."

Tir said, "Do you agree with him?"

Jared put his eating utensil down and leaned forward in his chair, resting his elbows on the table and folding his hands together. "Over the last several months, I've been asked over and over what it felt like to be there—inside Malum, standing in the midst of the warden. With Nho." Jared shivered as he recounted being inside the freezing cloud-being. "I've consistently replied that I felt something powerful, something I had never felt before. But that is only half of the truth." Looking off into space, he continued, "You see, I didn't feel something powerful. I felt some*one* powerful."

Tir and Vetta listened to him in silence. He went on. "I've never told anyone that part before, in part because I wasn't sure what I would have said if they'd asked me who it was."

"Sarco?" Vetta asked.

"Maybe. I don't know. I know that, whoever it was, it wasn't evil. I certainly know what evil feels like—Malum's warden was dark and terrible, and when you were in it, you could feel it through your whole body, like a great weight of despair. When Nho and I hoisted that staff into the air, it was like one being was purged from my body and another filled me in its place. Intuitively I felt like it was good, although I never heard a voice or anything as such. It was simply a presence."

Tir looked skeptical. "Are you saying we are to believe Malum and the mutiny are the work of"—she searched for the word—"the Ground Curser?"

"Ground Curser?" repeated Vetta.

"In Hazionite lore," Jared explained, "the Ground Curser was a celestial being who rose up against the Prime Maker but was exiled to the groundlands for his rebellion. The Sarconians carry a similar story, of one called the Outcasted who tried to unseat the One and was cast into the void."

He looked at Tir. "It's Nho's conviction that both Malum and the conditioning were the Outcasted's work. He's hard to argue with. Aside from the obvious effect of his staff on the warden and later the Aecrons of the mutiny, there is the additional, unavoidable fact that the Sarconians on board the *Hattan* were the only ones of their race not affected by the conditioning." Jared paused a moment. "This knowledge should make me feel better, but it doesn't. It bothers me. If the staff can defeat Malum and can also cure the Aecron conditioning, does that mean the Aecron government and Malum are somehow connected?"

"Do not forget," Tir said, "that Malum tried to destroy Aeroel."

Jared picked up a piece of bread off his plate and said, "Five hundred years ago, on Earth, the Central Territories waged a bitter war against the Northern Alliance. Both leaders were despots. Just because two groups are at war does not mean that one is good and the other is not."

"What are you suggesting?"

"He is suggesting," said Vetta, "that we may be facing evil on more than one front."

• • •

The Great Void was a vast empty region of space just beyond the borders of Ritican territory. In 1113, before the Riticans achieved interstellar spaceflight, the Aecrons dispatched a research vessel, the *Noeba*, into the Void. The *Noeba* never returned. Historians speculated that the ship may have been destroyed by the Invaders of 1124, and that the *Noeba*'s ill-fated voyage may have alerted the Invaders to the Aecrons' existence, which in turn precipitated the Invasion. If the Aecron conditioning that nearly destroyed the *Hattan* was a response to the Aecrons' fears of another *Noeba*-incited invasion, the government of Aeroel apparently shared this view.

The passing of the *Hattan* from Confederal space into the Void proper was more of a gradual understanding than a ceremonious event. Most of the crew was too anxious over the recent ambush and too busy keeping the ship in working order to try to demarcate a specific moment. A few, though—mostly Humans, but also a few Hazionites and Riticans—gathered one evening in one of the observation decks. No ship in the Confederacy had, to date, ever successfully crossed the Void. According to the estimates of the *Hattan*'s navigation team, it would take approximately six months to reach the nearest systems on the far side. The small group quietly marked what was an historic occasion in Confederal history.

Left unsaid was what would become of them all upon their return.

7

TITAN
EARTH INDEX 1306.151

Admiral Nhile Garvak arrived at his officer's box above the vast chamber of the Confederal Congress and braced himself for what was to come. For Garvak, this was a day long in coming, the inevitable outcome of a fateful decision that had remained a closely-guarded secret at Command. Politicians always seemed to have a knack for asking bad questions at worse times, and Garvak was quickly running out of believable answers. It might have helped had the Navy picked a less-conspicuous ship to send, but circumstances demanded the fleet's best, even if its apparent truancy would be harder to cover up.

Not surprisingly, the biggest maelstrom of activity—not to mention ferocity—came from the Aecron delegation. Some days Garvak wondered how the Aecrons' conditioning remained a secret, given that its more eccentric manifestations seemed so obvious. Surely no group of people could possibly be so paradoxically curious about science and fearful about leaving the Confederacy. And yet the Aecrons were both.

"Admiral Garvak." It was one of the Aecron delegates, her voice cutting through the Congressional concourse. "How thoughtful of you to take time out of your schedule to honor us with your presence."

Garvak brushed off the thinly veiled affront. "And how may I serve the Assembly today?"

The Aecron, an old politico named Roia Umaro, looked down carefully at her notes as she spoke, although Garvak knew full well she didn't need them. "Admiral," she said, "certain irregularities have been brought to my attention in regard to the deployment of Navy vessels. Irregularities that have my constituents quite concerned."

Garvak leaned forward, his large hands resting comfortably against the guardrail overlooking the cavernous chamber. "Congresswoman," he said, his voice carried easily by the chamber's brilliant acoustics, "Navy deployment orders are a sensitive issue to raise in an open session. If you have concerns about the placement of Navy resources, I suggest you pass those concerns on to the Navy Intelligence Committee, which can then confer with our staff behind closed doors."

Roia paced deliberately around the floor of the Assembly, looking up toward Garvak's chamber space with opaque eyes that seemed intensely focused on him. "This is not an issue I will defer to closed-door politics. The Navy's most ambitious vessel is unaccounted for. According to reports, the prototype *Hattan* ventured out toward the Ritican border months ago and has not returned."

"We have many ships on border patrol. The nature of the Malum threat necessitates some secrecy as to the exact locations of those patrols."

"But why would the Navy deploy its most powerful resource into obscurity? Instead of testing and perhaps mass-producing the innovations on board the *Hattan*, your office has assigned the most powerful ship in the Navy to guard duty."

Garvak's tone rose almost imperceptibly. "As I said, Congresswoman, these are matters best discussed behind closed doors. I will not comment on intelligence in front of civilian news agencies our enemies might be listening to."

"Even if you are violating Confederal statutes in the process?" A second Aecron representative—an older male named Huna

Vio—was now speaking. "Perhaps you would care to explain why Ritican intelligence now believes the ship in question is headed out of Confederal space?"

The chamber erupted into a cacophony of noise. Garvak could see delegates from the Ritican section marching angrily to their speaking podiums, voicing outrage over the revelation that Aecrons had acquired Ritican intelligence reports. Pockets of representatives from other races began talking among themselves or moved to add their concerns about the apparent inter-Confederal espionage. Above the din, Roia shouted at Garvak, "Is Congress truly in charge here, Admiral, or are we a military oligarchy?"

From above, a large boom rang out, drawing Congress quickly to silence. On the top concourse, Troye Carson—a Human delegate serving as a temporary chairman in the chairman's absence—rapped his gavel against the order stone. "We will have order," he said firmly, recognizing Huna to speak.

"Thank you, sir," said the Aecron male, his voice now softer. "Admiral, Chair Carson, and fellow sentients, this is not about politics."

Nonsense, Garvak fumed.

"This is about making sure that our planets and our people are protected from future attacks from the ones who created Malum. My planet was nearly destroyed by that device, and I owe it to my people to do everything in my power to make sure they are kept safe. Our request is not a complicated one. Bring back the *Hattan* so we may apply its technology, and send another vessel in its stead to guard the frontier. Chair Carson, I move for a motion to recall the *Hattan* to be remanded to Navy Research under the provisions of the Malum Defense Resolution."

"The motion has been made," came Troye's ethereal voice from above.

A chorus of approval came from the Aecron delegation.

"This body will have twenty Index minutes to vote on the motion," the chair decreed, a faint boom rippling through the chamber as the gavel again struck the stone.

Garvak closed his eyes and tried to suppress his anger. The Aecrons had rammed the motion in without giving him any real chance to present other options or even explain Navy policy. Of course, the truth was that the Aecrons were right; the *Hattan* was well out of Navy space. But a resolution to bring it back could be catastrophic on many levels. Normally Garvak would be able to resolve this through a closed meeting with the Congress's Navy Intelligence Committee, but the Aecron delegation would have nothing to do with that. The question was: would the other representatives accommodate them?

The call for a vote brought crowds of Congressional representatives into the chamber, joining the group already in attendance. The Humans, as always, exchanged idle pleasantries before taking their seats, a convention Garvak found unnerving. Hazionites, gifted in the sense of emotion, needed no introductions with each other and merely walked silently to their assigned positions. The Ritican delegation was already talking quite loudly about the situation, with one younger male Ritican making large gestures as he detailed the outrage of Aecron espionage to his newly-arrived colleagues. The Exos merely filed in and took seats.

And then there were the Aecrons. Most of them had already been on hand for the events of the last few minutes, but those who had not seemed to already know what was at stake, for they took their seats and lodged their votes without so much as a glance toward their colleagues.

As if they were machines.

The voting continued over the next several minutes as Garvak looked on. He was particularly concerned about the direction the Hazionite delegation might lean. It was no coincidence that this unexpected motion had taken place when the most influential Hazionites in the Confederacy—including President Trez Wheit and Admiral Wr Ghiri—were offworld tending to other business. Garvak's presence, far from filling the void, seemed to invite old Corridor War prejudices. And with the sentiments of the Humans and Exos being anyone's guess, Garvak needed every vote he could get.

Twenty minutes passed slowly, with each tick of the chamber's time display an eternity to an admiral who wondered if his very career would come to a close with the final second of the voting. Try as he might, Garvak could not read the sentiments of most of the delegations, and Confederal rules barred him from any last-minute pleas. The call for a vote had been made and assented to, and now it was out of his hands.

The voting ended a few seconds before time expired, and Troye Carson's voice rose up to declare the results. "The motion . . . fails, 247-251."

The chamber exploded into sound, cheers and shouts and screams co-mingling in a veritable political pandemonium. Garvak watched it all with quiet stoicism, though inside he was filled with relief. The *Hattan*'s mission and his career were both safe, at least for now. Most of the Hazionites and Riticans had, in an unusual show of unity, opposed the recall, supported by a few Humans and several Exos. That had been enough.

Now it was up to Jared Carter.

• • •

In the highest box in the chamber, Substitute Chair Troye Carson sat down, observing the various emotions playing out on the floor below. *These squabbles,* he mused, *are such petty ones.* The delegates obsessed over unimportant frivolities, the chairman pretended that those frivolities actually mattered, and fools like Confederal President Trez Wheit paraded in front of the masses as if they wielded real power.

Yet Troye entertained them all because they were a foothold to his greater destiny. The Voice—whose counsel had helped him gain his current seat as the temporary chair—regularly reminded him that the procedures he held in such disdain were helping to create the connections he needed to move beyond bureaucracy and into his destiny. That end was tantalizingly close: his secret dealings with the Others back on Earth were about to coalesce into action.

As if on cue—because Its timing was never wrong—the Voice spoke.

The seeds of discord have taken root, it said. *The time for your ascension is at hand. You are my building stone, and upon that mountain I will build my empire. Nothing will prevail against it.*

A Human female quietly walked up to his seat and slipped him a small, handwritten note. It said:

It is time.

Yes, it is, he thought. By tomorrow morning, Troye Carson would no longer be on Titan. He would be on his way to becoming a god.

8

Malum Terminus
Earth Index 1306.302

Jared stared out at the viewscreen, where the end of the fold was in sight. He looked at one of his displays, which noted the date: just over six months since they'd departed the Confederacy and crossed into the Great Void. And now he was staring, literally, at the end of the long succession of solitary jumps. Finally.

The fold parted, and the *Hattan* emerged into open space. A universe of stars crowded the main bidimensional screen, including one just off-center that seemed a little brighter than the others. As planned, the *Hattan* was on the outskirts of the system, nearly five billion kiltrics from its sun. Directly ahead was the terminus of Malum's particle transmissions.

This had been a long time coming.

Jared's hands gripped the arms of his command chair, an unconscious reaction to setting their first proverbial foot into hostile territory. Taking a breath, he relaxed his hold. "So here we are. Aioua?"

Aioua pored over the new, fast-growing mountain of data now overwhelming her displays. "Initial reports suggest no contacts in the immediate area. It will take a few minutes to analyze the system."

Jared stood and walked closer to the viewscreen. He took up a position immediately behind and next to navigation, a location he had often favored on board the interceptor *Retaelus*.

Kilvin Wrsaw, seated at navigation, asked, "How long has it been since a ship from the Confederacy has explored an uncharted system?"

"Under the terms of the Titan Accords, never," Jared said. "You'd have to go back to the first contacts of the pre-Confederal era, and even further if you include systems the Humans or Hazionites explored that the Aecrons had not already charted."

"It is a unique experience," said Aioua, sorting through the information that surrounded her.

Jared felt a peculiar sensation at that remark. Humans had long exhibited an impulse to discover, a curiosity about the unknown. The age of interstellar travel before the creation of the Confederacy had been a sort of legendary era in the romantic recollections of modern Earth, a time when Humans had emerged from darkness and into a whole new universe. Although few historians had articulated it as such, Jared wondered if the prohibitions of the Titan Accords against extra-Confederal exploration had been detrimental to Humanity's development and sense of self. Recent Human history was viewed in the public consciousness as a time of political infighting and stagnation.

It had not been all bad. The exchange of technology, commerce, and culture had strengthened the bonds of peace among the Confederal nations. Moreover, a number of Human colonies had been planted within explored Confederal space, so it was not as if Humans were affixed to their homeworld. But with Humanity focused on cultural convergence with the other sentients rather than braving new parts of the universe, something seemed to be missing in the Human experience, and it was something Jared did not fully realize until he was standing there, staring at that small star in the darkness ahead.

Looking at Aioua, Jared wondered if Aecrons also possessed such an exploratory impulse. Certainly they must have at some point. Now, though, with the influences of the conditioning, they seemed content to refine technologies and grow their influence among the Confederal races.

No, not content. Complacent.

He also reminded himself that Aioua was not under the influence of the conditioning. None of the Aecrons on board were. They were liberated. Did that mean that a desire to explore was also liberated?

Jared suppressed the thought for the moment and turned to Orel Dayail. "Is anyone talking out there?"

Orel's eyes were filled with awe. "Incessantly. It was not apparent during our approach, but there is an enormous amount of communication both inbound and outbound."

"I have a visual of the system," Aioua announced. "I am placing it on the tridimensional display now."

Off to one side of the main viewscreen, a full-bodied rendering of the system appeared in the air. Jared moved closer, examining it with a mixture of wonder and suspicion. It was an amazing sight, but it was also the destination of a transmission from a giant planet that had nearly destroyed the Confederacy.

Aioua narrated as the projection turned and various pieces of information superimposed themselves over the visuals. "There are four planets in the system and a number of smaller bodies. All of the planets are gas giants of varying sizes, not unlike those we have seen inside the Confederacy."

Jared paced a few steps around the visual to examine it from different angles. "Where are the communications coming from?"

"Most are coming from the vicinity of the largest gas giant, which is also the farthest in-system." Aioua scaled in the projection on a mockup of the innermost gas giant, along with small superimposed highlights in orbit around it. "Something near the planet is rerouting and amplifying the transmissions."

"Like a communications array."

"Possibly. Additionally, the communications profile does not match that of Malum. We are dealing with a completely different race."

Jared feared he knew the answer before he asked the question. "Who?"

"The transmissions are consistent with our understanding of Invader communications."

He mulled over the revelation. Malum's transmissions had been directed across the Great Void in the same presumptive direction the Invaders of 1124 had come from so long ago. Jared and his crew had long known that some sort of connection between Malum and the Invaders was possible.

He took a few steps back from the tridimensional display, still watching it. "So if I understand this correctly, you are saying that the Malum transmission is completely different than these transmissions, which appear to be Invader."

Aioua gestured to the affirmative. "They are unique and completely different methodologies of communication. Even in the Confederacy, various races now use standardized encoding. That is not the situation here."

"Yet we also know that Malum's transmissions were sent to this very place."

"Yes."

"The mere fact that the two languages are converging on the same point is a concern," Garo Ball rumbled. "It would be a realization of our greatest fears to learn that the two were allies."

Inside, Jared felt a chill. *Sarco, please don't let this be true.*

• • •

Rete and Rami sat at a table in the dining area. He was eating a modest meal of Earth vegetables; she was biting into meat encrusted by a pastry. Rami had just finished recounting her visit to the fabled Sarconian colony world of Teirel, which had been purged of life during the Invasion of 1124. Rete listened with rapt attention as she described their arrival at the uninhabited but revitalized world, and their discovery of a massive cache of Sarconian information: history, science, law, and other writings.

Rete noted that Nho had failed to mention any of this to him;

taking care of the crew's emotional needs continued to dominate Nho's life. Rete was especially curious to read what had been pulled from the Sarconian library. Rami promised to have it sent to him.

After spending some time talking about the contents of the cache, Rete changed the subject. "So, these transmissions. They have to be exciting for you."

"In some ways. Looking at this new species, watching their communications, trying to decipher their culture . . . it's the sort of thing every Human dreams about when they enter a life of interstellar travel."

Rete sensed she wasn't telling him everything. "But?"

"It's also overwhelming. Every moment we are here is a moment we risk being seen by these—these Invaders, and all of us feel the pressure of that. The Aecron research we acquired helps a great deal with the base language—a lot of it hasn't changed in two hundred years—but the Aecron lexicon says very little about Invader sociology."

"In other words, you're having trouble putting their words into cultural context."

She brightened a little. "Exactly. Just this morning, we came across a transmission alluding to 'going to war.' What does that mean? Even in our Confederacy, it can mean many things. A Human would be speaking of putting measured forces into play as a righteous cause, such as promoting freedom. A Ritican would see going to war as a means of defense, but one that would invariably involve the complete annihilation of the enemy. A Hazionite would view going to war as an extension of domination over Hazion Prime, purposing to conquer other planets. An Aecron would see going to war as a tool of scientific and influential gain, not military might."

"The Invaders attacked the Aecrons," Rete said. "Doesn't that give us insight into what they mean?"

"If all Invaders are of the same mindset, yes. But how can we be certain even of that? Consider the Sarconians. They're Aecrons, but when they spoke of going to war, they meant the war within, not without: fighting the lures of the Outcasted and prevailing against the desire to do that which was self-destructive. Their discussions of war were within the mind and the heart."

"I see your problem."

"And that is just one phrase. Imagine trying to determine the cultural context for an entire language without knowing the culture."

Rete took a tentative bite out of one of the more foreign-looking vegetables on his plate, then asked, "And the Aecrons' Invader lexicon doesn't offer any insight at all?"

"A little, but not much. It seems the Aecrons were primarily focused on deciphering the language for tactical reasons. They wanted it in case the Invaders returned, so they could possibly intercept enemy communications and anticipate their movements. Cultural understanding does not seem to have been a priority."

Rete pursed his lips. "I'm no strategist, but it would seem to me that cultural understanding is a valuable component of war. Knowledge of a species' culture can be useful in anticipating what they might do."

"No one ever said the Aecrons were superb tacticians. Their brilliance seems largely confined to science."

"To their credit, they did defeat the Invaders, and they managed to acquire much of the Invader language in the process."

"Fair point," she conceded. "They also were able to figure out how Invaders package and transmit sound and images. Without their work, we'd still be trying to figure out just how to make sense of these particle streams. That alone would take years."

Rami leaned forward and looked at him. "But enough about what I've been doing. What about the rest of the crew? How are they doing?"

"Excited, but nervous. I've heard your words echoed many times over. This is what they have long dreamed of. The Humans especially feel this way, but so do the Hazionites. The Aecrons are less direct about it, but it is clear they are also fascinated by these new developments."

"And the Riticans?"

Rete laughed. "Take a guess."

"They see the Invaders as a threat to their homeworld and they want to destroy them right now."

Rete nodded, glancing at a group of Riticans eating nearby. They looked like a lot of the Riticans he'd seen elsewhere on the ship: ready to kill something. Fortunately, that Ritican instinct was narrow enough that it hadn't been displaced toward any crew members. Rete hoped it stayed that way.

"And how about you?" Rami asked. "How are you?"

His face took on a more sober expression. "About the same as the last time we met. Tired, busy beyond measure. Most of the Aecrons are over the guilt and most of the others on board are over the resentment. Now we're dealing with an entirely new range of problems: the stresses of being deployed so far from home for so long, fears of the unknown, impatience over our current position, and a sense of being overwhelmed by the amount of work that lies ahead."

"The last one sounds like me."

"We've had a few from your department, but they are doing all right. They just need someone to talk to."

She rested her cheek on her hand. "Last time we talked, you were pretty overwhelmed by all the people who needed someone to talk to."

He smiled weakly. "I was, but it's better now. Besides, I have to do something to earn my keep on this ship."

• • •

Nho was sitting quietly in his quarters when the door chime rang. As much as the crew demanded his time, they were usually good at giving him his privacy when he retreated into his quarters. Usually. "You may enter."

The door opened and Rami walked in. "I just wanted to let you know that I compiled a new round of documents for you. I had them sent to your workstation."

"Thank you." He was so preoccupied with his counseling and spiritual work that he often forgot to check on her progress sorting through the massive information cache they'd discovered in the ruins of Teirel last year. She knew this was a deficiency of his, which was why she would often drop by to remind him. He asked, "Anything of interest?"

"Statutory records from the Teirellian government."

"Hm." As much as he appreciated learning about the Sarconians of Teirel, the minutia of lawmaking was not the most exciting topic, even for him.

"Don't be too quick to dismiss them," she warned, her finger waving in the air. "Some of these records appear to date from the years immediately before and during the Invasion."

He perked up a little. "What do they say?"

"You'll have to read it for yourself. Let's just say that if you ever wanted to learn what Teirel's policy was toward the Invaders, you'll find out."

"Extraordinary. Have you told the captain yet?"

"I wanted to wait until you'd read it first."

"I'll start on them as soon as I have time." He scratched his beard. "Rete mentioned that you were meeting him today for lunch."

"Yes. He's a nice person."

"He's a little old for you."

She placed her hands on her hips and glared at him. "Of course he is. It's not like that." When he didn't respond, she pressed her lips together in thoughtful concentration. "Look, I've been think-ing a lot about family lately, probably because everyone else on board is talking about how much they miss their own." Her voice changed; Nho couldn't tell if she was choking up a little or if it was just fatigue from a day of meetings. "It's started to really hit me just how much I've missed out on, both as a child and now in adult-hood. I have almost no family to call my own anymore. Mother and I have little in common now and I never knew my father, as you know. I've decided to take more control of that."

She sat down next to him. "You've been a good friend, and I've decided I want more friendships like that, people who can be . . . something like family. He's one of them."

Nho cradled his staff and leaned back a little on the couch. "He and I are different in many ways, but he is a good man. I know he appreciates the time." He hesitated. "Rete has no family or children to call his own."

Rami sharpened her gaze on him again. "Please don't tell him I told you this. I don't want him to think he's some sort of lab experiment in surrogate family."

Nho chuckled. "He already feels out of place on this ship. I wouldn't dare do anything to make it worse than already is."

• • •

The lights dimmed in the conference room and were replaced by a series of images: some still, some moving, all hovering above the table. The background hues were decidedly purple, and the objects or beings on display were decidedly alien. The sound that accompanied them was like an unpleasant cross between a swarm of Earth bees and a grinding of metal on metal.

Orel Dayail, standing at the head of the table, said, "These are some of the Invader transmissions we have decoded and compiled."

There were quiet murmurings as the other officers in the room leaned in to catch a better view of the imagery. The Invaders were a deep, dark purple, and had small dots toward the top of their bodies that might or might not be eyes. A series of whip-like extensions passed for limbs, radiating out of the creatures on all sides, and they moved like upright slugs. Even viewed through the varying aesthetic sensibilities of those in the room, the consensus was that the beings were hideous.

"We are still trying to develop an understanding of Invader society and culture," Orel continued, "but much of this appears civilian rather than military. There are some elements that resemble something that may involve weapons, but most of it seems almost personal."

Jared spoke. "What have you learned so far?"

One of the ship's xenosociologists, a Hazionite male, responded. "That has been an elusive question, sir. We know that various Invaders are communicating with one another, but we have little clue as to what the relationships are between those who are talking. Their correspondences do not conform to any social norms of any Confederal or Minor race, so trying to determine what institutions they have—occupations or family, for example—has been difficult. They do seem to adhere to some sort of hierarchy, but we are having a hard time understanding what shapes it or drives it. We are not even sure if there are one or more genders in play, or if they utilize any concept of family."

"Is there any mention of Malum or the Confederacy?"

"Not that we can tell," Orel said.

Tir Bvaso gestured to one of the floating images. "There are tens of different planetary settings to these visuals. Am I safe in assuming that they come from systems other than this one?"

"Most likely," said Aioua. "This system appears to be a hub for retransmitting and redirecting messages and other communications among a large number of worlds. Something inside the system there is managing all of this traffic."

Jared asked, "Is *any* of it from this system?"

"It is difficult to say, but if so, not a great deal. This seems to be more of a conduit for interactions between other systems than a location from which interactions originate."

"Is this conduit inhabited? Are we looking at a station of some sort? Or just an automated array?"

"We are too far away to take any direct readings, so we cannot be sure." Aioua brought up a tactical map showing lines spread out across the star system. "However, there are a few additional sources of communication coming from other points in the area. Based on our estimates, those are coming from open space, and they may be moving."

"Ships?"

"Possibly."

That could be a problem. "But the vast majority of the traffic is coming from the gas giant?"

"Either the planet itself or the immediate vicinity. I believe it is coming from something in orbit around the planet."

Jared paced around the table. "What would you say are the chances that we can learn what we need to from our current position?"

Orel answered, "We have discussed that question, and we are not optimistic. The communications we are analyzing do not, on their face, seem to relate to Malum. Without knowing exactly what is sending and receiving these messages, we have little sense of what we are dealing with."

Jared rested his hands on the back of a chair. "So how do we go about learning what we need?"

"We need," Aioua said, "to take the *Hattan* farther into the system so we can get more detailed readings."

Jared shook his head. "I'm not comfortable doing that, not with as little information as we currently have."

"We do have several short-fold probes at our disposal," Vetta said, speaking up. "They could be sent in to gather information."

"We also have two fully operational interceptors," added Redelia. "Either ship would be well suited to covert reconnaissance."

Jared cast a sideways look at Aioua. "What do you think?"

She considered the question briefly. "The probes may prove useful, but I would be hesitant to send them in blindly. An interceptor would be more effective at eluding detection, at least until it could get close enough to begin detailed sensory collection of the target planet."

Jared regarded Redelia, his senior interceptor commander, with an even expression. "Are you prepared to do this?"

"I was hoping you would ask, Captain."

9

Redelia Aroo took her seat on the bridge of the *Belico* for her morning shift. She held in her hands an Aecron drink, a soupy substance that was, like most Aecron drinks, served lukewarm. Bringing a beverage to the command chair was more of a Human convention than an Aecron one, but Redelia liked this particular drink and thought it was a convention worth trying. Anything to break up the monotony.

In front of her was a vista of debris: rocks, chunks of ice, particulates of dust . . . the same view she'd seen on the viewscreen each morning for the better part of the last month. Her ship was buried inside the rings of the system's innermost gas giant, protected from detection. The *Belico*'s journey into the rings a few weeks before had been a harrowing, tense journey to the back side of the gas giant, followed by a dangerous crossing through the rings.

Now boredom was the interceptor's greatest enemy.

For Redelia and her crew, the initial excitement of reconnaissance had long ago evaporated, replaced by interminable stretches of tedium. The only respite was the weekly sojourn to the far side of the planet to send updates to the *Hattan*, and after a few weeks even that had become routine. Redelia's crew had avoided the infighting that would seem inevitable in this situation, but she nevertheless worried about them becoming lax in their duties. She tried to keep them sharp by giving them daily projects to work on, everything from simulations of possible Invader combat to discussions on the content of Invader transmissions. There was only so much they could do, though, and as time progressed the monotony became more acute. She had already included, in her forthcoming data transmission to the *Hattan*, a suggestion to rotate in another interceptor.

In the meantime, a few unobtrusively placed probes along the fringes of the rings served as her window to the activities taking place around the gas giant. According to the Invaders, the planet's name, when modulated into a frequency that Humans could hear, was pronounced Ai'd'cam. According to the Invader lexicon, that name literally meant High Land, and it was a busy planet. A network of large artificial structures—Redelia's crew had determined they were communication relays of some sort—orbited around one of the giant's eight moons. The relays continuously transmitted to and from a large oblong-shaped orbital station. Teardrop-shaped ships—large, dark purple, and menacing—came and went from the station. All of it bore the markings of the Invader technology the Aecrons had faced two centuries before: tough bonded plate armor, efficient zero-point sublight drives, and hyperwave weapons that were lethal to life and—if the intensity were sufficient—degenerative to some ship materials.

Redelia closed her eyes and pushed work out of her mind. The first few quiet moments of each day were a chance to meditate on the One, and His Incarnate, Sarco. Her father was secretly Sarconian, providing legal counsel to other Sarconians and leading clandestine services in their home in defiance of Aeroel law. Redelia had witnessed her father's harrowing legal clashes with the Aeroel authorities, which had placed him at odds with planetary leadership. A unit daughter of a disapproved family within Aeroel's meritocracy had few prospects, so she had joined the Navy with the initial intent of pursuing Confederal law. As time went on, she found herself instead in the position of ship leadership. It was the last place she thought she'd be, but she was constantly in awe of how Sarco's power manifested itself through her career path, particularly over the last year.

This morning, she struggled to hold her meditative focus. She was not merely tired. She was weary. She opened her eyes, took a drink, and spoke to the only other officer currently on the bridge. "Any developments of interest?"

That other officer was Udos Beyole, the young sciences officer—and fellow Sarconian—who had been a part of the *Belico*'s crew during the incident at the Ramas-Eduj Manufactory. "A large Invader transport of some sort came in to dock a few hours ago. It does not match the profile of any of the ships we have seen so far."

Mildly interesting. "What is it transporting?"

"There are small habitations on board, sentient quarters of some sort."

"A passenger liner?"

"I am not certain. Everything about this facility suggests it is military. A passenger vessel does not fit."

"Invader culture is different," she reminded him, taking a drink. "Perhaps there is no distinction between military and civilian."

He reread some of his station's information on the new Invader vessel. "Nevertheless, I am skeptical that it is a simple sentient liner. The habitations, at least from what I can make out, are small and cramped, and there are barriers in place over many of the habitations. If it were a Confederal ship, I would say it matches the profile of a prison transport." New data flowed in front of him. "It is beginning to take on passengers."

Redelia felt a little less weary than she'd been a minute before. This transport was, relatively speaking, about the most exciting thing to have happened in a week. "Let me see it. Up front."

To the left of the main viewscreen, an annotated tridimensional image of the transport appeared, floating in the air. The display also captured part of the outline of the station. The transport was certainly large, and quite long; it stretched farther from front to back than one of the Invader warships that floated nearby.

"Commander," said Udos, "an unidentified sentient type is boarding the transport. Two of them. They are definitely not Invader. Preliminary evidence suggests something more polymer-based, not unlike the Exos, although their body structure is—by the Domes!"

She leaned toward him. "What is it?"

"Uxa251! I am reading Uxa251 on the unidentifieds!"

Redelia nearly dropped her drink. Uxa251 was an exotic compound known for its energy-redirecting properties. It was exceedingly rare in nature and well beyond the ability of Confederal scientists to reliably synthesize.

It was also the primary compound found on Malum's hull.

Redelia said to Udos, "How long until the transport departs?"

"It is powering up its sublight drive now."

Redelia keyed her link. "Bridge crew, report to stations."

Moments later, several officers streamed in to join Udos and Redelia, some of them shaking off the disorientation of sleep. Redelia quickly explained, "We have a transport about to depart the station that is carrying a new, unidentified sentient type carrying Uxa251."

"The transport has left its docking position and is setting a course," said Udos. "I would expect it to initialize a fold within the next few minutes."

Redelia processed her options. The *Belico*, originally designed to be a pirate-hunting ship, possessed trackers to affix to ships it wished to follow, but they were well out of range to use such a device on the transport. Every other option she considered ran into the same problem: exposing the Navy's presence to the Invaders. Right now that was out of the question.

The navigator let out a cry. Redelia looked up and immediately saw what had caused the commotion: something was moving on the viewscreen, something not far from the *Belico*. It was a small blur.

Another movement, from a different part of the screen. And another. At least three objects were on the move inside the gas giant's rings.

Redelia stood and stared at the screen. "What *are* they?"

"The rings make sensory data collection impossible," said Udos, "but they do not appear to detect us, either."

"Get me a clean visual. I want to know what they look like."

An image coalesced on the tridimensional viewscreen. It was small, dark, sleek, and flat, with a streaked dark purple hull. Redelia said, "It looks like an Invader craft."

"Could it be a patrol from the station?" the communications officer asked.

Udos sounded doubtful. "I have never seen a ship of that profile before. If it were a patrol, we would have sighted them around the station."

The navigator, Vidra Najik, pointed up at the screen. "It looks like they're moving in the direction of the station."

The weapons officer said, "Invader pirates?"

Redelia had wondered the same thing. She turned to the weapons officer and said, "There is only one way to find out. See if you can place a tracker on one of them."

"The interference will make it difficult."

"Try anyway. It may not matter, but I want to know what these things are and where they are going."

A slight rumble coursed the ship and a small tracker shot into space, weaving in and out of the debris as it chased one of the unidentified ships. Redelia watched anxiously as the tiny device quickly closed the distance between the *Belico* and its mark. The target was now very close to the edge of open space, and Redelia worried that if it cleared the debris, it might become visible to the small ships.

The tracker hit its target, impacting softly on the wing of the small ship. The Human weapons officer let out a quiet, victorious shout.

The three ships cleared the rings, where the *Belico's* relay probes could now perform detailed sensory analysis. The small vessels were Invader in design, similar to but slightly different from those in orbit around High Land. Their profile was more flat than the teardrop shapes of the larger Invader ships, suggesting that they, like interceptors, might also be capable of atmospheric flight.

And they were not alone. The three ships were soon joined by nine others, each emerging from different regions of the gas giant's rings. Redelia and her crew, observing through the *Belico*'s probes, watched as the twelve small ships, in nearly perfect timing, folded from just beyond the rings. Seconds later, they emerged from those folds nearly right on top of the transport. Because the folds were so short, the transport and other ships around the High Land station had only a few seconds of warning from the incoming fold distortions.

At once the twelve ships swarmed the transport, six of them latching onto different points across the larger ship's hull. A nearby Invader warship, which was escorting the transport, did not immediately attack the small ships.

"They must be afraid of hitting the transport," Redelia's weapons officer said.

The small ships, by contrast, had no such hesitations. Those not latched to the transport turned on the warship, raining purple bolts of hyperwave energy down from every direction. In the ensuing minute, both sides took heavy losses. The warship managed to disable two of the small ships and was on its way to doing so to a third, while the small ship attacks inflicted serious casualties and systemic damage to the warship.

Redelia pointed to a second High Land warship nearby, some distance from the first warship and the transport. "Why is that ship not moving to engage?"

"Any number of reasons," Redelia's weapons officer said. "It may not want to move away from protecting the station."

"Commander," said Udos, "several boarding parties appear to be moving from the small ships into the transport. Their physiology matches the profile of the Invaders on the transport. Preliminary evidence suggests that the boarding parties are now firing on those inside the transport."

Invaders were fighting other Invaders, and Redelia had no idea why. Her thoughts drifted to something else. "What about the unidentified sentients, the ones carrying Uxa251?"

"They are in the vicinity of some of the fighting. That is all I know."

On the display, a large fold distortion opened up in front of the transport. There was a collective gasp on the *Belico* bridge. If Invader technology was anything like its Confederal counterpart, blundering into a fold with multiple other ships attached to it could be catastrophic for all parties involved.

There was a flash, a bright purple spark of light from the front of the transport.

"Its hyperwave node just exploded," Udos reported. "I am reading heavy contamination to the forward compartments of the transport and a sharp decline in Invader life signs across the ship."

The transport pushed into its fold, the smaller ships still attached, and the fold closed and disappeared. The warship escort, left behind, continued to spar with two remaining attackers. "The warship's damage is serious enough," Udos reported, "it is probably not going anywhere anytime soon."

Redelia pulled up footage of the battle on her display. "I need to know where that transport went."

"I believe I have the answer." the weapons officer said. "One of the six ships attached to the transport was the one we placed the tracker on. It just dropped out of a fold farther out-system." He brought up a system map. "Commander, it's less than a billion kiltrics from the *Hattan*."

Redelia processed this information for a fraction of a second, then said, in a sharp voice, "Vidra, get us out of these rings as fast as you can."

• • •

On the bridge of the *Hattan*, Tir Bvaso was seated at the command station, reading over crew reports. It was already shaping up to be a difficult day. Earlier in the morning, there had been a heated altercation in the dining area between several Human and Hazionite officers that had required a full unit of security officers to break up. That made three such major incidents this week alone, to say nothing of the infamous *hutarl* competition brawl the week before, which Tir was still dealing with. Months of being ship-bound, combined with vast stretches of inactivity, were once again taking their toll. The captain was going to have to hold another round of ship-wide meetings.

Rami's voice interrupted her thoughts. "Commander, I'm receiving a transmission packet from the *Belico*."

That was unexpected. The interceptor was not due to send out an update for four more days. "Route it through to my display."

Tir studied the information in the packet for a minute, which included a brief, urgent message from Redelia. When the message ended, Tir began shouting orders to the stations around her.

• • •

Vetta said, "I have never understood this game."

Jared stood next to her, leaning against a bulkhead with his arms folded across his chest. They were on the sidelines of one of the *Hattan*'s larger open recreation areas. Before them, two opposing teams—each made up of Humans, Riticans, and Hazionites—were running back and forth across the open space, jockeying for control of a round ball that rolled along the floor.

"It's simple," said Jared. "Kick the ball into the net."

"It is a skill which has no application to any other context. It is not relevant to combat or even to daily survival activity."

"I beg to differ. It encourages tactical thinking, eases tension, and builds comradery."

"One game earlier this week almost led to a brawl."

Jared lifted a finger. "Almost," he pointed out. "They worked it out. That's an important distinction. How many officers are still in the brig from last week's *hutarl* competition?"

"Eight. Commander Bvaso would like them held over until next week." She looked at him. "You could hold them longer."

He straightened up, moving away from the bulkhead. "We don't have the luxury of keeping them in the brig for the rest of the mission, and I'd rather not execute good officers."

"There was another altercation in the dining area this morning."

Jared sighed. "I heard. Tir said she was going to speak with them after her shift was over."

Vetta leaned in and said, quietly, "I am not sure how much more of this idleness the crew can take. Even on a Ritican ship, this would be difficult."

Jared arched his eyebrow. "What do you want, an enemy attack?"

"No one does, but I fear the crew is beginning to forget who the enemy is."

At once alarms flooded the room. Combat stations. On the field, the players stopped, looking around in a moment of confusion.

Jared said to Vetta, "Be careful what you wish for," before rushing out the door.

• • •

The *Hattan* emerged from its in-system jump, staring down on the object of Redelia's message. "The vessel is approximately seven hundred trics long," said Aioua, "with bonded hull plating primarily composed of Pca112. It is seriously compromised. Its energy readings are erratic, biosigns are fading, and I am detecting pockets of hyperwave particles inside the ship."

Jared, sitting at the command station, looked at the technical information pouring in on his displays. Up ahead, on the main viewscreen, the Invader transport listed in space. It was sleek, with a nose like a dolphin and a stern like the bulbous end of a teardrop. The long hull was smooth, with streaks of gray stretching along the dark purple flanks of the ship.

"Do you think this was its intended destination?" he asked.

"I do not believe so. More likely it was aiming to fold out of the system, but something went wrong and it instead wound up here."

"Redelia said it was a transport of some sort, possibly a prison ship."

"I would agree. It contains substantial space for both cargo and sentients and is lightly armed. There is only one hyperwave node, located along the front quarter of the ship. The node appears to be badly damaged."

"Any sign of other ships in our area?"

"None, Captain."

Redelia's telemetry had indicated that the warship escorting the prison transport had been disabled, meaning it might not be able to initialize a fold for some time, perhaps hours, and it wasn't even clear the warship knew where the transport had gone. If the Navy hoped to learn anything, now was their opportunity.

Jared manipulated his station to show a close-up of the ship, moving it around in front of him. "Are there any points of entry?"

Aioua pored over the *Hattan*'s readings. "There are five locations that appear to be access points, but I do not know how their mechanisms operate. It is unlikely we will be able to manipulate them to open."

Jared knew the Exos could probably fix that. He said to Rami, "Deploy the boarding party and the *Shington*. When you are finished, send a message to the *Belico*. Order it to maintain its position in-system until instructed otherwise."

• • •

The large shuttle *Acebi* sailed out of the *Hattan*'s launch bay and glided toward the derelict transport. Close behind was the newly completed Navy interceptor *Shington* under the command of Lieutenant Brigg Drews, which had been ordered to escort the shuttle *Acebi* as it made its approach. On board the *Acebi* were ten sentients: a pilot, six security officers, two Exo engineers, and a medical officer. Vetta Quidd, one of the security officers, was the mission leader. Darel Weye was the medical officer. The six security officers—Vetta, three Riticans, and two Hazionites—were clad in durable Navy combat armor, while Darel wore an Aecron skinsuit. All seven were environmentally sealed.

The *Acebi* clamped onto one of the transport's probable entry portals, and the two Exos went to the task of cutting a way in. Despite the tough bonded hull, the two engineers had a working portal within a few minutes. Vetta ordered the two Exos to remain onboard the shuttle with the pilot unless called for.

The security team fanned out into the transport hallway adjacent to the *Acebi*, with Darel close behind. The atmosphere was cold and foreign; temperatures were hovering close to minus-eighty degrees Earth standard and the atmosphere was a concoction that included neither oxygen nor methane. Ultraviolet lighting fixtures curved along the walls of meandering circular hallways, and the walls and floors were smooth and seamless.

Vetta took the lead, her pulse pistol staring down the hallway. "Life signs?"

Darel consulted his sensor. "Microscopic life is abundant; we will need to decontaminate upon our return. There is, however, no sentient life on this part of the ship. There are several Invader life signs farther forward, but they are diminishing in number even as we speak."

"Are they dying?"

"Either that, or they are moving to a place where I cannot read them."

"What of the other life forms the *Belico* crew spoke of?"

"The Uxa251 readings are also farther forward, near where the Invaders are."

Darel sent his sensory information to Vetta and her team's combat visors, and within a few moments they all had a working model of the inner pathways of the ship, including the probable locations of the life forms. Their primary objective was to capture as much information as possible. They were also authorized to capture any life forms on the ship should the opportunity present itself, and a module had been affixed adjacent to the *Acebi* airlock specifically for that purpose.

Vetta ordered two of the security officers to stay behind and guard the shuttle, then led the remaining three, as well as Darel, down the meandering corridor. As the group pressed forward, the number of Invaders showing on Darel's sensor continued to drop.

• • •

Jared followed the security team's progress nervously from his place on the *Hattan*'s bridge. Vetta Quidd was one of the best in a situation like this, having demonstrated her abilities many times in the past, but he felt helpless. At that moment, he wished he were an interceptor commander again, where he could be in control of the situation rather than a bystander.

He heard a familiar walk-and-tap behind him, and turned to see Nho drawing near with his staff. Rete, who looked uncomfortable being on the bridge, was with him.

It was Nho who spoke. "I heard that Vetta and Darel had been sent into the Invader ship. I hope I am not an imposition."

"Not at all," said Jared, gesturing him over. "If you have any divine premonitions, I could use them."

Nho blinked. "From me? No, sadly. I'm simply curious to see who these people are."

"The Invaders?"

"I don't know if I like that word. They are the One's creations, just like we are."

"They wiped out an entire planet of Sarconians."

Nho shifted Sarco's staff over to his left hand. "I would not judge any Confederal race merely on the actions of a few or even their government. Why should we regard these people any differently? I've watched some of their communications, and I see sentients not unlike us. Foreign in their culture, yes, but not necessarily in an evil way."

"Aeroel's government would disagree."

"No disrespect, Captain, but I do not trust Aeroel's government. Right now none of us should."

Jared checked on Vetta's progress. Still moving, and through a part of the transport devoid of life. He said to Nho, "It's hard to be certain about anything regarding the Invaders until we understand their culture better. We barely understand what they mean when they say routine things."

Nho scoffed. "We *think* we do not understand, but that is only because we feel no certainty. It is possible their culture is not as unlike ours as we assume. Consider how much in common some of the cultures of the Confederacy had despite developing on independent worlds. Some of them may even hold the truth in them."

"Captain." It was Vetta's voice on his link, coming through from the Invader transport.

"Yes, Vetta. Go ahead."

"We have found two Invaders. They are alive."

• • •

Vetta looked down on the two dark, slick, tentacle-laden beings. Each of them was situated in restraints of some sort, and not for the purposes of the beings' protection. The two were in a small cell along the wall, one of numerous cells up and down this part of the ship. The other cells were also occupied, albeit with corpses. These two were the only living ones remaining in the entire wing.

"Astounding," mumbled Darel, watching the data pour in from his sensor. "Their physiology is far more complex than the *Belico*'s long-distance sensory data could adequately reveal. They have an inordinately intricate internal physiology that matches nothing I have seen before."

Vetta cast a wary look down the hallway. No signs of trouble yet. She looked back at Darel. "What is their condition?"

"About all I can tell you is that they are not dead," said Darel, "and I only know that because the dead melt into a chemical puddle. Beyond that, they could be healthy or dying and I would not know the difference."

"Were they exposed to the same hyperwave wash that killed the others?"

"For some reason, their cell barrier protected them better than the others before it failed. They have some exposure, not enough to be fatal to us. I do not know their tolerance for the hyperwaves, although, as we can see"—he looked around at the graveyard of nearby cells—"they do have their limits."

Ilva Forml, the Hazionite security officer, asked, "Can we communicate with them?"

"They do not possess anything that would pass as vocal cords, but they do seem to be organically broadcasting on some low-level wavelength. It might be an attempt to communicate."

Rami Del said, over Darel's link: "Aioua suggests using protocol four-twenty-one on your sensor."

Darel did so, and almost immediately a trickle of words lit up his portable.

"WHAT ARE YOU? / WHO ARE YOU? / (CONFUSION)"

Darel fed the translation matrix from his sensor to the rest of the security team. "We come in peace," he replied. "Who are you?"

This time his sensor modulated the words in an artificial voice across his link. "We are *fzzzttt* / We are harmed / (pain). What are you? / Who are you?"

Darel's large onyx eyes turned up to Vetta. "What should I tell them?"

"Tell them we are here to help them."

Darel repeated that to the Invaders. One of the Invaders replied, "We are harmed / We are failing / (anxiety)."

"Sir, there is motion coming from down the hallway," said one of the security officers, a Ritican male.

Darel turned his sensor that direction. "Uxa251, coming this way."

"Enforcers are coming / Harm is coming / (panic)," said one of the Invaders.

Two objects emerged from the far end of the corridor. They were floating low to the ground, less than a tric in the air. They were a deep black and geometrically complex. Their angular shapes seemed to rotate around and inside their center sections, spinning on various axes.

A spit of green, shaped like a ball of fire, discharged from one of the geometric objects. The green bolt collided directly into Ilva Forml, causing her combat armor to shatter.

The blast blew the other members of the team off their feet, the remaining four of them flying in different directions. Vetta crashed hard, first against the wall, then on the unyielding Invader floor, her pistol slipping from her hand and sliding along the floor. Across from her, Darel was face-down on the floor, his sensor next to him. Ilva Forml, the Hazionite officer, was face up farther down the hallway, badly disfigured and motionless. The other two security officers, both Riticans, were still off their feet, and at least one of them looked seriously injured.

A second bolt of green flame sliced down the hallway, striking Ilva's motionless body. Her form exploded in a mess of organic debris, the shockwave sending the rest of the Navy team sliding in different directions down the hallway.

Vetta's pistol, tossed about by the shockwave, skidded to a halt not far from her. Reaching with the opposable digits on her feet, she grabbed the pistol and fired. The pulse blasts flashed down the corridor, the first two shots missing but the third colliding with the attacker, knocking it off its axis and sending it momentarily to the ground.

The second geometric object fired a green bolt, and Vetta rolled away just as the fiery blast smashed into the area where she had just been lying. The explosion rattled the floor and kicked pieces of the wall into the air. Vetta retaliated with her pistol and was joined by Darel's handpulse and a pulse rifle from one of the Ritican security officers. The combined force of their pulse weapons chipped a section off of the second geometric object, which went spiraling into the wall and ricocheting onto the floor.

By now the first attacker had righted itself. The Ritican officer leveled his pulse rifle and fired just as the object did. The green bolt struck him dead-on, destroying his armor and sending him to the floor. The attacker, hit by the pulse, went bouncing off one of the walls.

Vetta scrambled to her feet, dropping her pistol and frantically drawing the ordnance-firing gibeon rifle off her back. Both of the hostile geometric objects moved into an upright position, sparkles of green forming along their centers. The gibeon rifle popped twice, and a moment later twin fireballs exploded right on top of the two attackers. The blast wave arrived a moment later, pushing Vetta nearly off her feet. She held her ground, the gibeon sighted down the hallway.

There was no need. As the smoke cleared, all that remained were scattered, charred chips of the two hostile sentients.

Vetta surveyed the carnage. The threat, at least for the moment, was over, but at great cost. Two of her officers, a Hazionite and a Ritican, were dead, and a third, another Ritican, lay dying, his combat armor cut open in several places from the shrapnel of the explosions. Darel looked bruised but was otherwise unharmed.

Darel got up and immediately made his way over to the dying Ritican, the security officer's armor hissing from the sound of leaking methane and body fluids oozing from various openings. Vetta hurried over, kneeling by Darel as he worked to save the other officer's life. "He has multiple internal and external injuries," said Darel, "and the pathogens on this ship are already attacking his internals. I do not know how to save him."

Vetta stood up and keyed her link. "Nolatrox, Centolox, make your way to our location immediately."

While Darel continued to work, Vetta ran over to the remains of the geometric attackers and scooped up some of their debris, placing it in a container located along her combat armor. Then, surveying the adjacent hallway to make sure it was safe, she backtracked over to Darel, holstering her rifle and scooping up her pistol from the ground. By now the two Exo engineers on the shuttle, Nolatrox and Centolox, had sped through the ship and were standing nearby.

Vetta pointed to the dying Ritican on the ground. "Nolatrox, get Deck Officer Borus back to the *Acebi* airlock immediately and affix him with a rebreather."

The Exo complied, hoisting the large-bodied Ritican male

quickly and easily. As it sped off back to the shuttle, Vetta moved up next to Darel. "Are you unharmed?"

He favored his arm but said, "I will be fine."

"What other sentient life remains on the ship?"

Darel consulted his sensor. "There are only a few left in other sections and they are not moving. I think they may be dying." He gestured to the two Invaders in the prison cell. "The two here do not appear any worse off than they were before the attack. They may be the only survivors at this point."

"I need to speak to them."

Darel manipulated his sensor. "Go ahead."

Vetta turned on the two Invaders, still confined to their cell, their tentacles wriggling rapidly. She spoke with deliberate precision. "We are going to free you from this cell. You will accompany us back to our ship. If you resist or attempt to harm us, we will kill you. Do you understand?"

The Invaders seemed to process that for a short time. Finally, one of them spoke. "We are being freed / We are following you / (understanding)."

"Correct. Will you attempt harm?"

"We will not harm / We are following you. We are peaceful / We are not enforcers."

Vetta took a step back, holding her pistol at the ready. "Centolox, free them."

• • •

The appointment of Lieutenant Brigg Drews to command of the Navy interceptor *Shington* was, in part, a product of circumstance. Redelia had initially recommended Eil Morichar, a savvy veteran with a decorated Naval career, for command of that ship. Eil, however, had contracted a resilient, recurrent Hazionite pathogen that had landed her on bedrest for two months. With a void to fill, the ship's senior staff had decided to hand off the command to Brigg, who had been Eil's understudy during the interceptor's field tests. The decision had rankled some of the interceptor commanders still awaiting their commands, but during a meeting held on the matter, Tir Bvaso had reminded the others that their time would come soon enough.

The son of Human merchant traders, Brigg had spent his entire life in space. He was easily the youngest of the interceptor commanders assigned to the *Hattan* battle group, but he was also regarded as one of the best, arguably better even than Redelia Aroo. Fearless and at times brash to the point of aggravating his subordinates, he also had an uncanny instinct for knowing exactly where his ship was supposed to be at any given moment.

His interceptor, the *Shington*, had been dispatched to escort and protect the shuttle *Acebi*, and now the *Shington* hung in a loose circular pattern around the Invader transport. The reports from the shuttle team had been grisly: two officers were dead and a third probably headed that way after a firefight with unknowns aboard the transport. The team had secured two live Invaders for their trouble and was nearly ready to disengage from the transport and return to the *Hattan*.

Brigg tapped his fingers restlessly on his chair. His instincts nagged at him, and not for reasons related to the shuttle. He was well aware that some two hours had passed since the *Hattan* had first arrived here. In his world, that seemed just the right amount of time for trouble to come folding in. He also distrusted the transport, which was practically a derelict but might still possess enough surprises to kill a few more officers before the day was done.

"I don't like it," he said aloud to no one in particular.

"So you've said fourteen times now," said the navigator. "You never like it."

"Not when things are taking a long time, a large enemy is right in front of you, and reinforcements are just a short fold away. If I had my way, we would torpedo that transport as soon as the shuttle is clear."

"The transport is completely disabled," said the sciences officer. "There are no Invader life signs beyond the two the shuttle crew has in custody."

Brigg shook his head vigorously. "I don't trust our sensory equipment with that bonded armor. Redelia's crew reported all sorts of problems getting through it."

"I know how to compensate for it, and I can assure you there is no one else alive in there."

"Run a deep scan of the transport bridge. Filter out the hyperwave residuals. Look for anything anomalous, even something that might otherwise just be background noise."

The Aecron started to object, then stopped. "Running a deep scan now. As expected, no signs of . . ." His voice trailed off.

"What?" snapped Brigg.

"An anomaly. Faint. One of them must . . . is it?"

"Now, not later."

The sciences officer pored over the data. "Something is moving at one of their bridge stations. It is wearing a barrier, possibly something to protect against hyperwave particles, although its life signs are fading."

"An Invader in some sort of protective gear."

"That is what I said."

"That wasn't a question." Brigg consulted his display. The shuttle *Acebi* had moved off and was about halfway back to the *Hattan*. He looked back at weapons. "Jenns, can our pulse cannons penetrate into that bridge?"

"Unlikely, sir."

"What about a torpedo?"

"Possibly, although we should probably contact—"

Brigg sprang out of his seat and made his way over to sciences. "Mulgara, bring us on a course away from the transport. Jenns, target the bridge with a rear torpedo and stand by for my order."

Brigg stood less than a tric from the sciences officer, his voice urgent. "If I was on my bridge dying and I only had time to do one thing, what might I try?"

"I—I—there is not much they *could* do, sir," stammered the Aecron. "The hyperwave node is not operational, the propulsion system is not functional, and their sensors are in such a state that they could not see to fire or navigate even if those systems were available."

"What about communication?"

"Their main transmitter is dormant."

"Wouldn't a ship like that have auxiliary ways to communicate?"

"I do not—well, wait, sir. Yes. There is something along the ventral flank, a . . . hold on." A pause. "Sir, I am reading a particle transmission. Very light, very faint, almost indistinguishable from the local background radiation, but something."

"Where is the transmission directed?"

The Aecron gave the equivalent of a gasp. "In-system, toward the High Land station."

Brigg nearly ran back to his seat. "Jenns, are all Navy elements clear from the target?"

"Yes, sir."

"Fire that torpedo!"

The bridge rumbled as a fusing torpedo shot out from behind the interceptor, crashing into the transport in a brilliant explosion that obliterated the bridge of the Invader ship.

• • •

"Rami."

Jared's voice was cold with anger. Inside he was confused and livid. Right before his eyes, the interceptor *Shington* had, without orders to do so, fired on and blown off a sizeable piece of the Invader transport, including the bridge and part of the front quarter paneling. Jared now regarded his communications officer with controlled fury, distantly aware that it might have been less controlled had he been talking to someone other than Rami.

Nevertheless, Rami would know exactly what was packaged in the icy, singular use of her name. She immediately contacted the *Shington* and ordered Lieutenant Drews to explain his actions.

Brigg Drews's face appeared on Jared's display. "Captain, the Invader transport was sending a low-power distress signal back to the High Land station. We traced the signal to a surviving Invader on the transport bridge. I recommend we withdraw from the area immediately."

Jared corralled his anger as best he could. This is what came with appointing the young man commander over an interceptor. For now, he accepted the wisdom of the younger officer's brazen, but not baseless, actions. There would be time later for discussion.

"Instruct your navigator to make for the rally point immediately," Jared said. "I'll give you further orders once we all arrive."

"Yes, Captain." The display winked out.

"Rami, send a message to the *Belico* ordering them to meet us at the rally point as soon as possible. Kilvin, get us out of here as soon as the *Acebi* is secured."

• • •

Slightly more than ten minutes later, two Invader warships descended upon the area of space where the prison transport had sent its distress signal. For just a moment, the warships detected two folds, one large and one small, each housing ships that did not match any in their ship records. Then, just as quickly, the folds closed and the two ships were gone. Left behind for the warships to examine was a large derelict prison ship, its bridge blown to pieces.

10

If the bridge were a Navy ship's mind, and the dining area its stomach, the commons was its heart. One-part social nexus and one-part mental haven, the spacious room offered respite from the stresses of Navy life. The ship's counseling department often carried on its work there, as did Nho and Rete, but it also played host to a variety of festivals, traditions, and other noteworthy occasions.

The area was far from joyous today. As first officer Tir Bvaso approached the commons, she smelled a grief so sharp and disheartening that she had to will herself to proceed.

At the front of the large room, a small casing housed the scant remains of Ilva Forml, the Hazionite female security officer who had died during the incursion on the Invader transport. Surrounding the casing were perhaps twenty Hazionite females of various statures. On Hazion Prime, the death ritual would consist only of near relatives. As this was not possible in space, all of the Forml tribe in the crew, most of them quite distant in relation, saw it as their duty to take part.

Sitting behind the women were a ring of Hazionite men, dressed in black. Tir knew most of them were part of the ship's counseling department, but that was only part of the reason for their participation. Like the women, men from the Forml tribe came together to serve out the role men had in the mourning ritual—that of servants and caregivers. It was a strange role for the males, stationed on a more egalitarian Navy ship far from the matriarchal world of Hazion Prime.

Yet they do, and willingly, Tir thought.

Rete Sorte, standing a few paces inside the door, noticed her. He walked across the threshold out to the hallway and spoke, his voice a whisper. "Do you need anything, Commander?"

"No. I wanted to come down for a moment to offer my scent to the family." One way to pay respects to the family of the deceased was to approach in silence, allowing one's emotions to drift into the room. It was Tir's understanding that such a show of emotional solidarity was popular among the Forml tribe.

Tir closed her eyes and let the emotions of the room flow over her. It was uncomfortable, but she knew the value of her presence to those in the room, male and female alike, was worth the effort.

"What's it like?"

She opened her eyes. It was Rete again. She looked at him. "What are you referring to, exactly?"

"For the women," he said with a light gesture toward the room. "I've always wondered what it is like to be in that state."

"You lived on Hazion Prime long enough to know that is a private issue."

Rete backed away, and Tir could smell a sharp embarrassment. "Forgive my forwardness. As transparent as Navy officers are, I thought it might be more acceptable to ask here."

"Generally speaking, no."

Rete offered a contrite nod and retreated to where he originally stood, just inside the door.

Tir looked back toward the ritual. The smell of sadness brought memories of her last funeral. It was an aunt, her mother's sister. The aunt had died suddenly, and Tir and her entire family had traveled halfway across the Bvaso region for the ceremony. That day, she sat down for the ritual and promptly fell catatonic. When she finally awoke, a full week had passed.

Tir stepped across the threshold and into the commons where Rete was standing. He looked up at her as she approached. "It is hard to describe," she said in a whisper. "You are not fully conscious. In many ways it is like Human or Hazionite sleeping, for you have visions of times past spent with the person. But at the same time, you remain aware that you are sitting next to that person's body. We stay that way until our body releases us to consciousness."

Rete thought for a moment. "What happens if you are disturbed before your body wakes naturally?"

"While we are in the state, it is difficult to be stirred," Tir said, "but it is possible. I have not personally experienced it, but I am told it is very traumatizing on the individual. For that reason, it is done only when the lives of those in the ritual are in imminent danger. Because our treehomes are relatively safe, this does not happen often."

Rete looked back and forth between Tir and the funeral gathering. "I'll make sure it doesn't happen here, either."

"That is part of the reason I told you," she said, then turned and left.

• • •

Not long after, Tir emerged from a lift onto the main bridge deck and began the long walk down the ship's central artery. There was a small but steady flow of traffic going each direction, and the smells of their various states of mind drifted in and out of her perception as they walked past. Coping with emotion perception for Hazionites was no different than the challenges other species dealt with regarding their own senses. Managing the influx of feelings was part of being a Hazionite, although most Hazionites were happiest in crowds that were smaller rather than larger. On Hazion Prime, Hazionites tended to live in distant treehomes, commuting to the urban centers only when necessary.

A familiar wave of feeling drifted into Tir's olfactory awareness. It was coming from her left, and it was equal parts fatigue and seriousness. The nuance of it was so well known to her that she didn't even have to look. Sciences officer Aioua Horae was walking alongside her.

Tir and Aioua shared a bond of friendship forged in the darkest days of Malum. The two females—one an Aecron sciences officer from a battle carrier, the other a Hazionite first officer from a cruiser—had formed a tacit alliance in the bowels of that evil planet, looking out for one another even as despair and occasional violence swirled around them. The bond had been life-changing for both of them, a sisterhood that no one other than the two of them would ever be able to fully appreciate.

What Tir had never said—but she knew Aioua must be intelligent enough to realize—is how the Aecron mutiny above Ramas-Eduj had nearly shattered her. In those moments, Tir had faced bitter uncertainty, wondering if her closest friend would be her assassin. When Aioua, a Sarconian, had saved her life instead of taken it, the clashing tides of emotion had shaken Tir to her very foundation. Even now she struggled to resolve her own skepticism of Sarconianism with what she had seen and what her good friend believed. Aioua, respectfully, did not press the issue.

Tir and Aioua stepped onto the bridge, then back into the conference room, which was filled nearly to capacity and humming with conversation. At the end of the table, Captain Carter silently reviewed information on a display.

Jared looked up and gave a brief nod as Tir took a seat next to him. Then he looked out at the rest of the room.

"Now that everyone is here, we can begin."

The room went quiet.

Jared rubbed his eyes absently. "I know you're all anxious to talk about our new guests, but before we do, I understand that medical has some preliminary information on our Uxa251 attackers."

Mollo Nairu, the Aecron medical officer, projected a still image from the Navy's incursion inside the prison transport. At the center of the image were the two geometric hostiles that had killed three members of Vetta's team. Tir could smell a spike in anger in the room, most strongly from the corner where Vetta sat.

"This sentient," Mollo explained, "is what one of our guests called 'enforcers.'"

Tir looked at Mollo. "Sentient? It looks like a machination. Are you saying it is living?"

"We believe so. It bears a distant chemical resemblance to certain nonsentient silicon-based life found in the Confederacy, although its internal organ structure has no analogue in our records."

"What about its surface?" Vetta asked, her calm voice belying the waves of anger flowing into Tir's nose. "Uxa251 is not organic."

Aioua Horae, sitting next to Mollo, said, "The Uxa251 may be one of the components of a protective coat, like armor. Their weapons are also nonorganic. They seem to operate on some sort of power cell that is distinct from the sentient itself."

"What else have you learned about them?" asked Jared.

"Not a great deal as of yet," admitted Mollo. "Darel's sensor had some difficulty collecting data on them. Our two guests, as you know, are another matter."

Mollo keyed a display and up came floating, tridimensional images of dark, gelatinous aliens surrounded by flowing tentacles. "These are the two Invaders in our isolation tank. At one point, we were not sure they would survive, given their state when we found them, and we were very concerned about inadvertently killing them while trying to help. Fortunately, they have some distant biological analogues in the Confederal databases. Combining that information with what we observed directly has enabled us—if nothing else—to do no harm. Their atmosphere is complex, as is their food supply. It is rather technical to explain here."

"I'll look at the report later," Jared said. Tir wasn't skilled enough to smell outright lies, but she knew the captain well enough to know he wasn't telling the truth. Few things interested Jared Carter less than discourses on chemistry.

One of the psychology officers, a Hazionite male, asked, "What about gender?"

"That is one of many mysteries we have yet to solve," Mollo said. "We have no idea how they reproduce or what constitutes gender in their society. We do not think they are asexual, but beyond that we do not know. We might benefit from having a larger cross-section of them to observe."

"We have asked," Orel added, "but the answers are confused. We're not sure they know exactly what we are talking about."

Jared looked at Orel. "Let's explore your conversations with them, then."

Orel gestured to the affirmative. "They go by the names Au'p and S'li. A foundational, and perhaps most fundamental, shift in our understanding has been the name we use to define their race. We call them Invaders; they, of course, do not. In fact, Au'p reacted in a way that strongly resembled indignation when one of my officers called them by that name. It—as Mollo already said, we know little about gender—stated emphatically that its species was not one of conquest, although it did admit that some individuals in their society were. The word Au'p used in self-description has no translation in Confederal common that we know of, but when modulated into our auditory range sounds roughly like 'Plury'be.' In conversations they talk of 'Us of Plury'be' or, in the case of their High Land captors, 'Those of Plury'be.'"

Jared scrolled through some information on his portable. "Your initial reports indicate that they have been cooperative in answering your questions."

"It would seem so, although some caveats are in order. One, there are elements of their language we have had some difficulty translating. This may indicate the lexicon from Aeroel is incomplete, or it may be the product of linguistic drift—their language may simply have changed over time, as many Confederal languages have. Two, there is always the possibility of prevarication, exaggeration, or some other misrepresentation."

Vetta asked, "How likely is it that they are lying?" Vetta's smell of anger had abated somewhat, but Tir could still smell what she might describe as a simmer.

Orel said, "That is a discussion we have nearly every day. We have no firm way of verifying what they say, but we do know this:

everything they say fits. It resonates with all the communications we intercepted back at High Land, and their stories are internally consistent."

Orel looked at Rami, who spoke next. "They may be trying to earn our trust. They have asked us if we understand what they are saying, as if they want to make sure they are being heard correctly. And when we explained to them the Invasion of 1124, they not only knew what it was, but they seemed to realize that our distrust stemmed from it."

Jared's eyes narrowed. "What do they know about the Invasion?"

"Only that some of the Plury'be factions attacked another society on the other side of the 'Place Beyond' and were defeated. They emphasize that they aren't experts on the history of that event."

"You mentioned factions of these . . . Plyru'be," Tir said.

"Plue-RYE-bee," Orel corrected.

"Plury'be," repeated Tir. "What are these factions, exactly?"

"That remains difficult to discern. To the best of our understanding, they are a society essentially governed by factions of power that have territorial control in various parts of the region. The factions all seem to have different beliefs, different aims, and complicated relationships with one another. Some coexist in a sort of collusion of power, while others are openly hostile toward all factions. We are still unclear on the motivations and dynamics of the various relationships. Some of us theorize that religious elements may be behind those dynamics."

Jared folded his arms across his chest. "Has anyone spoken to Nho about this yet?"

"Not yet," said Rami. "We wanted to learn more first. We also are aware . . . well . . ."

"That once Nho hears religion might be involved, he may not leave the isolation unit," finished Orel.

There were a few laughs in the room, and Tir could smell a lightening of the emotions around her. Next to her, she saw Jared smiling in spite of himself.

Orel continued. "Bear in mind that the religious supposition is still only theory. What is clear is that these two Plury'be come from one of the less popular factions. Somehow they antagonized one of the larger ones, which led to the situation we found them in."

Jared glanced over his portable. "Your last report said you were going to broach Malum with them."

Rami's voice softened. "When we showed them images of it, they became agitated. We were initially concerned we'd made a terrible mistake. They wouldn't talk for a long time after that, and when they finally did, it was with what the translation matrix described as contempt."

"They did not express understanding of the name Malum," Orel added. "They call the planet-ship a 'regulator.' Unfortunately, they don't appear to know much about how it works or what it does, but they did mention its creator—a name we believe is Dar."

Tir saw uncomfortable looks around the room and felt a corresponding rise in anxiety, including from herself. When all of them were trapped inside Malum, its cloud warden had repeatedly told them that Dar was now their master.

Jared took a deep breath and said, "Is Dar an Invader, a . . . Plury'be?"

Another exchange of looks between Rami and Orel. "We do not think so," Rami said. "We think Dar leads a neighboring empire that exerts great influence over the Plury'be, but we are not yet sure how strong that influence is. We're still weighing how to continue that line of questions, given how agitated they became earlier."

"I assume they also have questions for you," Tir said.

Rami nodded. "They've asked where we come from and what our intentions are. We've answered some of their questions, but we've been careful about how much we tell them. There is one question we haven't been able to answer, though. They want to know if we will be taking them home."

The word *home* brought out a wave of sentimental emotions from all around Tir. She suppressed the image of her husband-mate forming in her mind and said, "And where is 'home,' exactly?"

"According to them," said Orel, "their faction resides on a planet called Free Town. We believe that the Plury'be called S'li has some knowledge of navigation. Kilvin is working with S'li to create a common cartological understanding. He believes he is close to finding the world."

Tir glanced at Jared, then back to Orel. "Let us assume that we can learn the location of that planet. What would we do with that information?"

"These two appear to be part of a faction opposed to Dar," Vetta said. "Allies on this side of the Void would be a valuable asset."

"True," Jared said, "if they are telling the truth."

Tir's muscle core tightened involuntarily, even before the smells of distrust and suspicion drifted from the room into her olfactory system. She wasn't the only one who was skeptical.

• • •

"Here it is."

Navigator Kilvin Wrsaw manipulated the cluster of stars on the bridge's tridimensional display. A blue icon indicated the *Hattan*, while a yellow one identified a solitary star a fair distance away. "If S'li and I understood each other correctly, that star is the location Au'p calls E'reb."

E'reb was the modulated sound; according to Orel it translated as Free Town. Jared asked, "How long from here?"

"No more than a few days."

"So what are we going to do?" That question came from Tir, who was standing next to them.

Jared thought back to the words Au'p and S'li had uttered, repeatedly, to Orel:

"Free Town is our home / Free Town opposes Dar. Free Town can help you learn more about Dar / Free Town can help you fight Dar / (certainty)."

Jared rocked back on his heels, staring up at the floating map. "Let's presume for a moment that we don't go to this planet. What other options do we have?"

"Return to High Land," Tir said, "scout other systems on this side of the Void, or return to the Confederacy."

Jared shook his head. "None of those are good options. Returning to High Land is too dangerous now, and we've already spent a month there as it is. It's hard to know if we'd learn anything new. I also don't like just blindly following Plury'be transmissions from system to system."

"Returning to the Confederacy does not seem right to me, sir," said Kilvin. "Not with what little we know."

"It doesn't seem right to me, either," Jared agreed. "We're here to learn about Malum and its creators, and we haven't made much progress there yet."

"There is something else to consider," Tir said. "Seven months ago a fleet of Aecron ships tried to destroy us. Even if their actions were not sanctioned by the government, the Aecron delegates in Congress will do all they can to make sure no expedition like this happens again."

Or try to kill us again, Jared thought. "That means that if we want to learn about Dar and how to stop him, we have this one opportunity to do it." He gestured at the star map. "That brings us back to Free Town."

"It is the only option we have right now," Tir said. "That is our way forward."

Jared took a deep breath. "Forward it is, then."

11

Palace Imperial

"Master."

"Messenger."

"I bring important news from our Plury'be allies."

"Speak of it."

"There has been an attack near station High Land. A Plury'be transport ship departing the station was raided by another Plury'be faction. They penetrated the ship during its Exit. The transport lost control and Exited farther out in the system. When it was recovered four and one *nol* hence, all Plury'be on board were dead. Raiders and crew both dead."

"Speak of the transport contents."

"Harvests from High Land planet, supplies seized from faction designate No Greater, and No Greater prisoners."

"Speak of the Domain presence on the transport."

"One and one enforcers, Master."

"Speak of the enforcers' report."

"There is no report. The enforcers were destroyed."

A pause. "Explain."

"It is not clear. Internal ship records were sabotaged by No Greater, but another was also involved. Confederacy."

"Speak of evidence."

"Enforcers were destroyed by non-Plury'be weapons. Concussive packets, Aecron design, but also used by Confederacy combined forces. Command center of transport also destroyed, hit by projectile of Human design but also used by Confederacy combined forces. Plury'be warships entering later observed one and one ships on Exit, one large, one small. Large ship matches description of Confederacy ship-designate *Hattan*, which was disabled by Regulator-Malum forty and seventy and one *bonanol* antecedent. Small ship matches profile of Confederacy combined forces ship-designate interceptor design."

"Speak of what was taken by Confederacy combined forces."

"No cargo taken, two No Greater prisoners unaccounted for and presumed taken. One No Greater designate Au'p, profession rebel speaker. Other No Greater designate S'li, profession star runner. Speak of your orders, Master."

"Confederacy combined forces will join with rebels in probability. Kol confirms this. Plury'be of Kol will organize according to instructions from me. Regulators will deploy according to instructions from me. Confederacy will be forced to draw in with rebels so both may be destroyed together. So I have spoken."

"So you have spoken."

"That their bodies are free is only a soon-passing truth. Their souls already belong to me."

12

Jared stepped into the atrium adjoining the isolation tank. The tank was a large enclosure sealed off from the rest of the ship, and it could be flooded with any manner of atmospheres. They were standard on larger Navy capital ships and were used most often to confine pirates whose physiologies could not handle a standard Navy oxygen atmosphere or its accompanying gravity.

Trailing immediately behind Jared were Nho and Rete. True to form, Nho had immediately sought an audience with the two aliens once he had learned of the possible religious elements within Plury'be culture.

Nho walked up to the sciences officer on duty, who was busy at a workstation, and asked, "What are they doing?"

The sciences officer, a male Aecron, did not look up as he spoke. "They are eating."

"What do they eat?"

"It would take longer to explain than I have time for."

"How do I speak with them?"

"That is the work of the communications staff, not you."

Jared spoke. "Deck Officer."

The Aecron started at Jared's voice, looking up and realizing for the first time that the ship's captain was present. "Sir, I did not see you."

"I realize that. These two men are here to speak with the Plury'be. Please assist them."

The sciences officer pointed to a panel near the window. "Communications are all handled on the panel. The latest translation matrix was uploaded just this morning. Do you need assistance with it?"

"I don't think so," said Jared, "but I will let you know."

Jared stepped forward to the window. Inside the tank, viewable through a large, reinforced transparent window, the two Plury'be were pulling odd piles of a dark substance underneath their cylindrical bodies.

He manipulated the panel, which signaled that communication was now on inside the tank. "Au'p. S'li. This is Captain Jared Carter."

The panel and accompanying ship-generated voice translated the signals of communication emanating from the Plury'be. "Greetings Ship Master / Greetings Jared Carter," Au'p said.

Jared was tempted to apologize for intruding on their meal, but he caught himself. He had been told that the Plury'be did not perceive interruptions the way some races did; any time was a good time to talk, as far as these two were concerned. "How is the food?" he asked instead.

"It has improved / It does not make me sick," said S'li.

"It has improved / It could still use *spppzzttt* / (hopeful)," said Au'p.

Whatever Au'p had prescribed as an improvement to their food was lost in translation. "I will have our sciences officers look into it," said Jared. "I have brought two new people to speak with you. Their names are Nho and Rete."

"You are Nho and Rete / I am Au'p," said Au'p.

"You are Nho and Rete / I am S'li," said S'li.

Jared muted the conversation. "Their speech can be a little disorienting," he said. "I recommend you read the panel as well as listen as they talk. It will help you better understand their language structure. If you have clarifying questions, ask them. They do not take offense to seeking clarity."

Nho and Rete nodded.

Jared unmuted the conversation and gestured for the two men to speak. Nho stepped up to the window. "I am Nho."

Rete followed suit. "I am Rete."

"What is your role? / What is your function?" Au'p asked.

"We are . . . our function on the ship is different than others," said Nho. "Our work is to help the crew with their problems."

"I do not understand / What problems? / (confusion)," Au'p said.

"We help make sure there is not conflict between the members of the crew," Rete said. "If there is a disagreement, for example, we help them resolve that difference. We encourage the crew to talk and to repair disagreement."

"You create peace on the ship / You create order on the ship," S'li said.

"Yes," said Rete. "We create peace through communication."

"S'li is a ship runner / I create peace through communication," Au'p said.

"Ship runner?" Nho asked.

One of the communications officers sitting nearby, a Hazionite male, explained. "It is their word for a pilot or navigator."

Nho nodded and turned back to the Plury'be. "We came to ask about your culture. I wanted to ask you about your ... your belief system, your religious system."

"I do not understand belief system / I do not understand religious system / (confusion)," said S'li.

"S'li does not understand / I do not understand / (confusion)," said Au'p.

Nho tried again. "I wanted to ask about . . . let's see, how should I ask this? Do you have a deity or a god?"

The reply was a jumble of unintelligible phrases and implications of confusion.

"We have tried this line of questioning," the communications officer said. "We have not made much headway. Their factions seem to hinge around philosophical differences, and the phrasing suggests something religious to them, but they do not seem to understand our way of saying it."

"Let me try," Rete said. "Au'p, S'li, who created you?"

"We come from the nesting / The nesting produces Us of Plury'be," said Au'p. S'li signaled agreement.

"The nesting appears to be their term for family that produces offspring," the Aecron sciences officer said.

Rete continued. "When there was no nesting, who created the Plury'be? Who created the first of the Plury'be?"

"That Which There Is No Greater created the first / That Which There Is No Greater was the first," said Au'p.

Rete leaned forward, placing his hands against the tank's outer wall as if he sensed he was close to finding something. "Who is That Which There Is No Greater?"

"That Which There Is No Greater is the origin of Us of the Plury'be / That Which There Is No Greater is the origin of Them of the Plury'be. That Which There Is No Greater is the beginning of everything / That Which There Is No Greater is at the end of everything. That Which There Is No Greater watches over all / That Which There Is No Greater commands over all . . ."

Au'p continued, unimpeded, for close to ten minutes.

At some point during its exposition, Jared realized, suddenly and for the first time, Rete's value to Nho. Nho was a bright, earnest man and a devoted follower of Sarco, and he was the man whose faith had saved them all. But Rete possessed a skill with words that Nho did not. Rete was a communicator. What he lacked in Nho's ability to connect with people, he made up for in his ability to articulate ideas. It was Rete, not Nho (and not anyone else on the ship), who had known just what question to ask to open the floodgates of knowledge.

Au'p's explanation finally subsided and S'li had nothing to add.

Rete asked, "Has That Which There Is No Greater ever interacted with the Plury'be?"

That set off another monologue, this one lasting close to a half hour. Au'p told tens of stories, using names and terms that were wholly foreign to everyone in the room. Even the communications staff who had been working with the two aliens from the beginning had almost no idea what Au'p was talking about.

• • •

On the bridge, Tir Bvaso was wrapping up her shift as the watch officer. She was tired, and her mind was full of thoughts about their impending arrival at the Plury'be planet of Free Town.

Footsteps approached from her right. Aioua Horae, fresh on the bridge to begin her shift at sciences, walked up to her. "Commander," said Aioua, with slightly overstated formality.

"Lieutenant," said Tir.

Aioua stared at her for a long moment. "You look worried."

"We are headed toward an Invader planet to make intentional contact," mumbled Tir. "Tell me why I should not be worried."

"Because if we can survive Malum, I believe that same force can get us through Free Town."

As Tir searched for a response, one of her command displays lit up. It was a message from the captain, who was due to relieve Tir on the bridge in a few minutes. The message read:

Summon a watch officer to the bridge to cover me. I am down with the Plury'be. They won't stop talking.

• • •

In the atrium outside the isolation tank, the initial excitement of progress had given way to a more settled atmosphere of quiet observation. Jared was anxious to leave and report to the bridge to start his shift, but he was afraid of leaving. Nho would not soon forgive him if his departure somehow derailed Au'p's explications.

Au'p finished talking. Nho looked at Rete as if to say, *what will you ask now?* Rete looked to the aliens and offered the next question. "Has That Which There Is No Greater ever taken the form of a Plury'be?"

"That Which There Is No Greater came as the Seed Vessel / That Which There Is No Greater came as Ah'ey / (excitement)."

Nho leaned forward excitedly in his chair, unsure whether he wanted to sit or stand. "Tell us about Ah'ey," the old cleric said.

Here it comes, Jared thought. He then realized, too late, that he should have left the room during the brief pause in the Plury'be's explanation. *And I am going to hear all of it, whether I want to or not.*

Two more hours passed before Au'p finished talking.

13

"Stay calm, everyone," Jared said. His own heart, beating furiously, ignored him.

In the far distance, on the viewscreen, was the terminus of their fold. Beyond the fold was the planet that S'li said was E'reb, Free Town, a planet devoted to That Which There Is No Greater and Its Seed Vessel, Ah'ey. Nearly three days later, the communications and xenosociology departments were still arguing over what Au'p had been talking about. Nho, of course, had come away convinced that what Au'p spoke of was the Creator and His Incarnate.

The discussion was far from academic. If the Plury'be of Au'p and S'li were adherents to a theology like Nho's, the prospects of peaceable interaction would seem to be improved. From there, the potential for cooperation, even alliance, would also seem more plausible. That was not to say that the absence of such a religious connection would be fatal, but common beliefs would seem a potential point of contact.

Or maybe not, Rete warned. Not all of the Incarnate followers in the Confederacy bought into the idea that the Incarnate of other worlds was the same as their own. Some in the theistic cults of Earth rejected the idea that Sarco was one and the same as their Incarnate, and the reclusive Forger-Defenders of Ritica had no interest in interacting with the Sarconians, much less the few Dsori Barjak disciples left on the Hazionite worlds.

The Plury'be followers of That Which There Is No Greater might not accept that Sarco or Dsori Barjak or the Exo's Greater Task Master was the Confederacy's version of their Seed Vessel. If, at worst, they judged Sarconian beliefs as a heresy, it could turn Au'p's friends into the Navy's enemies.

That meant that, for now, the *Hattan*'s best point of contact with Free Town was a desire for peaceable interaction and a desire to oppose Dar, whom Au'p had made abundantly clear was also opposed by the Free Town leadership. It was a start.

"Ten seconds to fold exit," said Kilvin.

Jared sat in silence, waiting for the final moments to tick away. Presently, the fold's tendrils dissipated, giving way to open space.

A sequence of warnings cascaded throughout the bridge. One of the main tridimensional displays showed the *Hattan* flanked by a trio of large, menacing-looking ships. They were teardrop-shaped, with dark indigo hulls. Each of the large vessels possessed multiple hyperwave nodes, which even now glowed an ominous purple. The ships were prepared to fire.

"Three contacts in our immediate vicinity," said Aioua Horae, her sensory readings echoing the display. "They are comparable in size and strength to the warships we saw near the High Land station. Initial calculations place them at the equivalent of cruiser-level ships. I am also reading smaller craft farther off, identical in design to the ones we found attached to the prison transport."

"Now, Orel," Jared said.

Everything about this scenario had been carefully planned. They would fold in from a sufficient distance so their endpoint distortion would be visible for some time before their arrival. Such a lengthy fold would eliminate any element of surprise on the *Hattan*'s part, but surprise was the last thing Jared wanted. By giving Free Town advance warning, the *Hattan* was sending the message that it was not a threat. Moreover, the Navy cruiser's alien design would give the *Hattan* at least a few moments to make friendly overtures while the local forces tried to figure out just who or what they were.

Orel Dayail transmitted the message. It was in Plury'be language, announcing that they were peaceful visitors from the Place Beyond and that they had arrived at the counsel of Au'p and S'li to meet and discuss the possibility of an alliance against Dar. The message concluded with an offer to send down a small ship to meet with and talk to the Free Town leadership.

The message was sent. The *Hattan* now waited.

• • •

A few hours later, three interceptors emerged from the *Hattan*'s cargo bay. The *Belico* was at the lead under the command of Redelia Aroo. Just behind were the *Shington* and the *Ratha* under the command of Brigg Drews and Eil Morichar, respectively. The *Belico* proceeded onward, past the Plury'be cruisers and toward a waiting sortie of small craft. The *Shington* and *Ratha* took up patrol maneuvers around the *Hattan*, which remained in space out of orbit from the planet.

In the *Belico*'s cargo area, Au'p and S'li waited in a temporary holding tank. A small army of officers attended to the two Plury'be: a sciences officer, a medical officer, communications officer Orel Dayail, and four security officers, including Vetta Quidd.

On the *Belico*'s bridge, Jared, Nho, and Rete stood along the back wall as Redelia and her crew did their work. The looming planet, a near-complete swirl of grey clouds, dominated the interceptor bridge's primary bidimensional viewscreen. Cutting in and out of the view were a small fleet of Plury'be ships identical in design to those found attached to the prison ship.

"They look comparable to interceptors," Jared observed.

Udos Beyole, the Aecron sciences officer, said, "I would not want to face one, especially in close quarters."

"That's a lot more than one," said the navigator, Vidra Najik.

The swarm of Plury'be "flatboats," as some of the Human officers had taken to calling them, coalesced into a synchronized formation, bracketing the *Belico* on all sides. They were being funneled into a narrow approach vector.

Redelia turned slightly to sciences. "Planetary analysis?"

"It is an active world. Well over ninety percent of the planet is subject to precipitation at any one time and there is evidence of regular tectonic activity. Surface temperature at our target point is minus-sixty-four standard degrees. Atmosphere is similar to that seen on Plury'be ships. I can give you a full accounting of all the compounds if you wish."

Redelia looked over her shoulder. "Only if the Captain is interested."

Jared blinked, then stiffened. "No, no need to on my account."

"That was a joke, sir."

Of course. She was ribbing him over his loathing of chemistry. He took a deep breath and tried to relax. He was anxious—they all were—and Redelia was trying to break up the tension with levity. "I'll remember that the next time you try to requisition a stock of collider torpedoes."

A smile played across her face as she turned back to the viewscreen.

Their approach shortly brought them into contact with the planet's atmosphere. An eerie rattle spread across the bridge as the winds of Free Town buffeted against the interceptor's defense fields. At their speed, the clouds surged up to meet them, a momentary fog filling the viewscreen. Then the clouds cleared and the *Belico* could see the ground.

It was a bleak world. Ceaseless rain bore down, creating a brown, muddy mess of a surface. The cloud cover created a world of perpetual dusk, a land of gloom and foreboding in all directions. It was the sort of planet Human explorers would catalog and get off of as soon as possible.

The Plury'be flatboats leveled out and took a course to the magnetic north, skimming over the endless plains of mud. Most of the planet looked uninhabited, and Udos confirmed that there were only a few small pockets of life, the largest being the point they were headed to. This was less than a colony world; it was an outpost. That meant that either Au'p and S'li's faction had their main population elsewhere, or their faction was a very small one. It was too early to tell which.

The flatboat escort slowed as they approached the settlement. The flatboats guided the *Belico* to a raised landing platform which floated just above the muck, its circular black surface a contrast to the brown beneath. Vidra put the ship down on the platform, where it landed with a gentle thud. The ceiling of the interceptor roared dully at the sound of the persistent rains coming down.

Jared headed for the bridge exit. "Keep the engines warm."

"We will," Redelia said. Her voice grew quiet and serious. "Be careful out there."

Jared, Nho, and Rete took the lift down to the cargo bay, where other members of the landing party were already donning environmental suits. Jared and the two Sarco followers did the same, pulling on the requisite headgear and bodysuits to withstand the frigid, toxic world just beyond the airlock.

A few minutes later, the landing team descended from the airlock, led by the security team. At Jared's orders, Vetta and her unit were armed only with pulse pistols. They did not want to go unarmed, but felt the smaller weapons might appear less threatening to the Plury'be. The rain poured hard and loud, the amber-colored precipitation splashing everywhere before running in rivulets off the landing pad and down into the ground. It defied conventional wisdom how it could rain so constantly and the world not be an ocean.

Jared walked next to Vetta, who gestured discreetly ahead. There, near the edge of the landing pad, tens of Plury'be gathered in a broad a half-circle. The Plury'be's tentacles flowed among one another; Jared had the odd thought that they looked like analogues to Humans standing side-by-side, arms around each others' waists as if in a show of solidarity.

Floating just above the Plury'be were a sortie of glowing purple spheres. From this distance they looked to be the size of Human watermelons. Udos had pointed them out before Jared and the others disembarked, identifying them as floating hyperwave drones. At present they were not advancing on the crew, which Jared took to mean that they were intended as a defensive precaution.

Jared looked back just in time to see the airlock open again. Presently Au'p and S'li were on their way out, finally released from their necessary confinement. Au'p reached the base of the ramp first. The tentacled, undulating creature seemed somehow shorter now that it was out of the tank, standing no taller than Jared's chin.

The Plury'be slid up next to the captain, with Jared's translator receiving a message: "It is good to be out / It is good to be free / (satisfaction)."

Jared said, "What should we do now?"

"Our way is to meet at the Meeting Place / The Meeting Place is this way," said Au'p. "Be mindful of walking / Be mindful of staying on the pathways."

Au'p and S'li went ahead, joining the waiting crowd. The Plury'be encircled them briefly, brushing against the two. Jared's translator caught broken bits of words from the exchange but nothing more. The Plury'be then separated and, single file, wriggled their way over to a ramp that curled and sloped down into the settlement.

With the security team in the lead, the Confederals followed at a respectable distance.

Once Jared and the others reached the ramp, they could see the community in full view. It was not large; perhaps fifty or sixty small habitations connected by a network of black pathways. The habitations were no more than a few trics tall, of varying diameters, all of them circular with rounded domed roofs. The buildings were smooth and glossy, and the downward flow of rain was plainly evident on them, beading and running into the murky land. The pathways connecting the habitations stood just a few trics up from the planet's treacherous surface. The attending sciences officer warned Jared and the others that the muck below them was soft and deep, and could suck a person in like Earthen quicksand.

Among the habitations was one larger than the other, a bulbous structure that was wide but not tall. The contingent that had come to meet Au'p and S'li headed in that direction, joined by other Plury'be who converged on the room from the surrounding buildings. Jared judged that it must be the Meeting Place Au'p had spoken of.

"How many of them are there in total, I wonder? Plury'be, I mean," Nho mused aloud, his ever-present staff tapping along the path as he gripped it through his environmental suit.

The sciences officer, looking at his sensor, said, "There are four hundred and seven in this community, including the two that came with us."

"It would appear that we have an audience with all of them," said Vetta.

The Navy crew weaved along the pathways, stopping a short distance from the large building. Before them, a mass of Plury'be filed into the room.

Orel Dayail approached Jared. "Conversation inside that building could be complicated. Because of the multilayered way they transmit language, it may be difficult to sort it all out if they all start speaking at once. I recommend we ask them for a spokesperson. That may help avoid miscommunication or misunderstanding."

"Noted."

At that moment, one of the Plury'be came out of the Meeting Place. It was impossible to know on visual inspection if it was Au'p or S'li or one of the others; to the Confederal eye, they all looked the same.

The Plury'be said, "You shall enter / We are ready."

Jared exchanged looks with those standing around him: Nho, Rete, Vetta, Orel, the security officers, the sciences and medical officers. There was an air of nervous excitement: the fear of the unknown combined with the anticipation of doing something that had not been done in some time—making new allies.

Or perhaps more.

"Let's go see if we can make some friends today," Jared said, and directed them to head inside.

• • •

The Navy interceptor *Shington*, like all interceptors of its design, harbored living quarters in its center. The room consisted of various sleeping alcoves, a large table, a small lab and infirmary, and a bidimensional display surrounded by seating of various shapes and sizes. Other than the lavatory and shower in one corner, the room was largely absent any form of privacy. At the moment, the room was only dimly lit, with resting crew members occupying a few of the sleeping alcoves.

Lieutenant Brigg Drews, the ship's commander, stood on his head in the middle of the dark room, his legs pointed to the ceiling. From an early age, his father, a lifetime merchant trader, had impressed upon him the importance of keeping his body fit while in space. Like much of what his father said—more than he might admit to the elder Drews—Brigg had not forgotten the advice.

So here he was, the blood running to his head in a gravity slightly less than that of Earth. Brigg had found it a constructive morning routine to achieve a certain degree of physical and spiritual balance. His body complied with ease, thanks to muscle memory cultivated from thousands of sessions in this position. Inside his mind, he focused silently on the Creator and the Savior Heisus.

Brigg and his family were devotees of one of the theistic cults on Earth. The cults varied in the particulars of their beliefs, although most subscribed to worship of the Creator. Brigg's family members were Heisus followers, which, like the Sarconians, believed the Creator had taken the form of a person and lived among them. Little was known about Heisus; oral tradition held that there were once written accounts of His life, but they had been mostly lost at some point during the Dark Ages. It was generally accepted by those theists who followed Heisus—and even some who did not— that He had lived in a pre-industrial empire and had been executed when he was physically impaled onto wooden beams and left to suffocate.

Brigg did not discuss his religion with others, as it was unpopular among most Humans, including those in the Navy. Nor did he discuss it with Nho Ames, the old Sarco follower. Nho was convinced that Sarco and Heisus were one and the same, but Brigg's father had long viewed extraterrestrial religions cynically. Brigg was not sure he agreed with his father on that point, but Brigg also did not want to jeopardize his career prospects by saying something to Nho that might come back to haunt him later.

Some theists would have criticized him for his failure to proselytize—this remained a sharp divide within the theistic community—but most of the proselytizers lived on Earth. The Drews family had made a living moving cargo among various Aecron and Ritican worlds, where any attempt to convert would have meant a ban on trading on those worlds, if not outright incarceration. Perhaps someday, Hendry Drews once told his son Brigg.

Brigg finished his morning prayers and, after doing a few gentle maneuvers, lowered himself to his knees, got up, and dressed for the day's work.

The first part of Brigg's day proceeded uneventfully. It had been a full three days since Captain Carter had started meeting with the Plury'be leaders on Free Town's surface. Little information on the progress of those meetings had made its way to the *Shington*, but the news couldn't be all bad, as the local Plury'be remained calmly in orbit nearby and Brigg's orders had not changed.

On the viewscreen, a view of the planet Free Town alternated with that of the Plury'be garrison or the distant outline of the *Hattan* as the *Shington* ran its patrol route in a broad orbit around Jared Carter's ship. On the opposite pole of the *Shington*'s route, Senior Lieutenant Eil Morichar and the *Ratha* ran a similar path, the other sentinel in the night for the lonely Navy cruiser so far from home.

Up ahead, three-fold distortions opened in space. This was a fairly regular occurrence in the space above Free Town, with various Plury'be craft coming and going. Other than the three large cruisers the *Hattan* had encountered upon its arrival, most of the planetary traffic comprised small ships, including a fair number of the flatboats. The previous evening, Brigg and two members of his crew had engaged in a lively debate over which ship would emerge victorious in a hypothetical contest between a flatboat and an interceptor. The *Shington's* sciences officer had finally adjudicated the debate by constructing a simulation on the living quarter's tridimensional display. The flatboat emerged victorious. The navigator complained that the interceptor could have been commanded better.

"How long until those folds open?" asked Brigg.

"Fifteen minutes." The science officer sounded bored. "They started forming over forty minutes ago."

The navigator said, "That is a nice bit of work, to make a system approach from that distance."

Brigg agreed. A longer fold distortion wait time signaled an arrival from farther away. Most of the Free Town traffic had folded in from great distances, rather than folding in along the outskirts of the system and then completing the trip with a smaller jump. There were a lot of reasons why they would do so, the most likely being the desire to arrive more quickly by reducing number of jumps. The drawback was that longer folds could sometimes be less precise, so being able to fold in so close from so far away was a mark of both good navigating and an exceptional ship. An hour-long fold distortion, even by Navy standards, was impressive.

The sciences officer put up a schematic of nearby space on the tridimensional display. "By contrast, these four that just appeared behind the *Hattan* will open up in less than ninety seconds. They must be coming in from just inside the system."

Several uneasy thoughts stirred in Brigg Drews's head, all at once.

Four folds . . . Over the last few days, they had always come in either alone or in threes.

Four large folds . . . Most of the traffic had been small ships; these looked like cruisers.

Four large folds from in close . . . None of the Plury'be ships he'd seen here had used folds in-system like that.

Four large folds from in close right behind the *Hattan* . . . The *Hattan* was some distance away from the planet, and it made little sense to come in behind it; a shorter jump would presumably be more precise and therefore closer to Free Town.

Four large folds from in close right behind the *Hattan* . . .

Brigg grabbed one of his displays and begin working it in earnest. "Navigator, make for the new waypoint I am sending you. Increase speed to three-quarters and come around when you've reached it."

"Sir?"

"Now!"

After Brigg's heroics at the prison transport, the navigator knew better than to question Brigg twice. He began executing the maneuver.

Brigg had also learned from that experience. Although he'd helped save the fleet, he'd also earned a harsh reprimand from the captain. "You should have contacted the *Hattan* at the first sign of trouble rather than taking matters into your own hands," Jared had said. "You not only operated outside the chain of command, but you fired a torpedo on a ship we knew very little about—and that you knew even less about. Did you stop to consider what could have gone wrong, detonating a weapon like that against an unknown alien ship? Were it not for the fact that you helped alert us to the transport's signal, I would have stripped you of your interceptor command. As it is, consider this a one-time warning: do not *ever* do that again."

Although his ego had been bruised, Brigg wasn't in the habit of making the same mistake twice. This time around, there would be no operating alone.

"Sound combat stations," he said, "and get me the *Hattan* immediately."

• • •

Senior Lieutenant Venzz Kitt wandered leisurely around the bridge of the *Hattan*. Venzz was a curly-haired, slim, generally easygoing sort with a reputation for being the life of any social gathering. His record as an officer was above average but not stellar; some of his supervisors questioned his intangibles, including his instincts as a ship tactician. He was smart, though, and it was noted that, with experience, he'd gotten better at the nuances of leading a ship. He also had the right friends in the upper echelons of Navy Command, which some of his more cynical colleagues suspected was the real reason for his current appointment.

It was not enough to get him his own ship, at least not right now. Despite a long and respectable record as an interceptor commander, the Human was fifth in line among the five officers slotted as interceptor commanders in the *Hattan* battle group, behind Redelia Aroo, Brigg Drews, Eil Morichar, and a Ritican male named Amun Plau. Plau's ship, the *Binn-Phuna*, had not even been completed yet, so it would be some time still before Venzz would get his turn. In the meantime, Venzz had earned his keep as Redelia and the others had done, serving in the command chair of the *Hattan* as part of the bridge watch rotation. Those who knew Venzz well knew that he found it unsatisfying; being a watch officer carried the illusion of command, but Venzz also knew that at the merest hint of a crisis he would be unceremoniously pushed aside by Tir Bvaso or one of the other senior officers.

Still, he enjoyed looking the part. Venzz sauntered toward the communications station, ostensibly to check in on Rami Del. "Anything interesting to report?" he asked.

"No, Lieutenant."

Her voice was professional and distant, as usual. Unfazed, he added, "What are your plans for this evening?"

She said, without looking up, "The answer to whatever you're going to ask is no, Lieutenant."

He raised his hands in mock surrender. "How do you know before I even ask?"

"Because it's you, Lieutenant."

Venzz suppressed the urge to scowl. He was a man of many companions, and rumor had it that Rami had once been a kindred spirit. Unfortunately, something—that old man's religion, probably—had turned her into this dour thing now before him. Several times he had probed to see if the Rami of the rumors was still in there somewhere, but so far all he'd struck was the cold stone of her rebuffs. No matter; they were going to be on this ship for a long time. He would have other opportunities.

One of Rami's displays lit up with an ominous red. Her eyes darted that direction and she said, "We are being contacted by the *Shington*. Lieutenant Drews says it is urgent."

Venzz froze in place and his face darkened. He and Brigg Drews were about as different as two Humans could be, save for the dubious similarity of profound mutual dislike. Venzz thought Brigg to be reckless and arrogant; Brigg thought Venzz to be incompetent and lackadaisical. Tir Bvaso had warned them both to behave or risk being assigned permanent duty as commander of the ship's waste reprocessing department.

"Put him on," Venzz said irritably.

At Rami's command, one of the displays next to her lit up with Brigg's face. Brigg did not wait for a salutation. "I need to speak to Commander Bvaso right now. Those four fold distortions opening up behind the *Hattan* are cruiser-sized. They're too close, probably from in-system. Something's not right."

Venzz arched his eyebrows. "How is any of that a problem? We've had traffic in and out for days."

"I don't have time to argue with you, Venzz. Get me Commander Bvaso. Now."

"She's in a meeting," Venzz said. "I'll forward your concerns to her."

"We've got less than sixty seconds until those things open. If I'm right—"

"Right about what?" asked Tir, striding onto the bridge from her personnel meeting in the conference room.

"Four folds, in-system jump, forming directly behind you," said Brigg. "It's not right. They shouldn't be this far out."

Tir glanced over at Aioua. The Aecron sciences officer gave a quick nod.

Venzz glared at her. *Of course*, he thought. *That's how Tir knew to come out here.* The Aecron had bought into Brigg's story and summoned her. It was like the entire bridge was conspiring against him.

Tir turned back to Brigg. "Recommendation?"

"Take a defensive position. You have less than forty-five seconds."

Venzz snorted skeptically, but his opinion was immaterial; he was no longer the commanding officer on the bridge. "Do it," Tir said, taking a seat at the command station. "Navigator, bring the ship around to face the folds. Rami, contact the Plury'be and see if they are expecting these arrivals."

Alarms went off as crew scurried into their seats and activated passive restraints. Garo Ball's deep voice penetrated the noise. "Defense fields initialized, activating turrets. I can load torpedoes on your command."

"Do so," said Tir, pulling up Brigg on one display and calling for Eil Morichar and the *Ratha* on another. "Brigg, do not fire unless I give the order."

"Yes, Commander."

Venzz sneered. It was always good to see Brigg reminded that he wasn't infallible, although Venzz would have been happier had the captain actually stripped the cocky boor of command.

In front of Tir, Eil Morichar's face appeared, her visage stately and her hair a shock of white. She was smart, crafty, and famously laconic. "Commander."

"Sending your orders now," said Tir.

"Understood."

"No response yet from the Plury'be," Rami said, "but two of the

Free Town cruisers are coming about and making for our position, along with several flatboats."

"Let is hope it is not a trap set up by the local forces," Garo mumbled.

Almost in unison, the four folds split open into full spatial tears, and four ships emerged. Venzz Kitt's mouth fell open.

Tir leaned forward in shock. "What under the Moons is *that*?"

• • •

Jared and Nho stepped wearily out of the *Belico*'s airlock, flanked on each side by a security officer. Another day of meetings. The idea wasn't nearly as exciting now as it had been three days earlier. *This is why father went into politics and I didn't.*

One of his crew's first obstacles had been trying to explain to the Plury'be the notion of sleep. The Plury'be were dimly aware that some sentients experienced a physiological need for unconsciousness—apparently there were races on this side of the Void who also did so—but it was difficult for the Plury'be to understand the need to take breaks of any length, much less several hours, between meeting sessions.

On the first day, the leaders of Au'p and S'li's faction—they called themselves the "No Greater"—had questioned Jared and his team relentlessly for nearly fourteen hours. It was not an interrogation—no one was holding them against their will—but it was intense, with a variety of questions asked in the layered way the Plury'be used. Because Confederal speak was not so structured, answers took longer than the Plury'be wanted, and at times Jared and Vetta even took to trying to explain the same thing simultaneously to expedite the discussion. The Plury'be loved it; Jared and Vetta found it disorienting.

The Plury'be inquiries ran the gamut of topics, and Jared and his crew answered them truthfully for the most part, choosing to omit only things they felt could be a security risk to the Confederacy. The Navy crew explained the history of the Confederacy, the various component races, and how Malum (a "regulator," Au'p had called it) had nearly destroyed it all. They also spoke of the Invasion of 1124 and how the Confederacy had been uncertain if the Invasion and Malum were connected. They spoke of biological physiology and technological accomplishments (within reason), social structure, and planetary ecology. Orel Dayail was also hard at work with some of the Plury'be technicians to create a framework for exchanging large quantities of data on their respective societies, but that was still a couple of days off from being finalized.

After the first day, the Plury'be appeared satisfied that the Confederals were not an imminent threat. This allowed Jared and his team to ask questions of their own. Jared quickly realized that others among the Plury'be were more skilled at articulating the finer details of Plury'be life than Au'p and S'li.

The reason? Plury'be culture was thoroughly specialized, to the point where individuals were only skilled in a narrow range of abilities. S'li, for example, was the Plury'be version of a pilot and had little to offer in the way of explaining sociological or cultural knowledge. Au'p, meanwhile, was a speaker, a person whose primary job was to persuade other factions of the virtues of the No Greater ideology. Au'p was very good at dealing with those who already understood Plury'be life, but was not nearly so good at explaining ideas to those with little or no background.

In hindsight, some of Au'p's explanations back on the *Hattan* were misleading not because they were deceptive, but because they omitted certain small details which led the Navy to faulty conclusions. Au'p had failed, for example, to properly explain the complex relationship between religion and politics in Plury'be society. Had not Rete asked the right questions before their arrival, it would not have been clear if Au'p and S'li's faction possessed any religious beliefs at all.

Free Town, by contrast, offered a much broader range of specialists. Jared and his crew found that those best suited to answering his questions were of the tutor specialty, a branch of work dedicated to educating young Plury'be about their own society. In effect,

Jared and the others learned best from those tasked with teaching children.

The knowledge gained through the tutors' simple clarity was at once illuminating and sobering. The Plury'be were a race of factions with varying political, economic, cultural, and religious ideas. Some factions overlapped in many areas; others were completely distinct. Some factions were enormous and maintained alliances with other key groups; others were loners. Some factions cared deeply about technology at the expense of all else; others cared about several different subjects equally. It seemed on its face an almost overwhelming hyperpluralism of differences, but Jared and the others learned that a few key factions tended to dominate political—and, to a certain extent, cultural—control over the majority of the Plury'be, while other factions were more marginalized.

And what of Malum and its master, Dar? Dar, Jared discovered, was the high lord of a sprawling empire not far from the Plury'be. The Domain, as it was called, encapsulated hundreds of settled planets and at least thirty different races. Some of its component races were without spaceflight, while others possessed interstellar travel and engaged in trade.

All were closely regulated by the Domain's dominant race. The Plury'be called them the Supreme People; their self-ascribed name was not known outside of the Domain. Dar was of the Supreme People, as were the geometric enforcers Vetta and the others had fought on board the High Land prison transport.

The relationship between the Plury'be and the Domain depended on the Plury'be factions in power and the Domain's leadership. The Domain and the Plury'be collective enjoyed relative parity for centuries, until the failed conquest of the Aecrons. No one on Free Town could clearly articulate why certain Plury'be factions had organized the Invasion of 1124, but the losses made the Plury'be more vulnerable to Domain encroachment.

Dar's rise to power—Jared's crew wasn't exactly sure about the date, but the best estimate was perhaps thirty years ago—coincided with the Domain's increasing involvement in Plury'be affairs. Dar was the Domain's most powerful leader in recent history, having uprooted the Domain's almost Aecron-like meritocracy and replacing it with a single, indisputable leader.

Notably, Dar had not sought to conquer the Plury'be through military might; instead, his infiltration had been more insidious, proffering the Domain's many diversions, vices, and pleasures upon the Plury'be. Decadence had swept many Plury'be worlds, and when several of the minor Plury'be factions had tried to fight the Domain's creeping influence, a few of the major Plury'be factions had taken the incredible step of bringing in Domain forces to quell the uprising. The Plury'be homeworld of Mel'as'u—which translated as Sacred Home—was the most troubling example, having voluntarily accepted the police rule of Domain forces. Dar had gained cultural and military influence over the most important planet in Plury'be space without the need for invasion or attack.

The No Greater faction of Free Town had bitterly resisted the Domain's cultural takeover, arguing that it constituted the growth of evil among the Plury'be. A few factions, assisted by the Domain, had responded by seeking to systematically dismantle both the No Greater faction and others like them. Since then, the faction from Free Town had suffered setback after setback. That included Au'p and S'li's capture while trying to lobby against Domain facilities on a prominent Plury'be trade hub. Even the attempt to rescue the two had been—notwithstanding the *Hattan*'s involvement—a disaster, with all the No Greater forces sent to the prison ship lost in the attempt.

"They're dying, you know."

It was Nho, speaking to Jared. The two men and their party had descended the circular ramp from the landing pad and were headed to the Meeting Place. The rain, steady and endless, splashed over their environmental suits.

"What do you mean?" asked Jared, picking his way carefully along the elevated path.

"You know exactly what I mean. These people, this faction,

they are dying, and the hope of their entire civilization is dying with them."

"That's an extreme statement."

Nho stopped and stared at Jared, the rain hammering down on his suit helmet. "Is it? Is it really? You've heard what they've said. Dar is corrupting their society, destroying them spiritually just as surely as his Malum tried to destroy us physically. The sentients here are some of the only ones who can stop them, and other Plury'be factions, under Dar's influence, are coming after them because of it."

Jared raised his hands in a gesture of futility. "What are we supposed to do about it?"

"We need to help them."

"We weren't sent here to get involved in their politics. We were sent here to assess the threat level of Dar's empire to the Confederacy."

"Aren't they one and the same? Aren't we risking the Confederacy if we allow the Domain's influence over the Plury'be to become complete?"

Jared sighed. "What can we do? We have one cruiser and a few interceptors. Do you have any idea how big the empires are that we are talking about? I'm not sure I can even begin to comprehend the size of these things."

Nho held the staff out toward Jared. "And yet this staff—this 'shaft of wood,' as you once called it—overcame one of the mightiest entities one of those empires could produce." Nho knocked on the staff with his free hand. "And it had nothing to do with the wood it was cut from or the sealant that protects it." He paused, his voice at once weighted down by weariness and full of conviction. "This fight is not a physical one. It is a fight of another kind. I am convinced of this now more than ever. We know Malum can be beaten by the power of the One through Sarco. We know that the being these Plury'be call That Which There Is No Greater is the same being as the One, and we know that their Seed Vessel, Ah'ey, is the manifestation of Sarco here. They possess the same power to upend Dar that I do, that you do. We merely need to show them how."

Jared looked skeptical. "None of them have reported being able to do the same things to Dar's minions that you did. We have not even broached the subject of Sarco with them."

"Then let's do so." Nho paced a circle around Jared. "Let's open their eyes to the miracles we've seen, the power we have against the forces of darkness. We must, while there are still allies here to be had."

Jared's link chirped in his ear. "Redelia Aroo to Jared Carter."

"Jared here. What is it?"

"Sir, the *Hattan* fleet has just gone to combat stations."

Jared gasped. "Why? What's going on?"

"We are trying to find out. I have been monitoring fleet communications. From what I can gather, there are short-range fold distortions appearing behind the *Hattan* and there is some concern about them."

"Have they contacted the No Greater leadership?"

"I do not know."

Jared turned to head back to the *Belico*, motioning the others to follow. "Redelia, try to contact the leadership yourself. See if you can find out what's going on. We're headed back your way now."

• • •

The Navy interceptor *Shington* came to a point behind the four fold distortions and pivoted into position. Once Brigg had concluded that there was something amiss, he had decided that the best place to be was right behind the incoming ships. Should they prove a threat to the *Hattan*, it would give the attackers more than one angle to worry about. Tir Bvaso had ordered Eil Morichar to take up a defensive position, and Eil had taken her cue from Brigg's positioning by bringing her interceptor, the *Ratha*, up along the fold line's right flank.

On the *Shington*'s viewscreen, beyond the four folds, Brigg could make out a pair of Free Town cruisers heading toward them.

Was this part of an ambush orchestrated by the local Plury'be? If it were, the *Hattan* would be caught between at least six capital ships and quickly dispatched.

Heisus protect us.

He said aloud, "Time?"

"Less than ten seconds."

Brigg addressed the weapons officer. "Target the point I am sending, and relay it to the rest of the fleet." If Tir found a better target, it would be easy for her to countermand him.

At that moment four folds erupted open before him, and four large ships shot out into the emptiness of open space. Three looked familiar enough, but the fourth . . .

"Three cruiser-level Plury'be warships," said the sciences officer, "and a fourth ship not on record. Analyzing now."

Purple beams poured out from the three new Plury'be cruisers, splashing angrily against the *Hattan*'s defense fields. Hyperwave beams. The fourth ship spat waves of translucent energy toward the *Hattan*, waves that looked like pulse weapons, yet were different somehow.

The four ships had been clear of their folds for less than five seconds and the Navy cruiser was already taking a beating.

Tir's command had scarcely reached his ear when Brigg shouted for his weapons officer to fire. On the left side of the viewscreen, he could see the *Ratha* was also firing, with a fusing torpedo and a round of pulse shots ranging in on one of the Plury'be attackers.

• • •

The world around Tir Bvaso descended into barely organized chaos. The *Hattan* had come under fire from the three arriving Plury'be cruisers' hyperwave nodes, and was also being struck by an as-yet-undetermined attack from the fourth ship. Already the lethal hyperwave particles were beginning to seep through the fields, helped along by the fourth's ship's concussive shots. Three different sections along the forward decks were being evacuated, though it might already be too late.

On the viewscreen, the *Shington* and *Ratha* had launched their torpedoes and fired their pulse cannons from behind and beside the lead Plury'be ship, respectively. It was not enough to do a lot of damage, but it might get the enemy's attention. From the *Hattan* a flurry of eight fusing torpedoes, supported by a salvo from the pulse turrets, blasted out from the forward tubes, homing in on that same cruiser.

"Reload with the collider torpedoes," shouted Tir to Garo Ball. The *Hattan* had a limited number of the experimental weapons, which could deal damage much greater than a standard fusing torpedo. Expending some of them now meant having fewer to use later, but that point would be moot if there was not a later. "And saturate the siege cannon!"

The Navy's first fusillade exploded against the Plury'be cruiser. Tir turned her seat to face Aioua. "Analysis of the attacking fleet."

The left tridimensional display showed a projection of the battlefield. In front of the *Hattan* were the four attacking ships, labeled in red as Invader-1, Invader-2, Invader-3, and the unidentified ship, Invader-U. Behind them, the two advancing No Greater cruisers were in yellow, designated as Greater-1 and Greater-2. A large number of smaller Free Town flatboat cruisers were also advancing, including three that had accelerated and swiftly passed the No Greater cruisers.

"Three Plury'be cruisers, designed like those at High Land," said Aioua, her voice shaking. "Unknown ship . . . hull composed of Uxa251, some sort of proximity field, currently channeling a unidirectional force wave."

Uxa251. The same material as Malum. And a weapon similar to Malum's.

"A Domain ship," said Garo Ball. It was a speculative statement, but Tir did not doubt it was true.

Tir pulled up an enlarged image of the Uxa251 ship at her command station. It was sleek and angular, as if someone had built a spear head with square blocks save for the sharpened tip. Some of the square parts of the hull seemed to rotate as if on an axis, including an element on the bottom that appeared to be firing the focused force wave. Other than its glossy black complexion, it did not look like Malum, although the hull material and the weapon of attack certainly suggested a common origin.

Six smaller, spike-like objects ejected from the ventral and dorsal sections of the Domain cruiser. They flew past the *Hattan*, ignoring the Navy cruiser and quickly gaining speed. Since they were not an imminent threat, Tir decided to hold off asking about them for the moment. Instead she asked, "What is the status of our target ship?"

A schematic of Invader-1 appeared on Tir's display. "The bonded hull armor is showing significant fault lines from our attacks."

"Torpedoes ready," said Garo.

"Fire."

A barrage of collider torpedoes, pulsing blue from their reinforced fields, launched into the night, a shower of death bearing down on Invader-1. The cruiser turned its hyperwave nodes on the torpedoes, but it was fruitless; the eight projectiles exploded against its weakened hull, blowing the front of the ship to pieces. The back three-quarters of the craft careened aimlessly into the vastness of space.

• • •

Jared, Nho, Redelia, and the *Belico*'s weapons officer huddled around the tridimensional display on the bridge of the *Belico*, taking in the telemetry the rest of the fleet was forwarding them. The ship marked Invader-1 had just been destroyed, and now the fleet was turning its attention on Invader-2. The *Hattan* remained the focal point of the attack, with two remaining Plury'be attackers and the mysterious Invader-U concentrating their firepower on the Navy cruiser.

Jared was concerned about his ship, but he was also concerned about something else. "What are these?" he asked, pointing to six objects accelerating away from the center of battle.

Udos Beyole, the *Belico*'s sciences officer, enlarged them on the display. "They were launched from Invader-U," he said. "They are approximately twenty trics long and are on a direct course for the planet."

"Are they missiles?" Redelia asked.

"Based on the available data from the *Hattan* and the other interceptors, they do not contain anything identifiable as an explosive. Moreover, they have already pierced two different flatboats without detonating."

Jared furrowed his brow. "Pierced?"

"Right here and here." Udos highlighted the locations. "Two of the objects ran right through flatboats that were in their way. They pierced through them like a spear, apparently at only a marginal loss of speed."

"Against bonded armor?"

"Yes." Udos lifted his eyes from his station and stared at Redelia. "Commander Aroo, the encrypted data packet you received on Malum mentioned spikes like that."

A chill ran down Jared's spine. He hadn't had time to read most of that report. Jared said, to Udos, "Malum had those objects?"

"Malum never deployed them—it did not need to—but, yes, it was armed with them. At the time the Sciences Institute discovered them, they were dormant, so they did not learn much, but the report indicates that the spikes contained significant internal open space. They may be intended as transports."

The weapons officer drew up a trajectory on the objects on the tridimensional display. "Whatever they are, they're headed for the planet and it doesn't look like the Free Town garrison will be able to stop them. Based on their current courses, they appear to be targeting multiple points on the surface, including ours."

Jared looked at Redelia. "Can we get into space to intercept them?"

"Not before they reach the atmosphere. We are also missing our engineer. It is out with the Plury'be, helping to repair a transmitter."

That rules out that option, Jared thought. Engaging the spikes in Free Town's airspace was dangerous at best, and engaging in any combat without an Exo in engineering invited disaster. He looked back to Udos. "How long until one of them reaches this settlement?"

"A matter of minutes, Captain."

• • •

The reports came in from the *Hattan*'s engineering coordination station, and they weren't good. "Forward torpedoes are inoperable, and several of the forward turrets are also nonresponsive. Medical also warns that opening the siege cannon will flood the entire mid-section of the ship with hyperwave particles."

Tir Bvaso slammed her curled digits against the armrest of the command chair and let out a Hazionite profanity. The hyperwave attacks had been leeching through the defense fields, helped along by the pounding assault of Invader-U's force waves. The forward decks were becoming increasingly inhospitable, and at this rate, the entire crew would be dead before they could destroy the remaining attackers. Now the ship's offenses were being compromised.

"Garo," she said, "if we rotated on our axis, could we fire a concentrated broadside on the lead cruiser?"

The ancient Ritican was hard at work coordinating the available pulse turrets. "I would not advise it," he said after a short delay. "It would expose our flanks to the hyperwave attacks."

It kept coming back to the hyperwave attacks. Right now they were crippling the ship, and in short order would do far more than that. They needed to either find a way to divert some of the attacks away, or disable the attacking ships. The two Free Town cruisers and their flatboats had joined the fight against the invaders, but so far the situation had not changed: the *Hattan* remained the primary target.

"Rami," said Tir, "any reply yet from the Free Town ships?"

"No, Commander."

"Try again. Ask them if they would like to coordinate our attacks." Tir pulled up the faces of Brigg Drews and Eil Morichar on her command displays. Her voice was firm, urgent. "Our situation is becoming desperate. We cannot take this assault much longer. Is there anything you both can do about those hyperwave attacks?"

Brigg's serious face cracked a hint of a smile. "I have some ideas, ma'am."

• • •

In the early moments of the battle, the two Navy interceptors—Brigg Drews's *Shington* and Eil Morichar's *Ratha* —had tried to draw the attention of the attacking ships by coming in from different angles and hitting the enemy with what relatively few weapons they had at their disposal. They were virtually ignored, and for good reason; the interceptors did little damage against the Plury'be bonded armor and the Invader-U's proximity field.

Brigg had a growing sense that they needed to try something else, and he suspected Eil felt the same way. Tir's plea for help elevated his sentiment from sense to conviction. Along with that conviction came a firm plan, which he quickly shared with Eil.

"Your idea is insane," she declared, "but perhaps the situation demands it." Brigg took that as a vote of confidence.

With Brigg's ship in the lead, the two interceptors turned on their axes and made an attack run on the enemy fleet's three remaining ships: Invader-2, Invader-3, and, in between them, Invader-U. Brigg aimed to come in directly on the flanks of the ships, which were closing in on the *Hattan* in a line formation.

There were two targets on the attack run. The first was Invader-3, just leftward of Invader-U. Brigg's weapons officer selected one of the larger hyperwave nodes as the main target, unloading a torpedo and multiple pulse shots on the way in. Immediately behind came the *Ratha*, which did the same. The net effect of two torpedoes and a salvo of pulse rounds on the node was to blow it up, sending hyperwave particles scattering into space. The angle of the attack—which had been carefully calculated—pushed the hyperwave stream inward, directing it right at Invader-U and, to a lesser extent, Invader-3.

By this time, though, Brigg and Eil were already past Invader-3, wrapping up their attack run. From behind each of the ships came a second torpedo out of their rearward tubes, accompanied by a salvo of superheated attacks from their rear ardor turrets. This second attack struck a hyperwave node on Invader-3, causing the node to explode and push hyperwave particles back toward the other two invading ships.

Thanks to daring navigation and precise targeting, the two interceptors had managed to damage a pair of nodes and send their contents flying into the Navy's enemies in the process. It was a small victory, but it was also two fewer weapons trained on their flagship.

"As soon as the hyperwave particles dissipate," Brigg said, "we can do it again."

"It is still insane," said Eil, "but we are right behind you."

• • •

Jared and Nho raced out of the *Belico*'s airlock just in time to see the large, black, needle-shaped projectile spear itself into one of the pathways. From its blunted top end, a hatch opened.

Jared, standing just in front of the *Belico*, gripped his pulse pistol. Nho stood beside him, holding Sarco's staff with both hands. Off in the distance, down and away from the landing pad, a large number of Plury'be had streamed out into the open to see what had made all the noise. Among the mass of black sentients and their many tentacles, Jared could make out the forms of Vetta, Rete, Orel, and a few security officers.

Twelve sentients emerged from the hatch. The first eleven Jared had never seen in person before, but knew well from the footage. They were what the Plury'be called enforcers, geometrically dynamic floating objects with small frames and the capacity to fire potent balls of green flame. Just two of them had nearly wiped out an entire security team on the prison transport outside High Land.

As the enforcers fanned out from the projectile hatch, a stream of white smoke spiraled up and out into the torrential downpour.

Jared's mind registered shock, his body broke out in a cold sweat, and a profanity escaped his mouth as the gaseous being rose high in the air.

"By the Domes, it is a warden!" someone shouted over the communications channel.

It was a cloud-being, like the one that had terrorized the captives of Malum. The Navy officers, all of them former Malum captives, knew it as a warden. The Plury'be called it an overseer.

The thin tendrils of smoke coalesced into a cloud, which in turn became a ball of wispy fury. The overseer shifted laterally, taking a position above and in the center of the Plury'be settlement. The eleven geometric enforcers spread out beneath the overseer, a formation that strongly suggested a sort of hierarchy between the two different beings. The overseer seemed to be the leader; the enforcers were its platoon.

Up from the settlement, a cluster of purple orbs took to flight. Jared recognized them as the Plury'be drones that had so often floated above and around the local residents. Purple beams lanced out from the orbs and at several of the geometric enforcers. The enforcers shifted evasively in the air, returning fire with flaming green projectiles. Some of the hyperwave shots hit their marks, as did the green shots, though the initial results heavily favored the enforcers. A few of the enforcers sizzled under the hyperwave attacks, one even plummeted into the murky ground, while several of the orbs exploded in the first wave of fire.

Jared's pulse pistol was already out of his suit, and he was firing into the air, shouting into his link for all available officers to take up the attack. Within moments, he could see more pulse fire streaming from outside the Meeting Place as Vetta and one of the security officers rushed out into the open.

Jared, with Nho and a security officer trailing behind, skidded down the landing pad's ramp and into the settlement proper. He could see a mass of Plury'be scattering, trying to retreat into their habitations. In the air, it was already over; every orb drone had been all but destroyed, and there were still at least five enforcers remaining. The overseer remained high in the air, the cloud-being watching events unfold in detached silence.

Jared pushed his way through the mass of panicked Plury'be, his pistol shots landing on one of the enforcers, sending it spinning into the soft mire. Vetta fired down at Jared's target and it sank deeper, trapped in the ground. One of the other enforcers fired at Jared but missed, the green flame striking the ground nearby with a menacing hiss and shattering part of the platform. Jared did not like being in the open like this and began scanning the immediate area for cover, possibly in front of one of the habitations.

A large boom shook the entire settlement, knocking the Plury'be and several of the Navy officers onto the walking surfaces. Jared stumbled but was caught from behind by Nho, who planted Sarco's staff into the walkway surface to steady them both. Around them the four remaining enforcers had stopped firing, drawing into a formation approximating a square around the heart of the settlement. The overseer, the apparent source of the boom, had uncoiled its wispy body and descended straight down before coming to an abrupt halt right above the Meeting Place.

The overseer spoke. Jared could hear it, but his suit display also showed it was translating in the way of the Plury'be. Out loud Jared could hear:

"THIS WORLD BELONGS TO DAR NOW. SUBMIT, AND YOU WILL LIVE. RESIST, AND YOU SHALL BE ELIMINATED."

They were not unlike the words another overseer had used in Malum over a year ago. Then, just as now, the ground shook with the intensity of the demand. Out of the corner of his eye, Jared saw Rete running back into the Meeting Place.

Jared pointed his pistol at the overseer and fired several shots. His pulse rounds rose up against the rain, slicing harmlessly through the cloud.

The words of a nearby Plury'be reached his translator. "What are you doing? / You are doing that which will fail. You are asking for death / The overseer of Dar will bring death / (terror)!"

Jared flushed, his face hot with self-reproach over the ridiculous impulse. He'd brought unwanted attention on himself, the last thing a ship's captain should do. It was a mistake, perhaps a fatal one. Above him, however, the cloud did not respond, silently taunting Jared for his futility.

He felt a brush on his arm. It was Nho. The old man, the cleric of Sarco, looked at him placidly as he stood shoulder-to-shoulder with his captain, his covered hands holding Sarco's staff vertically. "The weapons of this war are not physical ones," Nho said, echoing words from earlier that day. "They are weapons of another realm. This is our chance to show the Plury'be what their Creator is capable of."

The cloud widened and thinned into a giant white ring, casting a halo over the area above Jared, Nho, and the others. Again its voice:

"THIS WORLD BELONGS TO DAR NOW. SUBMIT, AND YOU WILL LIVE. RESIST, AND YOU SHALL BE ELIMINATED."

Nho brought his aging frame to its full height and pointed defiantly at the gaseous overseer with the staff. "No!" he cried. "We will not submit! We will not surrender! Never! You have no power here, foul creature! You cannot stand against the power of Sarco, the Incarnate of the One! You cannot stand against the power of Ah'ey, the Seed Vessel of That Which There Is No Greater! He who created us all has given us the power to defeat you!"

The Plury'be nearby backed farther away from Jared and Nho, cowering to the ground, their tentacles writhing in what looked like panic. A clamor of terror, rage, and confusion assailed Jared's translator as the Plury'be berated Jared and Nho for bringing the overseer's wrath down upon them. In the sky above, the overseer rotated faster, creating a vortex that made the rain divert off at odd angles away from it. The four geometric enforcers slowly closer, making a straight line toward Jared and Nho.

Nho looked back at Jared, the old man's face a picture of serenity. "It is time for us to show them what it means to be free."

Jared nodded solemnly, placing his hands on Sarco's staff along with Nho's. "I trusted you before, and I'm willing to do it again. We're out of options."

Nho said, "It is when we are at our most desperate that our faith can yield the most power."

Up above, the overseer rumbled:

"SUBMIT AND LIVE. RESIST AND BE ELIMINATED."

Both men looked up at the cloud. Gripping the staff tightly, Jared fought the lump in his throat as he shouted, "We did not submit to Dar before, and we will not do so here!"

In perfect unison, the four enforcers fired. Their green bolts bore straight down on Jared and Nho . . . and hissed into four tiny wisps of smoke just a few miniscule centrics away from them. Jared could feel their heat.

Again the enforcers fired. Again the attacks fizzled in the air.

Sarco's staff took on a glow—a white, ethereal glow that Jared had seen before, at the moment of their deliverance inside Malum. Jared could feel its warmth radiating through his suit and into the air around him. Nho lifted the staff higher into the air and cried out, "Wicked agents of darkness, I give you the power of the One!"

Nho slammed the bottom end of Sarco's staff down on the walkway. The ground sparked, and a dome of light flared out of the staff, passing through Nho and Jared as it expanded out in all directions. The dome bloomed outward and upward, a radial front that collided mercilessly with the overseer and the four enforcers.

The geometric enforcers exploded into a fiery heat, their rotating bodies thrown haphazardly into the soft ground. The overseer shot straight up into the air in a feeble attempt to outrun the light, but the radiance ballooned into the cloud and consumed it until it was nothing.

• • •

Jared dropped into the *Belico*'s command chair. Redelia had ceded the chair graciously, not in an abdication of ship command, but out of recognition of Jared's complete exhaustion. Nearby, on one of the tridimensional displays, Tir's face hovered in the air. She looked as spent as Jared, her Hazionite features showing the lines characteristic of one who desperately needed a sleep cycle.

Jared took a drink of water out of a bottle and wiped his mouth, the fluids momentarily revitalizing him. "What is your situation?"

"It was a narrow victory, but the invading force has withdrawn," said Tir. "We managed to destroy one Plury'be cruiser and seriously damage another before the attackers folded out of the system."

Jared took another drink. "How is our fleet?"

"The interceptors are undamaged. The attackers completely ignored them. The *Hattan* suffered only minor structural damage; the unidentified cruiser pounded the defense fields with force waves, but they held. We have several fatalities and numerous injuries, however, and we suspect the death toll will rise before it is all over."

"Because of the hyperwave particles?"

"Yes, sir. They leeched through the fields, helped along by the force wave attacks. At one point, the particles forced the forward torpedoes and turrets offline and prevented us from opening the siege cannon. Were it not for our interceptors targeting the enemy's hyperwave nodes, we might not be talking right now."

Jared made a silent note to commend Brigg Drews and Eil Morichar later. Brigg, in particular, had distinguished himself, both for diagnosing the attack and helping to repel it. "What about the Free Town garrison?"

"They were some distance away, so they did not engage right away. They were instrumental in stopping one of the attackers, though they refused to communicate with us or otherwise coordinate an attack."

"Do you know why?"

"No. They still are not responding to us."

"I think I may have an explanation for that, sir." It was Orel Dayail, the Aecron communications officer, who sat next to the *Belico*'s communication officer. "I have been talking with some of our xenosociologists, and we have a working hypothesis."

Jared leaned his face against his palm, his elbow on the chair arm. "I'm listening."

"Based on what we know about their culture, the No Greater cruisers almost certainly were afraid to respond out of caution. From their perspective, the incoming folds might have been our doing. They may have wondered if we were colluding with their enemies."

Tir said, "That still does not explain why they did not respond to our communications even after we came under attack."

"We have a hypothesis on that as well. The Plury'be view combat differently than any other race we are familiar with. In most societies, the chief end of combat is to defeat the enemy as quickly and fully as possible. Among the Confederal militaries, for example, destruction of an enemy ship is either a high priority or the highest priority. The only exception is when a race wants prisoners of war; in those instances, ships are disabled to effect a capture.

"The Plury'be, on the other hand, see operable ships as a rare commodity and elevate the scavenging of equipment as the highest priority. They care less about prisoners; they believe any information a prisoner might have is probably readily available on the ship's systems themselves. As a result, they want the ships intact and the crews dead."

Redelia rested an arm on the communications station. "Hyperwave weapons serve that purpose well. They kill crew but their impact on ship systems is minor. It explains why they forgo explosive or ship-damaging weapons."

"Most likely, yes," Orel said. "Now, with that as context, consider what they see when they watch us. Our ships attacked the invading ships furiously, using torpedoes and pulse weapons. We even managed to destroy one of the invading ships. That sort of tactic would strike them, to use a Human term, as barbaric. They would be reluctant to get involved with a ship that fought like that, especially one they have just recently encountered. They did ultimately engage the invading forces out of a need for self-preservation, but they did it without coordinating with us."

Jared bit his lip. "We've learned a lot about them, but obviously that doesn't mean we know them."

"They would say the same of us."

Tir spoke. "What is the situation down there, sir? What became of those projectiles fired from the unidentified cruiser?"

Now that is a story, Jared thought. "We encountered an invasion team from one of those projectiles, but we survived. It was a platoon of the same enforcers Vetta's team fought on the prison ship, as well as one of the warden clouds from Malum." Tir's face registered shock, and Jared added, "Nho's staff was effective in dispatching all of them. The No Greater leadership has many questions for our cleric."

Tir paused to take in this new information. "So what are you planning to do now, sir?"

Jared rubbed his eyes. "We'll be on the planet for a little longer, at least. Nho and Vetta went out on a flatboat to combat the invasion teams that landed on other planetary settlements, although it may be too late for some of them. Beyond that, we have some difficult decisions to make. The No Greater have asked us to join them in forming a coalition to fight Dar and his Domain." Jared knew Tir well enough to know she wasn't going to like what he was about to say. "They want us to help them pull together an alliance of anti-Dar factions to liberate the Plury'be homeworld of Sacred Home from Domain control."

True enough, Tir looked at him with a sharp gaze of skepticism. "What sort of assistance would we be talking about? Diplomatic work? Military action?"

"I don't know yet. Possibly both."

Her pinprick eyes, small as they were, managed to narrow even farther. "Are you sure we want to entangle ourselves in that way? Forming alliances and involving ourselves in a civil war goes far beyond our orders? We have fulfilled our mission's mandate by collecting detailed intelligence on Dar and the Domain."

"I agree, but we also have a unique opportunity to safeguard the Confederacy from future attacks by undermining Dar's power on this side of the Void. If we walk away from this, we might never have another opportunity. You saw what happened today. The No Greater faction will not survive much longer without our help."

"That does not make it a compelling force to ally ourselves with, and it will potentially antagonize Dar against us."

"Dar has already attacked the Confederacy once," Redelia said, "and will do so again, regardless of who we side with here. The No Greater faction is small, but it is also our best chance to check Dar's power. They understand Plury'be politics better than we could. Accompanying them while they try to forge a coalition with other, more powerful factions seems like a worthwhile risk."

"There is something else, too," Jared added. "Nho believes that these people follow the same Creator he does. He believes they could come to find the same power he has. That is not a trivial matter. We watched Nho's staff dispatch an entire Domain unit today. If these people could also be taught to combat the Domain, we could do here what entire fleets could not do during last year's crisis."

Tir fixed her gaze on Jared. "If we are going to talk about people, Captain, we also need to talk about *our* people. The crew of the *Hattan* has already endured a long, dangerous mission into far space. Involving ourselves in this places them in far greater danger than what Garvak intended when we came here, and far more than anything we have done up to this point. We all knew that, when we enlisted in the Navy, we would be expected to follow Command's orders, even to possible death, but we are now talking of going beyond Command's orders. Providing the Plury'be with some understanding of Nho's . . . powers . . . is one thing. Entering into a political and military alliance is something entirely different."

Jared closed his eyes. "Let's put this conversation on hold for now while we both clean things up on our ends. We can discuss this further when I return to the ship."

14

E'REB / FREE TOWN

EARTH INDEX 1306.349

Jared crossed the threshold into one of the *Hattan*'s smaller recreational areas. It was empty, just as he had hoped it would be. He wandered over to a corner of the room, reached into a box, and pulled out a small rubberized ball the size of an orange. He absently tossed the ball against the wall, catching it on the first bounce, then repeated the action. It was mindless, just the sort of activity he needed to clear his head.

There was a lot of head-clearing to do. While discussion had continued between his team on the planet and the No Greater leadership, Jared had returned to the cruiser to check on the status of repairs, discuss the situation with Tir and other senior staff members, and, just as importantly, get a little rest.

But rest hadn't come easy. There was so much to do and so much to decide, both on the ship and on the planet below. For each decision he could make with certainty, there were two more that were so uncertain, he couldn't even begin to guess at the consequences of a wrong choice. It was not often that he faced such complicated, far-reaching pathways with so little insight into their ultimate outcomes. It wasn't hyperbole to say that this was the most consequential crossroads of his career. Even the difficult choices he'd faced during the heat of the Malum crisis seemed straightforward by comparison.

The ball hit the wall and came back at an awkward bounce. He moved to his left to pick it up, then straightened and threw again.

What made this situation different from past ones was the reality that he was out of communication with Navy Command. His ship had been sending regular updates back to the Confederacy by way of the *Hattan*'s experimental long-range communications array, but for various logistical reasons, the ship could not receive replies. For the first time in his career, he was having to make substantial command decisions with no option to consult his superiors. That he had a capable support staff—people like Tir, Redelia, Garo, and Vetta—did not lessen the burden. They could advise, but the decision was his. Surrounded by counsel, he nevertheless felt alone.

The ball ricocheted off the wall, this time bouncing off to his far left, beyond his ability to cut it off. It kept going, bobbing and rolling as it headed for the exit.

The door opened. Rami stepped in, saw the ball, and stooped to pick it up as it rolled to her feet. "Here you go, sir," she said, tossing the ball back to him.

"Hi, Rami," he said, raising his hands to catch it. "Is there something you need?"

"No," she said. "I just came down here to use the *vlexdrk*." She pointed over at the large, dark crate sitting next to the box Jared had retrieved his ball from. "No one seems to use this room as much as the others, and I worry less about accidentally hurting someone when I'm using it."

Jared shuddered. He'd decided long ago that Ritican recreational equipment was not for him. "You're braver than I."

She stretched a wide band of cloth over her head, then adjusted it to hold back her short hair. Without the fringe of hair to soften them, the angles of her cheekbones and jaw stood out, making her face seem austere. "Vetta introduced me to it once, years ago, right after the raid on Felseth 8," she said. "I was terrified the first time, to be honest, but I was too proud to back out once I'd told her I'd do it. The first time was the hardest, but once you get used to the primary arc, it's not too bad." She gestured to the ball. "Then again, maybe just a little of this might help, too. I just need to get away from my workstation for a little while."

Jared shrugged, then tossed the ball her way. She caught it with both hands. He asked, "How are you doing?"

"Other than the fact that I'm starting to see Plury'be language in my sleep, I'm well enough." She pitched the ball to him. He caught it one-handed. "How are you doing, sir?" she asked.

"I'm managing." He eyed the ball resting in his palm, weighing his words. After a long moment, he looked up and found her watching him with a concerned expression—the look of an old friend willing to share his burden. "I'm still trying to make sense of what to do about the Plury'be."

The ball flew from his hands to hers. "Orel contacted me from the *Belico* this morning," she said. "He said the No Greater are organizing to travel to some major Plury'be diplomatic planet and want us to come with them."

He knew a lot of crew members would tell him this as a preface to lobbying an agenda. That hadn't been part of Rami's personality, not in all the time he'd known her. If anything, that made him curious about what she thought.

"I have no idea," she admitted when he asked. She tossed the ball to him. "According to Orel, Redelia and Vetta believe we should go. Tir, on the other hand, isn't talking, which probably means she thinks we should return to the Confederacy. Orel also said you hadn't decided what to do yet."

Jared held onto the ball for a moment, squeezing it a little between his hands. "I'm still thinking about it. It's a tempting opportunity."

She cocked her head, as if studying his face. "But you're not sure."

He gave the ball a casual underhand toss. "No, and I don't know if I ever will be. How do you make a decision like this that has so many consequences for so many people?"

She eyed the ball for a moment, then gave it a strong over-hand throw. It went slightly off-course. He speared at it with his right hand, but it bounced off his fingers and went rolling toward a corner. As he went to retrieve it, she said, "There's always the Nho approach."

He picked up the ball and threw it overhand in a high arc across the room. "You mean pray, then go crashing in with a five thousand-year-old wooden staff?"

Running to receive the ball in both hands, she smiled, and the planes of her face softened. "Something like that." After she caught it, she added, "He's a strange man sometimes—"

He gave her a wry look.

Now she frowned. "Fine. He's a strange man most of the time. But if there's one thing I've learned from him, it's that I feel a lot better about who I am and the choices I make, now that I do the things Nho does." She held up the ball in one hand. "Except for the crashing in with the ancient staff part, of course."

He tilted his head, surprised to hear her speak so candidly about being a believer in Nho's faith. "Are you familiar with the colony on Axter?"

"The Lost Civilization of Nebs?"

He arched his eyebrows. "I'm impressed."

"I've been doing some reading," she explained. "Kilvin once gave me some trouble for my lack of history knowledge, especially of the ancient kind. I read about Nebs during our Void crossing. Very sad story. That entire society, lost."

It was a sad story. The Humans who had colonized Axter found ruins of a sprawling sentient civilization, possibly wiped out by their own devices. It was, not surprisingly, the most popular archaeological destination in the Confederacy, and one strictly regulated by Axter Colony, in collaboration with a consortium of Earth-based educational institutions.

Jared bounced the ball on the ground in front of him. "When I was younger—after my parents' divorce but while my father and I were still somewhat close—my father paid for a trip for me to visit

Axter as part of my tertiary education. There's a valley there that I traveled to during my last week. It's a long, narrow stretch of land, bracketed by mountains of exotic ore that completely disrupt guidance systems and link communication. The only way to travel there is by land or boat—a river cuts through the valley—and communications are only possible through physical transmission conduits. It's like a place out of another time."

He threw the ball to her and went on. "Archaeologists have reason to believe that the valley once housed a civilization separate from most of the rest of the planet. According to what they've been able to decipher, the valley dwellers were generally peaceful and just wanted to live independent of the larger civilization. But at some point, the valley was invaded by the larger civilization and overrun. The larger civilization appears to have imposed its culture on the valley dwellers, and as a result much of valley culture was lost. We know this because the larger civilization's records—such as we still have—were quite proud of this accomplishment. They were proud that they had eradicated another culture. Of course, now the entire planetary civilization is gone." Jared sighed. "I've thought a lot about that story the last two days."

Rami wiped some sweat off her brow. "You worry about history repeating itself."

Jared nodded. "When I saw Free Town under attack, I thought about that valley."

Rami nodded in return, and the two lapsed into silence. The only sound was their feet on the floor and the occasional sound of the ball hitting the same. Jared thought about what a basic exercise this was, throwing a small ball. It was the kind of game two children might play, yet that was what made it interesting. Fun, even.

He caught the ball in his left hand and looked at it. "I'd forgotten how enjoyable the simple things are," he said, tossing the ball back.

She sprinted over to catch it, this time one-handed. "Me, too. But I should get back to work." She held up the ball. "Thank you for the diversion, Captain. Not quite as exciting as *vlexdrk*, but

Darel won't give me as much grief the next time I stop by the infirmary."

Jared laughed. She flashed a smile, tossed the ball one more time, and headed out the door, which closed behind her. Jared caught the rubber sphere on a hop, holding it against his waist. He stared at the door for a long time, thinking. A lot of things had changed in his life during the last year. A lot of people, too.

• • •

Venzz Kitt sauntered down the hallway toward one of the smaller recreational areas. Ostensibly he was headed to get some exercise. Easygoing as he was in many respects, Venzz took a great deal of pride in his fitness level and the lean physique that resulted from it. Unlike his prudish rival, Brigg Drews, he found his motivation to exercise in the tangible rewards of companionship.

And, indeed, companionship was on his mind today. He had it on good authority that a certain communications officer liked to venture down here to use one of the pieces of Ritican recreational equipment, and he also had it on good authority that this was one of her favorite times of day, when the room was less busy. If he was fortunate, perhaps he'd have a chance—after his unsuccessful attempt on the bridge a couple of days ago—to find the companionable woman he believed was still somewhere deep inside Rami Del.

Sure enough, as he approached the recreation area, Rami came walking around the corner, a smile on her face, headed right in his direction. The moment she caught sight of him, however, her eyes narrowed and her smile vanished.

"Good afternoon, Rami," Venzz offered with a slow smile of his own. "Down here for some exercise?"

"Hello, Lieutenant," she said, her voice as distant as always. She sounded rather like a bored bureaucrat in a processing office. Still putting up a wall.

"I've heard you're well versed in the Ritican *vlexdrk*," Venzz continued, careful to keep his voice as innocent and light as possible.

He was good at scaling these particular walls. "I was hoping you'd be willing to show me how to play." This second part was a lie—the Ritican equipment terrified him—but his previous attempts with Rami had gone nowhere, and he was ready to try another line of attack. The best ventures, he reasoned, came only from great risk.

Rami gave him an implacable stare. "There are a lot of Riticans on this ship."

"They're not very patient with Humans." He lifted his hands in a gesture of surrender. "I'm just asking for ten minutes. Nothing else."

"If I learned from a Ritican, so can you."

She started to walk past him, but he took a half-step in front of her. Not enough to block her path, but enough to buy at least one more moment. "Will you at least think about it?"

She stopped, straightened up a little, and looked up at him with a pair of eyes that told him he was about to be scolded. "Lieutenant Kitt," she said. "I know you, how you think, and what you want. I want no part of it."

He sighed and brushed a finger against her upper arm. "I'd heard that, not so long ago, you had a more lively side. Surely you miss it."

Her face turned red, and he immediately realized that he'd made a serious tactical error. Far from planting seeds of hesitation, or even a faint longing, he'd unleashed something else entirely. Anger seemed inadequate to describing it.

"*Lieutenant.*" She stood her ground, but the word carried an authority of command he'd never heard from her before. He dropped his hand and took a step back. It was like talking to a different person. He momentarily forgot that, technically speaking, he was the ranking officer. "Whatever you think you know, know this: if you *ever* act like that again, or if you ever address me again in a way that is anything less than fully professional, I will break any finger you attempt to lay on me and our next conversation will be in the captain's office. Am I completely clear?"

He was speechless, in no small part because he believed every word. It didn't help matters that she'd worked with the captain far longer than he had. He had the very nasty feeling that if she did break his fingers, Jared Carter would find a way to rule that he deserved it and more. His mind swirled with everything that could go wrong. Would the captain deny him an interceptor command? Assign him to garbage reprocessing supervision duty?

All he could do was give a faint nod, then step aside. She stormed past, not casting so much as a glance back in his direction as she disappeared around the far corner.

As he stood there, contemplating his situation, he heard footsteps coming from behind him, back in the direction of the recreation area. He turned just in time to see Captain Carter rounding the corner.

"Good afternoon, Lieutenant," the captain said, and kept walking.

Venzz's blood ran cold. Had the captain overheard his conversation with Rami?

Captain Carter disappeared around the corner, leaving Venzz standing in the corridor, alone, the image of Jared Carter looking at him as he walked past frozen in his mind. Something about the captain's face disturbed him, even more than if Carter had been angry.

Had the captain been smirking?

• • •

Jared sat down at the command station of the *Hattan* bridge. The bridge crew around him was silent, all of them turned in his direction, all of their eyes watching him. Kilvin, sitting at navigation, watched him with confidence. Garo, seated at the weapons station, looked impassive, although Jared knew the Ritican supported him. At sciences, Aioua waited expectantly, as did Orel at communications. Rami, who was off-duty, nevertheless stood against a far wall of the bridge, watching him with her hands clasped behind her back and a half-smile on her face.

Not far from sciences, Tir waited, her face unreadable. Jared knew she didn't fully approve of what he was about to say, and he understood why. The two of them had debated this subject at length, and he recognized and shared her reservations. In fairness to her, she also understood his reasoning, even if she would have made a different decision in his stead.

"But I was not appointed to be the captain," she had said. "You were. I am not sure I will ever fully agree with this decision, but I will not impede you. Our lives depend on being unified, now more than ever. My opinions shall remain known only to you."

Jared suspected that she wasn't being entirely truthful—her good friend, Aioua, was likely to know Tir's objections—but if Tir trusted Aioua's discretion, Jared did, too. That might not keep some of the more observant crew members, like Orel and Rami, from speculating on Tir's opinions, but Tir would never speak openly of it. She would be the good officer, and Jared felt confident that would be enough. She wasn't above publicly disagreeing with her superiors—she had done so with the previous captain of the *Hattan*, Traves Walbirg—but her relationship with Jared carried much greater respect.

Still, Jared thought it wise to feel out the rest of the crew's sentiments. To both Jared's and Tir's surprise, the prevailing opinion of those on board was that they should press the alliance with the Plury'be. For some, like the Riticans, the reasons were obvious, but for others, like the Humans, it wasn't as clear. The best Jared could come up with was that the crew's shared experience inside Malum gave them a common desire to do all they could to stop the planet-ship's creator, even at the greater risk of their own lives. Jared wasn't sure if vengeance was the right word. Then again, for some of them, maybe it was.

Jared nodded to Orel, who keyed ship-wide communications. Jared cleared his throat and began speaking:

"Officers and crew of the *Hattan*, this is Captain Jared Carter speaking.

"When we were originally assigned to this mission, our primary objective was to ascertain the origins of Malum. We were to collect what information we could, and report it back to the Confederacy. We have succeeded, collecting an enormous amount of intelligence, not only on the Domain and its technology, but also on the mysteries of the Invasion of 1124. The Confederacy is safer because of our efforts. Each and every one of you has performed your duties admirably under the most challenging circumstances any Navy fleet has ever faced."

He paused, took a deep breath—he was a little nervous—and went on.

"We stand now at a difficult crossroads. Through either the work of fate or divine design, we now have friends on this side of the Great Void, friends who oppose the empire that created Malum. We have a chance to do more than just reconnaissance; we have a chance to ally with others who also face the wrath of Dar and his Domain.

"I realize this was not the mission any of us anticipated when we first departed home so many months ago. I also realize that involving ourselves with forces here places us in greater danger. Some might reasonably question if we are better off returning to the Confederacy.

"Our senior staff has weighed these issues carefully, and many of you have had a voice in those deliberations. It is in these discussions that our common shared experience of having been prisoners of Malum has been so important. All of us were forever changed by that event, and all of us want to make sure others do not ever share such a fate. Most of us agree that striking against the Domain on this side of the Great Void is the best way to accomplish that."

Jared glanced at Tir. She gave the briefest of nods. He nodded back solemnly, then continued.

"I will not hide from reality: this course of action has risks. Aside from the obvious risks to our own personal safety, we risk arousing the ire of the Domain and embroiling ourselves in a Plury'be conflict that is not ours. Given that the Domain has already tried to destroy us, we believe strongly that the potential gains of action here outweigh the drawbacks.

"We are now on a course for a Plury'be planet appropriately known as Wisdom. It is our hope that there we can find more who oppose Dar. If we succeed, we can further guarantee that our homeworlds will be free of the enslavement that the Domain certainly intends to bring. I have no doubt you are all up to the task."

15

To N'ht / Wisdom
Earth Index 1306.351

Rami speared a piece of meat with her eating utensil and took a cautious bite. Palatable, if plain. She directed the table to procure her some salt. Around her, the dining area buzzed with its usual sentient traffic. Across the table, Rete picked at his food, a distinct gloom hovering over him.

As she applied the salt, she glanced his way. "For someone who recently came back from Humanity's first newly explored world in decades, you seem awfully depressed."

He looked up and forced a smile. "I'm sorry I'm not better company today."

"Do you want to talk about it?"

"Why is it that every time we meet for lunch, you wind up being my counselor?"

"Because everyone needs a friendly ear now and then. Now start talking."

Rete stared at the table, then shook his head and gave a small shrug. "I'm disappointed with myself, that's all."

She cocked her head. "What are you talking about? I've read the transcripts. The meetings on Free Town went very well, thanks in large part to your contributions, both in the questions you asked and the ones you answered. Because of you, we now have an ally among the Plury'be."

"I'm not talking about that. Talk is something I'm good at. Where I fail is in what I do. It's always where I fail."

She put her utensil down and regarded him, her hands interlaced in front of her. "What happened?"

Rete tossed his utensil onto the table in a show of frustration. "When the Domain forces attacked the settlement, I panicked. I ran away. Nho ran right out there into the center of the settlement, and I ran away. I ran away because I was terrified, because I didn't want to die. I left him and the captain and all the rest and hid like some child."

She looked into his eyes. "I don't fault you for that. I've seen one of those overseers firsthand, and they are terrifying. Vetta would say the same of the enforcers."

"That's a small consolation when your friend is running toward danger with nothing but a staff and his faith. I claim to share that faith, but I doubted him. I thought he was out of his mind, and I ran. I cowered out of sight while Nho dispelled an entire platoon with a stick and a few words."

A Ritican voice nearby said, "The question is not what you did. The question is, what will you do now?"

Rete looked up and saw Vetta Quidd's sizable copper frame towering over them. "I apologize for intruding," she said, "but I would speak with you, if you have a moment."

Rete appeared caught off-guard. He looked to Rami, who shrugged deferentially, as if to say, *It's your decision.* Looking back to Vetta, he gestured to an open chair.

Vetta took a seat between them, the chair flaring out to accommodate her large body. "You are not the first to flee one of Dar's minions," she said to Rete. "You were not on Malum with the rest of us, and while we can describe what we saw, it does not substitute for the terror of being there and seeing it. You have now seen some of what caused such fear. You ran because it was your first time. When we were confronted by an overseer on Malum, all of us fled, including me and including some whose faith is the same as your own. Nho is the only soul who did not. You did as most do. The next step is to learn, to grow and develop the strength so that if you do face the terror again, you can face it with bravery and honor."

"How?" His voice constricted in his throat. "How do you face something like that?"

"I have some ideas, but perhaps the best one to talk to is your old friend. He knows a great many things about hope and courage."

Rete pressed his lips together. "I'll think about what you've said."

Vetta straightened a little in her chair. "There another subject I wanted to speak with you about, the true reason I came to find you today. It is about the one called Suda."

Rete's weary gloom vanished, replaced by a coldness. "What of him?"

"I spoke with him last year, while we were on Pane's Planet. He gave me a message to pass along to you, should I ever see you. I have intended to tell you for some time, but circumstance has prevented it. After the dangers we faced on Free Town, I determined that I should see to that task sooner rather than later."

"I'm listening."

"When I met him, he was a miner on Pane's Planet, scarcely better off than you were in the manufactory of Ramas-Eduj. He was sad and broken. Pitiable, even. Nevertheless, he requested that if I ever found you, I should tell you that he was deeply sorry."

Rete took a bite of food and chewed as he absorbed Vetta's message. "Thank you for taking the time to tell me," he said, although his voice was stiff.

"Of course."

Rete's voice softened a little. "And for your advice on the other matter. It has been good to speak with you."

Vetta stood and gave a Ritican gesture of one taking leave. She then walked away, leaving Rami and Rete once again alone at the table. A few minutes passed before either of them spoke.

Rami ultimately broke the silence. "Well?"

Rete looked up from his plate. "Well, what?"

"Your feelings on what Vetta said?"

"I'm not sure what to feel."

Rami smiled. "Vetta's a good soul. She's one of the most noble sentients I know."

"I've been told that. She also dealt with two very sensitive subjects."

"Nho and Suda."

Rete rubbed his nose with his thumb and forefinger. "At one time Tsi, Nho, Suda and I were like family, young and excited about what Sarco was doing for our enclave on Earth. We had the parchment pieces and the company of many good believers. Now Tsi is dead, Suda is a betrayer, and Nho has ascended to a faith I can't seem to find."

"And here you are, a freed slave now trying to find his way on a Navy ship in a part of the galaxy no Human has ever explored, all while facing the greatest of evils."

Rete laughed. "It sounds funny hearing you say it, but you're right. As much as I speak of the others, the truth is that I'm still trying to find my way. It does not help that I am my own worst critic."

Rami speared another bite. Holding her utensil up in the air, the vegetable still on it, she said, "I think Vetta's right. It is what you do next that matters." She popped the vegetable in her mouth. "So what are you going to do?"

• • •

Jared paid a visit to the infirmary on the way back to his quarters. The medical team was hard at work, treating the large number of officers still suffering from the aftereffects of the hyperwave attacks. The infirmary had been able to take care of the injured without the need for separate triage units, although not for reasons anyone would want; many of those exposed to the attacks never made it to the infirmary, perishing quickly under the biocidal effects of the Plury'be weapons. Tomorrow would be the first of the memorial services for those lost at Free Town, and it was going to be hard.

Jared watched the medical officers move among the injured, administering treatment or looking over diagnostic information. Along one wall, he could see Mollo Nairu performing a surgical procedure on a Ritican male. Closer to Jared, Darel Weye administered injections of varying sizes to a diverse group of crew members.

Jared's attention settled on a few Exos closer to where he was standing. Four of them were sitting on the floor, a large device attached to each of them by way of a snaking trail of cords. The cords appeared to be attached to the surface of their exoskeletons, and the whole apparatus hummed.

Jared walked over to the Exos. "How are you all doing?"

The one nearest him uttered a series of clicks and snaps, which Jared's link translated. "All of us will survive."

"What is this device?"

"A particle extractor. It removes hyperwave particles from our systems, allowing for normal function."

Darel Weye approached, adding, "They have a bout of food poisoning, sir."

"A bout of what?"

"Exo physiology ingests radioactive particles as part of their life process. As a result, hyperwave particles, which bear some similarities, are not as immediately fatal to them as to other sentients. Nevertheless, Exos cannot properly metabolize the particles, so they need to be extracted before they can cause too much damage."

"Were any Exos killed by the particles?"

"Fortunately, no, although Triphox was the most imperiled when it arrived here."

Jared took a quick intake of breath at the Exo name and looked down at the one sitting nearest him, the Exo who had spoken. It was indeed Triphox, the officer who had been Jared's industrious engineer on the *Retaelus* for so long. Jared had been so busy leading the ship that he had not interacted with Triphox directly in months. He felt a stab of regret at having all but forgotten the one engineer he knew best. Exos, because of their relatively task-driven personalities, were not particularly sociable and were easy to confuse with one another, so it was an easy mistake to make. Triphox would, by its very nature, take no offense.

That didn't make it right. "Triphox," Jared said, "are you all right?"

"I am harmed but will recover. The task of closing the torpedo tubes was successfully completed."

"They were in the forward torpedo bay," Darel explained. "Most of the crew working there died in the hyperwave attacks, but Triphox and two other Exos were able to manually close the torpedo tubes before we had a full particle breach in the forward compartments. I cannot begin to estimate how many lives they saved."

"The task was successfully completed," Triphox clicked.

Jared nodded to the engineers on the floor. Thanks meant little to them, but he felt compelled to express it anyway. "You have done this ship incalculable service, and I will see you are commended." He turned away.

He could only hope it wasn't for naught in the end.

• • •

Redelia Aroo and Brigg Drews stood next to each other in the main cargo bay, watching as Exos scurried over and inside the interceptors, examining them for damage and performing minor repairs and testing. Not much had been said between Aecron and Human in the few minutes both had been standing there; each was engrossed in the reports particular to his or her own ship.

Presently Redelia spoke. "I've read Tir Bvaso's report. You performed well back there."

Brigg looked up from his report and stared out at his ship. "I should have been able to do more. The Plury'be essentially ignored us."

"Interceptors are not warships. They have limits. You did well simply to alert the fleet to the attack."

"Right now, I feel like that's all these ships are good for. We're scouts and nothing more."

"That is by design," said Redelia.

"I know. This was supposed to be a reconnaissance mission, the kind of work an interceptor could handle well. Now our focus has changed, and our fleet is not equipped for combat."

"Do you have any ideas for what we can do about it?"

Brigg studied her profile carefully. Something told him she had ideas of her own already. The pretense irritated him—he was nothing if not direct—but he stifled those feelings. When it came to senior officers, he had to play the game.

"Our best option," he said evenly, "is to maximize our existing arsenal. We need to bring our remaining two interceptors to completion as quickly as possible. Five interceptors together would not be as powerful as a single cruiser, but they would be more potent than just three."

"Anything else?"

"I would love to have more firepower, but I don't see how we can do that without sacrificing what makes an interceptor effective. I grew up on a merchant ship, and if there was one thing I learned, it was that you never gained something without giving up something else. If we try to install additional weapons, we are almost certain to create liabilities that might actually harm us down the road. I wouldn't mind lobbying for Captain Carter to give each interceptor a couple of collider torpedoes, but I wouldn't go much beyond that."

"Is that it?"

Brigg stared pointedly at her. His patience with this exercise was just about at its end. "I know you have ideas of your own, sir."

"I do," she said, turning to face the ships in the bay, "although, they are not all that different from yours. Ultimately, I believe our best asset will be the allies we make here. That, and whatever other miracles the Creator can perform for us."

There was something about the manner in which she spoke of the Creator that made Brigg uneasy. What did she know about him?

16

N'HT / WISDOM
EARTH INDEX 1306.354

Located a considerable distance from the Great Void, the planet known as N'ht, or Wisdom, was one of several planets encircling a moderately sized star. While one of the inner planets was, incredibly, capable of supporting oxygen-based life, the Plury'be were sensitive to large quantities of oxygen or temperatures above minus-fifty degrees standard, so that planet was uninhabited. Wisdom was farther out, a cold ball of rock that glowed with a mysterious phosphorescent atmosphere. This gave the view from the surface an appearance of neither light nor dark nor even twilight. It was as if the heavens themselves created the light for a city at night.

Unlike Free Town, Wisdom was not the exclusive domain of a single faction. Rather, it was a collective of various power groups, the primary world of a few factions and the secondary world of many others. The inhabitants lived in an agreed-upon set of rules, including a yet-unbroken pact to never use weapons, either on the surface or in space. Wisdom was a place where factions were free to talk, it was said.

One of the major factions of Wisdom—and the object of the No Greater alliance campaign—was a populous known as the Way of Law. The Way of Law were governed by a litany of rules that crossed economic, political, religious, and cultural lines. Their daily lives were, apparently, a constant exercise in careful regimentation, as were their policies and actions.

The No Greater faction had cited them as a potential partner for many reasons. One, the Way of Law despised the corruptions the Domain brought to the Plury'be and had voiced opposition to Dar in the past. Two, they shared the No Greater belief in a singular divine creator, although they differed considerably in their understanding of that creator. Three, they possessed military potential (stationed, apparently, on planets other than Wisdom) formidable enough to challenge the factions sympathetic to the Domain. Four, a few within the Way of Law had recently converted to the No Greater faction, and those converts believed they could leverage their conversion to better reason with those on Wisdom.

Au'p and S'li were both converts from the Way of Law.

The *Hattan* emerged into open space a modest distance from the spectral planet. Three cruisers and several flatboats from Free Town had already arrived and were waiting. It had been previously decided that the Free Town entourage should arrive before the Navy ship; although Wisdom had a history of nonviolence, it was impossible to predict how area ships would react to the unannounced arrival of a completely alien warship.

The *Hattan* received approach instructions from the Free Town flagship: follow their heading, match their speed, and make no provocation. Defense fields and all weapons were to remain powered down, and no ships of any sort were to be launched from the cargo bay until told to do so. They would be observed carefully, the No Greater faction warned.

And they were right. Almost immediately the *Hattan* was assailed with sensory probing, the stellar equivalent of walking into a crowded room and facing a hundred curious stares.

Or more. In contrast to comparatively quiet space above Free Town, the approach to Wisdom was swirling with traffic. It was an awesome sight, like observing the thriving ecology of an ocean for the first time. Plury'be ships were the most common feature, but there were others, too, ships with propulsion and hull configurations that were new.

"That green bulbous transport," Aioua said, highlighting the ship on the tridimensional display, "is filled with liquid plastics. It has to be some sort of liquid-breathing species, not unlike the Ils of the Minor Races back home. And that small blue-green sphere just rightward of the liquid-breathing ship has the high-pressure environment of a gas giant."

"What about that dark brown cylinder, the one behind the green blob-like ship?" Jared asked.

"Dense atmosphere, large concentrations of Scr12."

Even Jared, who hated chemistry, knew what Scr12 was. It was the Aecron word for what Humans called ammonia.

Kilvin asked, "Are any of them oxygen breathing?"

Aioua parsed through her numbers. "Two models of ships show atmospheres comparable to ours."

"Oxygen breathers don't seem to be as common on this side," Jared said.

"Based on races we have observed, no. It is possible that other oxygen breathing species exist on this side, but are either not present here or lack spaceflight entirely."

Jared turned his eyes toward communications. "Any ideas where all these ships come from?"

"According to the Free Town database," Orel read aloud, "some of these ships match sovereign nations separate from the Domain or the Plury'be."

"But not all."

"No. That one"—Orel pointed to the liquid-breathing ship—"recently came under Domain influence, as did at least one other race represented in orbit. The Free Town database implies that, in both cases, it was not voluntary."

A shiver ran up Jared's spine. As if Malum weren't proof enough, here was yet another reminder of how dangerous Dar's empire was.

And that wasn't the only proof. Jared noticed a number of ships with a sharp geometric design closer to the planet. Aioua saw them, too. She said, "There are fifteen ships in orbit that have a similar profile to the Invader-U ship we encountered over Free Town."

The No Greater leadership had confirmed after the battle over Free Town that Invader-U was a Domain ship, specifically from its leading race, the Supreme People.

"The No Greater faction told us the Domain was known to make regular diplomatic visits to Wisdom," Orel said, "although this is a far larger contingent than the No Greater anticipated when we discussed this trip."

"One wonders if the Domain learned of the No Greater's intentions here," Garo said.

Jared shrugged. "We don't know enough about the Plury'be to say, but I'm not sure how much it matters. A Domain presence of any size is no surprise. We knew going into this that if we and the No Greater faction were going to convince the Way of Law to join the effort to oppose Dar, we would have to do so over the objections of Dar's diplomats. That's exactly what we will do."

• • •

The large shuttle *Acebi* debarked from the *Hattan* and made a course to the surface of Wisdom. Kilvin piloted the craft. Also in the shuttle were Jared, Nho, Rete, Orel representing communications, Vetta heading up security, and two other security officers, a Ritican and a squat Hazionite female named Bel Wrsaw. Darel was present as both a medical officer and a sciences officer.

Jared sat in quiet contemplation in the back of the shuttle. He rehearsed, silently, the possible scenarios he might face down below and how he might respond to them. His greatest fear was saying something that might unintentionally derail the No Greater cause, but staying silent was not an option. The Way of Law would be reluctant to ally with a small, remote Plury'be faction, but they might work with the envoys of a large multi-nation civilization like the Confederacy, especially one that had experienced—and stopped—an invasion from Dar.

Except he wasn't supposed to be here as an envoy.

Vetta Quidd took a seat next to him. "How are you doing, Captain?"

Jared stared at the floor. "I'm uncertain. About a lot of things."

Vetta leaned in, speaking quietly. "Let me attempt a guess. You are uncertain whether we know enough about Plury'be society to effectively negotiate with the people of this world. Or whether Free Town is capable of securing Wisdom as an ally. Or whether the Plury'be can stand up to Dar. Or whether we should be attempting such alliances in the first place, given that our mission was reconnaissance. Or, perhaps, whether we will be court-martialed by the Navy or assassinated by the Aecrons upon our return."

He looked up and smiled weakly. "You know me well. Every one of those things has crossed my mind." The smile faded. "It's a lot of unknown variables to risk our crew's lives on."

Vetta paused in thought. Then she said, "Admiral Garvak knew when he deployed us here that we might face unexpected circumstances—circumstances that might require us to make decisions outside the scope of our orders. That is an unavoidable element of operating in a place where conferring with one's superiors is impossible. The admiral would much rather us take the risk of bringing the fight to the Domain than squander an opportunity in the name of protocol or out of fear of possible loss."

"Tir felt Garvak might say otherwise."

"I have tremendous respect for the commander, but on this matter she is wrong. I am not speaking out of conjecture. It is fact. I know my people. Any Ritican militia commander in your place would do the same as you are doing. Admiral Garvak subscribes to the Code as we all do, and that Code elevates the defense of the state beyond protocol, beyond even the risk of failure. We have fulfilled our orders by sending our intelligence back to the Navy. It is now time for us to fight for our future with the opportunity that has been laid before us."

"She's right," Nho said, moving to a seat just across from them. "Sarco has opened a door for us to walk through, and we are fated to take it."

Jared exchanged looks with both of them. "So what do we tell them? What are the right words to tell a society whose cultural norms we barely understand?"

Nho lifted a hand, palm up, as if holding an invisible object. "Sarco once said that truth is the great liberator. That is our weapon."

• • •

The *Acebi* landed on a smooth, empty plain in the middle of a sprawling metropolis. There were a few other ships on the plain, all variations on the Plury'be flatboat design. The party on board the shuttle disembarked into the open, except for Kilvin and the Ritican security officer, who remained behind.

Jared took a moment to marvel at the sky as the last of the party emerged from the shuttle. The eerie glow of phosphorescent light radiated from above, massive streaks casting their ethereal prism of colors down on everything. There was no sun; the system's star was too far away to offer more than a pinprick of light.

"In the northern regions of the Earth's Western Territories, there are auroras like this," said Rete.

"I've visited that region," Jared said, "but I don't remember anything being this vivid. It's breathtaking."

A cluster of Plury'be slid along the plain up to where the Navy crew was waiting. Au'p was among them. "Welcome to Wisdom / This is the place of the Speaking Stone."

"Speaking Stone?" Jared asked.

"The Speaking Stone is a place to discuss / The Speaking Stone is a place to decide. The factions discuss at the Speaking Stone / We will seek the factions at the Speaking Stone / (hopefulness). We should go to the Speaking Stone / The factions are waiting at the Speaking Stone / (anxiety)."

Au'p and the group of Plury'be with it headed off. Jared and the others followed. In short order, they reached the end of the landing area, which gave way to crowds of habitations along narrow streets. Many of the habitations were low and round like those on

Free Town, although a few lean, tall towers stood out amidst the cityscape.

Plury'be bystanders were scattered along the edges of the street, watching as they walked by. Jared's environmental suit detected no communication; the city's inhabitants by all appearances were standing in silence. Other than a few glowing orb-shaped illuminators, there was little in the way of artificial light. Most of the illumination came from the multitude of colors in the skies above.

The Navy team walked in relative silence for several minutes, with only occasional chatter between Vetta and the other security officer over a private Navy frequency. Jared's eyes roved back and forth, soaking in everything before him. Walking in this city on a world so very far from Earth filled him at once with both a sense of profound awe and a feeling of smallness.

"One wonders what they must think of us," Nho said, gesturing to the narrow sideways along the street. "The inhabitants."

"I don't know." Then, a moment later, "I remember reading the accounts of the first Aecron envoys arriving on Earth tens of years ago. Humans were fascinated to see these short, large-eyed, blue-skinned beings descending from triangular spacecraft. Accounts at the time said that half of the Hattan population converged on the area just to catch a live glimpse of them."

"Hattan?" It was Bel Wrsaw, the Hazionite security officer with them.

Vetta explained. "Our ship is named for one of the large metropolitan centers on the Human homeworld."

"At that time, Hattan was the seat of the Western Territories," Jared added, "one of the regional governments on Earth. Every Earth government was there, as well as visitors from across the planet. The military was everywhere, trying to contain the crowds, which included more than a few protesters. Not all Humans were thrilled to be dealing with beings from other planets, especially since the Aecrons were widely suspected to have abducted and experimented on Humans centuries before."

Orel Dayail, trailing a few paces behind Jared, chimed in. "My unit father was an ambassador to Earth for many years. Resentment over those abductions remained a source of difficulty for him throughout his deployment. He rarely went an Index week without some Human reminding him of what our people had done, and Human leaders frequently tried to leverage that history in their negotiations with Aeroel."

"Humans hold long memories for indignities," Rete said, "especially when the offending party refuses to acknowledge or apologize for the offense."

"This is something my unit father understood that his superiors did not. Most Aecrons accept that the abductions happened, but do not understand the consequences of denying it officially."

Jared's eyes drifted briefly to Darel Weye, who was silent. Then, to Orel, he said, "Sociology has never been a strength of Aecron study."

Orel looked at him with a grimace. "I think it would be easier for Hazionites to teach Humans how to smell emotions."

"Captain," said Vetta. "Up ahead."

Jared cast his attention forward. Not far away, the road curled up and around a giant rocky plateau, which rose perhaps a hundred trics off the ground and loomed over the surrounding habitations. From their current position, there did not seem to be any structures on the plateau.

Rete's mouth fell open. "What *is* that?"

Jared took a deep breath. "Judging by the course we are taking, that must be the Speaking Stone."

• • •

Despite the implication in its name that it was unique, the Speaking Stone was actually one of many similar-looking gathering places in Plury'be civilization, facilitating an ancient practice among a society of factions who needed open venues to communicate and advance their ideologies. But the place known properly as the

Speaking Stone—this place—was among the more renowned and important of those gathering places. Wisdom's reputation as a safe place, combined with the large influence of the Way of Law faction who governed here, made the Speaking Stone the location where matters of the greatest import were decided.

Jared and the others ascended the road to the surface of the plateau. Up ahead was a dais, a slightly raised stone-like oblong stage some thirty trics long in the center of the plateau. A crowd of sentients surrounded the plateau. Most of them were Plury'be, but a few were species he had never seen before. There was a rustle of chatter as the Navy crew came into view, the locals and other visiting sentients discussing the strange newcomers. One cluster of wispy aliens began moving their tens of appendages at each other furiously; Jared wondered if it was some sort of form of communication.

Au'p and the No Greater approached and led Jared and the others to the edge of the dais, where they waited. Jared surveyed the perimeter of the oblong stage and at once his blood ran cold. Almost directly across from him was a group of geometric objects floating just above the ground.

"Enforcers," Vetta spat.

"I am not so sure," Darel said. "These beings bear noticeable proportional and physiological differences from the ones we saw at High Land and Free Town. They are also unarmed and bear no trace of Uxa251."

Jared attuned his communication so the Plury'be could hear. "Au'p," he said, "what are those beings across from us? The ones that look like enforcers?"

"Those are not enforcers / Those are emissaries. The Domain has envoys of many types / Emissaries are one of those types. Enforcers are envoys of another type / Overseers are envoys of another type. Domain ships are envoys of another type / Regulators are envoys of another type / (somberness)."

"Do the emissaries speak for Dar? Are they his diplomats or representatives?"

"That is correct / The emissaries speak for Dar."

Vetta said to Au'p, "So Dar has many ways of trying to carry out his will, whether it be the enforcers' weapons or the emissaries' voices? That is what you mean by envoys?"

"That is correct / Dar is powerful in many ways. His influence is dangerous / We are here to oppose that influence / (resoluteness)."

A group of Plury'be slid up on the dais, moving to a space nearly mid-center on the platform. Their words resonated loudly in Jared's environmental suit. "We gather at the Speaking Stone to discuss / We gather at the Speaking Stone to deliberate," one of them said. "A call to meet has been made by Those of No Greater / The call has been accepted by the Way of Law. Those of No Greater may speak / Others will listen. Others will respond / Those of No Greater will listen. Those of No Greater advance strange ideas / Others would know what they mean."

Au'p ascended onto the platform, alone, moving out to a space nearly mid-center, not far from the Plury'be party waiting there. Au'p's black surface rippled and its tendrils waved lightly as it gathered itself and began to speak:

I speak to those of the Way of Law / I speak to those who gather here who are not of the Way of Law.

We know that you seek truth / We know that you seek wisdom.

We know that you seek meaning / We know that you seek that which made us all.

We know who made us all / That Which There Is No Greater made us all.

That Which There Is No Greater made Us of Plury'be / That Which There Is No Greater made those of us who are not of Us of Plury'be.

That Which There Is No Greater does not need Us of Plury'be / That Which There Is No Greater is its own Master.

That Which There Is No Greater placed Us who live in the Worlds / That Which There Is No Greater came to Us of Plury'be as Ah'ey of the Faction of the Way of Law.

That Which There Is No Greater came to all that we might find Truth / That Which There Is No Greater came to us all that we might find the Good Which Comes After.

The Way of the Good Which Comes After is Truth in Ah'ey / The Way of Ah'ey is the path to the Good Which Comes After . . .

Jared chanced a look at Nho, who was deep in concentration. Jared wondered what the old man thought of those words. Ah'ey was, according to Au'p, the "Seed Vessel" of That Which There Is No Greater. Nho was convinced Ah'ey was the Incarnate, the same Incarnate who had come to other worlds, including to Aeroel as Sarco.

Au'p continued:

Ah'ey commands us to seek the Higher Way / Ah'ey commands us to seek That Which There Is No Greater.

The Domain commands us to seek the Lower Way / Dar commands us to seek That Which Distorts.

Ah'ey stands in opposition to Dar / Dar stands in opposition to the Higher Way.

Dar Distorts within the Domain / Dar Distorts on the worlds of Us of Plury'be.

That Which There Is No Greater seeks to save Us from the Lower Way / That Which There Is No Greater proved this with Ah'ey.

Ah'ey is the Life Being of That Which There Is No Greater / Ah'ey proved that it is the Life Being by returning from the Good Which Comes After.

Jared's link detected murmurs in the crowd. It was hard to parse out all that was being said, especially given the layered complexity of the Plury'be language. He thought he heard a few words of disapproval and at least one comment expressing a desire to hear more.

"What is a 'Life Being?'" asked Rete.

"A term the Way of Law use to describe their hope that one day the Creator will come and bring order to the Plury'be," Orel said.

"Au'p is trying to reach the Way of Law by speaking in their own terminology."

Jared grunted. It was hard enough keeping all these religious terms straight just within the Confederacy; adding Plury'be vernacular to the mix made his mind spin.

The Plury'be who had first spoken on the dais—Jared assumed from its earlier comments that it represented the Way of Law faction that largely governed this world—now spoke. "The ways of the Faction of No Greater already have been spoken / The ways of the Faction of No Greater are well known. The Way of Law accepts the Good Which Comes After / The Way of Law accepts It of a Final Power. The Way of Law rejects that Ah'ey was the Life Being / The Way of Law rejects Ah'ey / (disapproval). This is our way / This shall not change."

Au'p responded. "Us of the No Greater seek the Higher Way / You of the Way of Law seek the Higher Way."

"This is true / This is correct / (concession)."

"Dar corrupts our homeworld / Dar corrupts Sacred Home. Dar leads from the Higher Way / Dar leads to the Lower Way. The path is obvious / the path is clear / (certainty). Dar seeks to corrupt Us All / Dar seeks to distort us from the Higher Way."

A new voice said, "That is a fabrication."

One of the emissaries, the floating diplomats of Dar, came aloft on the dais, its spinning elements moving in clean synchronization as it made its way to the mid-center of the platform. The Plury'be crowd was quiet. In Jared's link, he could hear Rete and Orel chatting about the emissary's language, with Orel confirming what Rete believed: the emissary was speaking in a flat version of the Plury'be language, devoid of the layered nuances the Plury'be themselves used.

The emissary stopped not far from Au'p and the Way of Law delegation; one could draw a near-perfect triangle between Au'p, the Way of Law, and the emissary. The emissary spoke again. "All here know that the Domain and the leading Plury'be faction enjoy an amicable relationship. Conversely, the No Greater faction has continued to spread fabrications about Dar and the Domain and engage in destructive violence against the Domain. Domain lives have been extinguished for their actions."

"That is not true / That is a deception," said Au'p. "The Domain attacked the World of No Greater / The Domain attempted to subjugate Us of No Greater."

"You rearrange the facts to meet your conveniences," said the emissary. "Three and twenty *bonanol* ago you were apprehended after trying to incite a rebellion against Those of the Soul by destroying an Agro'ath House. Your allies in the No Greater faction attacked a prison transport to free you, extinguishing Plury'be and subjects of the Domain alike. You seek destruction."

Jared's mind clouded with confusion. Agro'ath House? Those of the Soul? What were they talking about?

Au'p's tentacles flared out in anger. "We do not extinguish / We never extinguish / (indignation). We sought to debate / Enforcers sought to destroy. Those of the Soul allowed Dar to corrupt Sacred Home / Sacred Home is no longer Plury'be."

The emissary rotated contemptuously. "Those of the Soul are here. They will speak to your actions at the Agro'ath House."

Jared remembered Au'p talking about Those of the Soul before; they were one of the major Dar-aligned Plury'be factions. The other term he'd never heard before. He linked privately with Orel and asked, "What's an Agro'ath House?"

"As near as we can gather, it is some sort of Domain establishment present on some Plury'be worlds. The No Greater claim it corrupts Plury'be."

Au'p addressed the crowd. "We did not destroy the Agro'ath House / The enforcers destroyed the Agro'ath House / (anger). They destroyed it because those inside had rejected the Lower Way / They destroyed it because those inside had chosen the Higher Way."

"More fabrications. Those of the Soul will speak otherwise."

"Those of the Soul seek the Lower Way / The Way of Law does not respect Those of the Soul."

The lead Plury'be from the Way of Law now spoke. "Those of the Soul are not of our alliance / We will judge their statements in due time / (patience)."

Jared felt a tug on his arm. Nho was looking at him with an intense expression, as if he had an unasked question. Jared nodded. It was time. "Nho, Rete, Orel, with me."

He climbed up on the dais. Nho followed, as did Rete, with communications officer Orel Dayail close behind. Their sudden appearance brought a wave of chatter from the crowds surrounding the platform. Jared walked purposefully to join Au'p, the Way of Law, and the emissary in the mid-center, attuning his communications to that of the Plury'be. "We would also speak of the Domain," he said.

The Plury'be of the Way of Law addressed him. "Identify yourself / Identify your business here / (interrogative)."

"I am called Jared Carter, and I am a representative of the Confederacy, an alliance of worlds from the other side of what you call the Place Beyond. We are here today because the Domain tried, and failed, to destroy our civilization. A regulator attempted to enslave large numbers of our people before we were able to stop it."

The emissary rotated as it responded, the colors of the sky splashing over its surface. "A regulator was dispatched as an envoy for Dar. It was sent to cross the Deep Reaches—the Place Beyond—and make amicable contact with the adversaries of the Plury'be invasion of *frgnot bonanol* prior. It was attacked by many ships and responded by making said attackers harmless. No life was extinguished by the regulator. The design was to collect enough knowledge to facilitate peaceful communication."

"That is not true. I was one of those inside the regulator, and it repeatedly declared that those who defied Dar's purposes would be extinguished."

"Dar's purposes are those of amicable communication," the emissary said. "Extinguishing happens only when there is a threat to safety. All present at the Speaking Stone know this to be true.

Conversely, your ship is one of destruction, using weapons to extinguish a ship of Those of the Soul at Free Town."

Jared suppressed his irritation. "Another lie. Your ships attacked our ship at Free Town."

"That is a fabrication. Your small ships attacked our vessels before we could make contact."

"Our reports would show otherwise. You attacked first, just as the regulator called Malum attacked us on our homeworlds."

The Plury'be of the Way of Law spoke. "You are foreign to us / We will judge your statements in due time / (patience)."

The emissary said, "Our regulator sent to the Confederacy determined that the Confederacy is preparing an attack of Plury'be space as retaliation for the invasion of *bonanol* prior. These members of the Confederacy are an advance party of that retaliation. They would seek to ally with the No Greater Faction and overthrow the major factions."

Clever, Jared mused bitterly. He looked at Orel, who stepped forward to speak. "I am Orel Dayail of the Aecrons, the people who were the target of that past invasion."

A ripple among the surrounding crowd.

"Not only is the Domain emissary's claim not true," he continued, "but it is in contradiction to the policies of my people. We have a strict policy of defense, and even ceased exploration following the Plury'be invasion as a precautionary measure. Our people do not desire to fight the Plury'be as long as they are peaceable."

"Your presence here and your attacks against Those of the Soul contradict that," the emissary said.

"Our presence here is because of your regulator's attack," Jared snapped. "We were dispatched here to ascertain the threat of the Domain, a threat that is apparently as serious as we believed."

"Those here know that is not the way of the Domain."

"Is it not?" said Nho, now stepping forward, Sarco's staff firmly at his side. "You continually demonstrate that you seek the Lower Way."

"Who are you? / What would you know of the Lower Way? / (interrogative)," said the Plury'be of the Way of Law.

"This is a risk," Vetta said quietly into Jared's link. "We do not know how this faction will respond to Nho's beliefs."

Nho looked directly at the Plury'be of the Way of Law. "I am Nho Ames, a follower of truth. I seek the Creator of the Universe, that which created all. I also seek that which is good and true, what you call the Higher Way. I have also been inside the regulator, the one that called itself Malum. There I was attacked by one of the overseers, which attempted to extinguish me. I only survived because of the grace of the One who made all."

The emissary pivoted to address the Plury'be of the Way of Law. "These outsiders seek to ally with the No Greater Faction and promote their ideas. This is a threat to everything the Plury'be and the Domain have sought to build, and it is based on a foolishness of ignorance and fiction."

Nho shifted his posture to glare at the emissary. "You are allies with the Outcasted, with—" Nho paused and cocked his head slightly, his face contorting in surprise. "Kol. That is your word for the Outcasted."

Jared blinked. He was sure the emissary had just flinched, a brief lift into the air. He, of course, knew next to nothing about Domain psychology, but was that surprise?

"Did you see that, Captain?" Orel said privately. "The emissary. That reaction."

"But how?" Vetta asked. "What is Kol?"

The tentacles of the Plury'be of the Way of Law flared out horizontally from its body, flailing in agitation. "This debate is at an end / This discussion is over / (finality). This is about the safety of Us / We do not countenance spreading of ideas from Outside. Your crew will depart / Your crew shall not return / (insistence)."

"Oh no," whispered Jared. His heart sank. Vetta's worst fears had been realized. He keyed his suit to speak aloud. "We implore you to consider the threat we have seen—"

"This discussion is over / We have already spoken of this

/ (anger). No further talk will be continued / You are to leave / (warning)."

Au'p rotated slightly and headed to the edge of the dais. Jared took a deep breath and followed. Just like that, it was over.

17

Nho sat hunched over in his seat, tears streaming down his cheeks. Ahead, on the shuttle's viewscreen, the spacescape of Wisdom teemed with traffic. Little had been said among the crew since they left the spectral world an hour earlier.

"I'm sorry," Nho said at last. "I've failed you and I've failed Sarco. I said what I felt was right, but in doing so I ruined all that we had worked for."

"Do not be so hard on yourself," Jared said quietly.

Nho shoved his staff miserably against the floor. "I should have remained silent. Or"—he glanced at Rete—"I should have let Rete do the speaking. He was more successful in reaching these people before. I was foolishly arrogant to think I possessed the right words for this situation."

Rete shook his head. "There is no guarantee that anything I said would have changed the outcome. We didn't appear to be winning."

Orel, who was sitting across from them, added, "The Plury'be are a deliberate people and are not easily swayed on policy matters. They regarded our voice, and that of the No Greater faction, as a minority voice. It was given little weight. For us to win, we would have had to be very convincing, perhaps impossibly so. We were not. At best we were scoring the equivalent of a draw against the

Domain's emissary, which in Plury'be politics all but guarantees we lose."

Bel Wrsaw, the security officer, said in a sour tone, "We did not simply lose. They forced us off the planet."

Orel regarded her with the Aecron equivalent of a scowl. "Whether they threw us off the planet or sent us away with presents is irrelevant. The outcome would be the same. The Way of Law has no intention of taking action against the Domain."

"The method matters. We were told to leave and never return."

"With respect, Deck Officer, this is my area of expertise, not yours. The Plury'be are not like you sociologically or linguistically. The No Greater faction was given a similar ultimatum on a past visit to Wisdom and yet they returned. Semantically the expression you heard connotes that we should not return with respect to that subject, not that we are forever exiled. They do not cease diplomatic operations out of petty anger the way your Hazionite diplomats do."

"Calm, please," Vetta said.

Orel lowered his head in deference. "Of course." He looked at Nho. "If the Confederacy were to enter trade negotiations with them at some future date, a delegation would most likely be permitted to land for that purpose, with an understanding that the subject of the Plury'be ceasing their trade alliance with Dar and the Domain is a closed matter. As the Riticans might say, you have lost the battle, not the war."

Nho wiped his eyes with one hand, his other gripping Sarco's staff firmly. "I appreciate your perspective. I am still sorry my words did not avail more."

"No words may have," said Jared. "It almost seems as if we were destined to lose."

Nho shook his head. "I still do not understand. Why would Sarco give me the name 'Kol' only to have it cause us to fail?"

"Captain," said Kilvin, "we are approaching the *Hattan*."

Jared stood and walked over behind Kilvin's seat. "How long until we arrive?"

240

"Less than ten minutes."

"Very well. Let them know that I need to meet with Commander Bvaso on the bridge. Vetta, I want you with me, too. As for the rest of you, you are officially off duty once we get back to the ship. It's been a long day, and you all could use some rest."

• • •

Jared and Vetta arrived on the bridge. Redelia was seated at the command station and Tir, apparently just arrived, was talking to her.

"Captain," said Tir as he approached, "I am told things did not go well."

"No, and I'm not sure what our next step is. We'll need to talk." He didn't add that he already knew what she would probably say.

"Sir," Aioua said, "the No Greater ships are breaking orbit. It looks as if they are preparing to fold out of the system."

That was unexpected. "Rami, try to contact them."

A pause. "They are not responding."

"Let's see them."

One of the tridimensional displays changed to show the small fleet of No Greater cruisers and their flatboat support. One by one, folds opened before each of the ships.

"Try contacting them again," Jared ordered. "Aioua, can you project their heading?"

"Their current direction does not match any known system in the region."

"They're not returning to Free Town?"

Aioua said, "They are headed in nearly the opposite direction."

On the tridimensional display, one of the ships disappeared into its fold. And then another. And still more, until the last of the No Greater ships navigated into their folds and out of normal space.

Almost as an afterthought, Rami said, "They never responded, sir."

The bridge was silent. Jared took a few steps forward, past the command station and up to where the navigator, a female Human named Nisshishothi Pessosollo, was watching him. Jared looked past Niss to the viewscreen. Heavy system traffic crowded the planet Wisdom. Although he could not see them from this distance, he knew the fleet of the Domain was out there as well.

At once Jared felt a sensation of foreignness, an acute awareness that his ship was alone in a sea of others that were nothing like them. Not only that, but his ship had no connections here, no advocates, no allies. Their only link to this part of the universe had just severed themselves from him and his ship with no explanation, leaving the *Hattan* a castoff in a faraway space. He felt alone, exposed, unsafe.

He realized that Tir was standing next to him; he had not heard or sensed her approach. "You said that we should talk."

He took in a deep breath. "Yes, but not while we are here, in this system. Niss, prepare for a fold jump. Make for a course out into deep space, a three waypoint jump so we aren't followed. I want us at a safe distance from the Plury'be and the Domain while we consider our options. Redelia, you have the watch."

• • •

Jared settled into one of the chairs in the bridge's rearward conference room and rested his arms over his chest. "I'll get right to the point: is it time to head home?"

The question hung in the air like a great weight. Tir said, "Even to someone who opposed coming here, as I did, that is a serious proposition."

"But a valid one," Vetta said. "Our negotiations failed, and we have been abandoned by our only allies here. It does not appear that there is anything more to be gained by staying. Moreover, now that our presence is known, we may be in danger, both from the Domain and from Plury'be antagonistic to the No Greater faction."

"Perhaps," Tir suggested, "we could return to Free Town. If that proved unsuccessful, we might also seek out other factions in Plury'be systems to ally with."

Jared tapped his fingers on the table. "That is a subject we can discuss with Orel and our xenosociologists, but I don't hold out much hope. I'm also wary of entering Plury'be systems now that we appear to have lost our diplomatic foothold here. That includes Free Town. Given what I've seen just now, I don't fully trust the No Greater faction."

"Understandably," Garo said. "And the last time we were at Free Town, we were attacked."

"Whatever course we ultimately take," Tir said, "I advise caution on being too hasty in making a decision. We are still feeling the sting of defeat, which could cloud our judgment."

Jared laughed bitterly. "Do I smell that obvious?"

"I smell it from myself, sir."

Jared regarded his first officer. The implication behind that statement was not lost on him. Tir, even in her objections to allying with the Plury'be, nevertheless had hoped for the venture's success. His defeat was also hers.

He leaned back in his chair and considered his own current state. He was tired and demoralized. His head hurt, both physically and emotionally. He said, at length, "You're right. Perhaps we should adjourn and meet again in the morning. We can further discuss things then."

• • •

To Redelia, the *Hattan's* bridge felt like the site of a funeral. A pall had settled over the place after the captain had ordered the ship to depart Wisdom. No one said it aloud, but inside everyone knew. Their mission here was over.

This should have brought some measure of relief. After months in the ship, alone on the far side of the galaxy, at last they were going home. Redelia was well aware of the positives surrounding returning to the familiar. Yet her emotions, such as they were, told a different story. The last months felt empty, a wasted effort that they were suddenly turning their backs on. There was also the matter of facing her people, and the conditioning that drove them, but that subject was too overwhelming to consider just yet.

"Thirty seconds to fold exit," said Niss Pessosollo.

Redelia consulted the map on one of the command displays. The navigator had plotted a simple three-jump course to an open spot some distance from Wisdom, as per the captain's orders. From there, they could easily make a course in any direction, including back across the Great Void. Redelia examined the nearby star systems on her display, a few of which were Plury'be worlds or points of interest. At this point, the farther they stayed from those places, the better.

On the viewscreen, the fold parted and they were back in normal space. Redelia could see Niss's station illuminating their next point of departure.

Redelia saw it before she heard it. On the viewscreen, prismatic tendrils of color formed at multiple points, spreading, opening.

"Commander, multiple folds forming all around us!" Aioua shouted.

• • •

Jared sat in a chair in his room, trying to decompress. He got himself a drink, pulled up a portable to read, and put his feet up, but it was futile. His mind was churning over the events on Wisdom.

Regardless of Orel's even assessment, it felt like a colossal failure. Regardless of Nho assuming the blame, it felt like Jared's failure.

The thought of leaving now felt like a poison pill, bitter and repugnant. He, like most of the others, had been hoping their mission would shortly take them home, but this wasn't the way he wanted to do it. It felt somehow empty. He told himself that it wasn't a failure—that they had learned and accomplished more than Admiral Garvak could have hoped for—but logic had no effect on his state of mind.

His thoughts drifted to the prospect of returning to the Confederacy, which only worried him more. Their exit from explored space all those months before had been marked by multiple brushes with death, first near the Ritican manufactory on Ramas-Eduj, and later by the mysterious Aecron ambush fleet.

How many groups would try to destroy them before they could even reach Titan? And what would happen to Jared and his crew once Command learned what had happened on this side of the Void? Would his presumptuous alliance with the No Greater faction and the debacle on Wisdom cost him his career?

Alarms pierced the quiet. Combat stations. The sound jarred him, leaving him momentarily disoriented. What was going on?

He sprang to his feet and ran out the door.

• • •

Jared rushed onto the bridge in time to see a fleet of Plury'be ships burst out of folds and into space on the viewscreen.

"They formed just moments ago," explained Redelia as she gave way at the command station. "Seven of them, coming in from all angles."

Jared took his seat. "Niss, how long until we can fold again?"

"Six minutes," said the navigator.

Jared looked at Garo Ball. The old weapons officer shook his head. There was no way they could survive that long.

"All right," Jared said evenly, "let's see what they want. Rami, try to make contact."

"Yes, sir. Also, two of the interceptors report ready to launch at your orders."

"Tell them to remain in the hold for now. Aioua, tell me what we have out there."

"Seven capital ships, six of them Plury'be cruiser level, comparable to what we have seen before. One of them is a new contact, much larger. Judging by the preliminary information, it appears to be the rough equivalent of a battle carrier."

"Let's take a look."

On the right tridimensional display, an image of a Plury'be ship appeared, similar in profile to what they had seen many times before but also different. For one thing, it was enormous, dwarfing the cruisers flanking it. It was probably fifty percent larger than the *Hattan*. It had the same indigo-streaked bonded plate armor of other Invader-style ships, but was not as teardrop shaped. It seemed flatter along its sides, ends, and top, like a rectangular box with rounded ends. Blurs of motion were visible along the top and both sides. Upon closer inspection, they appeared to be flatboats and other smaller Plury'be ships deploying into space. As battle carriers went, it looked the part.

"The ships' hyperwave nodes are powered up," said Aioua, "and they are moving to surround us. In less than a minute, we will be unable to properly open a fold."

"They may be preparing to mount a capture of our ship," Garo Ball said.

Jared tapped his armrest. "Weapons status?"

"Fusing torpedoes loaded, pulse turrets initialized, siege cannon will be saturated in three minutes."

"Continue saturating, but do not target or take any action that might be construed as hostile. We'll do what we have to, but I want to make sure I know their motives first."

"Sir, I've received a response," said Rami, "sent from the battle carrier."

"Put it on my display."

In front of him, the words appeared:

Captain Jared Carter will enter a shuttle / The one called Nho will enter the same shuttle / (demand). The shuttle will be unarmed / The shuttle will proceed to the primary ship / (demand).

Jared read the message a second time. They wanted Nho and him in a shuttle, alone and unarmed, sent to the primary ship, which was presumably the battle carrier. A simple, exacting demand.

Jared stood in time to see Tir rushing onto the bridge. "What is happening?" she asked.

"We've been ambushed and surrounded by Plury'be ships, and they want Nho and me in a shuttle, alone. You have command. I'm headed over there."

Redelia took a step closer to him, her blue skin glossy with anxiety, "Captain, are you sure about this?"

"No, I'm not, but it may be the only way to save the ship. Rami, inform them that we'll be over shortly, then contact Nho and instruct him to meet me in the shuttle bay."

Jared turned back to Tir, his voice quiet but authoritative. "Listen to me carefully. Under no circumstances are they to have the ship. Do not take any hostile action unless clearly provoked, but do not let them take it. Blow it up if you have to."

Tir's fluid body rippled just a little—a telltale sign of surprise, if not outright shock—but she kept her voice even. She knew, as Jared did, that if the Plury'be attacked, they weren't going to take prisoners. Hyperwave weapons were designed to leave only the ship intact. "Yes, Captain."

Rami said, "The Plury'be acknowledge your message, and Nho is on his way."

He gestured to her with his hand. "Rami, you're with me."

She looked caught off-guard, but only for a moment. "Yes, sir," she said, emerging from behind her station and walking briskly over to him.

Jared turned to lead Rami off the bridge, then briefly stopped. "Aioua?"

"Sir?"

"Find out how they tracked us here. If you—if we—manage to escape this mess, you need to make sure they can't do it again."

"Yes, sir."

• • •

Rami rushed off the bridge, accelerating her pace to match that of her captain. Inside, she was so nervous for herself and for Jared that she had to concentrate on walking. As soon as the bridge door closed behind them, Jared said, "Talk to me, Rami."

He looked pale, at least as worried as she felt. She swallowed and said, "Tell me what you need, sir."

They were walking quickly, with occasional surprised officers stepping out of their way to let them pass. Rami dimly realized others could hear what they were saying, but Jared didn't have the luxury of privacy at this moment. He said, "I've got two minutes to figure out how to deal with these Plury'be, and I've already failed once. I don't know what to do."

Her mind froze for a moment, locked between fear and processing of this impossible question. Her legs felt like lead. The weight of his burden was now hers, and her eyes began to well with tears as a flood of inadequacy threatened to overtake her.

She briefly considered suggesting to Jared that he contact Orel Dayail instead. Rami and Orel had worked closely together, but she freely admitted that Orel was better versed in Plury'be diplomacy. This moment seemed made for the son of an ambassador.

But she stifled the impulse. Jared knew all this but had, in the moment, called for her. Perhaps because she happened to be nearby. Or because she might put Nho more at ease when they met him at the shuttle. Or because she was Human. Or perhaps, she thought as she looked at him, he simply needed an old friend to walk with him as much as he needed the advice she might give.

Whatever the case, Jared needed *her*. She was his last lifeline as he prepared to cast off into darkness.

Sarco, help me, she pleaded.

"Umm—" She fumbled for words. "Let's think this through. We don't know what they want, and the one thing we know about the Plury'be is that there's still a lot we don't know. We can't—you can't—assume that you know what they want just because you interpret their actions a certain way through our cultural lens." Without the time to pick and choose, she decided just to let her words come out, in hope that somewhere among them was the key to all of this. "You don't know which faction this is, so let them do most of the talking. I was always told in our courses on diplomacy that you should never negotiate against yourself. I—I mean, you know that, of course, but I think the rule applies to the Plury'be as much as us."

The lift opened and they got in. She kept talking as the door closed. "They might want to interrogate you, but they also might not." She involuntarily wiped away a stray tear. "So the first thing you want to do is establish the faction. If it's a faction we've already dealt with, you already know some things, like the Way of Law's focus on self-discipline. If it's not a faction we know, see first if you can't tease out their factional motivations. They all have different priorities, and determining those priorities will be critical."

"What can I do with that?" Jared asked. There was no accusation in his tone; it was spoken as a man who was racing against time to soak up every molecule of knowledge.

"You have to trust yourself," Rami said. "Look for points of contact. They want you alive, which the Plury'be don't do when they're hostile, so don't assume the worst. I know it looks terrible, but maybe they just want to talk. Like I said, let them talk." She was rambling, but if she stopped talking she might not be able to start again, and the seconds were too few. "Don't act like a prisoner. Act as if you're right back on the Speaking Stone and you are equals. Answer their questions, but try to ask questions that will get them going."

The lift reached their designated deck and they exited. They were not far now from the shuttle bay. "And don't overplay it," Rami said. "The faction leaders seemed to have fairly fixed positions on things, so focus on establishing a diplomatic line first. Don't worry about trying to talk them into something. We've already seen that if you try to push them too hard, they might cut you off entirely. Probe and create a link, just like you did on Free Town."

Up ahead, Rami could see Nho waiting for them. She lowered her voice slightly. "And be mindful of Nho. He's going to think this is somehow his fault. He may not want to talk, but you might need him, especially if the Domain is somehow involved in this and you need the staff." Rami had no idea if any of this made sense, but there wasn't time to say more. They reached Nho and the three of them were in the shuttle bay, where crews were scrambling to ready a craft.

Rami stopped and Jared turned to her, giving her a look that said, *any final advice?* She knew that these would be the last words she could give, perhaps the last words any Human besides Nho would ever give Jared Carter in this life.

Her voice cracked a little. "I'll see you soon, sir."

His lips parted as if to speak, but he was silent. Perhaps in the moment, torn between the world behind him and the world ahead, he didn't know what to say. He finally nodded, then turned and led Nho to the waiting two-person shuttle.

As the buffer field formed between them, in preparation for the shuttle's departure, Rami whispered, "Go with Sarco."

• • •

Jared guided the *Swillow* out of the *Hattan* and into the darkness. His mind rang with all the words Rami had imparted to him before he'd left his ship. He tried to hold the sea of advice close, thinking more about Rami's desperate attempt to infuse him with hope. Even if her words proved futile, Jared would not forget the effort she'd made, and the raw authenticity of her parting. *I'll see you soon, sir.*

Nho sat quietly behind Jared, still bewildered by the sequence of events that had him sitting in the shuttle. He gripped his staff tightly. It was the closest thing to a weapon they had with them right now.

Jared brought the small shuttle on a course toward the Plury'be battle carrier, which looked even larger now than it had on the bridge's tridimensional display. Around it, flatboats and another type of Plury'be craft—one Jared had never seen before, perhaps a fighter?—drifted in what clearly looked like a protective patrol pattern. A few of the fighter-sized ships broke off and took up an escort posture around the *Swillow*, nudging it toward an opening on the battle carrier's side—its upper-left side, from Jared's current orientation.

At one point, Jared consulted the shuttle's display to make sure he was noting the passage of time correctly. He was—it was simply taking much longer for him to reach the battle carrier than he would have estimated. The behemoth vessel gave the illusion of being at a lesser distance than it was because it was much larger than it appeared to be from afar.

"Do you know what they want with us?" Nho finally asked.

Jared didn't look at him. "No idea. I don't even know which faction they belong to."

"I'm sorry, Jared. I fear I've brought this upon us."

Jared remembered what Rami had said about Nho. "Don't assume that, not right now. What does your intuition tell you about these Plury'be?"

"Sarco is silent, if that is what you're asking. I'm as lost as you are."

Jared regarded the open battle carrier hangar door that waited to receive them. "One way or another, our answers are coming."

• • •

The interior of the ship looked similar in design to the footage Jared had seen from the prison transport at High Land. Ultraviolet fixtures dotted curved hallways that meandered throughout the ship. The hallways were relatively narrow, with branches at seemingly arbitrary locations, unlike the t-styled interchanges that Humans had popularized on Navy ships or the radial design of Aecron vessels.

Ensconced in their environmental suits, Jared and Nho marched through the carrier's hallways, escorted on all sides by Plury'be guards and their floating purple hyperwave drones. At last they rounded a corner and were herded into a large room with an open space in the center. A handful of Plury'be were waiting in the middle, their tentacles flowing between and around one another. The room looked vaguely like the Speaking Stone they had seen on Wisdom.

"Step forward, one called Jared Carter / Step forward, one called Nho / (request)," said one of the Plury'be.

Jared and Nho walked forward. They were in the center of the room now, surrounded on all sides by a ring of the dark, gelatinous aliens.

"You know who I am, of course," said Jared, surveying the room. He thought about Rami's words. "Who am I speaking to?"

"I am B'aha / I am of the Way of Law. I am the Ship Master / I am the Fleet Master."

Knowing it was the faction from Wisdom was a small comfort. At least he had a framework of understanding from which to work. "From one fleet commander to another, I greet you," said Jared with a slight bow. He figured a little formality couldn't hurt. "Why have we been brought here?"

"Speak of Kol / What do you know of Kol?"

Jared looked at Nho, who said, "I am a follower of the Creator, what I call the One and what you call That Which There Is No Greater. His Incarnate, which I call Sarco and the No Greater call Ah'ey, spoke to me. He told me the Domain's master is called Kol."

"The No Greater do not know that name / Few know that name. The name is hidden from the Plury'be / How do you know that name? / (interrogative)."

"As I said, it was spoken to me by the Creator. I did not know it before then."

The Plury'be withdrew momentarily into the crowd, perhaps to consult with others, then re-emerged. "The No Greater say you have destroyed a regulator / Have you destroyed a regulator? / (interrogative)."

"I've defeated one, yes," said Nho. "Or, rather, Sarco did so through me. I am merely His vessel."

"No one has destroyed a regulator / How did you destroy a regulator? / (insistence)."

Nho held out Sarco's staff. "Through a series of events, we were led to this staff, which we believe came from Sarco, the Incarnate. Captain Carter and I placed our faith in the staff and it destroyed the regulator's—Malum's—overseer. Once the overseer was destroyed, the regulator ceased to function."

For the next few moments there was discussion among the

Plury'be. Jared's suit could not make out what was said among the many voices speaking at once.

Finally B'aha spoke once more. "You have been brought here to discuss the Domain / You have been brought here to discuss Sacred Home."

Sacred Home was the name for Mel'as'u, the Plury'be home-world that was under the cultural sway of Dar and the Domain. Jared asked, "What about them?"

"You have said the Domain is a danger / The Way of Law agrees they are a danger. We do not share the ideas of No Greater / We are followers of the Way of Law. We do not believe in Ah'ey / We do oppose the corruptions of Dar / (frustration)." A pause. "You have asked for an alliance to liberate Sacred Home / We ask for your alliance to liberate Sacred Home / (request)."

Jared took a moment to digest this. When he looked at Nho, he was met with a blank expression. Looking back at the Plury'be he said, with deliberate caution, "If you meant to enlist our help, why were we thrown off of Wisdom? And where did the No Greater faction go?"

B'aha's tentacles wriggled higher in the air. "The events on Wisdom were a deception / The deception was necessary to conceal the truth from Dar. The Way of Law was skeptical of your claims / The Way of Law was convinced after the one called Nho spoke of Kol."

Jared looked again at Nho, who looked thoroughly confused, as if he didn't fully understand—or believe—what he was hearing. Jared wasn't sure he did, either.

"The No Greater faction had to leave you / Their departure was necessary to complete the deception," explained B'aha. "A tracer was placed on your shuttle while on Wisdom / The tracer was used to follow you here. We met here to maintain the deception / We met here to form an alliance. We have long wished to liberate Sacred Home / We cannot liberate Sacred Home / (candor)."

An alliance, thought Jared. Out loud, he asked, "Why can you not liberate Sacred Home?"

"A regulator orbits Sacred Home / We cannot defeat a regulator. Us of the Plury'be cannot defeat a regulator / You of the Place Beyond can defeat a regulator. Those of the Soul control Sacred Home / Those of the Soul invited a regulator. We can defeat Those of the Soul / We cannot defeat the regulator."

So the Plury'be homeworld, Jared mused, was now guarded by another Malum—one of the regulators. Au'p had told him the Domain had much influence over that planet, but the presence of a planet-ship was much more than just influence. It was control.

Nho said, "Those of the Soul . . . that was the faction the Domain emissary spoke of on Wisdom."

"Those of the Soul are a powerful faction of Us / Those of the Soul have corrupted Us of Sacred Home / (frustration)."

Things were slowly coming into focus for Jared. The Way of Law were of a different belief than those who followed That Which There Is No Greater, and indeed they denied Ah'ey, the Plury'be's version of the Incarnate. They nevertheless recognized that Nho held a special power and, critically, needed that power. The Way of Law believed they had the ability to unseat the faction controlling the Plury'be homeworld—Those of the Soul, the faction was called—but the Domain made that impossible.

And Nho could change that.

Next to Jared, Nho smiled in delighted surprise. In an instant, the cleric had gone from bearing the guilt for a failed diplomatic mission to being the one who had turned the tide for their efforts. His utterance of the name Kol had set in motion what was now an alliance of multiple factions with the Confederacy against the Domain.

• • •

"Commander, the *Swillow* has just emerged from the Plury'be ship."

The bridge exploded with chatter. Tir looked up sharply. "What is its status?"

Aioua's voice was emotional as she read the data before her.

"The shuttle is unharmed, as are the captain and Nho. The shuttle is on a course back to us."

Tir initiated a secure connection with the shuttle. "Commander Bvaso to Captain Carter. What is your status, sir?"

Jared's face, looking back at her, was calm, focused. "We have a lot to talk about. And a lot of work to do. Everything has changed."

18

Rami Del scooped up a bite of her dessert and popped it into her mouth. Even better than anticipated. "What I don't understand," she said as she chewed, "is why they are asking for help from something they don't believe in."

Rete looked at her cynically. "You have depended on Nho to work his miracles even though you aren't Sarconian. What the Way of Law is doing is not different."

"How do you know I'm not Sarconian?"

"Are you?"

"That's a personal question."

Rete laughed. "You asked for it."

"That's true," she admitted, taking another bite and speaking around it. "But you still haven't answered *my* question. How does the Way of Law justify seeking the help of an Incarnate whom they explicitly reject?"

"Think about it. Plury'be factions are a complex assemblage of political, religious, social, and economic ideologies that rely on intra-faction solidarity for their strength. To concede that the religious beliefs of a marginal faction like the No Greater are true would undermine the Way of Law's considerable power and influence."

"But the Way of Law already accepts the idea of a universal creator. They're halfway there."

"Don't expect them to get any further," said Rete. "According to Au'p, the Way of Law was the religious group that Ah'ey—the Plury'be Incarnate—was born into thousands of years ago. When Ah'ey questioned the Way of Law's teachings, it was the Way of Law who executed Ah'ey for its heresy. If what Au'p says is true, the Way of Law literally has thousands of years of animosity against the No Greater and other like-minded groups. You don't simply undo that."

"If that's the case, I'm surprised they gave the No Greater an audience."

"They earned an audience because of us. The Way of Law wanted to see what we were all about. Otherwise, I don't believe it would have happened, since the Way of Law sees the No Greater as a splinter of the true way."

"As in," Rami said, "the true way of the law."

Rete chuckled. "Yes, as their faction name suggests. It's a telling name, too. Their faction is defined by what they do rather than who they serve. It clearly shows their priorities. They care more for self-discipline than the mystical devotion the No Greater favor." He folded his hands together. "So what about *my* question?"

"What was it again? I don't remember."

"Clever. Are you Sarconian?"

Rami rested her face on her free palm, her elbows on the table. "Is it enough to say that I'm trying to keep an open mind?"

"It would have been a year ago. You've seen enough by now."

Rami pointed her eating utensil at him, half-seriously. "Are you trying to proselytize me?"

Rete raised his hands in a gesture of mock surrender. "Have I ever?"

"No, you have not. You've been a perfect gentleman."

Behind them there was an outbreak of Ritican laughter. Both of them looked that direction and saw a group of security officers engaged jovially in their own separate conversation. As Rami watched them, she also caught sight of two people sitting next to them. One was Kilvin, and sitting across from him was a female Hazionite, a short deck officer with a shock of blue-gray hair atop her head. Rami searched her memory for the female's name: it was Nenkin Fiwdl, from cargo bay maintenance. From one of the minor tribes, Rami thought. Kilvin and Nenkin were engaged in an animated conversation, and, it seemed to Rami, laughing.

Rami looked back to Rete, who shook his head in disbelief. "The atmosphere in here is so different than it was a week ago. It's almost as if we're on a different ship. I've heard more laughter in here the last two days than I've heard the last six months combined."

"The crew has a sense of purpose now," said Rami. "That's not to say they didn't before, but it's more focused now. A week ago, we were still trying to find our way in this region, and after Wisdom, we thought we might even be headed home without completing what we felt we needed to do. Now we have a target and a goal."

"Sacred Home," said Rete.

"The transliteration is Mel'as'u, but I'm probably the only one not named Orel Dayail who calls it that. Anyway, yes, that's the target. We get to help liberate a planet from the cultural domination of the Domain, and we even get to face another Malum planet."

"It will be my first."

"I always forget that." Rami raised her eyebrows. "Let's just say that seeing one of those massive things is an experience."

Rete relaxed in his chair, hands folded on his lap. "So how is Nho going to stop this giant ship, exactly? Is he going to charge at the planet and get sucked in?"

"I suppose we'll find that out when we meet with the factions at Watch Tower," said Rami. "And since you are his assistant, you'll probably get to accompany him."

Rete's face fell, as if he hadn't thought of that. "I can't wait," he muttered.

• • •

Jared straightened the collar of his dress uniform. He rarely wore it except during weddings and funerals, and at this moment he was fully conscious as to why. It always seemed like he was fighting it rather than wearing it.

At least the occasion wasn't a funeral. There had been enough of those on this trip already. Instead, the commons was gaily decorated in a flurry of bright colors, with ribbons of reds and greens and blues strung along the ceiling. The chairs were arranged in rows pointing to the front of the room and faux flowers, replicas of those found on the Human colony world of New Tessee, were scattered among the tables near the back wall.

Each of the different Confederal societies approached the subject of pairing and reproducing differently. Aecron family units were built around complex contractual arrangements between prospective partners, a meritocratic system where the best competed among one another for the most qualified companions. Hazionite pairings were traditionally arranged, with powerful females seeking male partners from other local matriarchs in exchange for such currency as political support or property. Riticans were steadfastly devoted to family—it was thoroughly intertwined with their unshakeable desire for self-defense—but the exact context and manner of how unions were decided was equivalent to a state secret. Exos were asexual and had no concept of family or pairings.

Humans alone made a public ceremony of marriage. The event was usually a communal affair, with large numbers of guests and a program presided over by an officiant. On Human worlds, the conductor of marriages was usually a local legal official, such as a magistrate, but Human law, both on Earth and on the colonies, permitted other methods when no such official was available. Marriages were rare on Navy ships—this was the *Hattan*'s first— but when such occurrences did take place, either the ship's captain or another person of the couple's choosing oversaw the ceremony. As long as the ship's legal officer was present, the marriage was considered contractual regardless of the officiant.

The prospective couple, neither of whom had any known

religious ties, had nevertheless asked Nho to speak. They had also requested that Jared be present.

The room was packed, with various Humans, Hazionites, Aecrons, and Riticans sitting and standing around. Even a few Exos were in attendance, though this was probably because the bride worked in engineering and had asked them to be there. Human weddings on Navy ships, when they happened, were well-attended by other Humans, but they also almost always drew large, curious crowds of non-Humans.

The door on the far end of the commons opened and the bride and groom walked in arm-in-arm, both dressed in their formal uniforms. The Humans in attendance stood and, realizing the other sentients had no idea what to do, gestured wildly for the audience to join them. A haphazard rising of bodies followed until at last everyone was on their feet, watching the couple as they walked forward through the center of the commons and up to the front where Nho was waiting, flanked on his right by Jared.

Nho began the preliminaries, avoiding any direct mention of Sarco or the Incarnate, but speaking nonetheless of the miracle of marriage and the bond brought together by the Creator. Nho seemed not only buoyant but also comfortable in his delivery; Jared wondered if the cleric had performed one of these ceremonies before. The bride and groom, both of them young deck officers, were radiant. Perhaps the happiest two people Jared had ever seen.

Jared looked out at the sea of familiar faces in the audience, all of them in formal dress. Some of the Riticans were wearing adornments associated with family, though no non-Ritican knew exactly what they stood for, and history had shown probing about the matter to be a bad idea. Hazionite males stood behind the females, a sign of deference even in the egalitarian Navy. Several of the Aecrons had their eyes closed in prayer, a telltale sign they were Sarconian: Aioua Horae, sciences officer Udos Beyole, interceptor commander Redelia Aroo, and . . . Orel Dayail?

Jared knew the communications officer had been profoundly affected by the mutiny over Ramas-Eduj, but had not realized he had become a believer. Jared did not see Darel Weye, but would not have been surprised if he, too, was in prayer.

Jared caught sight of a Human with his eyes closed. Brigg Drews, the young, hard-nosed Human interceptor commander. So Drews was religious. That was interesting. His parents were merchant traders, and they were not always seen as the faith-based kind. Perhaps they were of the theistic cults.

Nho continued into a short discussion of the importance of devotion and commitment in marriage. This hit close to home for Jared, who had watched helplessly as his own parents' marriage had collapsed. He was reluctant to admit, even to himself, how deeply their separation had affected him, but his extraordinary caution with respect to romance was clear evidence enough. He was not going to proceed into marriage until the time was right and the person was right.

Out in the audience, about halfway back, she opened her eyes and made eye contact with him, looking at him with tranquil happiness. He offered a calm smile in return.

Maybe.

19

Nah'ca / Watch Tower
Earth Index 1306.361

The *Hattan* sallied forth out of a fold and into normal space. It was a dark place, a billion kiltrics distant from a lowly, planetless dwarf star. Ahead, visible on the viewscreen, a flotilla of Plury'be ships huddled around an ancient space station, a rod-shaped object perhaps five hundred trics wide and ten times as long. The Plury'be language, properly rendered, called it Nah'ca. It translated roughly as Watch Tower.

Watch Tower had been one of the early constructions of the Plury'be collective as it spiraled out into unexplored space some thousands of Index years before. It was, by turns, first a frontier station and later a staging ground for expansion outward, a way-point for the many factions scrambling to establish colonies on ever more distant worlds. As time went on and the Plury'be more firmly established themselves beyond their homeworld, Watch Tower fell first into disuse and finally into wholesale abandonment, all but forgotten.

At least, forgotten to almost all. As Jared learned, one of the Plury'be factions, the Silent Ones, had continuously and surreptitiously kept the station alive. Their purpose in doing so was not clear, but the Way of Law speculated that the Silent Ones believed the wholesale demise of Plury'be civilization to be an ever-present possibility and saw Watch Tower as a potential repository for critical Plury'be history and knowledge. Few even within the Silent Ones knew of the station's current operation, and fewer still knew its exact location, although most factions, even if they had known, would have thought little of an antiquated place with so little apparent strategic or practical value.

What most factions would not realize was that the Silent Ones, in addition to establishing a store of information, had also established a means of observation. At multiple points on and above the Plury'be homeworld were image-gathering devices which sent telemetry back to Watch Tower. How this was accomplished without detection was unclear, but the net effect was that the Silent Ones were able to keep a careful eye on the planet Sacred Home.

The Silent Ones shared some of the philosophical beliefs of the No Greater, though they were very different in many other respects (they were agnostic about whether there was a Creator) and historically had little interest in aligning with other factions for risk of exposing their operations. The recent Domain influence—some would say occupation—on the Plury'be homeworld had divided the Silent Ones; some concluded that the Domain's corruptions were a threat to the Plury'bes' existence as a species. After contentious debate, the Silent Ones leadership had decided that the time of passive observation was over. It was time to move toward saving their people.

An agent of the Silent Ones had been present during the debate on Wisdom and had observed the pleas of the No Greater and Jared's crew. The agent made contact with a trusted element in the Way of Law and was initially rebuffed . . . then later told to meet a Way of Law ship in the emptiness of space. From that meeting came the agreement which bonded the Way of Law, the No Greater, the Silent Ones, and a few other Plury'be factions in a conspiracy against the factions of Sacred Home and their Domain allies.

Jared's excitement over fomenting a revolution was tempered by deep uncertainty and more than a few suspicions. Could a conspiracy of this scope, for example, be accomplished without being discovered by the Domain or its Plury'be allies? No one on the crew could offer a satisfactory answer, not even those who had devoted themselves to studying Plury'be sociology.

Another question: if Watch Tower were so sacred and important to the Silent Ones, why invite the various factions—and the alien races of the Confederacy—to its heretofore secret location? Again, no one could answer with complete certainty, although the ship's lead weapons officer, Garo Ball, had the most plausible theory. "Our presence would indicate that it is neither as sacred nor as exclusive as the Silent Ones would have us believe," he said.

Those speculations aside, the reality was that Watch Tower offered a window into the situation on and around the Plury'be homeworld of Sacred Home, and the old station was to be the place from which the planet's liberation would be planned and executed. In cosmic terms, Watch Tower was right next door; travel to the Plury'be homeworld from there would take less than one Earth Index day.

• • •

The captain and a few select members of the Navy crew watched as an assembly of Plury'be filed into a large, open space somewhere deep within Watch Tower. The station itself was a patchwork of old and new, with some sections reflecting the style and technology seen on Free Town and Wisdom, and others showcasing bizarre bright indigo coloring that looked like something from a different race entirely. This room, with its darker purples, was more modern.

Some of the more important figures among the insurgent Plury'be factions were in attendance. Au'p, S'li, and a cruiser captain named Sa'ba were among those present from the No Greater. The battle carrier captain B'aha stood with the Way of Law. The reputed leader of the Silent Ones was also present, as was the leader of another lesser faction that apparently had a longstanding animosity toward Those of the Soul, the faction that controlled the Plury'be homeworld. Representing the Confederal Navy along with Jared were an interceptor commander, a weapons officer, a communications officer, and a Sarconian cleric: Redelia, Garo, Orel, and Nho.

Suspended in the air in the middle of the room was a live image of Sacred Home as observed from a point near the planet. The Plury'be homeworld was a mishmash of purple hues and copper elements covered in places by clouds of angry red. The entire planet, Jared had been told, was an almost-unbroken city, the product of thousands of years of unceasing expansion. Other than what was necessary for Plury'be survival, most other life had been discarded to extinction.

On the far side of Sacred Home, hanging over its figurative right shoulder, was a regulator. Jared shuddered involuntarily at the sight of what he forever would think of as Malum, an artificial sphere in orbit above this planet. Unlike its dead counterpart in orbit around Aeroel back in the Confederacy, this one was very much alive.

Once the room was full, one of the Plury'be began speaking, laying out the plan of action. Sacred Home's liberation would take place in multiple waves, with advance parties followed by various fleets to deal both with the regulator and any Plury'be ships in orbit that might contest the insurgency. From the outset, it was clear this was not some hastily assembled plan. At least one of the factions (it was not clear which) had been developing this for months, maybe years, and had been waiting for the means and opportunity to implement it. The arrival of the *Hattan*, and specifically Nho, was the missing link.

When the Plury'be came to the part where it was to speak of Nho's role, it did so dispassionately and unambiguously. Jared looked uncertainly at the cleric, who looked back at him with serene confidence. This, Nho said without saying anything, is exactly the way I think it should be done. The way Sarco has ordained that it be done.

• • •

The lab on the *Hattan* vibrated loudly, rattling various instruments nearby against their tables and each other. Aioua knew she would hear complaints later from adjacent researchers even though she had received permission to perform the test. She did not care. This was more important.

"Elevate the output," she ordered.

Ovocitox complied, increasing the energy flow into the asymmetrical Malum piece floating in the air. The noise grew, as did the visibility of the translucent force waves flowing from the piece.

"The input is at forty-five megabiis," said the Exo.

Darel Weye, standing a few paces away from Aioua, examined the diagnostics on the makeshift defense fields. "Impressive," he admitted. "There is only a five percent distortion in the formation alignment of the defense fields. Brought to scale, the Hattan could maintain its fields for up to fifteen Index minutes against even a high-output regulator."

Aioua turned to the Ritican security officer nearby. "Fire."

The pulse rifle discharged, striking the Malum piece and knocking it out of the air, sending it in a flying arc to the floor, where it landed with a haphazard half-roll. At once the force waves stopped, as did the noise.

Everyone in the room—Aioua, Darel, Ovocitox, and the Ritican—stared silently at the object, a piece taken from Malum over Aeroel. It represented all the frustrations of fighting Dar, all the intimidations of the regulator now orbiting Sacred Home. Now it lay dormant on the floor of the lab.

"Ovocitox," said Aioua finally, "have these adjustments taken to engineering. I want them implemented on all fleet ships before we arrive at Sacred Home."

"I will complete the task at once."

"Deck Officer Fonus, you are also dismissed."

"Yes, sir," said the Ritican, following the Exo out the door.

That left Aioua and Darel alone in the lab, both still looking at the piece of Uxa251 on the ground in the middle of the testing area. Darel shut down the makeshift defense field and walked over to where she was standing. "You have come a long way on this research," he remarked. "Realistically, you have increased the operative time of a capital ship defense field against a regulator by more than thirtyfold, to say nothing of the interceptors. The implication for fighters and bombers is even more interesting, although we will not be able to demonstrate that until we return to the Confederacy. You need to make sure these results are forwarded to Navy Command with today's report packet. This is a crucial development."

Aioua looked at him with satisfaction. "Your comments are appreciated, as is your assistance in the research. I will note your own contributions in the report. I would never have made this progress without the ideas you developed from your time on board the *Retaelus*."

"I am only a medical officer here to offer my help. You are the sciences officer."

She sensed a certain dissatisfaction in the tone of his answer. She tipped her head, inquisitive. "I must ask: why did you accept a medical position? I have seen you in the infirmary and I have seen you doing research, like the work here. You are far more passionate about technical analysis than sentient physiology."

Darel picked up the Malum piece and placed it back in storage. "My family unit has a long history of medical work. My unit parents are both physicians on Aeroel, as were their parents. My specialization is in medicine because they made sure it was. My interests were not a concern to them."

Most family units, Aioua knew, were that way. Her family was not, but they were an exception. And in her case, there were also other reasons.

"I am fortunate, however," continued Darel. "The Navy has allowed me to pursue my interests within the context of my position. And I do not hate medicine; it is challenging and interesting. It simply is not my highest interest."

Aioua paced to one of the readout displays and began shutting down some of the equipment. "Is this the right course of action?"

Darel looked surprised. "What action do you mean?"

"Is it the will of Sarco for us to be relying so heavily on our own technological ingenuity? We know that Sarco has the power to defeat the Domain. At times this work feels like the dark path that our people have walked down so many times."

Darel picked up some of the tools to file them away. "I can understand your concern. You and I grew up idolizing the technological genius of the Aecrons; now we are part of a faith that looks at technology more carefully. Some Sarconians even view it to be the province of the Outcasted."

Aioua's face turned indignant. "I never said I believed technology to be evil. You know better than to suggest it. I merely wonder if we rely too much on it."

He stopped what he was doing, his face tightening. "I never said you did, and I do know better. The evidence of that is clear enough right here in this room. We both believe in the value of technology. But I also see your struggles with Sarco's teachings in the fears you expressed. Some Sarconians might say that your innovations here indicate not only a lack of faith in the One's greater plan, but a dark dalliance in self—the trap of the Outcasted—rather than in Him who saves. It is that which you fear."

"You presuppose too much. How can you claim to know what I fear?"

Darel stared at her. "Am I correct?"

A pause. "No. Yes. I do not know. By all that is under the Domes, this has been difficult." Aioua tapped her blue fingers against the palm of her opposite hand. "I rarely suffer from such moments of uncertainty."

"That is because the question is not merely intellectual. Intellectual prowess is one thing you and I possess in large measure. Spiritual discernment is still a new art for both of us."

When Aioua spoke next, it was in a lower voice. "My unit parents had very strong opinions on both of those issues."

"Is that not true of most families?"

She didn't respond. Darel looked at her for a moment, then sat down on one of the nearby stools. "What happened?"

"So be it," Aioua said, as much to herself as to him. "When I was a child, the contract of my unit grandparents, maternal order, was dissolved."

Darel looked at her with astonishment. "Dissolved?"

"Yes."

Aioua knew what Darel was now thinking: that Aecron merito-cratic pairings were painstaking in their crafting, and a dissolution of such a pairing suggested one or more sides was intellectually inept. Unlike Humans, Aecrons almost never ended their unions.

Darel asked, "Why?"

She sat down on a stool opposite him. "One day my grand-paternal was gone. No one of the family spoke of it, although I know my unit parents and my unit grand-maternal spent years searching for him. They never found him."

"Did he leave for another sentient colony?"

"There were no emigration records."

"Then what you are saying would seem impossible, unless he died in the ocean or the wilds."

"He did not die. The government still recognized him as alive, and years later my unit grand-maternal received formal notice of the dissolution."

Darel said, "That makes no sense."

"I have tried for years to make sense of it. When I was older, I joined the search. There are a few possibilities that explain the circumstances, but I have no proof of any of them."

"What is your best guess?"

Aioua took a short breath to find calm. Even now, this part hurt. "During the course of my investigation, I uncovered that my grand-paternal had Sarconian connections."

"Was he Sarconian?"

"No, but he was sympathetic to the plight of Sarconian persecution."

"That in and of itself would not seem grounds for what happened."

Aioua tapped her hand again. "It is not, but he also had par-ticular engineering skills that, in the right context, might serve government purposes. I believe he was conscripted for clandestine government activity, although my evidence is fragmentary and circumstantial. It would be . . . embarrassing . . . if any part of this story were shared."

"I will not share it." Darel hesitated before asking, "Were you close?"

Aioua was hurt by the question, though through no fault of Darel's. "He was, at the time, a better unit parent than my own. He encouraged me to pursue my interests. My unit parents disagreed, until he disappeared. When I began to train in sciences that would allow me to search for him, they did not stop me."

"I see."

Aioua knew that Darel would put the pieces together. Aioua was a skilled sciences officer with a reputation for making sense out of incomplete or disparate data. It was that skill that had won her a place on the battle carrier *Sidney*, and a skill that had brought her to the *Hattan*. A skill honed in years of searching for her lost grand-paternal.

Darel asked, "Do you blame the Sarconians for his disappearance?"

"My family appeared to, but I did not. I blamed a government that would do such things. Our encounters with hostile Aecron forces has only made me feel stronger about that." Attempting a less somber tone of voice, she said, "We were talking earlier of technology. What do you believe? Is it, as some Sarconians say, a dark art?"

Darel stood up and returned to the task of filing away lab tools. "I cannot say for certain what Sarco would say, but I have talked with Nho and Rete. While Nho in particular is no great fan of Aecron ingenuity—or most technology, for that matter—he also maintains that Sarco can work through the hands of invention. If your hands are Sarco's and your desire is Sarco's, I believe this work here is also Sarco's."

Aioua's link chirped and the flat voice of an Exo translation spoke into her ear. "Nonocentiphox to Lieutenant Aioua Horae."

"Aioua Horae here. Go ahead."

"Report to the cargo bay."

"I will be there momentarily."

She looked at Darel. "It appears I am needed in the cargo bay. Thank you for your help, and for our conversation."

"Of course. And"—he hesitated, as if weighing whether to proceed—"should Sarco allow us to survive these next few days, I would like to speak more. I, too, am new to this, and I would appreciate someone else to learn with."

Aioua did not speak, but she gave an Aecron gesture to the affirmative, then hurried out of the room.

• • •

Jared had an office, but he rarely used it. Most of his days were spent in one of a hundred other places on the ship, whether it be the bridge, his quarters, or the many places in between. Today was an exception. Jared wanted to review the plans he had received from Watch Tower, and he wanted to do it apart from the distractions of the crew or the temptation to sleep in his bed.

He took some of the information from his portable and projected it in the air above his workstation. This was the first time he'd been able to review the plans since hearing them, and upon second review, he noticed things he had missed in his first viewing. The most obvious was the critical role several elements in his own battle fleet played in the final outcome. It was as if the Plury'be had the makings of a plan but were missing key elements to make it work . . . only to have the *Hattan* and its fleet suddenly, miraculously, appear to fill the gaps. More likely, Jared reasoned, the arrival of the Navy fleet had enabled the Plury'be to tweak the plan to fit what the *Hattan* offered.

His door chimed. *Never a quiet moment*, he groused quietly. "Come in."

The door opened and Orel stepped through. "I apologize for the intrusion, Captain. I suspect you are reviewing our plans from Watch Tower."

"I am. What is it?" he said, sounding more impatient than he intended.

"I have been studying the histories of the Watch Tower passed along to us by the Silent Ones. I have some information from them that I think you should know. It involves the Invasion of 1124."

Orel knew well Jared's weakness for history. The captain put down his portable. "Have a seat, Lieutenant."

He did so. "Thank you."

"So what have you learned?"

Orel had no images, graphs, or charts. He simply spoke with the even cadence of a storyteller—or, as Jared knew him to be, the unit son of an accomplished Aecron diplomat.

"What we call the Invasion of 1124," Orel began, "is known to the Silent Ones as the Failed Conquest of the Place Beyond. Their histories contain some of the details of the reasons for the Invasion and its impact on their future policies. The Silent Ones appear to know more about it than the other factions we have interacted with so far."

"Go on."

"The Invasion was orchestrated principally by Those of the Soul, the same faction currently dominating the culture of Sacred Home. According to the histories, Those of the Soul have long been an influential faction on the Plury'be homeworld. This influence has grown in recent centuries as other factions have departed for less crowded colony worlds."

Jared leaned back, his elbows resting on his armrests and his fingers interlaced. "It begs the question, then: why is the liberation of Sacred Home so important if the other factions have abandoned it for other worlds?"

"Because the other factions do not approve of Those of the Soul ceding Sacred Home's influence to the Domain. It is still their homeworld, even if its political and economic importance has diminished. How would Humans react if the Hazionites occupied Earth, even given the presence of Human colonies elsewhere?"

"A fair point. So what is the story behind the Invasion?"

"Those of the Soul are the dominant faction on Sacred Home," said Orel, "but they are not particularly powerful elsewhere. They have long sought to change that, but there are not many unsettled colony-friendly worlds near Plury'be space, and there have not been for centuries. They also do not appear interested in integrating with established colonies, especially ones as rigid as Wisdom. Those of the Soul are an old faction with a reputation among other factions for dabbling in what outsiders might classify as dark, forbidden arts. They practice a variation on what Humans call hedonism, and seek out ways to expand influence and power through practices which appear spiritual."

"If Nho were here, would he say they worship the Outcasted?"

"Perhaps so. Au'p made similar intimations when we were on Wisdom."

"Au'p said they followed the 'Lower Way.'"

"Yes," said Orel. "Au'p equates the Lower Way with That Which Distorts, which is the Plury'be counterpart to the Outcasted, or what the Domain calls Kol. Since Au'p claims Dar is in the service of Kol, you can figure out the rest."

"So Those of the Soul somehow came into an alliance with Dar and the Domain, which precipitated the Invasion?"

"It is the other way around. The Invasion helped precipitate the alliance. More on that in a moment."

"I'm listening."

"Over two centuries ago, Those of the Soul—this hedonistic Plury'be faction—determined that the immediate galactic region was inadequate to their dreams of expansion, so they began looking farther afield. They began establishing small societies on other Plury'be worlds to expand their knowledge of the factions, and built the High Land station to begin looking beyond the Great Void."

Jared thought back to High Land, the station where they had first arrived after crossing the Great Void. "So High Land is under the control of Those of the Soul."

"Yes, which explains why Au'p is so contemptuous of that

faction. They were the ones responsible for Au'p's capture and imprisonment. And High Land has a history relevant to us: nearly two centuries ago, it became the staging area for the Invasion of 1124, which Those of the Soul organized after encountering the Aecron research vessel *Noeba*."

Jared thought on that for a moment. "That would reinforce the prevailing belief back home: namely, that the *Noeba* inadvertently alerted the Invaders to the Aecrons' existence."

"It would seem so. The records are not clear, but I would not be surprised if the *Noeba* stumbled upon the High Land station after crossing the Void. There is no evidence in the histories of any Aecron captives, so we must assume the garrison at High Land destroyed them, then decided to organize the Invasion using information they had about the *Noeba*'s point of origin: Aeroel. Perhaps they were able to extrapolate it using the research vessel's approach heading. Of course, the Invasion failed, in part because Those of the Soul underestimated the Aecrons' defenses. It also seems that few other factions supported the Invasion."

Jared arched an eyebrow. "Perhaps to our good fortune."

"My people would have been overwhelmed by the full might of the Plury'be. That was not the case, though, and the politics of Plury'be society make such unified attacks unlikely in any event."

Slowly, gradually, Jared's mind began to process the full ramifications of Orel's story. It was as if a great curtain were being pulled back on some of the prevailing mysteries of the pre-Confederal era. What he was hearing would be the envy of every historian on the other side of the Great Void. He asked, "So what happened after the Invasion?"

"The defeat greatly diminished the military and political influence of Those of the Soul," said Orel, "although they maintained control of Sacred Home. Later, when the Plury'be came into formal contact with the Domain, Those of the Soul saw an opportunity to regain their lost influence and complete what they had begun.

"An actual alliance took some time. The failed invasion helped catalyze discussion between Those of the Soul and the Domain, but it was only under Dar that those plans began to truly coalesce. Apparently Dar's predecessor, whose name is not mentioned in the histories, was reluctant to get entangled in Plury'be intrigue. Dar had no such reservations. Those of the Soul worked with Dar in collecting intelligence on the Confederacy in advance of the Malum attack; this suggests scout missions into our space but the records are not specific on this. Those of the Soul also coordinated with Malum through High Land with the understanding that they would share in the control of our region of space."

Jared sat forward, resting his interlaced hands on his lap. "So Dar colluded with this Plury'be faction, the one dominating their homeworld, in sending Malum to conquer us?"

"Yes."

Jared puffed his cheeks and blew out a shot of air. "That is an incredible story. All of it. You know this will shake the foundations of Confederal history."

"That is why I felt this was worth interrupting you."

"I'm glad you did. Make sure this information is in today's report packet. Navy Command needs to know this."

• • •

Tir Bvaso and Aioua Horae stood silently in the *Hattan*'s main cargo bay, marveling at the spectacle before them.

"I cannot believe it," Tir said.

"They said they could do it," Aioua said, "and they are not ones to overpromise."

The two walked farther into the bay, making their way past scurrying bands of Exos putting the final touches on their work. The bay, as large as it was, felt crowded with the crew and equipment taking up so much space. From their vantage point, the five interceptors all stood in a perfect row, their designations clearly visible.

Belico.
Ratha.
Shington.

Binn-Phuna.

Falcon.

"How?" Tir asked. "Just last week we were hoping to have the fourth one ready by the end of the month."

"They said they would have five, remember?"

"Are all five of them really ready for flight?"

One of the Exos standing nearby turned to her. "All five are ready for flight," it clicked.

"Pending test flights," Aioua said.

"All five are ready," repeated the Exo. "They will pass test flights."

Tir looked at her Aecron friend incredulously. Aioua looked back at her and said, "As I told you, Exos never overpromise. You should know that by now."

"This is a miracle."

"No," said Aioua, her face grim. "The real miracle is yet to come. We still have to defeat another Malum."

20

MEL'AS'U / SACRED HOME
EARTH INDEX 1306.364

To Kebrun, my husband-mate,

I do not know when, or even if, you will receive this letter. Nor can I tell you where I am, although I am not sure you would believe me if I did. I can say that we are far away, and I feel that distance now more than at any time before, perhaps even more than when I was trapped inside of Malum.

I could deceive you by telling you that I am safe, and I will be home soon, but I do not think you would believe me. You do not even need smell to know whether I speak truth. Instead I will tell you as much truth as I can without risking the Navy refusing to deliver this message to you. I am headed into great danger, into an unknown no one in the Navy has faced. But I do it because, if I succeed, I have a chance to make you and our offspring safe. I cannot pass up that opportunity.

The Human called Nho is fond of saying that hope is a powerful thing. (You must find me amusing for drawing wisdom from one of the criminals of the Bvaso Mountains. It speaks of how much things have changed in the last two years.) I find myself thinking of these words often. I hold tightly to the hope that what I do now will save you, and that I will live to see you and our family once again. And I hold to the hope that, even if I do not return, that the honor of protecting you was greater than any fortunes of the Sky Walkers.

From Tir, your wife-mate

• • •

Tir steadied herself as the flatboat accelerated out of the fold and into the normal space above the Plury'be homeworld. The small ship, which belonged to the Way of Law, did not have areas to sit in, since the Plury'be did not sit. Instead, the ship projected small gravitational pools along the room where individual sentients could stand and be insulated from the forces of travel. The Plury'be assured her and the others that they would be perfectly safe inside the gravitational circles, although her instincts cried out for a chair and a good set of passive restraints.

The flatboat had a display for seeing what was ahead, although its contents were not natively visible to Hazionite eyes. Tir's environmental suit did the work, though, and through its filters she could make out the looming world ahead and the flow of space traffic around it. She could also make out a massive artificial moon—a regulator—which was just now peeking around from the far side of the planet.

She could smell nothing but her own emotions, and it unnerved her. Each Hazionite reacted differently to being encased in an environmental suit. For some it was only a nuisance, being unable to smell the emotions of those nearby. For others it was debilitating, the monotonous feedback of smell leading to madness. She was closer to the former than the latter; she would not go mad, but she would not stay in this suit one second longer than she needed to.

"Commander?"

Tir looked over at one of the other Navy officers with her, another Hazionite female. All seven of the Navy officers present were Hazionite females; that was by design. "What is it, Lieutenant?"

"Is this going to work, sir?"

"This is a poor time to ask that question."

The Hazionite lieutenant—like Tir, a member of the Bvaso province—regarded her anxiously. "I do not intend disrespect, Commander. I simply am concerned. We all are."

Tir surveyed the others and saw that the lieutenant was right. Worry, even fear, were visible in their body language. Some of them were moving their limbs erratically—a telltale sign of tension from smell deprivation.

This was not exactly the ideal team for a mission with so much uncertainty and danger. She would have preferred a team of battle-hardened security officers, perhaps even with a few Riticans. But the parameters of the mission required a skill set other than shooting things. That was why she was leading a team of xenopsychologists and communications officers. Officers unaccustomed to environmental suits and proximate danger.

"I understand your concern," Tir said. "Most of you are used to working behind the scenes, not on the front lines. This is not what you were trained for." She paused before adding, "Even I am apprehensive, and I am trained for these missions.

"But," she continued, "you are the very best we have for this. The Plury'be need Navy officers who can speak to the atrocities of Malum and communicate the gravity of the Domain threat."

"I know," said the lieutenant impatiently, "and I know we are the only one of the Navy races who has a chance to slip through Sacred Home's port security. I understand those facts, ma'am. I am simply communicating my feelings."

Tir's eyes narrowed. She did not always share Jared's patience in these moments, and certainly did not feel gracious given her own unease. "That is enough, Lieutenant," she snapped.

The officer recoiled slightly in surprise. Tir regarded all of them coolly. "That goes for all of you. You are Navy officers and we have work to do. The fate of our people depends on it. You are all trained to do this work, and your job today is to act like it. I will not hear any more such talk. You are not a tribe of infant vola. You are Navy officers. Am I clear?"

The other six replied crisply in assent.

"Now," said Tir, gesturing with the Hazionite equivalent of impatience, "I would remind you of your roles. Your task is not to fight. That is the Plury'be work. Your job is to speak the truth of what the Domain has done to us. Your job is to tell the Plury'be the horrors of Malum and the threat they were to us. You have all studied Plury'be culture extensively, and you all know how to communicate effectively."

She paused, trying to soften her voice a little. "If you do what you are tasked to do, you will live to see the worlds of the Hazionites once again."

• • •

"We are in position," announced Kilvin, seated at the *Hattan*'s navigation station. "From here we can reach Sacred Home in less than seven Index minutes."

Jared mirrored his own display to the current image on the tridimensional, which showcased a live feed of the view over Sacred Home as captured by the Silent Ones and their surveillance. "Orel, what are you hearing from our allies?"

"The first wave has infiltrated Sacred Home and is headed to the surface. The second and third wave Plury'be fleets are in position and waiting. It is just a matter of timing. They expect second wave action in three Index hours equivalent time. The third wave will respond as needed."

Jared fully understood the Plury'be plan, but remained ambivalent about its success. He knew he was not the best judge, since he was no expert on Plury'be tactics or psychology, especially in a scenario like this one.

He manipulated his command station to show the *Hattan*'s left flank, where B'aha's massive Plury'be battle carrier loomed, along with hundreds of other ships. The fleet looked formidable now, but he wondered how it would look once it was staring down the forces around that planet.

Especially that regulator.

• • •

At Redelia's command, the *Hattan* bridge conference room darkened. Above Redelia and the other interceptor commanders, Malum appeared—Malum as it had been over a year and a half ago, during the Battle of Aeroel. Fleets of ships—Aecron, Navy, and others—fired from all sides at the giant planet, their weapons more often than not swallowed up by wide-ranging swaths of pale light. As the seconds ticked away in the recording, the pale beams consumed ship after ship, thinning the defensive ranks and the firepower coming from them.

She manipulated the footage to zero in on one particular quarter of the combat zone. There, a cluster of interceptors was moving around erratically, strafing away from the pale beams and firing off pulsing blue torpedoes.

"That was your battle group, wasn't it?" said Brigg Drews.

Redelia nodded. "The *Retaelus* battle group, under then-Commander Jared Carter."

"Those are collider torpedoes," said Amun Plau, the corpulent Ritican sitting in a squat heap not far from the table.

"That is correct. We were authorized to take them from the derelict *Hattan* when it was left in orbit around Obaiyo Colony."

"Why have I never heard of this before?" Brigg asked.

"It was a combination of factors. I think much of the chaos of the Battle of Aeroel has been lost in the official reports."

Eil Morichar, the Hazionite interceptor commander, scoffed. "'Lost,' indeed."

"What are you insinuating?" Brigg said, his tone sarcastic and rhetorical.

Amun Plau did not recognize Brigg's sarcasm and answered matter-of-factly. "Admiral Garvak was operating outside of his purview in allocating those torpedoes," he said. "Those are the manner of details that are easily hidden in the aftermath of such a catastrophic crisis."

"Who cares?" said Venzz Kitt, leaning back with his feet

propped up on the table. "It's not as if any of this matters. That fleet was wiped out just like everyone else."

"Valuable lessons can be learned from a loss," said Brigg, looking directly at Venzz. "If that weren't the case, some of us would never learn anything."

Venzz's feet dropped to the floor. "Excuse me, *Lieutenant?*"

Redelia's large onyx Aecron eyes bored into both men. "There are at least ten other senior officers on this ship who are willing and able to command an interceptor if neither of you is suitable for the role."

"My apologies, Commander," said Brigg.

"Sorry, ma'am," Venzz mumbled.

Redelia glared at both of them before continuing. "Now, my reason for showing this footage should be self-evident. We need to determine what advantages we have should we find ourselves in combat with the regulator."

Amun Plau asked, "What is the state of our pulse weapons and defense fields?"

"The Exos have made modifications based on Aioua Horae's experiments. They are confident our pulse cannons will pierce the force waves and our defense fields will hold."

Eil looked doubtful. "We should not rely on that assumption."

"I agree," Brigg said.

"As do I," said Redelia. "To that end, I have spent considerable time talking with several people on board who served on the *Retaelus* battle fleet to consider the tactics we developed during the Battle of Aeroel and how we might improve them. Of particular help were Vetta Quidd and medical officer Darel Weye, both of whom served on the *Retaelus* and developed the defensive combat doctrine you are seeing here. I also spoke with navigator Kilvin Wrsaw, the *Retaelus's* navigator and the one who implemented the maneuvers on that ship."

Amun Plau gestured at the still-moving footage. "I do not see a pattern to the movements."

"For the most part there is not. The captain encouraged us to be unpredictable against Malum, so most of our movements were erratic and arbitrary. His hope was to keep us on the battlefield for as long as possible so we could expend as many torpedoes as possible."

"The idea appears sound," said Brigg, "but it didn't play out well. Most of your group was wiped out in the first two minutes, and the damage total was small."

Redelia's face fell ever so slightly. "Yes. In my subsequent conversations with officers in the *Retaelus* battle group, we all concluded that, by operating independently, we inadvertently made it easier for Malum to focus on one of us at a time. Had we been able to do it over again, we would have employed a more coordinated, algorithmic attack pattern."

"Linked maneuvers, as if you were small fighter vessels," Eil said.

"Precisely. It is not the sort of attack strategy interceptors normally would employ, given their role within the Navy, but it would be not difficult to effect. The patterns would still aim to be unpredictable. Rather than using synchronized formation as fighters or torpedo bombers do, we would be using asynchronous but planned patterns, ones that would be harder to decipher. But by coordinating, those patterns could actually be used to assist one another and increase our collective damage potential."

"Or using one ship's maneuvers to draw attacks off of others," Brigg said.

Amun pushed his large midsection against the table, "If there is one thing I can support, it is finding a way to keep that *bkslah*'s weapons off my ship."

Redelia shifted the floating image to one of hypothetical maneuvers against a simulated regulator. At one point, one of the simulated interceptors appeared to be drawing pale beam fire away from a larger group while the rest fired off torpedoes and pulse weapons. "Vetta and I ran up a few simulations where we might do just that."

• • •

The Plury'be flatboat rumbled as it penetrated the atmosphere of Sacred Home. Below, the clouds parted to reveal a landscape of endless city. Tir watched on the Plury'be display as the ground grew steadily closer, showing increasing details of a planet given almost totally over to civilization. There was no sign of natural spaces on the surface, not even of the barren kind. Everything looked taken over by sentience, a world covered by a single city.

"There is nothing left," said one of the Hazionite officers nearby, of the Wrsaw province. "They have completely destroyed it."

Tir, as a Hazionite, was sympathetic to the cultural context behind that statement. Hazion Prime was famous for its tree-covered, natural ecosystem, something retained even as the Hazionites industrialized and expanded. To turn a planet into such an artificial wasteland was, to a Hazionite, the height of abomination.

"This planet is smaller than most homeworlds, including ours," noted one of the other officers. "Even we would have trouble maintaining that ecosystem."

"That is no excuse," another said. "It is an offense to the planet's life force."

The planet's surface fell to the bottom of the view as the flatboat pulled up, flying parallel to the ground. "We are nearing the landing / You should prepare yourselves / (urgency)," said the Plury'be pilot.

Tir reached for the bulky contraption affixed to the floor next to her, which released easily into her hands. It felt considerably heavier than the last time she had held it. The gravity on Sacred Home was higher than the standard on Navy ships, and while her environmental suit was designed to compensate by augmenting her movements, she could still feel the difference.

The contraption was a haphazard construction that, once placed over her, would cover her entire body. The Selitin were, according to the Plury'be, a tribe of crafters and dealers that had long ago been subsumed under the Domain. Because of their prowess in developing small, efficient equipment and their even greater prowess at selling it, the Domain allowed them limited rights of trade with other races, including the Plury'be.

The Selitin, like most sentients, could not breathe the atmospheric mix present on Plury'be worlds, and the contraption was a reproduction, visually, of what Selitin wore when visiting such places. Shorn of their equipment, the differences between Tir's party and actual Selitin traders would be obvious, but with the equipment on and with the right attention to detail, a Hazionite female could pass for one of the traders. Everyone accompanying Tir had spent time reviewing footage of the traders to adequately duplicate their mannerisms and movement style.

Tir's contraption locked into place above her head and flowed down over her body, briefly cocooning her in darkness. After a moment, her environmental suit interfaced with the contraption's optics and she could see the world around her. It was a little disorienting, like looking through a short tunnel, but she had practiced with it back on the *Hattan* and believed she could manage. In fact, she had discovered that this visual perspective actually helped her better mimic the Selitin, for reasons she could not quite place.

"How are you all faring?" she asked her crew.

"Much like I did when I tested it on the ship," said one. "I feel like I am in the tree hole my clan mother forced me into when I trespassed into a neighbor's *cosorast* pen."

"I never realized clan mothers in other regions did that," said another.

There was a bit of Hazionite laughter, and Tir could sense—if not smell—the tension in the room dissipating, at least a little.

• • •

Rami Del arrived on the *Hattan*'s bridge and took her place next to Orel Dayail at the communications station. The *Hattan* was about to enter a battle zone where it would need to coordinate with two different fleets speaking two different languages and operating with two distinct combat styles. Rami, it had been decided, would coordinate the actions among Navy assets, including the *Hattan* and its five interceptors. Orel would orchestrate communication between the Navy battle group and the various Plury'be factions.

At the command station, Jared noted silently that part of the fleet waiting at Watch Tower was beginning to stir. By now the operation's first wave—the Way of Law flatboats, including the one Tir Bvaso was on—were on the surface, its members preparing to fan out to Sacred Home's various speaking places. Sacred Home had places not unlike the Speaking Stone they had visited on Wisdom, locations where policy and alliances could be made, and the first wave's personnel would converge on those simultaneously to begin their part of the operation. If all was going according to plan, that wave had not yet been detected; it should have been seen as little more than a normal part of the planet's traffic. As the operation continued, that would change.

That's where the second wave came in. The second wave was a collection of Plury'be ships encompassing several factions, including the Way of Law, the No Greater, and the Silent Ones. This wave's primary purpose was to prevent the orbiting Plury'be factions from interfering with the first wave's work. The prohibitions against violence on Wisdom did not exist on Sacred Home, and the threat of orbital strikes against the first wave—and any sentients unfortunate enough to be near them—was very real. There was also the matter of possible attacks by Dar-aligned Plury'be factions already on the surface, but the strategists among the Silent Ones believed that those risks were lower. Orel indicated to Jared that it was due to the complex nature of Plury'be sociology.

That left the matter of the regulator, the Domain planet-ship orbiting high above Sacred Home. Assuming the regulator was comparable in design to Malum, its threat to both the first wave on the ground and the second wave in space was considerable. The third wave's task was to engage the regulator directly, and it would involve a fleet of various Plury'be ships combined with the *Hattan* and its fleet.

And Nho.

Jared looked over at the old man. Nho stood not far behind the weapons station. His eyes were closed and his hands clasped around Sarco's staff, holding it close to his chest.

"Orel," Jared said, orienting himself to face communications, "how long until the second fleet moves out?"

"Less than three Index hours equivalent time. The fleet is powering up now in case there is a need to move early."

Move early. In other words, if something failed to go according to plan.

• • •

Tir stepped out of the gateway leading from the landing area and was nearly knocked over. Around her, under Sacred Home's bright red sun, a sea of Plury'be moved in all directions, their forms brushing against one another as they slid along their various paths. Tir lowered her center of gravity slightly to compensate; through her link she could hear one of her officers helping to steady another officer. Their Selitin coverings disrupted their sense of balance.

"I have never seen so much life in one place," one officer said.

"Try visiting one of the cities on Earth," said another.

"Essential talk only," Tir admonished. "Stay focused, keep your balance, and follow our guide."

The *Hattan* first officer set off after the ones who had brought them here. Among the mass of Plury'be it was virtually impossible to differentiate them by visual inspection alone—the Plury'be all looked the same. Her suit's optics, however, marked their allies with green auras that were clearly visible. She pushed her way through the masses, her fellow officers close behind.

Tir had been told that the cities of this planet were crowded and that it was appropriate simply to force her way through, but the actual sight and feel of so much life nevertheless overwhelmed her. The Plury'be here did not use any form of traffic control or protocol. Floes of the beings moved to and fro in essentially random directions. Within her first minute of walking, she was forced to ford two virtual nexuses of traffic, and in each case the Plury'be were passing through from five or six directions simultaneously. The streets were wider here than on Wisdom or Free Town, but they felt insufficient to handle the local masses. If this was indicative of other parts of the world, Sacred Home's population had to be immense, small planet or not.

Tir and the others pushed on. The wide streets were bracketed by structures of various shapes and sizes, some of them small round-like habitations like those on Free Town, others surprisingly jagged constructions that stretched into the sky. Having seen so much uniformity of architecture on the previous two Plury'be worlds she had visited—Free Town and Wisdom—she did not expect to see such diversity here.

"DAR BRINGS PEACE / PEACE UPON ALL OF YOU / (SINCERITY)."

Tir stifled a gasp and kept walking.

"Did you hear that?" one of her officers cried. "Where did that come from?"

"Keep your heads moving forward," said Tir. "As far as we are concerned, this is a normal occurrence." Even as she said it, though, she could see one of the clouds—an overseer—up ahead, floating just above a large, shining structure.

. . .

Jared's visual feed of Sacred Home winked out. He stared absently at it, waiting for the image to come back on. When it did not, he attempted the time-honored—if ineffectual—tactic of tapping the device. Nothing. He cycled through the other available feeds from the Sacred Home system being sent from Watch Tower. Still nothing.

"Aioua," he said, "I believe something is wrong with one of my displays. My live feed of Sacred Home is down."

"The problem is not with us. We are no longer receiving telemetry from the planet."

"No one is," Orel said. "The Plury'be factions are asking the same questions. The Silent Ones are telling them that they have lost contact with their probes around the planet."

Jared reverted his dormant display to the last tactical information sent from Sacred Home, a still image of an unassuming world. "Could it be some sort of malfunction?"

"The Silent Ones are saying the problem is with the probes themselves, not their receiving systems at Watch Tower. The nature of their responses gives the impression that the technology is not prone to failure."

"That is suspicious timing," Garo Ball said. "The advance teams are on the ground and the second wave has not yet deployed. They are vulnerable."

Nho opened his eyes and said, "Dar has already shown he can anticipate our plans. The Outcasted informs him well."

Jared cut off the profanity about to spill out of his mouth. Instead, he said, "Orel, what are the Plury'be going to do?"

"They are accelerating their plans. The second wave ships are preparing to initialize their folds within the next few minutes. B'aha is sending orders to the third wave to prepare to move immediately thereafter. We have received our target coordinates."

"Feed them to navigation. Aioua, where will those coordinates deposit us?"

"Extrapolating from the last telemetry, they will interpose us between the second wave fleet and the regulator."

Jared keyed his command station to broadcast ship-wide. "Officers and crew of the *Hattan*, this is Jared Carter speaking. Circumstances are bringing us into a battle zone sooner than we anticipated. In a moment we will be going to combat stations. You all have given me your very best in these last months, far more than any captain could ever hope or wish for. I need your best one more time. It's time for us to strike a blow against Dar. This is for Ahtog 3, for Obaiyo Colony, for all of the Confederacy. That is all."

Jared keyed for combat stations, and the ship's alarms responded accordingly. As they did he spoke into his link. "Carter to Aroo."

"Redelia here, Captain."

"Have the interceptor crews report to the hangar immediately and prepare for launch on my command."

"Already on my way, sir."

As the connection closed, Jared took a last look at Nho. "May the fortunes of the Sky Walkers go with you," Jared said.

"Fortune is for those wishing for hope," Nho replied. "I have hope. Sarco is with me."

Nho turned and headed for the bridge exit.

• • •

AGRO'ATH HOUSE.

Tir's suit projected the sign's translation in front of her eyes. The suit also projected annotations on the term, pointing out that it had been used by the Domain emissary during the debate on Wisdom, and that it referred to a Domain establishment of some dark design, although the Plury'be had difficulty clarifying exactly what it did. Tir's best assumption was that it represented some form of self-indulgence or debauchery.

It did not lack for business. The influx and outflow of the building's patrons were, improbably, even more congested than along other parts of the street. It was impossible to ford straight through, even by way of pushing sentients aside. The Plury'be leaving the Agro'ath House waved their tentacles more slowly and showed less balance as they moved into the less packed traffic. Tir thought they looked debilitated.

"DAR BRINGS PEACE / PEACE UPON ALL OF YOU / (SINCERITY)."

Tir gazed up to the sky. The overseer floated benevolently above the Agro'ath House, its cloudy tendrils interlacing with the upper spires of the building.

"It is so different than the one inside Malum," one officer said. "It looks so . . . benign."

"Such is the nature of Dar's deception," Tir said. "We need to get around this traffic. Follow me."

Tir cut a wide arc around the Agro'ath House's crowd, eventually emerging on the far side of the congestion and back in the wake of her Plury'be guides from the Way of Law. She resisted the urge to look over her shoulder as the overseer again issued its placid declaration.

Now clear of the Agro'ath House, the group's pace increased. They cleared a run of tall buildings and were now passing a series of short flat ones.

"Commander," said one of the officers, "look over there. Left of us, over the horizon."

Tir focused her attention in that direction and there it was—a large, black sphere coming into view far above in the bright daylight.

A regulator.

The planet-ship seemed to suck all light around it out of existence, even as it glossed with a brilliant sheen. *Just like Malum.*

Even as she watched it floated across the sky, showing a pace she had never seen in any natural moon. In fact, it almost seemed to be headed to the point above them.

• • •

Nho arrived at the shuttle hangar where a Human pilot, a young male, met him. "We need to hurry," the pilot said.

Nho nodded. There was much to be done and little time. The pilot pointed to one of the small two-person shuttles, the *Swillow*, which would take Nho to his next, most crucial destination.

A chorus of voices filled the shuttle bay, most of them Aecron, but some others as well. Nho listened as several officers nearby chanted, softly, the prayer of Sarco:

> *My paternal, the greatest One,*
> *Your name is sacred.*
> *Your leadership flows,*
> *Your grand plan be borne,*
> *Among us as it is in Paradise.*
> *Provide for us our needed sustenance,*
> *And forgive us for our failings,*

As we, in turn, forgive those who fail us,
For you are the righteous empire,
All that is mighty, you fill the galaxies,
For all time.
It is true.

Nho momentarily closed his eyes, then opened them again. "May the peace of Sarco be with you all," he said, then rushed to his shuttle.

• • •

The Plury'be leading Tir and her officers came to the door of a building and stopped. The door was short but wide, and the sign on the street in front of it translated roughly as Trade Room. One of the guides brushed against the door, and it receded to reveal a small circular entrance. The room within was of plain construction, with some lighting, a few surfaces, and very few Plury'be.

The Way of Law followers moved through the building's main foyer and into a tube-styled hallway that terminated at another door. That door also receded, and Tir's Plury'be guides slid through. Tir and the others followed. This room was much smaller, with spherical and cylindrical objects stacked about. A storage room of some sort.

"You may speak here / It is safe here," one of the Way of Law said. "We should not speak long / Our time is short / (urgency)."

Tir activated her external communication. "What is this place?"

"It is a way to resistance / It is a way to spread our message."

The Plury'be who spoke moved its tentacles slightly and part of the floor slid aside. Underneath, a tubular chamber lay on the sub-flooring. One of the other Way of Law immediately got into the tube and took a position flat on the chamber's surface. The first Plury'be then moved its tentacles again and a pale glow—a familiar, terrifying pale beam flooded the small chamber. When the glow receded the Plury'be lying there was gone.

Tir recoiled. "What is this? Is that—?"

"It is the tool of the Domain / It is the tool of the regulator," said one of the Plury'be. "The Domain uses this tool for darkness / We use it to fight the darkness / (defiance). We enter here / We exit in another place."

One of Tir's officers said, "We are expected to *use* one of those?"

"This is the path to the resistance / It is the only path to the resistance. It is safe / It does not harm / (insistence)."

Tir crouched down and examined the device. So the Plury'be had reappropriated the regulator's pale beam and used it to transport sentients across distances.

She looked up at the others. "If they say it is not harmful, then we will take them at their honor. I will go first."

21

Underground

An evil light gave way to darkness, and Tir found herself on the ground. Her stomach tract churned sickly. She brought herself to a sitting position, her Selitin garb shifting over her.

She was surrounded by a group of Plury'be on the ground and, up in the air, a cluster of purple hyperwave spheres. She was in a small cave tunnel, dim and damp. She could hear liquid dripping somewhere in the distance.

One of the Plury'be said, "We are safe / We must still hurry / (urgency)."

Tir nodded and got up slowly, out of a small indentation in the ground. As soon as she cleared the indentation, a shaft of pale white light poured into the space and another Hazionite officer appeared. Within minutes, the entire Navy party was through, nauseated but otherwise unharmed.

Once all of them were accounted for, the Plury'be began to move, beckoning Tir and the others to follow. They made haste down a long passageway. It was solid rock on all sides with liquid dripping from the ceiling in places. Along the way, small light fixtures cast an indigo glow along the tunnel, casting shadows at everyone who passed in front of them.

As they walked, Tir asked, "What is this place?"

One of the Way of Law answered, "This is a refuge / This is the work of the Silent Ones."

"Is it a secret base of some sort?"

"This is designed to preserve / This is designed to protect. This is a part of our history / You will understand / (urgency)."

The passage continued, almost in a straight line, for fifty or more trics. There were no intersections, branches, or signs of anything other than an unbroken tunnel. The Plury'be moved quickly—more quickly than they had above ground.

At last, the tunnel dipped slightly and came to an end. The Plury'be went through first. Tir followed, emerging from the tunnel into one of the most astonishing places she had ever seen in her astonishment-filled life.

It was a giant cavern, perhaps hundreds of trics high and several times larger in width and depth. The enormous room was filled with color—indigoes, crimsons, oranges, and even some greens and blues. All of it was alive, the ground and walls covered in an array of exotic fauna unlike anything Tir had ever laid eyes on. Moving among the growth, and sometimes flying through the air, was life of all sorts, from the small to the massive. The ground shook as one particularly large living organism—a giant thing ten trics high and roughly the shape of a deflated sphere—rolled past, collecting various pieces of growth with sticky cilia.

Up at the ceiling, the cave was alight with a bright sphere, a rich red just like the sun of Sacred Home. It cast a light that was so real, it seemed as natural as its real counterpart, though Tir knew this could not be.

"This is unbelievable," one of the Hazionite officers said. "It is a living ecosystem."

Tir asked, "What is this place?"

"This is the life of Sacred Home / This is the remnant of Sacred Home's life. Watch Tower is a repository of knowledge / Under World is a repository of life."

"So this is the life that was on this planet before your cities overran the surface?"

"You speak sadness / You speak truth / (profound sorrow)."

One of Tir's officers asked, "This cave is under the surface, then?"

"The surface is above / We are below. This cave is hidden / This cave is isolated. There are no entrances / There are no escapes."

"Except for the pale beams," said Tir.

"The only entrances are the pale beams / The only exits are the pale beams. This cave serves as a sanctuary / This cave serves as a transit. Follow Us / We must continue / (urgency)."

The Plury'be resumed their movement, taking a course along the outskirts of the cave where a flat pathway rose a few trics above the main area. Ahead, along the cavern wall, were round holes that seemed to exit to other places.

"You said this was a transit point," said Tir, speaking to one of the guides. "Can you get to other parts of the planet from here?"

"The Silent Ones established other pale beam connections / The Silent Ones wanted many connections. We can leave here using other portals / We can emerge in other places."

They reached a junction with one of the holes. The Plury'be stopped briefly to address the Navy officers. "Each one of Us will enter a cave / Each one of You should follow one of Us. We will divide / We will move."

Tir turned to her colleagues, who all looked back at her in their strange, decorative coverings. "May the fortunes of the Sky Walkers go with you," she said.

They responded in kind and separated, each Hazionite officer moving off with one or more of the Plury'be. Each headed for a separate exit tunnel, where pale beam transporters led to different parts of the planet's unbroken city.

22

The Battle at Mel'as'u / Sacred Home
Earth Index 1306.364

As the *Hattan* dropped into normal space above Sacred Home, two things happened immediately:

First, the cruiser came under the merciless force waves of the regulator.

Second, a pale beam struck directly at the ship.

The *Hattan* quaked. Cold light poured over and around the cruiser's defense fields, probing for a point of entrance by which to extract the ship and its crew from this plane of existence. The bridge viewscreen showed nothing but the sickening light. The bridge crew froze in their seats.

The light subsided, and the *Hattan* was still there. The ship rumbled under the force waves, but the defense fields held.

Jared exhaled.

The left tridimensional display lit up with the tactical situation above Sacred Home, and it was chaotic. The second wave, hundreds of ships strong, had arrived at Sacred Home only to come under immediate attack by a garrison that included Those of the Soul, its allied factions, and several Domain cruisers. The massive regulator, far from watching passively, had taken to the offensive, making a direct course for the second wave.

The third wave, whose legions included B'aha's battle carrier and the *Hattan* battle group, were tasked with shielding the second wave from the regulator while the orbital garrison was dealt with. Jared's fleet had almost arrived too late, having underestimated the ferocity by which the regulator would spring into action. Even as Jared watched, a pale beam lanced past the *Hattan* and focused on a second wave cruiser, pouring its wrath into the ship's bonded armor.

The Plury'be were not defenseless against the regulator. The bonded armor employed by Plury'be ships was resistant to the pale beam and could hold out against it for a while. Eventually the beam would shear off the bonding, at which time the Plury'be ship would be vulnerable. The third wave's job was to keep that from happening to the second wave. It was theorized (but by no means certain) that, if second wave could defeat the garrison, the regulator might withdraw.

For Jared, the sensation of the moment was at once one of dreaded familiarity and uncertain newness. He had faced a regulator once before in the form of Malum, and the vibrations of the planet-ship's force waves were as unsettling now as then. This time, though, it was different: a different planet, a different ship, different allies, and a different level of preparation.

And the knowledge that Nho had the power to stop it.

"The interceptors report they are clear of their folds," shouted Rami above the din. "They are linking up for their attack pattern."

Over on the right tridimensional display, a detailed schematic of the giant planet-ship appeared in the air. Jared silently asked for the courage to do what needed to be done next. "Kilvin," he said aloud, "bring us on a direct course toward the regulator. Garo, bring everything we have to bear on that thing and fire at will."

• • •

The small No Greater flatboat rumbled under the regulator's force waves, giving Nho the illusory sensation that he would fall. Somehow he did not. Still, he planted Sarco's staff firmly in front of him and held on to it with both hands.

Nho's role was simple: get close enough to the regulator to get absorbed into the planet-ship by way of the pale beam, then do to the regulator what he did to Malum. To accomplish this, S'li and Au'p had volunteered to fly him directly at the monstrous sphere in a flatboat, firing its weapons and attracting attention.

Next to Nho stood Rete, also encased in a gravitational pool. Nho had earlier taken stock of the state of his old friend, and decided not to do so again. Rete was petrified, his eyes closed as if he were trying to shut out everything unfolding around him. Rete had only joined Nho out of obligation—or perhaps fear of shame—but he looked as if he would rather be anywhere else. Part of Nho could not blame him; another part of Nho wondered if Rete truly possessed the faith he had claimed to have for all these years.

"We are drawing closer / The waves will grow louder," S'li said.

"I understand," said Nho. "Thank you for your courage."

"We are fearful / We are uncertain," said Au'p. "We will trust That Which There Is No Greater / We will trust Ah'ey / (hope)."

• • •

Redelia sat on the bridge of the interceptor *Belico*, watching the battle unfold around her. From behind, an eruption of fusing torpedoes streaked from the *Hattan*, weaving past the interceptors in the erratic maneuvers for which they had been programmed. Other attacks—hyperwave beams from other third wave Plury'be ships, pulse shots from the *Hattan*—sprinkled through the void of space, making a direct line toward the monstrous planet-ship looming ever closer. In reply, the regulator's multiple pale beams lashed out at the ordnance, hitting a few but missing others. And the force waves pounded against everything. So far the defense fields of both the *Hattan* and the five interceptors had held, but there was no way to know how long they would last.

The five interceptors—*Belico*, *Shington*, *Ratha*, *Falcon*, and *Binn-Phuna*—had linked together in a seemingly arbitrary—but complexly designed—attack pattern designed to augment their collective attacks while staying out of harm's way. The fruit of that strategy bore out as the first salvo from the interceptors struck the regulator's surface, followed closely by a fusillade from the rest of the fleet. Distant splashes of light indicated successful hits.

Redelia said. "How much damage on the target?"

"Very little so far."

Not surprising. The regulator was enormous, and a few fusing torpedoes were not going to do a lot.

The communications officer said, "The *Hattan* is directing us to use collider torpedoes."

"Do it," said Redelia. The collider torpedoes were exponentially more powerful than the traditional fusing torpedoes, but were also fewer in quantity. They were being held in reserve specifically to use on the regulator. Each interceptor was armed with five.

"Commander, multiple objects are launching from the regulator," said Udos Beyole from sciences. "Spike-shaped, each around twenty trics long. At least three hundred in total, matching the profile of the objects deployed from the Domain ship over Free Town."

Redelia had long wondered if those would show up. The encrypted data packet she had received from the Aecron Sciences Institute spoke of similar objects, but the original Malum had never used them. If they were like the ones used at Free Town, what was inside them was as dangerous as the objects themselves.

She pulled the visuals on the spike-ships to her display. "Where are they headed?"

"They are targeting ships all along the third wave line, but a disproportionate number are on a course directly at B'aha's battle carrier and the *Hattan*."

"How disproportionate?"

"At least forty."

Redelia took in a short breath to keep calm. "Contact the other interceptors. Change of plans."

• • •

The spikes flew directly past Au'p's flatboat, ignoring it entirely, just like every other regulator attack. S'li fired the hyperwave node repeatedly at the Domain planet, striking the target but garnering no response. Either the regulator saw the ship as too small to be important, or it wanted nothing to do with who was inside.

• • •

Another flash of pale light splashed against the *Hattan* and faded. The defense fields were still holding.

"Captain, a number of the garrison ships are converging on us from behind," said Aioua. "They appear to be breaking off from the second wave to engage us."

"Composition?"

"At least thirty are moving to attack the fleet. Seven of that number are bearing directly for the *Hattan*: two cruiser-level Plury'be ships, four flatboats, and a Domain cruiser. They will be within attack range in moments."

"Garo, target the Domain cruiser with the rearward weapons and prepare to fire on my command. Time on the siege cannon?"

"Twenty-four seconds."

"We have another problem," said Aioua. "Numerous objects inbound from the regulator. Spike-shaped, twenty trics long, similar to what we saw at Free Town. I count three hundred. Over forty of them are specifically targeting the *Hattan* and B'aha's battle carrier."

"*Belico* reports that the interceptors are moving to engage the spikes," said Rami.

"Tell Redelia to proceed," said Jared. "Garo, target the spikes with our turrets. Maintain torpedo attacks on the regulator."

Orel said, "Several third wave flatboats and fighters are moving to intercept the spikes. B'aha's ship is continuing its attack on the regulator."

One of the elements on Jared's displays turned bright green. At once Garo Ball said, "The siege cannon has reached saturation."

Jared stared at the regulator with the intensity of a man who knew he was about to throw his best punch. He gave the order to fire.

• • •

"Unload the collider on the regulator," Brigg Drews ordered, "then find us one of those spikes to hit."

Brigg did not like where this battle was going. It was bad enough facing a foe as peerless as a regulator, but trying to do so with the additional challenge of these attack spikes and imminent reinforcements from the planetary garrison had turned a suicide mission into a potential massacre. Redelia's order to focus on the spikes was the only correct option in this situation; the capital ships, with their firepower, had to be protected at all costs.

A flash of light consumed the viewscreen, momentarily blinding him. Ahead, a large, surging, vicious ball of fury shot away from the *Hattan* and past the *Shington*, streaking off into the darkness. Despite its impossibility, Brigg was sure he heard it roar as it went past. It was alive with power, a rainbow of colors flowing through its surface and rippling out in vibrant lashes.

"Go. Go," Brigg's navigator whispered, as if words could will the weapon on.

The blast rapidly closed the distance to the regulator. The planet-ship responded by training no fewer than four pale beams on it. If the ball shrank under the beams' gaze, it did not show. Unerringly the attack closed in on the planet-ship, giving light to a regulator that seemed to absorb light.

At last there was a collision as the siege cannon's attack smashed against the regulator, an unstoppable force against a titanic object. A flash of light blew up on the screen, nearly blinding Brigg a second time. The flash receded, revealing a discernible hole of perhaps a few hundred trics across the equator of the regulator. Brigg almost thought he could see a glow of light from the regulator's inner sun beyond.

• • •

Jared watched the scene play out with unvarnished awe. "Analysis?"

"Pale beam effect on the siege cannon packet was negligible.

The attack struck with full yield. Damage to the regulator was significant but localized. The Uxa251 hull was able to dissipate some of the blast, although there is a breach. The regulator is already repairing at a rapid rate; the hole will not be open long."

Jared said, quickly, "Garo, see if you can sneak a few torpedoes through that hole before it closes, and ready the cannon for another round as soon as possible. Aioua, how many spikes are still out there?"

"At least one hundred, with fifteen in our immediate battle zone alone. I am also reading more deploying from the regulator; preliminary number is more than one hundred and ten. Projected impact of the new wave within a minute."

Jared traced a finger along the edge of his chair. "If one of those things hits our defense fields, what will happen?"

Aioua parsed through the data in front of her. "Uncertain."

"Speculate, Aioua."

"The Uxa251 embedded in their exterior may redirect our fields when they impact."

"May?"

She looked him in the eye. "Will, sir. They will breach our fields and pierce the ship."

"How badly?"

"The fields should slow them enough to keep them from passing clear through as they have done to the flatboats, but they will nevertheless breach the hull."

"Captain," Garo said, "I recommend redirecting our torpedoes to the spikes."

Jared looked out at that gaping hole in the regulator, which was even now, before his eyes, beginning to close like an opportunity about to be lost.

"No," he said. "Focus on that hole."

• • •

"Terrible idea," Brigg shouted, watching another round of collider torpedoes race from the *Hattan* toward the regulator.

The weapons officer looked at him. "Sir?"

"Captain Carter is going for the deathblow on the regulator while those spikes are bearing inbound. Serious mistake."

Brigg shook off the thought. Critiquing a decision already made during the heat of battle was a waste of time. "Forget it. How long until we can target the next spike?"

. . .

Tir stepped onto the large round disc under Sacred Home's bright sun. It was a platform, much like the dais on Wisdom. It was not on a large plateau, but rather in the center of a cluster of towering buildings. Tir had been told it was a speaking location for influential members of Plury'be society; the implication was that it was the closest thing to a seat of government on the planet. Her fellow officers were, at that moment, arriving at other, similar locations across Sacred Home.

On the disc upon which Tir now stood, several Plury'be from different factions were engaged in an argument over the situation developing above in space. Tir had seen the pinpricks of light in the sky and knew it must mean the second wave—and possibly third wave—had arrived and was in combat. These developments were much, much earlier than originally planned, which meant something must have changed. Or gone wrong.

Some of the Plury'be, likely of Those of the Soul, turned on her as she mounted the stage. "You cannot be here / Traders are not allowed here. This is for Us of Plury'be / This is not for You / (indignation)."

Several purple spheres—Plury'be hyperwave weapons—converged on her, taking on a glow as if they were about to fire. They were immediately cut off by other spheres, the ones of the Plury'be accompanying her. One of her companions, of the Way of Law, said, "This one comes from a distance / This one speaks urgency."

"This one may not be here / The reasons are immaterial."

Tir pulled at her Selitin covering and disconnected it from her environmental suit, the unwieldy, asymmetrical shroud falling in a heap beside her. That brought all manner of surprised utterances from the local crowd.

"I am Tir Bvaso, and I am no Selitin," she declared. "I come from what you call the Place Beyond, and I am here today because Dar and the Domain are out to destroy you all. I know this well, as Dar tried to destroy our people. I also offer a hope, for we know where Dar gains his power and how to stop it."

She pointed to the large artificial sphere—the regulator—orbiting almost directly overhead. "Our people stopped a regulator once before and we can do so here. We can return independence to you."

The disc devolved into a cacophony of voices, with Those of the Soul denouncing her, the Way of Law denouncing the denouncements, and other factions offering their own commentary. Tir remained silent for the moment, considering what to do next.

A rush of wind, and suddenly a large cloud drew forth from between the tall buildings, hovering directly over the disc.

A warden. An overseer.

"DAR IS HONORABLE / THIS ONE SEEKS TO DESTROY OUR PEACE."

Tir's body shook, but she held her ground. Pointing to the cloud, she shouted, "You lie! You do not seek coexistence! You seek dominion, just as you sought to do to us!"

"YOU ARE AN OUTSIDER / YOU WILL NOT DESTROY THE PEACE."

The cloud moved toward her. She had a small pulse pistol on her suit but she knew, based on the reports from Free Town, that it would be useless. She had no means to defend herself and Nho and his staff were far away. The Way of Law was next to her, but it was uncertain if their weapons could hold off the cloud.

"YOU WILL NOT DESTROY THE PEACE / LEAVE OR BE EXTINGUISHED."

Her feet froze beneath her as the nightmare of death filled her entire field of vision.

• • •

A single collider torpedo struck the regulator, missing the hole created by the siege cannon entirely. Jared swore loudly. The pale beams had swallowed up all but one of the *Hattan's* torpedo barrage, and the one surviving torpedo had failed to find its way inside the planet-ship. The regulator had waited until the last possible second to consume the torpedoes, catching them as they were crowding in toward their destination. The regulator's interior remained unharmed, and the hole was now half its original size.

He felt foolish now, wasting the torpedoes on the hole in the regulator even as the spikes drew near. And behind the first wave of spikes, another wave was incoming. "Reload with fusing torpedoes and see what you can do with the spikes. We'll take another shot with the siege cannon—"

The bridge rocked forward, nearly throwing Jared from his seat.

• • •

"The planet's garrison has engaged the third wave," said Udos, sitting at the *Belico's* sciences station. "The *Hattan* and B'aha battle carrier are both coming under fire from the rear."

Redelia watched as her interceptor's pulse cannons obliterated one of the spikes. Beyond, on the screen, she saw one of the regulator's pale beams finally shear through the forward hull plating of a Way of Law cruiser and soak into it, carving it up into oblivion.

"Our defense fields are weakening under the force waves," the weapons officer cautioned. "I do not know how much longer they will hold."

"Then we need to do what we can while we are here," snapped Redelia. On her display, she noted that two Plury'be cruisers were targeting B'aha's battle carrier, while a Plury'be cruiser and the Domain cruiser were firing on the *Hattan.* Some of B'aha's flatboats were surging in to assist, but most were tied up trying to shoot down the spikes, which by now were almost on top of their targets.

The spikes . . . something was not quite right. She manipulated the tactical map, homing in on one group that looked separate from the rest. Those three looked as if they were going to miss both ships entirely. Where were they going?

• • •

A volley of fusing torpedoes from the *Hattan* hit the rearward Domain cruiser dead-on, followed by multiple rounds from the rearward ardor turrets.

Aioua's voice broke in. "The battle carrier has been struck!"

Jared shifted his attention to B'aha's ship, which the large spikes had impaled in multiple places. One of them appeared to have hit the forward section precariously close to the bridge.

Wait—that *was* the bridge.

"Orel, contact B'aha. Ask if they need assistance."

Orel worked his station, then announced, "No response, Captain. Their communication with the fleet has been severed."

"Garo, can we blow those spikes off with our turrets?"

"Not without endangering the battle carrier."

"B'aha's ship is no longer actively maneuvering," said Aioua. "Its last course change sent it heading toward Sacred Home. If it does not make a correction, it will burn up in the atmosphere in a matter of minutes."

Jared winced. He knew the force waves were too great to send a shuttle over there, and the interceptors were barely keeping the remaining spikes at bay. That battle carrier was about to burn in the atmosphere, and they couldn't do a thing about it.

• • •

Brigg's interceptor *Shington* was on its way back to the *Hattan* while firing at spikes. Ahead, the *Hattan*'s flank turrets were blanketing the sky with pulse and ardor flak, striking other spikes and lashing out against the two enemy ships coming up behind it. A brief, violent flash heralded another round from the siege cannon, which barreled past, making a line toward the regulator.

The battlefield was in complete turmoil now, with all semblance of organized combat vanished. Redelia had long ago ceased giving specific orders to the other interceptors, since the goal of stopping the spikes had superseded other matters. The *Hattan* had largely been spared any spike impacts, but the flatboats had failed to effect the same protection for the battle carrier. It had been gored in several places and was falling into the planet's gravitational pull. B'aha's ship seemed destined for destruction, along with whatever section of the planet's unbroken city was unfortunate enough to be in its way.

Brigg panned back to the *Hattan*, taking in its situation, which was increasingly in danger from the rear, especially now that B'aha's ship was disabled. There were other Way of Law and No Greater ships in the third wave fleet, but they were not the equal of the battle carrier and had their own problems to deal with.

Out of the corner of Brigg's eye he noticed something amiss. Three spikes were hurtling past the *Hattan* in a clean miss. That made no sense. The spikes could navigate at will and should have adjusted to hit the *Hattan* dead-on. Unless . . .

They had already started to pivot when he opened a channel to the *Hattan*. "*Shington* to *Hattan*, three spikes making for your rearward quarter!"

• • •

S'li bore back toward the fleet with dismay. After trying in vain to attract the regulator's attention, the No Greater pilot was retreating to the rest of the group to help deal with the new flurry of spikes and the garrison fleet. Farther beyond, a few second wave ships had finally arrived to take on the garrison from behind, but the assault on the *Hattan* and B'aha's battle carrier continued.

Everyone on S'li's flatboat watched in horror as several of the spikes slammed into the battle carrier, including one deathblow to what S'li said was the ship's bridge.

"The ship is adrift / The ship is drifting toward the planet," said S'li. "Control has been struck / Control crew may be dead."

Nho said, "That is terrible. There are so many sentients in there."

"Perhaps the *Hattan* could send a team over," Rete suggested.

"The force waves are too strong," said Nho. "They would never make it."

"There are enforcers in those boarders / The enforcers will overrun the ship of B'aha," said Au'p.

Nho stood up straight, bringing his staff in close. "Then we need to go and help them."

Rete nearly fell off of his gravity disc. "Us?" he exclaimed. "What are we supposed to do?"

"Sarco has chosen to keep us out here for a reason. There are legions of Plury'be in danger, both on the ship and on the planet below if the ship crashes. S'li, how easily could this ship dock with B'aha's vessel?"

"The connections are the same / Docking is simple."

"If we were able to access its navigational controls, could you restore it to orbit?"

Rete's voice was a near shout. "Have you lost your mind?"

"Ships of Us use common systems / We can restore it to orbit," S'li said.

"Then take us there," said Nho. "If we can get to the bridge, perhaps S'li can find a way."

Rete couldn't believe what he was hearing. "This makes no sense. There's a huge crew in there. If they can't take care of themselves, what do you expect us to do?"

"None of them have what we have," said Nho. "Trust me when I say that they need us."

• • •

Tir could see nothing but swirling darkness from the overseer all around her. The cloud did not speak, but she could feel its wrath. Her oxygen tract crushed in on itself. She was choking and freezing to death inside of her own, fully pressurized suit.

"THEY BELONG TO DAR," it rang out, this time in Confederal Common, "AND YOU WILL NOT DESTROY WHAT HE HAS BUILT HERE."

She was knocked to her back, her breathing constricting still further. She instinctively grabbed for her airpipe, but it was a reflexive, ineffectual act. Nothing she could do would save her.

In a flash of impulse, she choked out, "Dsori Barjak, planet avatar of the Prime Maker, *please, help me.*"

• • •

A loud crash reverberated through the ship, pushing Jared forward again.

"Hull breach!" the engineering coordination officer announced. "Engineering is reporting intruders emerging from the spike. Security is moving to respond."

Jared surveyed the damage on his display. They had managed to destroy two of the three spikes that tried to ambush the ship from behind; the surviving one had impaled the *Hattan* just below several of the rearward torpedo tubes. "Defense field status?"

"The field is compromised at the point of impact. The remaining fields are destabilizing."

"I estimate no more than a few minutes before we are fully exposed," said Aioua, "and another round of spikes is closing in. First impacts from those in less than two minutes."

On the viewscreen, the mighty shot from the siege cannon had blown open another hole in the regulator, although that one, too, would likely close in a matter of minutes. It seemed like for every hit the *Hattan* scored, the enemy was scoring two. The battle was minutes away from being over, with the Confederacy among the losses. And with the force waves still crashing against the ship and that spike puncturing the engineering section, a retreat was out of the question.

Aioua spoke again. "We have another problem. Hyperwave particles from one of our attackers are leaking through at the spike impact point. It is flooding into the rearward compartments."

Jared felt the blood drain from his face. "How long do we have?"

"Once our fields collapse, it will be less than a minute before the entire ship is flooded. Prior to that we could be looking at up to sixteen percent of the ship uninhabitable nearest the point of entry in under five minutes."

"That will also kill the intruders from the boarding party," Jared said. But he already knew the answer to that dilemma—the Domain simply did not care, as long as the *Hattan*'s crew was dead.

• • •

Redelia sat on a conference channel with the other four interceptor commanders, trying to regroup and deal with the multiple problems facing them. The *Hattan* was compromised and mere minutes away from a catastrophic end. B'aha's battle carrier was incapacitated and headed for a fiery death. The regulator had destroyed three more ships in the second and third wave fleets. And another volley of spikes was incoming. Amun Plau's interceptor had lost its defense fields and was beginning to suffer system problems, and the others were not far from the same scenario.

Redelia sent out her new orders. Eil Morichar and Amun Plau were to continue to defend the *Hattan* against the incoming regulator spikes, while Brigg Drews and Venzz Kitt were going to see what they could do to draw fire from the ships attacking the *Hattan*'s rear quarter.

As for Redelia . . . she was still deciding what to do with the *Belico*. Her second option was to assist Eil and Amun in parrying the spike attacks, but her first hope was to see if there was something she could do to help B'aha's battle carrier.

A pale beam sliced past, missing Amun Plau's exposed interceptor by a few trics and lancing into a Plury'be cruiser. *That was close.*

She looked to Udos. "Is there any way we can help the Way of Law flagship?"

His voice was grim. "I do not see how. We do not have a locking mechanism installed on this ship that will interface with them, and we do not have the force to stop their drift."

Redelia used her chair display to hone in on one of the battle carrier's airlocks, inspecting it to see if there was something in its appearance that might suggest how to rig a way in. As soon as she did, her view was occluded by a flatboat moving in to connect to it.

"Udos, whose flatboat is that docking with B'aha's ship?"

"It is a No Greater flatboat, Commander." Then, "It is the ship carrying Au'p, S'li, Nho, and Rete."

Redelia and Udos exchanged looks. She knew they were both thinking the same thing. *Sarco, protect them.*

That made her next decision more clear. "Vidra, bring us about on an intercept course for the next round of incoming spikes. Taulcar, lock on to the closest one and prepare to fire."

• • •

When Nho stepped through the orifice from S'li's flatboat to B'aha's battle carrier, he saw a world much like and much different than the ones he had seen on Free Town, Wisdom, and Watch Tower. He saw similarities in the interior design, especially to buildings he had seen at Wisdom. Yet there were differences, too, not only in the more cramped, meandering architecture, but in the general state of panic that permeated the vessel.

The situation on the battle carrier was critical, and the crew apparently knew it, as they were scurrying around much more quickly than Nho thought physiologically possible. The Plury'be hordes rushing by looked more like a confused stampede than the crew of a military vessel. Nho and Au'p tried to speak with crew to gather information, but were ignored. Either they were not considered worthy of conversation, or B'aha's officers had more important things to do. Ironically, for a group of strangers who showed up unannounced on the ship, they attracted precious little attention at all.

"Why won't they help us?" Nho said to his friends after several failed attempts to ask for directions.

Rete said, "Would you care about a small band of boarders if your ship was about to burn up in the atmosphere?"

Nho said to S'li, "How long do we have?"

S'li gave an answer that Nho's translator converted to a few minutes, with the caveat that S'li could not be sure.

There was a commotion nearby. Nho looked in time to see a floating, dynamic geometric sentient fly around a corner, green balls of flame-like energy surging from its midsection. The attacks hit several Plury'be, blowing them into a sticky goo that splashed against the floors and walls. A purple hyperwave sphere came up behind the sentient and started to attack, but the geometric sentient—by now Nho recognized it as an enforcer—pivoted effortlessly and blasted the sphere to pieces.

Nho ran toward the enforcer, shouting, "Minion of Dar, I stand against you in the name of Sarco!"

As he spoke, Sarco's staff suddenly came aglow, and a sparkle of radiant power—a rain of white light—streamed from the staff, impacting against the enforcer and shattering it. Even Nho seemed caught off-guard by the staff's attack, skidding to a halt.

The Way of Law Plury'be standing nearby spoke amongst themselves, onlookers to a miracle they neither expected nor understood. Nho could hear their questions in his suit. What had happened? What manner of attack was this that could stop an enforcer?

He looked out on a small crowd of them. "Listen," he said urgently, "We are here to help save your ship, but we need to get to the bridge—to Control—so we can stop it from falling into the planet."

One of the crew said, "Control is exposed to space / Enforcers have overrun Control / (futility). B'aha is dead / Others cannot reclaim Control / (despair)."

"Then lead us there. We will stop them and save your ship."

• • •

Vetta Quidd had two problems. First, a contingent of enforcers—the same foot soldiers that had wiped out most of her team on the prison transport at High Land—were making their way into the engineering section, firing at anyone or anything in their way. Second, hyperwave particles were beginning to leak into the ship's rearward compartments, including engineering, killing any crew unfortunate enough to be caught in their way. The particles were spreading inexorably forward, penetrating bulkheads and safety doors, and would overwhelm all of engineering in a few minutes. This would probably kill the enforcers if they were still present, but if the enforcers were able to destroy critical systems before that happened, the *Hattan*'s demise would be greatly accelerated.

Vetta coordinated several security teams that converged on the engineering section from various angles, including a team of Ritican warriors she led personally. All of her officers wore environmentally sealed combat armor and wielded pulse rifles. Vetta would have preferred explosive gibeon rifles, but the risk of discharging them in engineering was too high.

The teams poured into engineering and were immediately assailed by shockingly accurate green projectiles from the enforcers. The shots killed three officers within seconds, and even their errant shots did damage by exploding against walls and damaging equipment.

Vetta took a position on an upper catwalk and, joined by her platoon, fired a volley down at one of the enforcers. Their volley hit the mark and the enforcer spiraled back into the bowels of the large room. Nearby she could hear fire as other units engaged other targets.

A burst of green flame struck just behind Vetta. The explosion knocked her forward, sending her careening off the catwalk and down toward the engineering floor. Her hands and feet grasped for something, anything, but could not find purchase, and she quickly dropped to the ground where she hit hard. Her pulse rifle bounced away from her and came to a rest in a far corner.

She looked up in time to see an enforcer emerge from behind a bulkhead, its attention still focused on the catwalk above. She pulled a pistol out of her armor holster and keyed the trigger, pulses flickering out. The enforcer must have either heard or sensed her action, because it strafed away from the shots and, pivoting, fired back. By then Vetta was no longer where the explosions hit, having sprung to her feet and raced behind a bulkhead. Still sprinting, she emerged from the other side and, now just a few trics away, sprang off her feet, leaping through the air at the Domain solider.

The enforcer, apparently expecting more weapons fire, was caught off guard by the close-quarters physical attack. It spun awkwardly to avoid the airborne Ritican but failed, and Vetta got a hand and foot on it, bringing it down backward toward the ground.

Vetta was on what amounted to its back now, the two of them falling and Vetta's own back striking the ground. She pulled hard at the enforcer, trying to rip something off, but nothing would move—it was surprisingly durable, even to a Ritican. The enforcer rose off the ground, hovered for a moment, and then threw itself back, slamming Vetta's back against the ground, the enforcer pushing down on her from above. The enforcer did it again: rising, then crushing Vetta against the ground. She howled and, with one hand, brought her fist like a hammer on one of its shoulder-sections. She thought she felt it give slightly but could not be sure.

The enforcer flipped upright, the force of the motion so great that Vetta was thrown over its shoulders like a rock from a catapult. She flew head over heels across the room, crashing into a wall. Scrambling to an upright position, she had enough time to look up as the Domain soldier, an arbiter of death, brought its weapon to bear on her.

A blur of motion, and suddenly the enforcer was in the air, held aloft by a large, tall, black object. It took a moment for Vetta to recognize the object.

It was Triphox. Triphox, the Exo that had been her crewmate on board the *Retaelus*.

The Exo engineer grasped the enforcer with multiple hands along both ends, and, pulling, snapped the Domain solider in two with a sickening crack. The soldier's spinning parts immediately stopped moving.

Triphox discarded the two pieces and looked down at Vetta. "You must leave this compartment immediately," it clicked. "The hyperwave radiation will be here in seconds."

"Agreed," said Vetta, taking one of Triphox's hands and pulling herself to her feet. She added, "Never again will I doubt the strength or bravery of an Exo."

"The Greater Task Master said that some tasks are more important than others."

The Exo Incarnate. "So there are," Vetta said aloud. "And there is still much more to do. Let us go."

• • •

A flurry of powerful collider torpedoes launched from the rearward torpedo bays of the *Hattan*, racing through the night before smashing into the Domain cruiser. The Domain ship's proximity field buffered it against some of the attack, but not enough; the high-yield torpedoes shattered significant sections of the hostile vessel's front quarter. The Domain ship reversed course, backing away from the *Hattan*.

One down, Brigg Drews mused. His *Shington*, along with Venzz Kitt's *Falcon*, was on a direct line into the area behind the *Hattan* to help with the rear assault on Captain Carter's ship. Now that one of the two major capital ships had been dealt with, they had an obvious target: a Plury'be cruiser belonging to Those of the Soul, which was firing a single hyperwave stream directly into the weak point where the regulator's spike had pierced the *Hattan*'s defense fields.

The *Falcon* would arrive first, as it was closer to the *Hattan* when Redelia's orders had gone out. That left Brigg to watch from a distance as his rival and fellow interceptor commander took the first shot. It was not hard to guess at Venzz's attack plan; Brigg's display indicated that the *Falcon* was gaining speed at a dramatic rate. Brigg noted with mild contempt that Venzz, by all appearances, was about to copy the same hit-and-run tactic Brigg had used against the attackers at Free Town. No doubt Venzz would get in close and try to destroy the hyperwave node as he passed by. *Predictable as always*, Brigg said to himself. *Never smart enough to come up with something original.*

Almost immediately Brigg felt agitated, suspicious. It was the feeling he got whenever something seemed wrong, and most of the time it meant something would go wrong. He focused on Venzz's ship and looked at the readouts. The *Falcon* was continuing to accelerate toward the attacking Plury'be cruiser but was holding its fire, no doubt to surprise the enemy by striking out at the last moment.

No, that wasn't the problem.

He redirected his focus on the target, the Those of the Soul cruiser that was attacking the *Hattan*'s rearward quarter. Jared Carter's ship was still firing ardor from its rear turrets, but the torpedoes had ceased, either because of battle damage or, more likely, because of the hyperwave particles seeping in. Brigg inspected the enemy ship closely, trying to divine what the problem was, why he was so unsettled.

Then he saw it.

"*Shington* to *Falcon*. Venzz, break off the attack run now."

"You're a *groshoro*, Drews. I get to be the hero today."

"It's a trap, Venzz, break—"

Three hyperwave nodes, which had been lying dormant on the Plury'be cruiser during its attack on the *Hattan*, came to life, a purple trinity of death soaking into the *Falcon*. The interceptor, having lost its defense fields a minute earlier, took the full force of the attacks unprotected. The hull lit up with an unnatural, ghostly purple glow.

"Status on the *Falcon*," Brigg said. In spite of his animosity toward Venzz, the order came out choked, emotional.

His sciences officer spoke quietly. "No signs of life, not even the engineer. They are all dead, sir."

On the screen, the *Falcon* flew past the Plury'be cruiser and kept going along its last plotted course, its systems still functioning but its crew now gone, a speeding coffin headed away from the battlefield and out into the emptiness.

• • •

Tir opened her eyes. Directly in front of her was the copper sky of Sacred Home, with its red sun and long, thin streams of cloud cover. At the top of her vision she could see the regulator moving in its orbit.

She sat up and realized she was surrounded by a crowd of Plury'be onlookers. She checked her suit, which appeared undamaged. Brushing herself off, she got to her feet.

One of the onlookers, one of the Way of Law that had escorted her there, asked, "Are you harmed? / Are you hurt? / (concern)."

"I am unharmed," she said. She then looked around. "Where is the overseer?"

"It withdrew / It left."

She was not sure whether to be confounded or relieved. For the moment, she was both. "Why? What happened?"

"We do not know / We thought you might know. It was surrounding you / It stopped surrounding you / (confusion). We thought it would kill you / It has left the area."

Tir tried to process this. She should be dead. She was not. The overseer had her on the ground, suffocating her, and suddenly it was gone. What happened? Why had it not killed her as it so easily could have? Did someone summon it away?

Or did she somehow do something?

She thought back to her last words. She had cried out for the Incarnate of Hazion Prime. *No*, she thought, *that could not be it*, although part of her wondered if that was exactly what had happened.

She was still standing on the speaking platform. All around her the Plury'be were staring at her, waiting, not moving. They appeared as lost, as confused, as she. For the moment, she had their complete attention.

"Let me—" She fumbled for the right words. "I—I know that you live in fear of Dar. I know he gives you what you desire, but you fear him, too. You fear him because he brings darkness with him. I know, for I have seen that darkness, including here, today. But I still live. Let me tell you how we have faced Dar, and how you might, too."

• • •

The *Shington*'s weapons officer looked at Brigg. "What are your orders, sir?"

Brigg wiped the involuntary tears from his face. In his mind he could still see the image of the *Falcon*, bathed in the glow of biocidal destruction. His voice was strained but firm as he croaked, "We have to stop that cruiser."

"We do not have much time," the sciences officer said. "The hyperwave particles have penetrated most of the *Hattan* engineering section. They are about to flood the first of the crew compartments as well as the siege cannon maintenance area and turret guidance. There are at least one hundred and twenty officers in those areas."

"How long?"

"A minute, perhaps less."

Brigg eyed the cruiser's hyperwave nodes. One of the nodes was still firing at the *Hattan*; the others, the ones that had killed the *Falcon* crew, had once again gone silent. His mind raced through the various options, with all of them coming up short either on success or the time necessary to execute them before large numbers on the *Hattan* perished.

That left just one possibility. It was the worst of them all, but it was also the only one.

He straightened in his chair. "Navigator," he said crisply, "I'm sending you a course now. Make for it, maximum speed. Engineering, I need you to disable the safeties on our torpedoes immediately."

The navigator checked his orders and immediately went pale. The weapons officer looked at him incredulously. "Sir," she said, "what you are ordering is tantamount to suicide."

"No," said Brigg, "it *is* suicide. But it is also the only way to save those people. There are only six of us. It's easy arithmetic."

A dead silence permeated the bridge. "I do not want to die," the navigator whispered.

"I don't, either." Then, to the weapons officer: "I'm open to other options."

The weapons officer was silent, staring back at Brigg without expression. Finally she said, to the navigator, "He is right. Make the course now, while there is still time."

The navigator did not answer, but turned and set the course.

As the ship accelerated toward its terminal target, Brigg said, softly, "Take courage, all of you. Death is not the end for those who believe."

· · ·

Twenty-four seconds later, the *Shington* collided directly into the Plury'be cruiser's bridge. All hands on board the Navy interceptor were already dead, having been cut down by the lethal hyperwave nodes on its final approach, but the course had been fixed beforehand and the cruiser was not nearly nimble enough to avoid it. As the *Shington* hit its mark, the torpedoes inside it—both conventional fusing torpedoes and three collider torpedoes—destabilized and exploded, along with the collider plant in the interceptor's engineering section.

The explosion did more than even Brigg Drews could have hoped for. Not only did it destroy the Plury'be bridge, but the cascade effect rippled through the entire cruiser, splitting it down the middle and cracking the vessel open like a giant egg. The *Shington* sciences officer had incorrectly estimated the number of Navy lives saved by the maneuver; it was closer to one hundred and fifty.

· · ·

Nho stopped and stared at the translucent wall. The Plury'be had hastily erected an environmental barrier in the area leading to the battle carrier's bridge, or what the Plury'be called Control. Control, apparently, had been blown open by a spike and was exposed to the vacuum of space; the barrier apparently kept the ship's atmosphere intact while allowing sentients to pass through. Beyond the barrier was a contingent of enforcers, guarding the room while the ship fell to its destruction. Several waves of Plury'be soldiers had already stormed Control in an attempt to retake it.

"Many have gone in / None have come out / (hopelessness)," said one of the Plury'be officers standing nearby.

"We can't do this," Rete said, his voice tight and panicked.

Nho faced him and replied, in a gentle voice, "Hope is a powerful thing, my old friend. Never forget that."

Then Nho turned back to the barrier. Taking a firm hold of Sarco's staff, Nho closed his eyes in silent prayer, then opened them and stepped through. Au'p and S'li followed.

Rete, his whole body trembling, followed a few seconds later.

The bridge was large and spacious, with a high ceiling and various stations in loose orbit around a central table. Plury'be bodies littered the room: on the floor, draped over consoles, lying against walls. The collective deaths of both the bridge crew and the units sent to liberate the bridge was astounding.

On the far wall, sticking through from the outside, was a large, black, spike. Up close, the spike was not as smooth as it appeared from a distance, and its sheen was incredible, even though it had the paradoxical quality of absorbing the light from around it. Above the spike, part of the battle carrier's hull wall had been torn away and a clear view of space was visible. Nho could see splashes of light from the battle outside, and beyond that the outline of the regulator.

There was no sound here other than that of one's own breathing. The vacuum of space was complete. Rete felt a dull vibration at his feet, which he suspected was the work of the regulator's force waves impacting the ship. Au'p, wearing a thin, transparent protective barrier, was standing a few paces ahead, next to S'li. Nho was several paces beyond them. Rete was still less than a tric from the entry barrier.

Eight enforcers rose from among the various consoles. They were glowing dimly in green. They had no faces, no way of showing emotion, but Rete nevertheless thought they looked angry. Certainly their master was one of anger.

A voice rang in Rete's ear. It was coming through the same frequency the Plury'be communicated with, but was in Confederal Common. It was not flat as the Plury'be translations were. It had emotion, and it spoke in a tone that was brutish, vicious.

"Leave now while you still can, Human."

Rete blinked. It was the first time he knew of that an enforcer had ever spoken.

Nho replied, "It is not your master who will prevail today, but mine. You have no power here."

"It is you who have no power. This is not as it was on Malum. On this side of the Great Void, the power belongs to Dar."

Rete stood there, momentarily dumbstruck. Not only was the enforcer speaking, but it did so with knowledge of events from the Confederacy.

Nho said, "The power of the One knows no borders, foul creature. I will not permit you to destroy the lives of the people on this ship."

"Their souls belong to Dar."

"Not anymore."

Nho stepped forward. Immediately a barrage of green fire rained down on him, eight enforcers firing at once. Nho raised the staff defensively, and the shots struck an invisible barrier no more than a tric in front of him, taking on the appearance of a green dome as they piled up against the shield erected by Sarco's staff. Although Nho appeared unharmed, he staggered under the blow, the heat of their attacks felt even through the cold of space and the insulation of his suit. The staff glowed hot white and a light haze almost like smoke floated around it.

Nho took a step forward, holding the staff perpendicular to the ground. The enforcers kept firing, but the green fire again and again came up short.

Nho shouted, "Your rule over these people ends today! They belong to Sarco now!"

Rete watched as Nho brought the end of his staff down on the floor. There was a bloom of light, and a wave blew the enforcers up and away, some hitting walls, others out into the open of space. The threat was over.

Nho turned to S'li. "Now, quickly."

The Plury'be pilot moved to one of the stations and began working the controls. "I understand this / It is responding," it said. "Reversing direction / Stabilizing orbit / (relief)."

An enforcer rose up from the ground and rounded on S'li, its center glowing in anticipation of an attack. Nho, standing several trics from S'li, raised his staff and pointed it at the enforcer.

A white burst shot out from the staff. The attack struck the side of the enforcer, sending it spinning off just as it ejected a green bolt. The errant enemy shot, knocked off course by Nho's attack, split the air between S'li and Nho, smashing into a console and causing it to explode into pieces.

Nho's head flinched violently and he fell to his back. He did not move.

Several trics behind, Rete screamed. He ran over to where Nho had fallen and immediately realized that the faceplate on Nho's environmental suit had been shattered. The old man's face had been struck by a large piece of shrapnel from the exploding console and was disfigured beyond recognition. His body lay lifeless, devoid even of a face by which to stare out of death.

Nho Ames was dead.

A dazzlingly hideous light erupted onto the bridge, streaming in from space. Rete looked up just in time to see the power of the regulator's pale beam surge over the room, bathing the bridge in cold, bright terror. Rete tried to cry out, but heard only an echo of his own voice, as if through the end of a long tunnel. And then everything became nothing.

23

REGULATOR

"Imagine," Nho once told Rete, "being shoved into a giant glass bottle, shaken one hundred times, and then tossed onto a stone floor. That was what it was like."

Rete found himself facedown, gagging up small bits of stomach fluid onto the inner surface of his suit helmet. His body would have ejected an entire meal had it been able, but the steep anxiety he'd experienced earlier that morning—in the hours before boarding Au'p's flatboat—had already taken care of that. Instead, his insurgent digestive tract was content to spew clear fluid. The unmistakable smell of vomit filled his helmet.

Rete brought himself to a sitting position, his insides still wrenching. The environmental suit's self-cleaning systems were already working to remove the smear and purge the smell, and Rete fought to keep from adding to the mess. He closed his eyes and took several deep breaths, one of them nearly interrupted by yet another upheaval. Eventually his digestive system calmed.

He opened his eyes and looked about. A rough, textured surface, punctuated by small green pools of liquid. A hazy, crimson atmosphere. A landscape that seemed to curve up slightly on all sides. Looking up, he saw a small, bright sun raining a cold, mirthless light down on everything. A large, almost living cloud orbited that sun, at times partially obscuring—but never fully occluding—it.

There was no question where he was. It was almost exactly like the Malum others had described to him, the Malum Nho had once fought.

Nho. Rete looked to his left and there he was—at least, what used to be him. The body lay on its back, the arms spread apart at haphazard angles, the helmet smashed open, the face unrecognizably gory. For some time Rete could do nothing but stare at the horrific scene, his head throbbing in pain as tears welled up in his eyes.

"Can you hear? / Are you injured? / (interrogative)."

Rete looked for the source of the voice. He found it, directly behind where he was sitting. It was Au'p, bringing itself upright. A short distance behind it was S'li, who looked like a pile of gelatin on the ground.

Rete blinked away the tears that stung his face. He wished his helmet was off so he could wipe them, although he could not trust that the atmosphere here was safe. He noticed that Au'p and S'li were both still wearing the thin atmospheric barriers they had taken on before entering the battle carrier's bridge.

He said, his voice strained, "I am unharmed. Are you injured?" Both Plury'be replied simultaneously that they were not injured, although S'li still seemed to be struggling to get off the ground.

Rete decided it was time to test his own balance. He brought himself to a slow crouch, then to his feet. He was shaky and slightly nauseated, but after a few moments the sensation passed and he felt it would probably not return.

He felt an unexpected wash of numbness. He observed, aloud, "There are no others here besides us."

"The regulator is large / There may be others in other places," said S'li. "B'aha's compartments resist the pale beam / We may be the only ones from the ship of B'aha."

"So perhaps only the bridge was hit by the beam."

"Other ships have been taken / Other crews may be here," said Au'p. "We should— / We should— / (interrupted). The overseer is moving / The overseer approaches / (fear)."

Rete looked up. The cloud swirling around the sun had pulled away from the light and was now descending toward them. Given the distance, Rete found the speed alarming; the overseer would close the gap in a matter of seconds.

Frantically, Rete searched for a weapon. He felt his suit for a pulse pistol, the one Nho had discouraged him from taking but that he had brought anyway. It was gone. He looked around for it—or any other means of defense—and could find none. He looked at the Plury'be. "Do either of you have your weapons? Your probes?"

"My weapon is not here / My weapon is not effective on overseers / (futility)," said Au'p. S'li said something to the same effect.

"There has to be something we can use . . ." Rete's voice trailed off as, just beyond Nho's body, something caught his eye.

Sarco's staff.

Rete hurried around the body and swept up the staff, nearly dropping it in his haste. He secured it with both hands and turned around to see the overseer, the cloud-warden, hanging just a few trics above him. A boom rang out from the cloud that almost blew Rete off his feet. Then, a voice:

"YOU BELONG TO DAR NOW. SERVE HIS PURPOSES, AND YOU SHALL LIVE. DEFY HIS PURPOSES, AND YOU WILL BE EXTINGUISHED."

Rete opened his mouth, but no words came out. He was paralyzed with fright, his body trembling so badly he nearly lost control of the staff again. He had heard an overseer speak once before, on Free Town, but he had been hiding inside a building then. This one was directly in front of him.

"YOUR FRIEND IS DEAD BECAUSE HE DEFIED DAR'S PURPOSES. YOU MAY YET CHOOSE ANOTHER PATH."

Rete's heart palpitated. The cloud-being was talking directly to him, its wispy tentacles even gesturing at him as if for emphasis. He felt utterly alone, cast off from the world he once knew, staring up at a life form that held his existence in its grasp. His brain contemplated a hundred different things at once and failed, instead simply locking up.

The cloud flowed left and right, swirling higher as it towered over and around Rete, stretching out to show its full size and depth. It hovered there for a moment, an angry storm so close Rete could feel its wind pushing against his suit. He was barely conscious of the fact he held Sarco's staff in his hands, although his mind could not connect it with the work Nho had done. Rete was not Nho.

"WHOM DO YOU SERVE?"

That question was, paradoxically, both unexpected and unsurprising. Of course it would ask. Why would it not? Rete again opened his mouth to speak, and again nothing came out. He faintly remembered that he had once been known as the one of great speech, the one who could articulate things that even Nho Ames could not. That seemed as if it was aeons ago.

"WHOM DO YOU SERVE?"

The question was louder now, more insistent, if that was even possible.

Rete thought on that for a moment. He served no one. Himself. No, he served something, but he did not know what it was. No, that was not correct, either. He *had* once served someone, but now he was unattached, unaffiliated. He had once been in the employ of someone, but that was in the past, during a time long lost.

He saw a stir of motion to his right, and Au'p was beside him, the Plury'be drawn up to its full short height. Its tentacles waved gently around its cylindrical body as it said, "I am Au'p / I serve That Which There Is No Greater. I defy your master / I defy Dar / (indignation)."

Rete's mouth fell open and he stared at the Plury'be, trying to understand what had just been said. Inside, his mind raged in fear. *The Plury'be is trying to kill us!*

"DAR REIGNS HERE. LOOK AND SEE. THE ONE WHO FACED MALUM NOW LIES DEAD BEFORE YOU. THAT POWER HOLDS NO PLACE HERE."

"I will not submit / I will never submit," said Au'p, the toneless translation in Rete's suit belying the passion in its voice. "I defy That Which Distorts / I defy Dar / (anger). I stand against the Lower Way / I stand for the Greater Way. That Which There Is No Greater knows no limits / That Which There Is No Greater is not limited here / (stubbornness)."

The cloud shifted perceptibly, as if to turn and face Rete.

"DO YOU STAND WITH THE PLURY'BE?"

Rete swallowed, his mouth so dry that now, even as he tried to speak, he was not sure he physically could. He looked at the staff in his hands and glanced at Nho's body. *There was once a power here*, he thought, *but it has died. It died in me long ago, and it died in Nho today. I do not know if it can be found.*

"DO YOU STAND WITH THE PLURY'BE?"

The overseer was nearly close enough to touch. Rete's body felt cold.

Au'p drew nearer to Rete but said nothing. S'li, standing behind them both, was also silent.

"I—" began Rete, "I am not Nho. I will never be Nho. But I loved him as a brother. He risked his life to save—"

"DO YOU STAND WITH THE PLURY'BE?"

But Rete continued to speak. "—me, when all reason would say he should not. He convinced a group of strangers to shield me from the darkness, and I now call those strangers friends. I may never have the faith that Nho had, but I"—he was crying now—"cling to a hope! Maybe it is a vain hope, but it is a hope! I once claimed to serve the One, the Incarnate. Sarco. I still doubt, but I will not give up my faith."

"DO YOU STAND WITH THE PLURY'BE?"

The answer came out as a whisper. "Yes."

The cloud drew up and around them, covering them like a great dome. The rest of the regulator's interior, including the sun, was blocked out, hidden from view by that which served Dar. The cloud dome began to shrink, drawing closer, like walls closing in. Au'p said, "Nho stopped Dar / You can stop Dar / (conviction)."

"I am not Nho."

Several of Au'p's tentacles gently reached up and clasped the staff. "You are not Nho / You are Rete. I am not Nho / I am Au'p. We are what we are made to be / We are what That Which There Is No Greater has made Us to be. Do not draw on your strength / Your strength will fail. Draw on That Which There Is No Greater / Draw on the One."

The cloud walls crushed in on them. Instantly Rete's world was a hurricane, the wind whipping against his suit and his skin underneath exploding with the pain of a thousand shards of ice. His body experienced a dramatic increase in gravity, bending under a weight that made him feel like he was carrying another man on his back. He felt like he was drowning, and he gripped the staff as if it were the only way out of the water.

"Sarco, help me!" he shouted. "Help my unbelief! Save me!"

The staff glowed dimly.

Au'p tried to speak but could not. Rete could tell it was not from a lack of desire; the weight of the gravity was crushing the Plury'be, and it could not properly formulate communication.

Rete pleaded further. "Sarco, He of the One, please! Save us!"

The staff flourished with light, a spiraling array of pinpoints spinning out and away from the staff. They impacted points on the cloud, causing the cloud to retreat slightly. The weight still came down, crushing Rete under a burden of ice and dark.

"I cast my faith with the Incarnate," croaked Rete. He hit the staff against the ground as he had seen Nho do.

Almost immediately the staff came alive, its righteous light billowing out and into the cloud. The cloud withdrew, pulling out into first a great dome, and then into a ball that withdrew back up into the air. The light from the staff pursued it. Rete took a step forward, holding Sarco's staff higher in the air as its glow continued to shoot forth.

A very different light, a pale light, erupted from below and enveloped them. It was the same evil light that had flooded the bridge of B'aha's ship, washing over them and through them, although

Rete sensed intuitively that the staff was insulating him against the fear the pale beam usually brought. The regulator was preparing to move them again, Rete realized.

And there was darkness.

24

The Liberation of Mel'as'u / Sacred Home Earth Index 1306.365

For the second time in less than ten minutes, Rete Sorte spewed uncontrollably into the helmet of his environmental suit. His head throbbed and his body felt battered. He winced, then ventured a look at his current surroundings.

He was back on the bridge of B'aha's battle carrier. Nearby, he could see Au'p and S'li, as well as Nho's lifeless body. Rete's mind, still muddled, tried to make sense of the sudden turn of events. As best as he could tell, the regulator had sent him back here. It was not clear why.

He looked down at Sarco's staff, which was still in his right hand, although it was no longer glowing. His first, best theory was that the regulator, having been challenged by the staff's power, had wanted no part of it and had sent him and the others away.

But if that were the case, why even bring them into the planet-ship in the first place?

The answer came to his mind almost immediately. Perhaps the regulator had taken them from the battle carrier thinking that, without Nho, they would surrender. Rete was not sure he could point with great pride to his actions on board the regulator, but he was alive. Au'p was alive. S'li was alive. Nho was not, but Nho would have approved of Rete's defiance, shaky though it was.

Rete brought himself to a sitting position. "Thank you, Sarco," he whispered, "for helping one of such little faith as I."

• • •

Two spikes slammed into the front quarter of the *Hattan*. One of them had passed straight through a flatboat which had valiantly, but vainly, tried to stop it. On the bridge, Jared received multiple reports of hull breaches; both engineering and security teams were amassing to confront them. The hyperwaves coming from the rearward quarter had ceased, but Vetta and her team were still dealing with enforcers in that area.

On the viewscreen, a pale beam struck out from the regulator and settled on the bridge of B'aha's ship. This struck Jared as odd; the regulator had fired a beam in that same place just a few minutes earlier, right as the Plury'be battle carrier was finalizing maneuvers to stabilize itself back into orbit. The pale beam retreated . . . and then the regulator opened a massive spatial tear. Jared bolted to his feet, watching as something absolutely unthinkable happened.

The regulator retreated.

All around the *Hattan,* the spacescape filled with spikes, the objects drawing out of the Navy cruiser and other nearby ships. The spikes made a direct line back to the regulator, moving with extraordinary speed through the emptiness of space. The regulator by now having drawn fairly close to the *Hattan* and its allies, the spikes returned to the planet-ship before most of the bridge crew had time to process the events taking place.

The giant planet of Dar drew into the fold, and the tear closed behind it, hurtling away from Sacred Home.

• • •

Once the regulator departed, so did the other Domain ships, and once the Domain ships departed, the collective morale of the Sacred Home garrison collapsed. Within a brief ten-minute span, Those of the Soul went from standing on the cusp of victory to transmitting a request to surrender.

On board the *Hattan*, there was no time for rest, at least not yet. There were hull breaches to patch, damage to assess, and a few scattered enforcers stranded on board to deal with. None of the enforcers went quietly; all of them died in a blaze of weapons fire. Once the intruder threats had been eliminated, it was up to the Exos to swarm the damage, repairing it with the tireless efficiency the race was so legendary for.

Even for their skills, though, the work was daunting, for just as one problem was solved, it seemed another arose in its place. Many more of the internal systems had been damaged than was immediately apparent, and the engineers found themselves rushing to deal with life support and power systems even as they were coping with hull damage and defense field integrity.

The infirmary was crowded, more so than during the mutiny over Ramas-Eduj or the Aecron ambush in the Far Outerlands. Darel and the other doctors worked nonstop for what would become days, treating every malady from simple scrapes to nearly fatal hyperwave exposure. The room became a carousel of diagnoses, interventions, prescriptions, and, in some cases, surgeries. More good officers died in those next days, numbers on top of the numbers already lost in the fighting.

Darel, as most doctors do, tried to put the scope of the tragedy out of his conscious, but his calculating Aecron mind could not help but keep a brutal count of the losses. By his estimates, the *Hattan* fleet had suffered at least sixty deaths, and over three times that many crew members had moderate to serious injuries.

• • •

Down on the surface, meanwhile, a revolution was underway. The envoys of the first wave had been engaged in conversations of varying success across the planet. Some, such as Tir Bvaso, had earned large audiences, while others were struggling simply to be heard.

The moment the regulator left the sky, everything changed. Suddenly the Hazionites' detractors found themselves without the authority that came from overseers and the planet-sized regulator, and their courage failed them. The Way of Law speakers seized on this, pointing to the regulator's retreat as proof that the Way of Law's cause was a righteous one.

Tir, for her part, stood in disbelief as she watched the regulator, hanging in the sky directly above her, depart in a large fold that lit up the sky. She still had work to do, but an end was in sight. She would soon be headed back to her ship, and not as the same person who left it.

EPILOGUE

Jared fell onto his bed, exhausted. His head throbbed, his feet hurt, and his body ached. All of that, though, paled in comparison to the pain in his heart. True, his fleet had freed the Plury'be homeworld from the grip of the Domain, but it had come at a terrible cost.

The crews of two interceptors, the *Shington* and *Falcon*, had been lost. Brigg Drews and Venzz Kitt were good commanders, and their absences would be deeply felt. Drews, in particular, had been a hero of the highest order: his final self-sacrificing act had saved the lives of as many as one-sixth of the *Hattan*'s crew.

But another loss dwarfed the others. Nho Ames, the old cleric who had stood up to Malum—the one who had brought the power of Sarco to bear on the forces of the Domain—was dead. Sarco's power was not Nho's alone—Rete had already demonstrated that—but Nho's loss nevertheless created a hole that would be difficult, if not impossible, to fill.

Nho had been an enigmatic, at times distant man, and that had made him difficult to get to know. Still, Jared had counted him a friend. In his earliest meetings with Nho, Jared found him somewhat adversarial and intentionally cryptic. As time passed, Nho became more approachable and more understanding. He grew to be the sort of follower that he claimed Sarco wanted him to be.

Jared was not one to cry; he could not remember the last time he had done so. He almost wished he could here. Crying might be cathartic, help him release the bevy of emotions now tumbling through his head. His mind hurt and his heart felt as if there were a hole in it.

Jared's link chirped. "Kn Ghiri to Captain Carter."

He sat up slightly. "I'm here. What is it?"

"Captain, come to the bridge immediately. We have a development."

• • •

"It appeared less than three minutes ago," explained Aioua. "The size is consistent with a large cruiser or similarly situated capital ship."

Jared relieved Kn, the Hazionite watch officer, at the command station, his attention fixed upon the fold distortion spreading across the viewscreen. "How long until it opens?"

"Thirty-six seconds."

"Any idea who it is?"

Rami Del was at communications. "The Plury'be report they are not expecting any ships. A few Way of Law vessels are moving to monitor the fold."

Jared looked around. The crew was still reeling from the previous day's battle. They did not look ready for more combat, although they might not have a choice. "Garo, what is our tactical readiness?"

"Some of our turrets are still down, as are four of our forward torpedo tubes. The siege cannon and rearward tubes are inoperable. Our defense fields are ready, but not at optimal performance."

It would have to suffice. "Initialize the fields and stand by on available weapons."

The distortion erupted into a full tear and a large ship glided out into open space. Several members of the bridge crew immediately reacted in obvious shock.

"It—it cannot be," said Garo.

Jared took a deep breath. "Aioua, verify what we are seeing."

Aioua's data filled the space before her. "Confirmed, sir. One Ritican battlecruiser. Ksinti-level. According to our records, it is the *Rkshla-Voun*, under the command of Ritican militia captain Tolar-fsiff-crosta-margawen-Dor."

"Sir, the ship is contacting us," said Rami.

Jared nodded. "On my display."

At the command station, an image of a battle-scarred Ritican militia captain appeared, enshrouded in a hazy atmosphere. The Ritican spoke. "Captain Tolar Dor, battlecruiser *Rkshla-Voun*, Ritican militia."

"Captain Jared Carter, Navy cruiser *Hattan*. What are you doing on this side of the Void, Captain Dor?"

Tolar Dor's face was impassive. "We need to speak immediately. I bring grave news regarding the Confederacy. It is no more."

APPENDIX

A GUIDE TO THE PLURY'BE

1. Historical Background: The Plury'be

The *Hattan*'s campaign into the region across the Great Void marked a turning point in the understanding of the species long known in the Confederacy as the Invaders of 1124. Because of both the relative brevity of the 1124 war and (in all probability) the Aecron government's reluctance to be fully transparent on the subject, very little was known about the Invaders beyond the fact of their invasion and a few scattered details on their technology. This changed as the *Hattan* interacted with the mysterious race and collected information on their histories and ways of life.

The Invaders, who call themselves *Plury'be* (Plue-RYE-[brief pause]-bee), are an ancient race whose histories rival anything within the Major or Minor races. Their small homeworld of Sacred Home is so developed that it exists essentially as a contiguous city, and their technology is as advanced as the Aecrons in some ways, surpassing it in others. Plury'be interstellar travel predates its Aecron counterpart by at least a thousand years, although the Plury'be were much slower to establish colonies than the Aecrons, perhaps because of political or cultural reasons. Whatever the reason, once the Plury'be expanded, they did so in advanced fashion, adapting uninhabitable planets to their uses through forms of atmospheric modifications not known even to Aecrons.

Physically, the Plury'be stand less than a tric tall and are similar in height to the Aecrons. Their surface has an opaque gelatinous appearance, not unlike that of the reclusive Tullasph, one of the Minor Races near the Confederacy. Their bodies are a round cylindrical shape with a rounded top that is encircled by tentacles on all sides. The tentacles appear to have a multiplicity of functions: as tools of physical labor, means of sensation and perception, and the place from which they transmit their communication through short-range radio-style wavelengths. Because their bodies are relatively fragile, they are often augmented with protective technology, including thin barriers that can serve as the equivalent of environmental suits.

The Plury'be physiological system operates by processing a few different gases, absorbing them through their surfaces in a complex way that is also used to process their food. Their internal organ system is still a deep mystery to Navy medical officers, as is their neural system, which appears to be spread out across their entire interior. A proper understanding of Plury'be gender and reproduction has been hampered both by language difficulties and what might be a taboo or prohibition against discussion of the subjects.

2. Sociological Background: The Plury'be

Plury'be governance is not formalized in the way that many other known races are. Instead, their power shifts among various factions whose views on political, cultural, social, and religious norms differ. Factions are not ethnic and are not fixed, so there is transience among them, although each faction retains a core of followers who, as a matter of practice, do not convert to other factions. Many of the factional beliefs are more or less fixed, while others are more fluid. Which areas are fixed versus fluid depends entirely on the faction and, to a lesser extent, the current faction leadership, which emerges by way of popular consensus, military power, or one of hundreds of other factors.

The total number of factions is unknown, as are the total number of living Plury'be. If such a census-counting faction exists, the *Hattan* did not discover them and their information is not stored in the Watch Tower annals maintained by the Silent Ones.

Below is a summary of some of the major factions the *Hattan* did encounter during its campaign.

Silent Ones. The Silent Ones are, as their name suggests, a faction that prefers to observe rather than speak. In contrast to many other Plury'be who thrive on debate and dialogue, this faction prefers to operate independently and alone, involving themselves in politics only when they see it necessary either for their interests or, as was seen during the Sacred Home revolution, what they see as the larger interests of the Plury'be. Politically isolationist, they practice an economic system that appears largely communal. Religiously they seem to be predominantly agnostic, although spirituality is not one of their primary fixed beliefs and it is believed some Silent Ones are practitioners of ideas similar to that of the Way of Law or the No Greater.

One major tenet of the Silent Ones is the preservation of that which the Plury'be have been in the past. The Silent Ones operate under a persistent fear that Plury'be society may one day be destroyed, either by anarchy from within or by forces from without. They are particularly suspicious of the Domain, which they believe (with ample reason) to be out to remake Plury'be culture.

The Silent Ones have sought to effect the preservation of Plury'be life in different ways. They have, for example, established a repository at Watch Tower (and, most likely, in other locations) chronicling Plury'be history, including its origins at Sacred Home and its expansion to other planets, including the failed Invasion of 1124. The Silent Ones also maintain ecological histories of areas where they believe local nonsentient life is endangered; the most important example of this is the clandestine underground chambers on Sacred Home where ecologies of the planet prior to its complete urbanization are preserved for such a time when they can be re-introduced.

Those of the Soul. Those of the Soul orient themselves around a range of beliefs that often emphasize self-discovery and self-gratification. They are often involved in merchant and trade endeavors, and their research and development is frequently associated with entertainment, pleasure, and communication. Religiously they are variable, with some of the faction deeply involved in mystical self-discovery and others with no interest in religious matters at all.

Large in population but limited in expansion, they were one of the few factions that did not emigrate in large numbers to colonial worlds in the early centuries of Plury'be interstellar colonization. The best evidence suggests that the faction remained on Sacred Home with the long-term goal of dominating the homeworld after other factions had left, which in turn would give them leverage over the colonies. Events did not quite come to pass in that way; as the faction colonies grew, the influence of Sacred Home instead declined, although it still retained enough of an identity as the root of Plury'be society to warrant the revolution that the *Hattan* witnessed.

Once Those of the Soul determined that their conquest of Sacred Home would not translate into control of the larger Plury'be society that they had planned, their leadership turned their attention to other means of cultivating power. They seeded small groups on other colonies to better understand—and perhaps exert some influence on—rival factions, and they established the station at High Land in part to create a network of communication that others would come to depend on. In time, products and services by Those of the Soul were used more by other factions, although that, too, did not necessarily translate into the level of influence the faction hoped for.

Alongside their plans to influence their own species, Those of the Soul also sought to expand their power outside Plury'be borders. In 1113, the Aecron research vessel *Noeba* stumbled onto the High Land outpost; while the crew's fate is unclear, what is certain is that, in 1124, Those of the Soul crossed the Place Beyond (the Great Void) to seize control of Aecron society. Their attacking fleet, which included a few ships from some other, more minor factions, was turned away with heavy losses. This dealt a serious blow to

Those of the Soul's financial and political situation. (Other factions later became aware of the Invasion but expressed little interest in matters beyond the Great Void, seeing the Void's great distance as an obstacle not worth bothering with.) Those of the Soul never again attempted an invasion, although they would later come to ally with the Domain and agreed to allow Dar the use of High Land as a staging ground. It was from there that Malum would launch its incursion into the Confederacy.

Those of the Soul's alliance with the Domain extended beyond the military. The Domain came to identify this faction as being the most compatible with Domain belief and practice and was able to cultivate trade with and cultural influence over Sacred Home. That arrangement persisted until the Battle at Mel'as'u (Sacred Home) in 1306.

Way of Law. The Way of Law is one of the oldest factions, its history stretching back before recorded Plury'be history. As a faction of self-discipline and relative austerity, it would be easy for an outsider to posit it as an antonym to Those of the Soul. This would be an oversimplification; while it is true that the self-gratification element of Those of the Soul is repugnant to the Way of Law—and this difference was, in part, a catalyst for the Sacred Home conflict—in other ways the two factions are similar, especially in some economic and hierarchical areas. Both factions, for example, cultivate trade with other factions. In some cases the two factions have even cooperated, such as the linking of the High Land communications system with those operated by the Way of Law, or collaborative product transportation. While some within the Way of Law disapprove of these collaborations, the complex nature of factional differences means that, to some, Those of the Soul are no more different from the Way of Law than a hundred other factions.

Religiously, most members of the Way of Law accept the idea of a higher deity, which it refers to as "It of a Final Power," although a few in the faction apply self-discipline apart from any religious elements. Those that do accept the religious elements do not view

It of a Final Power as being overly active in the lives of Plury'be, but they do hold out hope that one day the Final Power will send a "Life Being"—a sort of interfactional leader—that will bring order to the whole of Plury'be society. While Ah'ey, the Seed Vessel, claimed to be a different kind of Life Being, the Way of Law rejects this interpretation. These differences separate them from groups like the No Greater.

The Way of Law maintains a presence on multiple Plury'be worlds, but none is more well-known than Wisdom. The Way of Law prides itself on maintaining Wisdom as a planet free of violence where various factions can discuss or debate any ideological subject without fear of harm or retribution, with the caveat that the Way of Law may curtail discussion on a particular subject if it deems the discussion to be at an impasse. Wisdom is also open to non-Plury'be, both for trade and for debate, and many other sentient nations travel there for economic, political, religious, or cultural reasons. The Way of Law is able to successfully maintain this peace on Wisdom thanks to both time-honored tradition and one of the Plury'be's more formidable militaries.

No Greater. By the best Confederal estimates, the No Greater faction emerged as a splinter group from the Way of Law some five thousand years ago when a leader named Ah'ey led a movement that shifted the focus away from many of the Way of Law's core tenets. While the No Greater faction does not represent the totality of Ah'ey followers (other factions and other Plury'be within factions claim Ah'ey devotion), they are one of the more visible examples.

The No Greater share the Way of Law belief in self-discipline, but they teach that self-discipline as a consequence of Ah'ey devotion rather than an end in itself. Ah'ey, they allege, was a "Seed Vessel," or a planting of the deity called "That Which There Is No Greater" in Plury'be society. The concept of That Which There Is No Greater appears broadly similar to "It of a Final Power" in Way of Law lore, although the No Greater describe that deity as much more involved than the Way of Law do. The No Greater are vocal critics of Those of the Soul, which has occasionally brought the two factions into conflict: Au'p's imprisonment at High Land and the raid on Free Town by Those of the Soul are examples.

While the No Greater emphasis on religion is higher than most other factions, it also has its own range of views on other topics. Their economic system focuses on more specialized production, filling niche markets in the colonies in areas such as food production, waste removal, and specific ship parts. Some members of the faction are essentially communal while others are almost singularly individualistic.

Because of their relatively small population, the No Greater have not vied for power on planets so much as sought to influence larger factions. They will also join larger coalitions of smaller factions if the situation presents itself, especially if those coalitions offer them an opportunity to advance their religious cause. Their unofficial homeworld of Free Town is sometimes a gathering place for smaller factions to discuss ways they might pool their influence in dealing with larger factions, and the No Greater have adopted some of the ideals of Wisdom in their managing of debates there.

ACKNOWLEDGMENTS

I would like to offer my appreciation to:

My wife and best friend, Rachael. Throughout the writing process she was an invaluable sounding board, cheerleader, and asker of just the right questions. As an added bonus, she graciously combed through the entire manuscript with her professional proofreader eye. I frequently remind her that she's awesome.

My family, for their unwavering encouragement and support.

My beta readers. As with the first book, they graciously gave of their time to help me with this one, offering important feedback that made the novel better than it ever could have been with just me alone.

My editor, Reagen Reed, who, with her usual good humor and grace, worked her wizardry to make me up my game.

Gilead Publisher Dan Balow, whose tireless efforts are the reason Gilead exists today. *Into the Void* would not have made it to press without him.

And Enclave godfather Steve Laube, who believed in *Edge of Oblivion* and has continued to champion its science fiction universe and the universes of so many other authors.

Joshua A. Johnston was raised on science fiction television and film before being introduced to the wider universe of sci-fi literature as a teenager. A graduate of Truman State University with a bachelor's degree in history and a master's in social science education, he's an American history and American government teacher, a novelist, and a ruminator on everything from video games to parenting to Aldi.

Joshua lives in St. Louis with his wife, Rachael, and their two daughters. When he's not watching *Star Trek* or pining after Nintendo's latest games, he enjoys hiking, camping, and other forays off the grid.

Edge of Oblivion, the first book in the Chronicles of Sarco series, was released in 2016.

Connect with Joshua!

Website: *joshuaajohnston.com*
Facebook: *facebook.com/joshuaajohnston*
Twitter: *twitter.com/jallenjohnston*
Google+: *plus.google.com/+JoshuaAJohnston*